Sex in the Sanctuary

Sex in the Sanctuary

Lutishia Lovely

KENSINGTON PUBLISHING CORP.
http://www.kensingtonbooks.com

DAFINA BOOKS are published by

Kensington Publishing Corp.
850 Third Avenue
New York, NY 10022

All Kensington titles, imprints and distributed lines are available at special quantity discounts for bulk purchases for sales promotion, premiums, fundraising, educational or institutional use.

Special book excerpts or customized printings can also be created to fit specific needs. For details, write or phone the office of the Kensington Special Sales Manager: Kensington Publishing Corp., 850 Third Avenue, New York, NY 10022. Attn. Special Sales Department. Phone: 1-800-221-2647.

Dafina Books and the Dafina logo Reg. U.S. Pat. & TM Off.

ISBN-13: 978-0-7582-1751-6
ISBN-10: 0-7582-1751-X

First Kensington Trade Paperback Printing: February 2007
10 9 8 7 6 5 4 3 2 1

Printed in the United States of America

This book is dedicated to the angelic sisterhood
who I know watches over me:
My grandmother Amanda,
My great-grandmothers Alma and Lutishia,
And my great, great-grandmother Fredonia Yates.
Good lookin' out ladies . . . I appreciate you.

With Gratitude

When I think of gratitude, acknowledgements, thank-yous, and of all the people and experiences that ultimately helped me co-create this moment, I am reminded of just how blessed I am, of how amazing this journey called "life" is, and of how everything and everyone is connected. All of those thank-yous would equal the size of this novel!

But there are those whose thoughts, words and deeds are intricately woven into the fabric of this particular work. Your talent, energy, positive attitudes, senses of humor and love helped it happen. And it is you I thank now.

To Spirit, the I Am, for allowing and enabling me to reflect Your light in the earth. In the beginning was the Word . . . and we're still writing. I am so grateful . . .

To my earliest mentors and, in addition to being my parents, two of my best friends: Willie and Flora Hinton. I love you! To my nieces, nephews, brothers and especially my sisters, Dee and Marcella, for our crazy conversations, laughter and tears, down through the years. Y'all know. To Aunt Ernie (Jackson), for believing in my writing and for living in New York, one of my favorite cities.

To my special family of friends: Sherri Roulette-Mosley, Kai Aiyetoro and Fadzo Chanakira (Wu-Wu!) for your invaluable input, feedback, suggestions and critiques through the rewrites, and through life. To my twin, Storm, for being a much needed sounding board and breath of fresh air. To Micki Guzmán and Tino Struckmann for the unexpected yet treasured friendships during our literary journeys. You're next! To mi amigo Hugo Perez. Gracias para todo. And to my heart, Cuezalin; my world shines brighter with you in it . . . *tlazohcamati*.

To the Kensington crew: My fearless and flawless editor Stacey Barney (there I go with the adjectives!), Karen Thomas, the pivotal

Hilary Sares, *Are you sure you don't want me to read this?* Also Lydia Stein, Karina Mikhli, Barbara Bennett and Brendan Finnel.

To Kristine Mills-Noble, Jo Tronc and Tracy Marx for the reason this book is flying off the shelves . . . the cover! Speaking of shelves, to bookstores and booksellers everywhere.

To my legal counsel and the Author's Guild, Robin Davis Miller and the amazing Anita Fore. Your commitment to writers is first class! To agents Sha Shana Crichton and Natasha Kern. What you women do is no joke!

And to you, yes you, the one who's so graciously picked up this novel and turned the page. What would a writer be without a reader? Exactly. I pray God's blessings on your life and your dreams.

If you didn't see your name, and you believe yours is a name that should be seen? The sequel's coming, darlins'. Keep reading . . .

Mr. Snakeskin Boots

It squeezed her booty without apology. But that was only part of the beauty of a St. John suit. The other was its flawless design—its intricate stitching—its wrinkle-free fabric. The way it hugged every inch of her curved, firm body. She was a perfect St. John size six. Thirty-eight years and two children later, a perfect St. John size six and she was proud of it.

Vivian Elise Stanford Montgomery stepped back and briefly inspected her image in the mirror. She moved to the dresser and, pushing aside the two-carat diamond studs, decided on the round ruby dangles with matching choker. The black onyx jewel setting provided a fitting backdrop to the precious stones and complemented the black piping around the jacket as if they had been designed specifically for the occasion.

The ruby and the black and the herringbone all worked to complement Vivian's unblemished, coffee-colored complexion. Well, coffee with a wee bit of cream. She'd been pretty her whole life, although she didn't always think so. It took Sistah Lillie and Brotha Benson's son Titus to convince her she was really pretty, worth a Snickers candy bar and the faux-pearl ring he got out of his Cracker Jack box, but that's another story. To this day she still wasn't sure whether Titus really thought she was pretty or if he just wanted her to play hide-and-go-get-it behind Brother Armstrong's toolshed, but again, that's another story. She could remember being in the Sunbeams and having the mothers of the church comment, "Ooh, ain't she a pretty little black thang?"

Her shoulder-length black hair framed her face softly in a trendy flip style, a style that accented the Asian slant of her wide, brown eyes. Sitting at the vanity, she finished her make-up, adding just a hint of blush and a subtle layer of ruby red lipstick to her full, well-defined lips.

Vivian opened the set of double doors to her dressing room and grabbed a snazzy pair of Manolo Blahnik pumps, black with a patch of ruby and black herringbone fabric encased between the leather toe and heel. She slid into them effortlessly while eyeing the matching bag on the lower shelf. She glanced briefly at her watch, and amidst the dazzle of diamonds that caught the light from every direction, was the message that she'd better hurry.

Crossing to the dresser, Vivian splashed on a generous amount of Spikenard, a present from her best friend Tai's most recent visit to the Holy Land. With one last glance in the full-length mirror, rather a stop-pivot-turn, stop-head-back-pivot-turn again, Vivian exited the spacious master bedroom and entered the hallway.

"Derrick! Elisia! Let's go!" She never stopped walking as she knocked on each child's door and headed for the stairway. She knew that Anastacia, the housekeeper and children's nanny, would have them dressed and ready to go. "We're down here, Mama!" yelled Elisia, all satin and lace. Derrick was sitting on the settee in the foyer, already looking like a deacon at the ripe old age of seven. Why did he insist on dressing like that? Because it made him look like his father, that was why, and his father was his hero.

His father, Dr. Derrick Anthony Montgomery, was many people's hero. Senior pastor of Los Angeles' latest soul-saving sensation, Kingdom Citizens' Christian Center, he was a preacher's son, preacher's preacher, scholar, teacher, much-sought-after conference speaker and one of the finest brothers this side of glory. Vivian smiled as this last thought popped into her head. But how could she help it as she looked at her husband's spitting image, albeit thirty years younger, in front of her?

You know how people say when you meet your husband you'll know? Well, Vivian had that very experience when she laid eyes on D-2's daddy fifteen years ago. Lord! Where had the time gone? And why did the moment seem like yesterday?

It was back in her home state of Kansas at the Kewana Valley District's annual Baptist Convention. Vivian hadn't wanted to go. The only reason she, a twenty-one-year-old communications graduate on her way to becoming the first Black Barbara Walters, had agreed to revisit her old religious stomping grounds was because her best friend's husband was being installed as the new and youngest assistant moderator of the district, and her friend thought Vivian's attending would add a bit of "celebrity" to the affair.

Her best friend was Twyla "Tai" Nicole Brook. Vivian and Tai (so named because her goddaughter and namesake couldn't say Twyla. It always came out "tie-la," so they eventually settled on Aunt Tai, and the name stuck) had been friends since the ninth grade. That's when Vivian's father, Victor L. Stanford, had made a sizeable contribution to Kewana Valley District's Higher Learning Scholarship Fund, and in doing so had become even more important than his propensity for eloquent speech and impenetrable loyalty already afforded him. Her father had been invited to join the district's board, and shortly thereafter invited to a board meeting, family included, in the Florida Keys. Vivian dreaded the trip because she thought she'd have to endure a week of "old fogies" and was delighted when she met fourteen-year-old, auburn-haired, freckle-faced Twyla in the lobby of the posh Hilton Keys Hotel. They had run off to their rooms, donned modest two-piece swimsuits, headed to the beach and shared lifetime secrets, dreams and aspirations that only thirteen- and fourteen-year-old girls could share. They were fast friends from that very day, and even a hundred-mile distance—for that was how far they lived from each other at the time—could not separate them. They wrote each other every week and talked on the phone almost every day from the ninth grade through Vivian's first couple of years of college.

Just before her senior year in high school, Tai informed Vivian that she was getting married. Vivian was not surprised. Tai's singular goal after graduating was to become a wife and mother, and she had talked nonstop about King Wesley Brook from the moment she met him. She surmised after their first kiss that he would be her husband, and after their first unofficial date a short time later, a surreptitious meeting in the church parking lot during a midnight revival, said he would be the father of her children. She was right on both counts and became Mrs. King Wesley Brook shortly after her nineteenth birthday and six months before their first child, Michael Wesley Brook, was introduced to the world.

Tai had asked Vivian to deliver a motivational speech at the Saturday Night Youth Extravaganza. Vivian went to the Friday night services to gauge the type of crowd attending the meeting. She wasn't sure whether to be more spiritual, religious or political. It was a fine line during this time, the '80s, and with her ever-increasing personal relationship with God and widening social and political views as a news correspondent, she was always walking that line.

She tried to sneak in after the devotional (which she found boring) and before the offering (where she wanted to be sure and give back to God). She excuse me'd down to the center of the pew three rows from the back and had just opened her program when the lady to the left tapped her and nodded toward an usher who was motioning, for her to follow him. She looked around and saw Tai's widened eyes which said "come *on* girl," so she dutifully excuse me'd back down the row, avoiding a few angry eyes but not missing the "umph"s and "tsk"s of a few sisters before bowing her head and following Mr. Black-Suit-White-Shirt-Pinstriped-Tie down to the second row.

She barely had a chance to squeeze Tai's arm, giving her a little pinch, when she saw him. He came in with the pastors and others designated to participate in the evening's program. She was staring without knowing it and, even after she knew it, couldn't stop. She checked him out from the top of his s-curled, collar-length hair to the soles of his buffed and polished snakeskin boots. Snakeskin boots! Who was this brother?

"Who's Mr. Snakeskin Boots?" she hissed at Tai. Tai just smiled and rolled her eyes while rocking to the choir's fiery rendition of "Jesus Is A Rock." Vivian tried to regain her composure, but snakeskin boots had cooked her collards. He was wearing a dark navy, double-breasted suit that emphasized his broad shoulders which narrowed down—*can we say "vee"*—into a highly huggable waist and then fanned out, oh-so-slightly, to reveal a perfectly shaped, hard butt . . . Jesus! What was she thinking? And in the middle of church service no less. Right in between "rock in a weary land" and "shelter in the time of storm." *Pull yourself together, girl!*

She tried to divert her eyes as he sat down and even joined Tai in a rock, clap, rock, clap as the choir bumped it up an octave. She threw in an "amen," raised her arms and closed her eyes, trying to capture the image of Jesus as a rock. But all she could see was curly hair and snakeskin boots, and it was making her hot! She opened her eyes just in time to see Snakeskin staring at her intently. She closed her eyes again and tried to start singing, but since she didn't know the words it just looked as if she were singing in tongues, and they didn't play that at the Baptist Convention in 1985! When she stole another peek Snakeskin was smiling broadly, as if he knew she'd been thinking of him.

Vivian was thankful when a lady two rows behind her got happy and started jumping up and screaming, "My Rock, my Rock!" That brought other members of the audience to their feet, and before she knew it Tai was on her feet, thankfully blocking Vivian's view of Snakeskin. About this time Tai's husband, King Wesley Brook, mounted the podium along with his father, the Reverend Doctor Pastor Bishop Overseer Mister Stanley Obadiah Meshach Brook, Jr., Vivian's father and a group of other board members. The song had reached a feverish pitch, and the choir was rocking, literally. Just before delivering the song's final lyric, they paused. The choir, director with hand in midair, pianist, organist, drummer, lead singer—everybody stopped. It seemed everyone in the audience was frozen, too, holding their breath, all except for the "happy" woman two rows back whose "My Rock!" had toned down to a quiet "Rock" between sobs as she was furiously fanned by two ushers in white. Oh, it was on now! The Holy Spirit was moving, people were remembering how Jesus had been their Rock and there was shouting and crying and dancing going on all around. All that time the choir remained frozen, as did Vivian, but she for a totally different reason. Slowly the lead singer, a Karen Clark-like soprano-alto, sang the final line. She hit every note on the musical scale as she brought the song to its dramatic conclusion. Adding several syllables to each word, she belted out, "Jesus is my Rock."

The drummer started a roll on the snares, the guitarist held on to a string, the note reverberating in the air, the pianist and organist seemed to be in a competition as to who could hit the most keys in the shortest amount of time and the lead singer had gone on a journey to find notes that heretofore had not been hit. The song never really ended. It just faded away. The lead singer started her own personal praise as she walked back to the choir loft, the musicians were in their own player praise and the audience added their adorations to the Lord.

Vivian had sat there quiet and still, a small smile playing on her face as she felt the power of God. She stayed that way a long time, through the shouting and the clapping and the praise pause and the player praise. She opened her eyes when she heard the voice of a man that reminded her of her father's soothing tremor, but the voice was raspier, lighter. She cocked her head as she opened her eyes and stared into those of Snakeskin Boots himself, Derrick Anthony Montgomery.

"Are you ready to go?"

Vivian jumped, shaken from her walk down memory lane. She was sitting in the living room, waiting for her husband to come down. And here he was in front of her, still melting her just like he did fifteen years ago when she watched him deliver his eloquent tribute to King Brook at the Kewana Valley District's Baptist Convention.

"Yes, I'm ready," she responded as she grabbed her purse, and, rising from the couch, kissed him lightly on the mouth. They headed to the garage and the iridescent, pearl white Jaguar waiting there. They all settled in as Derrick hit the garage door opener, started the car and drove down the long, winding driveway.

"King called," Derrick began after a brief silence.

"When?"

"Just now."

"Must have been important," Vivian pondered aloud. "He knows how busy Sunday mornings are. What did he want?"

Derrick's brow creased slightly as he tried to figure that out himself. "I don't know. I told him I'd call him later today, between services maybe."

Vivian leaned back and looked out the window. It was a beautiful Sunday in Los Angeles with clear blue skies, fluffy white cumulous clouds and picture-perfect palm trees lining the streets. Her mind drifted to the conversation she and Tai had a couple days ago. Tai had seemed unusually quiet and reserved, and when Vivian asked her if everything was okay, Tai had said she was just tired. Since they had four, Vivian had assumed it was the children. Now she was wondering if it was the kids, or something else?

I think you got something that belongs to me

Tai feigned illness to get out of morning services. Well, she didn't really lie. She was sick—sick of perpetrating a fraud, acting as though everything was hunky-dory when it wasn't. She just didn't think she could go through the motions of blessed-first-lady-with-out-a-care-in-the-world today. She went downstairs and crossed the lovely yet cluttered atmosphere of the living and formal dining room and entered the large, ranch-style kitchen. At one time this had been her favorite place.

She poured a cup of coffee and even though it was only ten in the morning added just a touch of Bailey's Irish Cream. Tai didn't drink often. In fact, she'd never drank alcohol before until a friend's baby shower, when she was twenty-six. Not that she thought it was a sin. It was just something she'd never been exposed to, or interested in trying. But this morning she felt that she had some serious soul-searching to do, some decisions to make. And she didn't think God would mind too much if she asked Mr. Bailey to join her in the process.

Tai leaned back on the island counter and stared out the window into their spacious backyard. She didn't really see the large oak tree or her children's brightly colored swing set and battered jungle gym. She didn't hear the sounds of the robin and crow vying for attention in God's feathered friends' choir. Tai didn't notice that the tulips she and her daughters had planted were budding open with bright color swatches of pink, purple, yellow and red, and had formed a nature necklace around the oak tree's huge trunk. When Tai looked out into this Sunday morning all she could see was Hope Jones. Petite and powerful, funny and fiery, spiritual and seductive, she was in many ways the exact opposite of Tai's subdued, almost shylike personality. Hope reminded her a bit of Vivian, except Vivian had more class in her toenail than this woman did in her whole body.

It was, in fact, her similarity to Vivian and her zeal for God that Tai had initially appreciated when Hope had come to the church as a transplant from Tulsa, Oklahoma. She even had the same hourglass figure as Vivian, much to Tai's weight-gaining chagrin. Hope had landed a job in Kansas City and said the second thing on her agenda after finding a place to live was finding a church home. She'd fit in immediately with the members of Mount Zion Progressive Baptist Church, a place where the membership, two thousand strong and growing, was more like family than anything else. Hope had attended the same type of close-knit church in Tulsa, though that congregation was much smaller, and she was always searching for the things of God. She had been active in her home church from the time she was baptized at the age of seven, until she left Tulsa. She'd been first a student and later a teacher in their Sunday School, a member of the drama department and lead singer and codirector of the church choir. Her father was head of the Deacon Board, a group of men who carried out the business of running the church under the pastor's direction. Her mother had been the pianist for years, until she and Hope's father divorced and her mother had moved her membership to the Methodist church on the other side of town. Hope had stayed at the Baptist church with her father and her friends and by the time she left had become a leader who was now sorely missed. At least those were the facts as told by Mrs. McCormick, and Juanita normally got her facts pretty straight.

Hope had literally exploded onto Mount Zion's small scene, a kaleidoscope of energy and enthusiasm, just what the church's youth department needed. She'd immediately become invaluable to its director, Sister Juanita McCormick, and—although Tai didn't notice it at first—to her husband as well.

It wasn't his first affair. That had happened years ago, right before Princess, their second child, was born. That one she had seen coming a mile away. Tootie "the Floozie" Smith had been her nemesis since high school, a woman who always wanted what she couldn't have. She'd had an on-again, off-again relationship with King until Tai and King got married. And she was a sore loser. Not only that, but Tai thought Tootie had as much use for God as a blind man for reading glasses. So when Tootie Smith walked into a Wednesday night prayer meeting wearing a loud, multicolored jacket over what basically amounted to a cat suit, Tai knew that one of the devil's helpers had just entered the building.

She didn't blame Tootie entirely. It took two to tango, and like Tai always told King, "She didn't make a vow to me, *you* did." Things had been a little rough during the first part of their marriage. After much soul-searching she'd finally admitted that one, maybe she had been too young to get married, and two, they'd had no time to really adjust to being a married couple before their son Michael was born. At that time King was working sixteen-hour days trying to get the church established, and Tai, along with being a new mother, was supplementing the income with a full-time secretarial job at Sprint. They barely saw each other those first three years, and when they did they were either too tired or too frustrated or both to share quality time.

Like Michael, Princess wasn't planned. She came along on one of those rare Friday evenings when King came home early and Tai wasn't tired. They'd shared a nice dinner and then moved to the den to watch a movie. King popped popcorn while Tai put Michael to bed, and it wasn't long before their own passion surpassed that of the lead character in Spike Lee's *She's Gotta Have It*. That movie had stirred up controversy in the Baptist circles, and some clergy had urged their members not to see it. Well, King and Tai had rented it to see what the fuss was about. But they never saw the ending. Nine months later, the King had his Princess. But not before Tootie had him.

Tai, seven months pregnant, had taken Michael and headed to Chicago to attend her brother's graduation from Northwest University. King had planned to go, too, but a last minute crisis at the church had prevented him from leaving. Tootie could barely wait until Tai got back to give her the news. She and King had slept together, at their home, in their bed. Tai never slept in that bed again. In fact, she and King moved to a new house and bought all new furniture shortly after Princess was born.

Tai had been devastated, but she never thought about divorcing King, although she did move to her parent's home for a couple of months. She was pregnant when she found out about the affair, and it was over before the delivery. King swore it was a one-weekend fling, a seventy-two-hour period where in Tai's words, "He lost his frickin' mind!" Indeed, Tai saw Tootie only once or twice after the incident. Word had it she moved to Los Angeles to pursue a singing career. King promised her it was a mistake that would never happen again, and for the next few years, they were very happy. That happiness led to twins Timothy and Tabitha, born three years after Princess. This pregnancy was planned; having twins was not. Yet having been fruitful and having multiplied, the Brooks felt their family was complete. King then visited the doctor for a little "snip-snip" to ensure their childbearing days were over.

The twins were almost a year old when Tai found out about Karen Ward. Like Tootie, Karen was not a member of their congregation; in fact, Karen never stepped foot inside the church. That placed her a miniscule step ahead of Tootie in the class department, but still won her no brownie points. She occasionally attended The Good Shepherd Community Church, with a mostly White congregation, on the city's north side. Tai and King met her when they went to Byron White's Fourth of July party. Byron was King's best friend at the time. Karen was Byron's cousin from the small town of Iola, about one hundred miles from Kansas City. When King met Karen, Tai had almost put his and Tootie's affair behind her—almost. She still remembered feeling just a twinge of something when during the course of the afternoon she saw King and Karen laughing together and then later saw Karen staring at King before Tai caught her eye and Karen quickly looked away. Thinking she was just being oversensitive, Tai shook off her feelings of discomfort, and if not for the innocent ramblings of a little child, she may never have learned the truth.

She'd agreed to take the Sunday School's beginner's class, those between the ages of six and eight, to the park and then for pizza. This in celebration of their successfully completing the "I'm in the Lord's Army" study course, which included among other things, memorizing the Lord's Prayer and Twenty-third Psalm. She and the two other chaperones had spent a vigorous, yet for the most part unchallenging, day at the park and were chomping on pepperoni pizza from Chuck E. Cheese when little Danielle, Byron's daughter, walked over to her.

"Hi there, Miss Angel," Tai cooed as she opened her arms for a big hug from Danielle.

"Hi, Queen Bee," the child cooed back, using the title the church family had bestowed on their much loved first lady. "Where's Pastor King?"

"He's probably at the church or at home studying. You like our pastor, don't you?"

Danielle nodded her head yes and inched even closer into Tai's embrace. "Aunt Karen likes him, too. She likes him a whole bunch."

Tai became stock-still at that point, and Sharon, one of the other chaperones, almost shushed the child. But Tai held her hand up and encouraged Danielle to keep talking.

"I'm sure she does," Tai continued, smiling pleasantly at the little cherub-cheeked messenger whom she was sure God had sent. "All of God's children are supposed to like each other, right?"

"Uh-huh," the girl conceded. "But I didn't know we were supposed to kiss and hug the way Pastor King and Aunt Karen do when they see each other."

"Where did you see them together?" Tai asked, her voice barely above a whisper and her hand absently stroking the little girl's long, twisted braid.

Danielle, happy to be the center of attention with what was obviously a pretty important story since it held two adults spellbound, continued on in the blind ignorance that only six-year-olds enjoy. "Oh, at Daddy's house, and one time when I was staying with Aunt Karen, Pastor King came over to her house and helped us bake cookies."

"Really?" Tai whispered, her eyes shining with tears but not spilling over.

"Yes," Danielle replied thoughtfully and in a whisper, too. "Then they went in Aunt Karen's bedroom while I watched *Barney.* Then I fell asleep."

Tai hugged the child close while wiping her eyes quickly. Sharon grabbed her hand and spoke silent volumes of "sistah-girl sympathy." Tai looked at her with the obvious question in her eyes. Sharon, a longtime member of the church and staunch supporter of her first lady, leaned over and whispered, "As God is my witness, I won't tell a soul." She never did. About a year later her husband was promoted and their family moved to Texas. Tai still marveled at Sharon's trustworthiness and ability to keep a confidence. She no longer, however, liked Chuck E. Cheese.

Tai never knew when the affair started or how long it lasted, but again, King promised her it was the last time. That it had been only a physical thing that meant nothing to him. Tai didn't believe

him. Nor did she care. At least that was the lie she told herself. He
had taken the very thing that her life with him had been built on,
trust. He'd destroyed her self-esteem, already eroded after four
children and fifty extra pounds.

This time it was King's mother, Sister Maxine Brook, who
saved the marriage and Tai's sanity. She and King had again separated following his adultery. This time King moved out, or rather
got kicked out, by his very pissed off wife. Hoping other people's
problems would lessen her own, Tai immersed herself in *Oprah,
The Young and the Restless* and white wine. King returned, but the
children became her primary focus, and if not for them, she'd have
had to look strenuously for a reason to go on living. Mama Max
had phoned one day when Tai was feeling particularly low. Two
hours later, she knocked on the door with a meatloaf, a pot of
spaghetti, a huge apple cobbler and a dose of age-old attitude that
only a mother of the church could possess.

"Baby," Sister Maxine began as she warmed the food on the
stove, pushed up her sleeves and started cleaning a kitchen that
hadn't seen soap for days. "I know you're hurting. I understand.
And I also know you can let this do one of two things. Break ya or
build ya."

Tai reached for her glass of wine and countered, "But, Mama,
you don't understand, you've never been down this road."

"Oh, yeah? You think you're the first one who's had to deal
with one of them bitches!"

Tai almost choked on her chardonnay. In all this time of knowing Sister Maxine, she'd never heard her say so much as "darn." Yet
here was this matronly diva, still the epitome of style with straight-
legged black pants, an extra-large jungle print top that reached
midthigh and coiffed hairdo swept up and secured into a fashion-
able French bun, rolling "bitch" off her tongue as if it wasn't the
first time. Tai stared at her wide-eyed.

"Mama Max!"

Mama Max just gave her a look and then swiveled around to

stir the spaghetti. "You got any more of that?" she asked without looking back.

"What?" Tai asked, still amazed Mom had "gone there."

"That what you're drinking." She replaced the lid on the spaghetti and reached for the loaf of French bread and butter. "Pour me a glass and I'll tell you a story. And shut your mouth before a fly gets in."

Mama Max went on to tell her about the time almost twenty years earlier when "the Rev acted like a plum fool." It had been while they were out of town, at a convention in the big city of Dallas, Texas. Sistah Max had been born and raised in a small town and moved to an even smaller town when her husband got his first church. Their marriage experienced its share of ups and downs, but she'd been happy. She'd gone back to the hotel right after service and was in a sound sleep when the phone rang. "Sistah Brook," an unfamiliar voice had whispered into the receiver. "I don't mean to be nosy or rude, but I just saw your husband come into the lobby, and I don't think he's headed to your room."

"Who's this?" Mama Max demanded, now wide awake and sitting up.

"You can just say . . . I'm my sister's keeper." Then the line went dead.

Mama Max jumped out of that bed as if lightning hit and started praying in tongues. "Give me the spirit of discernment, Holy Ghost," she intoned as she paced back and forth and around the room. After about fifteen minutes a number came to her clear as day—915. Without hesitation, Mama Max slipped on her caftan, pulled on her slippers and checked her always perfectly coiffed hair in the mirror before leaving the room and heading for the elevator. When she reached room 915, she knocked on the door. After a moment, a quiet voice asked tentatively, "Who is it?"

"It's your worst nightmare!" Sistah Max explosively responded. "Wife of Bishop Stanley Obadiah Meshach Brook and mother to his four children: King, Queen, Daniel and Esther." Sistah Maxine was yelling for the world to hear. "Open up this door, you two-bit hussy. I think you've got something that belongs to me!"

Tai was incredulous. She'd never have that kind of nerve. "What happened?" she squealed, leaning forward as though she were watching a thriller on television.

"What do you think happened? She opened the door. My husband came out, and by this time a few more guests had come out of their rooms as well. Assured that I was the center of attention, I made an announcement. I said real calm and quietlike, 'You low-life trollop, if I see you or anyone who looks like you with *my* husband again? I will kill ya and tell God I did it!'" Sistah Maxine's eyes were twinkling as she relived the story. She buttered the last piece of bread, placed the bread back in the foil and placed the foil in the oven. Before continuing, she took a long swallow from her glass.

"Well, you know that the next fastest way to spread a message besides telephone is tell a church member. The story was on more people's lips than that night's sermon. I became a hero of sorts to the married women and someone not to be messed with to the would-be husband-stealing floozies. It probably didn't hurt that I signed up for a gun permit as soon as I got back home."

"You did what?" Tai exclaimed. No longer able to sit still, she jumped up and reached for a knife and a tomato to begin the salad preparations.

"Oh, I never got a gun," Sistah Max went on calmly as she plucked lettuce leaves and placed them in a colander. "But word got out that I had *applied*." She took a delicate sip of wine before continuing.

"The Reverend was in the doghouse for about six months, and I got some of the best jewelry of all our years of marriage. I told him I would not forgive him a second time, and even though vengeance belonged to God—the next bitch I caught him with would think it belonged to me. To this day, to my knowledge anyway, he's never strayed." She turned off the fire under the spaghetti, eyed Tai with a slightly raised eyebrow and sly smile, announced that dinner was ready and said she'd "fetch the chil'ren." Then she drained her glass, patted her coiffed do and walked out the kitchen while humming "I'm a Soldier in the Army of the Lord."

Tai smiled at the memory of her mother-in-law all those years ago. That particular heart-to-heart had influenced Tai's decision to stay married. Mama Max had always been a pillar of strength, but after that day, their relationship took on a new meaning, a more sisterly bond. Tai and King got back together, and although it was different, they were able to pick up the pieces and put them together reasonably well. To his credit, King had gone out of his way to assure her of his love for her and their children. He'd cut back on his overloaded schedule, brought her flowers and gifts, spent more time with her and the kids, and they'd even splurged on a two-week vacation to Orlando, Florida, and Disney World. But Tai never got over the betrayal totally, and after that, all women were suspect. She even felt she'd developed a sixth sense where women who might threaten her marriage were concerned, and that was why Hope Jones was not a surprise.

Remembering Hope made Tai's smile disappear. She rose from the couch where she'd downed her second cup of coffee with Bailey's. She opened the refrigerator but deciding she wasn't hungry, poured a glass of water instead. She wanted to call Vivian but knew they would still be in church. She needed her friend desperately but didn't know if she wanted to have this conversation with her. Again. To this day, King denied anything was happening with Hope Jones. Something was going on. King came home later and later. When he was home, he stayed in his office. Fool me once, shame on you. Fool me twice, shame on me. Tai's intuition told her King was using strike three. She would not be fooled.

Hearing from God

The hip-hop sounds of gospel artist Tonex blasted out of Hope's canary yellow Mazda MG as she sped down I–35 on her way to Kansas City, Missouri, to see her cousin and new best friend, Frieda. *"You are my personal Jesus,"* she crooned along with the hip-hop singer with much enthusiasm and excitement if just a tad bit off-key.

Hope felt good. Not only was it a sunny March day in the Midwest, but it was also Sunday, her favorite day of the week. Church had been inspiring. Her praise dance troupe, the Angels of Hope, had performed for the first time and had been heartily received. Their performance alone had been a miracle. It had taken much prayer and a private meeting with the highly opposed Mother Bailey before she convinced this tradition-inclined church matron and others that dancing could be holy, not a matter of "branging that devil's music into 'de Lawd's house" as Mother Bailey had more than implied. Even so, Hope had choreographed a conservative routine. She'd prayerfully chosen the music, an updated gospel classic, "I Surrender All." And rather than have too many steps or other dance movements, she'd decided to use her knowledge of sign language and incorporate a large amount of dramatic hand movements and facial expression into the presentation, combining drama with dance. Not only that but she, along with Sistah McCormick and Pastor King, had codeveloped and taught a two-month praise and worship study course for all who would be a part of the dance or drama department so they would understand the difference between performing for the secular world and performing for the Kingdom. They explained how one's body could be used as an instrument of praise to God.

All of the instruction and the rehearsing and the fasting and the praying had paid off. The Spirit of God was evident, even tangible, in the church as the group of eight graceful young ladies danced in their flowing white costumes. Tears flowed from a dancer's eyes as she remembered her own surrender. One dancer's face reflected joy, another showed serenity, another, reverence. Their bodies moved as one, twirling gracefully. *All to thee, my blessed Savior . . .* Their hands reached toward heaven. Audience members stood with their arms raised in worship. They, too, surrendered everything to God. Problems. Pain. Disappointment. Fear. Their voices rose to join the uplifted arms as saints told God their dreams, desires, needs. The final confirmation of acceptance and proof that God was indeed present was when Mother Bailey, who couldn't fake getting the Holy Ghost if she tried, had stood crying and moaning reverently, "I surrender, Lawd, I surrender!"

Pastor King's message was the crème de la crème. "How To Turn Mourning Into Dancing" was a fitting topic, undoubtedly penned with the dancing troupe's debut in mind. Had he been inspired after watching their rehearsal earlier in the week? Hope thought so. Perhaps God had spoken to him, as He'd spoken to her. It gave her a warm, fuzzy feeling to think she was on the same page with her pastor because it proved, in her mind, that she was indeed hearing from God.

Those who tried knew that hearing from God wasn't always easy. For instance, Hope had been sure she'd heard God say Shawn

Edmunds, her former neighbor, first love and boyfriend all through college, was to be her husband. Why else would she have given him anything so precious as her virginity?

It had happened a couple years ago, during the annual convention hosted by Perry Carlson, a leading minister in Tulsa with a "mega-church" of over ten thousand members. The opening services that Monday night had been extraordinary, and both Hope and Shawn were glad they'd been a part of it. Shawn, a talented bass guitar player with dreamy hazel eyes, filled in for the church's regular guitarist who'd gone on the road. Known for her original gospel plays and praise dance teams, Hope was seated in the area reserved for special guests, second row center. It offered a perfect place to see and hear the choir and guest speakers, and it gave her two to three uninterrupted hours to stare at and appreciate God's gift. That was what she considered Shawn to be—a gift from God with her name on it.

The message that night was entitled "Having by Asking." The preacher's text was taken from the Book of James where he, a half brother of Jesus, was explaining that sometimes people didn't have what they desired simply because they didn't ask for it or they asked for the wrong reasons. Hope went home, got on her knees and asked God for Shawn to be her husband. Then she got up, crossed the room to her desk, grabbed her Bible and plopped on the bed. She asked God for a sign, a confirmation that He'd heard her prayer and that the answer was yes. She closed her eyes, opened the book, placed a finger on the page, opened her eyes and read the words beneath her finger. "Wherefore they are no more twain but one flesh. What God has joined together, let not man put asunder. Matthew 19:6." The Bible fell out of Hope's hands. She was taken aback, couldn't believe where her finger had landed. But a clearer message could not have been received. She felt God Himself had spoken.

The next day, Hope felt a confidence and freedom with Shawn she'd never known before. Although she felt that sex before marriage was a sin, she became more and more amorous in her affections toward her husband-to-be. Not one to complain, Shawn embraced this new and improved Hope as a sign that finally she believed he loved her and in return, just maybe, she'd let him hit it.

Hope hadn't planned it to happen. But after the Friday night services were over she, Shawn and another couple had gone out for a late dinner. This couple had just gotten engaged. Hope was elated for them. Hearing this news on the heels of her revelation that Shawn was to be her husband was further proof the season of marriage was here and her turn was coming. Shawn had given her thigh a little squeeze, and Hope squeezed right back, running her hand down to his knee and back up the inside of his thigh just beneath his manhood. She remembered almost touching it and jerking her hand away as if she'd touched a hot oven. At that very moment she thought of one of her grandmother's sayings, "If you keep playing with fire, you gon' get burnt."

They'd gone back to his place, a two-bedroom apartment not far from the university campus they both attended. Shawn put on a Babyface CD. "I just love this song," he whispered as he gathered Hope in his arms and began a sensual slow dance across the living room floor.

To this day, Hope didn't remember exactly what happened next. It was like one minute they were dancing and the next minute she was in his bed, naked. It wasn't the first time she and Shawn had fooled around, but she'd never taken all of her clothes off before. Lying next to him as he slowly outlined her body with the tips of his fingers, she recited in her mind the Scripture she'd read just days before. There was little resistance when he began kissing her mouth, eyes, ears, breast, and just a slight hesitation as he continued to tease her with his tongue down her stomach, hips, thighs . . . She covered her eyes then and was surprised to feel the weight of his physique when he covered her body with his own while placing his hand behind her knee and raising her leg in a slow, languid motion. She could feel him pressing against her and took her hands from her eyes, wrapping them around his strong muscled back and hugging him tightly. She didn't remember a word being spoken, but she knew this time would be different. Shawn must have sensed it, too, because he continued gently, almost reverently, as if to make a hasty move might break the mood and change the atmosphere and Hope's acquiescent mind. He grabbed his dick and rubbed it against her, higher at first and then lower and lower, positioning himself for entry. *Could it be?* he thought as a slight layer of perspiration broke out on his brow, and his heartbeat quickened. Suddenly Hope's hand was against his chest.

"Shawn," she whispered, a mixture of longing and fear in her voice, "do you love me?"

"With all my heart," he answered. And the two became one.

Life had been heavenly after Hope gave herself to Shawn. She was sure that marriage was their relationship's destiny, even though no date had been set or ring given. But the summer after Shawn's graduation, several months into this new level of their relationship, Hope noticed a change in his behavior toward her. It was almost imperceptible at first, like a smell that you notice but can't quite define. There were sudden and unexplainable mood swings. They spent more and more time apart. Hope grew worried and questioned Shawn about the way he was acting. He became agitated. She did, too. Hope had thought by now they'd be making wedding plans.

Summer passed. Shawn announced plans to relocate to Dallas and pursue a career in sports broadcasting. It wasn't that Hope hadn't known about his desire for such a career; she'd often encouraged it. It was the fact that she didn't find out he actually had a job and was leaving until two weeks before he got on the plane.

The signs became even more glaring once he moved. For instance, he insisted she not come down, saying he needed to get settled first and focus on his career. When after two months she still wasn't welcome, Hope asked if he was seeing someone else. He was, a Dallas Cowboys cheerleader named Tiffany. Hope never saw his apartment. Six months after this heartbreaking news and mere weeks after graduating from college with a degree in English, she moved to Kansas City.

Hope was sure she'd heard God this time. As soon as she put the wheels in motion to leave Tulsa and the experience with Shawn behind her, good things began to happen. She'd been devastated by their breakup, but was determined to move on with her life. Rather than pining away about a past that could not be changed, she threw her energy into creating a new, more favorable future. However, a lesson had been learned. Hope would not compromise her beliefs with another man. She wouldn't get ahead of God. The next time she made love, she'd be married.

She'd barely put her resume on the Internet before receiving calls to schedule interviews. Then, as God would have it, a cousin she hadn't seen in ten years and who was the assistant to a human resources director ran across her resume. A month later, she was putting her English degree to work as a copy editor for the city's newspaper, the *Kansas City Star*.

It was this same cousin, Frieda Moore, who'd told her about Mount Zion. Hope had asked her about churches within days of her arrival. Although not a member, Frieda had attended Mount Zion with friends a few times and had enjoyed the new way they told an old story. The preacher was fortyish and fine. And they had a band, a real live band that backed up the choir. "Sometimes," Frieda had gushed enthusiastically, "it feels more like a party than church!" Hope had smiled at this comparison. A Holy Ghost party was right up her alley.

From the time Hope hit the steps of Mount Zion, she knew she'd found her church home. It wasn't just the music, a wonderful blend of contemporary and classic gospel that was audible a block away from the church, but also the feeling that enveloped Hope the moment she parked her car and stepped into the parking lot. It was the smiles on the faces of the other people entering the sanctuary, the joy that pulsated up the steps and down the aisle as she entered. It was the courtesy and warmth that exuded from the usher as she placed a program in Hope's hand and led her up the aisle. It was the hug from Sis. Wilma Stronghart who, upon finding out that she was a visitor, grabbed Hope and clutched her tight to her ample bosom, planted a loud smack of a kiss on her right cheek, leaving an apple red lipstick imprint, and said loudly, "Welcome, welcome, welcome!" It was First Lady Brook, affectionately known as Queen Bee, and the warm way she'd smiled as their eyes met after Hope stood and was welcomed to the services of the Zion family. And it was the pastor, King Brook, a man whose words seemed to come from the very mouth of God, who spoke from the depths of his spirit to the pit of her soul. She'd been amazed by his sermon on that first visit to Mount Zion. How it so resembled what she'd gone through that the sermon could have been titled "Hope's Story." So uncanny, she would have questioned her cousin about spreading her business, except that she hadn't shared her business, especially the breakup, with Frieda.

Pastor King spoke on starting over. He talked about turning life's page when one didn't like the writing and beginning a new chapter. Hope tried to remain impassive as the pastor spoke of broken hearts and shattered dreams, and how with God, all could be made new. But her eyes filled with tears as she remembered past pain, including the callous way Shawn had told her about his new girlfriend. Hope's parents' divorce had been heartbreaking also. Scars remained, but the message encouraged Hope, confirmed that she could begin a new life, one filled with love and happiness. Pastor King promised, "The darkest hour is just before day."

It was Hope's daytime. When the invitation for membership was issued, when Pastor King asked if there was anyone who wanted to "progress with Mount Zion Progressive," her legs had propelled her upward before her mind knew what was going on.

The congregants in her row encouraged her forward. Several others joined her as she walked down the aisle. She'd felt the Holy Spirit so intensely her knees had almost given out as she made her way to the altar. She stood before the altar, basking in the cleansing presence of God. Her heart filled with peace as the remnants of pain faded. Pastor King had come down from the pulpit then, looked her straight in the eye and said simply, "The Lord is going to use you, woman of God." Then he'd laid his hand gently on the top of her head. The next thing she knew she was lying on the floor, staring up at the ceiling, covered by a large piece of black cloth. As the ushers helped her up and onto a seat in the first row, she realized she'd been "slain in the Spirit." That had never happened before. She knew she'd heard from God, and she knew she was home.

The CD player switched from Tonex to Fred Hammond. Hope exited the freeway and trekked through the streets of Kansas City toward the famously popular eating establishment, Gates Bar-BQ, where she was meeting Frieda. She was still thinking about Pastor King and her beginnings at Mount Zion as she pulled up to a red light.

"Hey, baby girl, can I come?" she heard from the passenger in the car on her left side.

"Jesus is going to be there, is that all right?" she answered with a slight smile as she turned up Fred Hammond just a little more on her stereo.

"Hell yeah, that's all right. I don't care if He come, long as He bring you."

Thankfully the light turned green, and Hope purposely slowed behind a big, pink Cadillac, giving the Range Rover time to jet ahead of her. She shook her head and sighed, turning into the Gates Bar-BQ parking lot at a faster speed than was prudent. Her father always told her she had a lead foot where the accelerator was concerned. She checked her make-up and jumped out just in time to see Frieda walking over.

"Hey, girl," Hope said, giving Frieda a hug.

"What's up, Hope? How was church?"

"If yo' butt really wanted to know, you'd take me up on one of my many invitations to come join us."

They entered the restaurant. It was noisy and crowded, as it was most weekends and every Sunday.

"May I help you, please?" the worker shouted from behind the counter when they'd stepped inside the door.

"Just keep praying for me so I don't go to hell," Frieda replied with a smile, before she shouted back to the woman behind the counter, "I'll have a short end with fries and—what do you want?" she asked Hope. "And a chicken dinner and two strawberrys." There was nothing like the strawberry sodas at Gates.

Hope and Frieda grabbed their orders and wound around counters and customers to a red leather upholstered booth by the window. A handsome older man with a short, salt-and-pepper cut and an expertly trimmed goatee smiled at Frieda. She smiled back, waving a rib between her fingers before placing it in her mouth and pulling it out clean. She quickly grabbed another, this time wrapping a sauce-soaked piece of white bread around it before taking a more ladylike bite, quickly followed by a thick, golden fry.

"Girl, church was the bomb this morning," Hope began, spreading a liberal amount of the spicy sauce on her chicken leg before cutting it with her knife and fork.

"Well, I'm glad your time with God was the bomb this morning, suga' pie," Frieda countered, licking her fingers and sucking bits of meat from between her teeth. 'Cause my date was sho' an explosion last night!"

Hope shook her head and rolled her eyes.

"Girl," Frieda began, drawing out the word and lowering her voice to a whisper. "Let me tell ya—brotha man is no joke." She related detail after detail in a conspiratorial tone, and although Hope listened with genuine interest, she couldn't help but think that this was way too much information. The last thing Celibate-Till-I'm-Married needed to hear was about a night of sexual escapades. Still, she leaned forward, not wanting to miss a word as Frieda recounted her torrid evening.

"Girl, shut up!" Hope exclaimed after hearing a particularly juicy tidbit, even though that was the last thing she wanted Frieda to do.

Hope left the restaurant two hours later, thankful for her crazy cousin's friendship. She planned, in time, to tell her about Shawn, and prayed for a way to subtly steer Frieda toward a less promiscuous lifestyle. At the very least, she'd make sure Frieda was using protection. These days, it was a matter of life and death. Still, she didn't judge her cousin. Hope missed the physical love that Frieda was getting, and prayed for a solution to that as well.

His "spiritual thing"

"Man, this sounds serious," Derrick groaned as he loosened his tie and rested his head back against the chair in his large home office. He methodically rubbed his eyes and then his head, realizing too late that after preaching in two services he didn't have the energy for this conversation.

"It is, Brother, it is," King responded, his voice low and equally fatigued. They were silent for a moment. Then Derrick cleared his throat and sat up, his head in his hand.

"So what are you going to do?"

"I don't know. What can I do?"

"That's a question for you to answer."

King sighed. He'd been dealing with this issue by himself for months, and while glad to be able to unload and get the advice of his dear friend, he didn't feel any better. "You know I love Tai."

"Yeah, I know," Derrick replied. "That's why I don't understand this whole thing, because I know you love her. She's the mother of your children, man, four beautiful babies."

King sighed again, but was otherwise silent.

Derrick continued, "Does she know?"

"She suspects. But then she always suspects."

"She has her reasons."

"I know, but that other stuff happened a long time ago."

"When it comes to affairs and a woman's memory, a long time ago is like yesterday."

"Yeah, I guess." King leaned back into his wing-backed chair. He was still at the church, in his office. He'd changed out of his suit, which was wet from the sweat of the last service, showered and was wearing a pair of casual navy pants and a white polo shirt with navy ribbing around the collar and sleeves. His shoes were off, and his feet rested on the edge of his massive maple desk. He picked absently at the fish dinner that his staunchest supporter and oldest member, Mother Bailey, had brought him when she found out he'd be staying through until the evening service. His Bible lay open on the other side of the desk along with a copy of the day's program and a picture drawing of Jesus surrounded by lambs that Mother Bailey's great-grandson, five-year-old Joshua, had colored in Sunday School. A yellow legal pad of paper was to the left of it with unfinished notes for the Sunday night message written in outline form.

"You got to think of your family, man," Derrick was saying as King picked up the pen on the legal pad and began to doodle. "That's your obligation—to God and to them."

"That's all I've thought about for the past six months, in fact, the past few years. I'm trying, Dee, I'm really trying. Like I said, I still love Tai; I'm just not *in* love with her. And this other thing, well, it may be too big for me to control."

"What do you mean, too big for you to control?"

"It's like no matter what I do, it won't stop."

"Ah, come on, King, this is Derrick you're talking to. I've known you for twenty years, and I know you can do anything you set your mind to."

"This isn't a mind thing."

"It's a dick thing, right?"

"That's cold, man."

"Well, isn't it?"

"It's a spiritual thing. She's gotten into my spirit and I can't get her out."

Derrick was unmoved. "Start by getting out of her bed, King. That's the first step to getting her out of your spirit and your life."

King changed the subject after that, confirming that everything was set for Derrick to be the guest minister at their Leadership Conference coming up in July. They talked about their children: "Yeah, Vivian's fine, kids growing like weeds." King congratulated Derrick again on his church's mass choir CD debut, *Kingdom Citizens' Christian Center Sings Thy Kingdom Come!* Derrick reiterated his continued support for the Total Truth Association, an organization of Baptist, Methodist and other churches who'd broken away from their more traditional organizational umbrellas to embrace practices not recognized in their denominations, like miracle healing and speaking in tongues. King told Derrick about the Angels of Hope, and Derrick told King about the Kingdom Kick Boxers, a martial arts program for the church's young men. Finally King looked at his watch, then at the pad, and realized he needed to get back to work. He'd had a sermon prepared, but as so often happened, God had another one in mind.

"Take care, bro', I'm praying for you," Derrick said to his brother, whose pain resonated through the telephone.

"Me too, Dee, me too." King hung up the phone and pushed the half-eaten fish dinner aside. He crossed his arms on the desk, put his head down on top of them and started silently praying in tongues. He had been praying for about thirty minutes, had started feeling his spiritual and physical strength return, when the phone rang. The red private call light lit up. King raised his head, looked at the caller ID. Slowly, resolutely, he picked up the receiver. His "spiritual thing" was on the line.

Blessed

"Daddy!" Elisia's high-pitched voice rang out cheerfully as she knocked on the door. "Daddy, Mama says to tell you dinner's ready."

"Come in, honey bunch," Derrick replied, smiling as his angel bounded through the door and into his lap. He kissed her cheek and playfully tugged at one of her long hair twists as she beamed appreciatively. She studied her father's profile thoughtfully for a few minutes, outlining his eyebrows with her finger, and then crossing his forehead and continuing down his nose to his mouth, where Derrick playfully bit her finger and held it tightly between his lips for a moment before releasing it.

"Mama's got a surprise for you," Elisia whispered as she continued to trace her father's definitive features, over his cheek-bones and around his ear.

"What's that?" he whispered back conspiratorially.

"Daddy," Elisia chided somberly. "If I tell you, it won't be a surprise." With that, she jumped down off his lap and grabbed his hand. "Come on."

"I'll be there in a few minutes, little one."

"What's wrong?" Elisia questioned as she paused by the door.

Derrick had again leaned back in his chair and closed his eyes. He didn't know she was still there.

"Nothing for you to worry about, baby." Derrick's conversation with King was still weighing heavily on his heart. He knew King and Tai had had their share of problems, but he also knew there was a lot of love in that marriage, and the last few years, he thought, had been especially good all the way around. King's ministry was flourishing—he'd just been elected President of the Total Truth Association, Mount Zion had completed a major church renovation and expansion and Tai had been by his side all the way, encouraging, nurturing, taking care of him and the family. Tai had always been a quiet first lady, a silent but undeniable main thread in the fabric of King's life and ministry. She'd never been out front, singing or teaching as was the role of many pastors' wives. She preferred, even enjoyed, staying in the background. Her forte was in the area of organizing and overseeing, creating and delegating. Her priority and focus had been King from the time she was sixteen years old and then he and the babies as they came along. Most people wouldn't have guessed it if they just looked at outward appearances, but Tai's love was the foundation upon which King's success had been built.

Derrick leaned forward, suddenly aware that Elisia was still at the door, watching him silently. He offered a small smile as he got up to join her. They headed down the hall hand in hand.

"Daddy," Elisia said quietly as they neared the bottom step before entering the downstairs area and crossing through the living room to the dining room. She'd stopped and was now looking up at her father seriously with big, clear brown eyes.

"Whatever it is, God can fix it. He can fix anything."

Derrick swallowed as his heart swelled and eyes misted at the perceptive words of his little girl. *And a little child shall lead,* he thought, smiling. "You're absolutely, right honey bunch," Derrick replied as he entered the dining room now overflowing with people, food and conversation. Because if God couldn't fix it—nobody could.

Sundays were a celebration at the Montgomery residence, and this Sunday was no exception. The table was set beautifully with fine bone china and Waterford crystal. A floral arrangement of calla lilies provided an eye-catching centerpiece.

A large platter of blackened red snapper lay on one side of the lilies, an equally large platter of baked lemon chicken on the other. Surrounding these meat choices was an array of vegetables including corn, spinach and summer squash, a large bowl of mashed potatoes with sprigs of fresh parsley and dashes of paprika for color, a pan of Vivian's famous dressing made with apples and olives and a bowl heaped with a variety of rolls. On the buffet behind the large dining room table was another Vivian dinner staple, a salad bar. Also on the buffet were a variety of sodas and a pitcher of tea. Lastly there was Derrick's surprise, his favorite dessert besides Vivian, sweet potato pie.

The classical music in the background could hardly be heard amid the din of voices. There was Mother Faye Moseley, a pillar at Kingdom Citizens' and Vivian's play mother who practically lived at the house, and her husband, Brother Clyde. This couple, married for forty years, had been one of the mentors of the Montgomery marriage, and at times Vivian wondered if it would have lasted without them. Other Kingdom Citizens' members around the table included Darius Crenshaw, the minister of music, and his sister Tanya, who worked with the youth ministry. Next to Tanya was Stacy, a good friend and fellow worker in the youth ministry. Stacy dreamed of changing her title from "friend" of Tanya's to "sister-in-law." Her sly yet seductive glances to Darius throughout the meal underlined this fact. Rounding out the dinner guests was Cy (not only pronounced "sigh" but evoking many) Taylor, Derrick's associate minister, confidant and friend.

Cy was a bit of a phenomenon at Kingdom Citizens' for many

reasons. First, he was one of the most intelligent men Derrick had ever met, having graduated summa cum laude from Howard University with a degree in Business Administration. He'd received his master's in Organizational Leadership from Biola University and had been an irreplaceable asset to Derrick and the ministry since joining the team full-time, three years ago. Secondly, he was a man of integrity—gracious, unpretentious and humble. He was one of those rare breeds of men unafraid to show his emotions. People felt special around Cy.

Then there was his outward appearance. Cy Taylor was one of the finest men God ever created. When God stepped back and said "it is good," his eye had rested on Cy. At six-two, with bedroom eyes, cupid-shaped lips and a dimple, Cy wasn't just handsome; he was fine. Or as Stacy said it, "fa-eye'een," figuring that one syllable just wasn't enough.

Cy was wealthy. He'd made his money as a financial advisor for a large investment company and, following his own advice and intuition, had invested heavily in the computer and Internet markets when both were in their infancy. When he sold his Internet stock several years later, he was a millionaire many times over. That was when he decided to leave the business world and assist Derrick and Kingdom Citizens' full-time. He was adored, admired and envied by men and women alike. He was God's man, single and celibate.

Derrick blessed the food, and everyone filled their plates. Mother Moseley had taken only a few bites before starting a litany of anecdotes from her Sunday service observations.

"Lawd a'mercy," she said, wiping her mouth on a napkin. "It's just pitiful how these women keep throwing themselves at the man, just pi-ti-ful!" She looked at Cy and shook her head.

Cy knew what was coming. Although he would have preferred to not be the topic, he couldn't help but laugh at the comical and accurate way she told a story.

★　★　★

As usual, groups of people milled about after church, with more than a few waiting on a chance to see and or speak to Cy Taylor. One of the regulars was Millicent Sims, who'd been in hot pursuit of Cy since he joined the ministry. Unfortunately for Cy, he'd made the mistake of going out with her a few times, and although he thought she was a wonderful person, he discovered quickly she was not his wife to be. And a wife was just what Cy was looking for. Millicent, however, felt differently and had made it her mission in life to become Mrs. Taylor. She tried everything, including becoming active in every area of ministry even remotely affiliated with the man. When she found out the bookstore fell under his branch of leadership in the church, she became the manager. If Cy pledged a thousand dollars for something the ministry needed, she'd also pledge a thousand, even though for her this often meant a bank loan. When he signed up for the singles cruise to the Bahamas, she booked a ticket. When he offered to conduct a seminar to educate church members on investment, budgets and economic freedom, Millicent volunteered to be the coordinator. She always dressed impeccably in designer suits, shoes and handbags. Her best shopping buddies were MasterCard and Visa. Millicent always had a number of admirers swooning around her. But she had eyes only for Cy.

When she saw him exiting the church after service, she made a beeline in his direction. Unfortunately, she was trying so hard to act as though she wasn't approaching Cy that when she casually looked behind her, she almost knocked down another member. Even more, her heel caught on a cobblestone, and when she grabbed a post to steady herself, everything she'd been carrying—purse, briefcase and a box of flyers for an upcoming book sale—went flying. Cy had his back to her and missed the entire spectacle, except for the fluttering flyers. Mother Moseley, who didn't miss much, had seen it all.

★ ★ ★

"Lawd, I thought the child was gon' fall and hurt herself or somebody else. She was trying to unhook her heel, grab the flyers and keep an eye on Cy all at the same time. She looked like a human pretzel!" Mother Moseley wiped her eyes, which were tearing up from her laughing so hard. "God's got a wife for ya," she continued as she grabbed another piece of chicken and put a scoop of potatoes on her plate. "You just wait and see."

Stacy, who'd been staring at Cy, now glanced at Darius and then at Mother Moseley, wondering if she had a word on Darius's wife, and if her name was Stacy.

Stacy had had a crush on Darius from the beginning. She remembered when he first came to the ministry, when it was still called Good Rest Baptist Church, the name before Dr. Montgomery left the National Baptist Association, renamed the church Kingdom Citizens' Christian Center and aligned the ministry with the Total Truth Association. He'd joined the ministry as a keyboard player but also played saxophone and drums. He was married then—to a very possessive, diminutive woman. She sang in the choir, a powerful soprano, and led many of the songs. Darius quickly became an integral part of the music ministry, writing many of the choir's songs and charts for the band members. He also traveled several times a month as part of Dr. Montgomery's evangelism team.

It was upon returning early from one of these trips that Darius came home and found a strange car in the driveway. That wasn't unusual. Gwen was always inviting people over. But the car belonged to Bobby Perkins, Gwen's former, and it would seem present, lover. Things looked normal enough as he opened the door, but Gwen's greeting seconds later was a bit too hurried, a bit too forced. She seemed breathless, her make-up smudged, hair thrown back in a hasty ponytail. She couldn't look him in the eye, and when a toilet flushed, and Bobby came out moments later heading straight for the front door with a quick "Hey Darius! Nice to see you again," and "Gwen, thanks for letting me use your rest room," he knew without a doubt the rumors that had been circling about his wife were true. She fought for the marriage valiantly, but in effect it ended when the toilet flushed. They divorced some months later. Darius had been cautious since then and had rarely dated. Rumors had him dating Vanessa, the praise team captain. But Stacy had always had a crush on Darius, and after her most recent relationship ended, she again hoped that Darius was "the one." Of course, like everybody, she thought Cy was "all that and a bag of chips," but when it came to the women who were vying for the title of Mrs. Cy Taylor, the line was way too long.

Derrick watched Cy gracefully handle being the topic of conversation. As pastor of a mega-church, he knew firsthand what it was like to have one's business, or what others assumed was one's business, discussed openly. He thought of King and hoped his friend's indiscretions didn't become dinner chatter for Mount Zion Progressive. That was a conversation that clearly belonged between King and Tai Brook.

After dinner, with company gone and children playing, Derrick and Vivian enjoyed some time alone.

Relaxing in the den, Vivian studied her husband a moment. "You were quiet at dinner."

"I talked to King."

Vivian waited. Derrick remained silent.

"What's going on?" she finally prompted.

Derrick hesitated. "He's seeing somebody."

Vivian sat up, more attentive. "Seeing somebody?"

Derrick stood and slowly paced the room. "Yes, King's having an affair."

Vivian sat back, closed her eyes. "Not again."

"Yes," Derrick said, rejoining her on the couch. "Again."

"With who? Don't tell me one of the members."

"I don't know. He didn't say much. I didn't either. Except to tell him to end it, think of his family."

"Oh, Tai," Vivian whispered, thinking again of how distracted her friend had sounded when they talked earlier. "I'll call her," she said to Derrick.

"Let her bring it up, though," Derrick cautioned. "Getting in the middle of this . . ."

"I know, you're right," Vivian said. "When she's ready, she'll tell me about it."

Derrick reached over and hugged her tightly. "We're blessed, baby."

"Yes," said Vivian, returning his embrace. "Blessed."

Mama can usually smell that coming

"Missed ya at church Sunday." Mama Max's stare was speculative and penetrating as she gazed at her daughter-in-law over a cup of coffee. "Feeling better?"

"Not really," Tai replied, leaning forward to refill her cup from the carafe on the living room table. Mama Max remained silent. So did Tai. They both sipped their coffee, each deep in thought. Finally, Mama Max drained her cup, cleared her throat, placed the cup down on the table, leaned back and folded her hands across her stomach. She turned to eye Tai with compassion.

Tai felt her stare. "I can't go on like this, Mama Max. Before, the babies were small, I was younger; things were different. I was different."

"Different how?"

"Stronger, more positive. Before, I felt like each woman was one of the devil's little flies and I was the fly swatter. I don't feel like swattin' anymore. I'm tired. So the flies are just buzzing around and around, getting on my last nerve."

"You know I talked to King," Mama Max replied, again filling her cup, adding two teaspoons of sugar and a generous helping of cream before continuing. "And he tells me there's nothing going on between him and that Hope girl."

"Famous last words . . ."

"Maybe, but do you think it's possible that there isn't anything happening, that you're imagining things because of how active the girl is in the church, how enthusiastic she is about the ministry? Now, I admit she's a bit feisty and she could let out the hem of those skirts an inch or two, but, baby, she's never given me a reason to believe that something was actually going on with her and my son. And you know Mama can usually smell that kind of thing coming."

"Well, something's going on," Tai replied, then walked over to the big picture window that almost covered the entire front wall. She watched the neighborhood children playing with abandon, unable to remember how such innocence felt. She turned back to Mama Max and crossed her arms. "King is different, and he's been this way for a while. It's nothing major; it's the small things, things that only someone who's been with him as long as I have and loved him as much as I do would recognize. "And," Tai added, smiling at Mama Max, "I can smell pretty good myself."

"Look, I'm not one to doubt a wife's intuition. I've been right about something with only a feeling to go on too many times. I was just thinking that . . ." Mama Max's voice trailed off, and she took another small sip of coffee.

"Thinking what?" Tai quizzed.

"Well, I know with the twins in school you've had more time on your hands, feeling a bit, less involved. Trying to find your place again. In the meantime, this Hope girl has come in like gang busters, and it seems like every time you look up at the church, there she is. And she is a pretty girl."

"One of many with stars in their eyes every time they look at King."

"Maybe it's just admiration."

"Maybe it's just infatuation."

Mama chuckled. "Tai, I'm gonna give you some advice that you haven't asked for. Don't fear something into happening. King is your husband, and in the name of Jesus, it's gonna stay that way. You, in the meantime, need to get with God and find out what you're supposed to be doing for *Him*."

Mama Max shifted in her chair. "I also know you've been feeling down on yourself for gaining weight. And I'm one to talk with my big butt spread all over your love seat here, but you could drop a pound or two."

"Now, look," Tai began, walking over to the love seat and plopping down beside Mama. Mama reached out her hand and placed it on Tai's arm to stop her response.

"Darling, I love you no matter what size you are, and I know King does, too. It just might make *you* feel better, more confident, that's all. You know Mama Max loves you. I'm only trying to help. And I'm not thinking you should do this alone."

"And just who do you suggest should do this with me?" Tai asked, grinning broadly.

Mama Max just pointed to herself, and smiled.

The Full Workout Fitness Center was one of the newest exercise facilities that the suburb of Overland Park, Kansas, had to offer. Not only did it have every type of equipment known to man, but there was also a full line of workout classes including regular aerobics, step aerobics and water aerobics in their Olympic-sized swimming pool. There was kickboxing and Tae-bo. There was yoga, jujitsu, karate and tai chi. On the other side of the building was a full-line spa complete with a variety of massages and body treatments, a hair and nail salon and juice bar. The center was relatively quiet but still busy for a weekday, with a group of twenty or so women milling about, waiting for some type of aerobics class to begin, and others spread out on the various fitness equipment. A way-too-cheery employee with a perfect smile, size four body and flawless face literally sang out her greeting as Tai approached the counter.

"Welcome to the Full Workout Fitness Center. My name is Daphne. How may we help you become the best body you can be?"

Tai suppressed a wide range of sarcastic responses to say politely, "I'm interested in starting an exercise program to lose weight."

"Well, you've come to the right place!" Daphne continued in her singsong voice that in another time and place may have been nice but was presently grating Tai's next-to-last nerve. "We've got a variety of programs available to fit just about any need one wanting to become physically fit could have. In addition, we have a nutritionist and full-time psychologist on staff to balance your exercise program with healthy eating habits and a positive mental focus."

Tai stifled a laugh as she remembered who this woman reminded her of, one of the robotic Stepford wives.

"What I'd like to do," the robot named Daphne continued, "is give you a tour of the facility, explain our programs to you and when we're finished, have you answer a questionnaire that will help us place you in a regimen that will best suit your needs and goals." Daphne-robot bounced from behind the counter, grabbed a clipboard, then turned and with a dazzling smile back at Tai said, "Right this way, please." Another employee behind the counter nodded encouragement as Tai turned to begin the tour.

An hour, a smoothie and a manicure/pedicure later, Tai left the land of physical fitness behind, actually feeling better having joined. She'd decided on a beginner's program since it had been a while since she'd exercised, and also with Mama Max in mind, that included water aerobics and calenetics, a series of stretching and toning exercises. She also scheduled a session with the nutritionist but passed on the psychologist. She was going to work on some of the machinery for abdomen toning and, if she really got into it, hire a personal trainer. *Thank you, Mama Max,* Tai thought as she returned to her car, turned on the radio and bobbed her naturally auburn curls to the sounds of 91.5, the Oldies Station. Tai felt a little better, but even as she sang "I Can See Clearly Now" with Johnny Nash, that sixth sense feeling in her stomach would not go away.

Good, good

King sat at the head of the table in the church's tastefully furnished conference room. A committee of Mount Zion Progressive members joined him. Associate ministers, deacons, his personal secretary and others waited to give their progress reports on the upcoming conference.

"As you know," King began after a lengthy "Baptisized" prayer by Deacon Nash, "this year's leadership conference will be the largest and I believe best one so far. The speakers are dynamic, the workshops specific and explicit, and it seems that most of the details are in place. If anyone disagrees, now's the time to voice what needs to be done. I don't want any surprises at the last minute. Is everybody with me?" Everyone nodded or said yes. "Charles, let's start with you. How are things looking with respect to our speakers and other guests?"

Charles was the church's director of business affairs; organized, detailed and concise. His report reflected these attributes. "As you all know," he said, directing his gaze at King, "we've had a few challenges. But as of today, almost all of the leaders we've invited have been confirmed. We're still waiting on final word from a few session speakers and from Dr. Myles Monroe out of the Bahamas. And we've not finalized the contract for Dr. Hayden's Economic

Empowerment course. That is proving to be one of the more popular sessions." He checked his notes quickly and concluded, "Everything's falling into place."

"Good, good," King intoned, pleased as always with Charles's work. Quick and to the point, that was what King liked about him. Deacon Nash could learn a thing or two from him, especially where "quick" and the deacon's long prayers were concerned.

"Remind me to put in a call to Myles when we get back to the office," King directed Joseph, his assistant, before turning to his secretary. "Denise, let's have a rundown of the conference schedule to date."

Denise Williams, who had been taking notes, opened her folder and shuffled a few papers before beginning to read. She was an attractive woman in an understated way.

"Okay," she began, sitting up straighter and taking a deep breath. "The preconference begins Tuesday night with a dinner for the guest pastors and their wives, special guests and others on the list to be provided by Pastor King. Registration begins Wednesday morning at 10:00 A.M. in the church lobby. Over five hundred people have preregistered already, so we hope there'll only be a few stragglers who don't make the deadline. The first worship service is Wednesday night, and on Thursday morning, there are four sessions available: Follow the Leader, Strategies for Spiritual Success . . ."

As Denise continued with her report on sessions and special guests, Youth Minister Mark found himself paying less attention to the words being said and more to the mouth the words were coming from. He'd always found Denise attractive, and he loved her quiet, sweet spirit, but here, seated at the conference table with only a few chairs between them, it was as if he was seeing her lips for the first time. They were full and thick, not so big as to be soup coolers, but in perfect proportion to her face, which was heart shaped and glowing. She wore an almost translucent lipstick, a whispery pink, or was it beige? Through the glimmer, Mark couldn't tell for sure. He leaned forward, almost involuntarily, to inspect further.

"Of course, Friday is Young Adult Night," Denise continued, excitement in her delivery. She licked her lips unconsciously as she turned the page to continue.

Pink, Mark decided, following her tongue as it traced the outline of her sumptuous mouth. And as if to confirm his decision, the color of her blouse grabbed his attention. His eyes traveled south of their own volition, and without meaning to, he visually caressed her neck, adorned with a thin gold chain that sported an equally thin cross that dipped down and hovered just above her breasts. Mark sat back and gazed at her eyes, large and inviting as they scanned back and forth over the notes she read. Her nose was lovely, and Mark noticed it turned up just slightly at the end. As if to say, "Kiss me, I'm cute." Denise licked her lips again. Mark found himself wondering if she liked Mexican food, and if she was doing anything Friday night.

". . . so with the dance performance by the Angels of Hope, the steppers, Mixed Blessings, and Imani's dramatic presentation, that as they say in show business, will be a wrap!"

"Good, good," King replied. He went around the room then, asking specific questions relative to each person's responsibilities and assignments. Work regarding volunteers, security personnel, hospitality for out-of-town guests, and even the budget was under control. One of the assistant pastors was conducting a series of outreach endeavors for people who may not have considered church as a place they could receive instruction for practical living, in addition to food for their souls. Mark and a group of specially selected and trained teenagers and young adults were passing out flyers at the local schools and youth hangout spots. Deacon Nash had prayer covered, and Hope had designed an excellent and energetic schedule for Young Adult Night.

"As you know, Pastor King," Hope began, having given a more detailed outline of the extravaganza earlier in the meeting, "Righteous Rebel will be a huge draw for the young people because of his popularity and visibility when he was a secular hip-hop artist and because of his latest hit, "Holy Ghost High." With him performing, there will be tons of young people there, many of whom may have never stepped in to a church otherwise. He's got an awesome testimony about how God spared his life in a gang-related shootout where his best friend died. And with your approval of course," she added, looking at King and flashing a megawatt smile, "we might be able to talk him into doing a midnight concert just for the kids."

King had been watching her intently and leaned forward as she finished, forming a praying hands pose beneath his chin. "Good, good. Excellent idea, Hope. Let's get together after this meeting is over so you can give me more details. How's my schedule?" he asked Joseph, who grabbed a day planner and scanned it quickly.

"You've got about forty-five minutes, it looks like, before your meeting with the councilman."

King nodded and turned to the others. "I want to thank everybody for the hard work you're putting into this conference. When everything's over and everybody's commenting on how blessed they were and how successful the meeting was, know that each of you played a vital part." On that note King stood, as did the others except for Hope, who sat patiently waiting as King spoke to Joseph first and then to Mark. Her legs were crossed and she was shaking the top one gently, the only outward sign of her inner excitement at Pastor King's approval of her plans.

She wasn't the only one excited. King had barely been able to concentrate on the conference details, still caught up in a conversation he'd had with a certain female before the meeting started. She had detailed the plans she had for him later, plans that sounded good, good.

Ladies first

Vivian scooped the last bite of butter pecan cheesecake onto her fork and moaned audibly as it melted in her mouth. Her eyes were closed, and they stayed that way as she chewed, swallowed and reached for her napkin, dabbing her mouth before falling back against the plush, wicker chairs at Whispers, her favorite beachfront restaurant. "It should be illegal for a piece of cake to taste that good," she said as she grinned, shaking her head and reaching for her almond mint tea. "I feel like a stuffed pig."

"Well, you definitely look like you were enjoying yourself," Carla commented as she downed her last bite of deep-dish apple pie and pushed the plate away. "And if you're a stuffed pig, I must be a beached whale!"

Carla was often referred to as "big pretty" in private male conversations. Carla had never been a skinny girl, nor had she ever suffered low self-esteem. She was big boned and shapely, like an oversized coca-cola bottle, with expressive eyes and a ready smile. Her personality attracted both men and women like bees to honey. Even after many years in Los Angeles, her Georgian twang was as strong as ever, and when she got excited, which was often, it became even more pronounced. There was not a jealous or pretentious bone in her body. Carla enjoyed life and came as close to being an angel as anyone Vivian ever met.

They had met three years ago when her husband, Reverend Stanley Lee, was appointed to a local Church of God In Christ, COGIC, assembly after serving in an Atlanta suburb affiliate for five years. A progressive and contemporary thinker, Reverend Lee had consciously sought out like-minded religious leaders of other denominations with whom to network and possibly bring about a much-needed spiritual change in the city's atmosphere. One of his first phone calls had been to Vivian's husband, Derrick, and after inviting them to dinner—an evening that lasted from seven that night until two in the morning—Vivian and Carla were fast friends.

It was also during this first meeting that the seeds were sown for Ladies First, a group of pastors' wives from different churches all over the city meeting once a month to discuss ways to best serve God, their husbands and the female members in their congregations. Carla was very attuned to the women in her church and empathetic with their needs both spiritual and emotional. She was particularly sensitive to single women, including single mothers, wanting to get married. She had been both. And when it came to loving yourself no matter what your weight, Carla could have been the poster girl. She was beautiful inside and out, and she saw herself that way. She believed she was made in the image of God and that "God don't like ugly so he sho' didn't make it."

Vivian's forte was with women looking for their spiritual purpose in God, as well as overcoming issues of self-doubt, self-worth and self-esteem. Other core members of Ladies First included Chanelle Robinson, Terri McDaniels, Ruth Edwards, Pat Lange and Rebecca Collins, the only ordained minister in the group.

It was this group who sat fat and happy, having stuffed themselves with the delicious cuisine at Whispers as they planned their quarterly women's fellowship meeting. It was a one-day affair, including various seminars, symposiums and discussions and a special luncheon speaker, held at the Beverly Hilton Hotel in a beautiful, chandeliered ballroom. Each quarter, a specific topic was selected, and all of the activities, including the luncheon speaker, centered on this subject. Vivian thought she had a poignant, if a bit explosive, topic for an upcoming session.

"My proposed theme for the fall fellowship is called S.O.S.," Vivian began, having sat up from her reclined state and looking from one face to the next, before continuing.

"S.O.S.?" Terri questioned.

"That must stand for Sick Of Somethin'," Carla bellowed. " 'Cause God knows we are all . . . Sick—of—Somethin'. Sick of no-good Negroes, sick of hard-headed kids . . ."

"They are blessings and not curses," Minister Rebecca injected, only half teasing. "Watch your witness!"

"Sick of cookin', cleanin'—first our house and then the Lord's house," Carla went on dramatically, although now she had taken on the intonation of a plantation slave. "I's so tired, massa," she moaned. *"Nobody knows de trouble I see,"* she began to sing, so loudly that some of the other diners turned around with a mixture of curious, comical or censoring looks on their faces. Carla couldn't have cared less. She was enjoying herself.

"Girl, will you shut up," Vivian whispered loudly, barely able to keep an unladylike guffaw from erupting. The other ladies at the table were giggling, and Chanelle held a dainty hand up to her mouth to suppress a belly laugh. "You're right, you know, we are all sick of something, but that is not the meaning behind this S.O.S." Vivian paused, still smiling, and took another sip of tea. The table became quiet, waiting for her to go on. "S.O.S.," she continued, "stands for the Sanctity of Sisterhood." She waited a beat while everyone replayed the name in their minds.

"As you know, sanctity means set apart, holy and sacred, among other things. I believe that we as sisters, as women of the faith and as women in general, have gotten away from the sanctity and solidarity that our being female used to mean. I've had this on my heart for a while now, and recent conversations have only served to stir it up again.

"What exactly do you mean?" Ruth asked, leaning forward and tilting her head slightly as she squinted against the sun sparkling off the ocean waters. "Are you talking about women being more Godly, treating themselves with more respect?"

"Themselves and each other. Following the golden rule of doing unto others as you would have them do unto you. It seems we don't respect each other anymore, we don't care about each other anymore, and I guess that does come from not being Godly and not caring about ourselves. Even more to the point, ladies, I'm talking about our behavior with the opposite sex. The standard of decency has been lowered dramatically, and now it's survival of the fittest when it comes to relationships, both forming and sustaining them. For instance, I remember a time when it was not okay to go after someone else's boyfriend, much less her husband. Those times, sadly, are a thing of the past."

"It still ain't all right to go after mine," Carla insisted with a look of indignation.

The ladies nodded and murmured their agreement as Vivian continued.

"Of course it's not all right, Carla, but try and tell that to Susie Q. Single down the street. We used to respect what belonged to other people. We used to think more of ourselves than to try and entice a husband away from his family, or a man away from a committed relationship. And if we knew someone who was like that, that person was not popular. They didn't flaunt their actions for the world to see because other women just wouldn't stand for it. Older women would give her a piece of their mind and younger ones would shun her company. And I'm not putting all of the blame on women, because there used to be a higher standard for men, too. However, I am focusing on women because that's whom this fellowship is designed to reach. Now, I'm not saying that we were perfect, but there used to be a time when we didn't just open our legs for every Tom, Dick and Harry that came along."

"You better preach, sister," Minister Rebecca intoned. "I counsel women all the time who are hurting behind some aspect of male/female relationships. And it usually centers around three things. Usually they are single and celibate wanting to get married, single and fornicating wanting to get married, or married and not happy often because of the constant self-applied pressure to keep her man."

"Been there, done that," Carla replied.

"I have these conversations all over the country, *all* the time," Rebecca repeated for emphasis. "Most of the pain I encounter centers around either the need or desire for a relationship, or the pain caused by one that is not working well."

"Exactly," Vivian continued, her friend's comments confirmation that she was on the right track. "I became filled with all these questions. Why is this happening? Why do we not value ourselves more? Why are we so careless with other people's feelings, with our own? Why is it no longer unusual to have multiple partners—even in this age of AIDS—for some women to sleep with five, ten, even fifteen men or more during their lifetimes? Why is virginity such a rarity and celibacy so unappealing? Why are there so many single women in the church? Why aren't there more marriages? Why is there adultery in so many Christian marriages? Why is the divorce rate in the church the same if not higher than that of the general society, and why are seventy percent of Black children born out of wedlock with an inordinate amount of those pregnancies happening within our church walls?"

"That's a lot of questions!" Carla exclaimed.

"Seventy percent?" Ruth inquired incredulously. "Are you sure?"

Chanelle, petite and soft-spoken, nodded. "I heard that statistic recently. It was while listening to one of those talk shows on my way home, the *Larry Elder Show*. Most of the time I can't stand the man, I think he's arrogant and ignorant, but on this topic we were in total agreement. Seventy percent is too many kids, Black or otherwise, to be born without intact families. But that rate is only in the Black community. I think for Whites it went down to fifty-five percent and for Hispanics it was in the twenties or thirties. Don't quote me, but the percentages were in that range."

Vivian held out her hand, counting on her fingers as she went on. "One. Men aren't getting married because they don't have to. Like my grandmother used to say, 'Why buy the cow when you can get the milk for free?' We don't make them wait anymore, or want anymore; we give it up too easily and too frequently. Sex is like chewing gum these days—everybody's got a piece. Two. When a woman is married or in a committed relationship leading to marriage, other women don't consider these men off limits. Instead of seeing it as a chance for another sister's happiness, they see it as a challenge to their own. And don't let the sister try to do the right thing and remain chaste until marriage. Sex becomes the carrot the other woman dangles to get the greyhound around the track. Three. Because relationships are being entered without commitment, they fail easily, leaving behind a trail of broken hearts, bruised spirits and empty promises. All of this gets put into a nice grocery bag to be carried into the next relationship. Oh, and there might be a child or two in that grocery bag, and that's a whole 'nutha issue."

"I don't know if this is an issue we can tackle in one Saturday," Carla twanged. "Just trying to get women to keep their panties up and their dresses down could be the whole day."

Vivian smiled. That was one of the things she loved about Carla, that she was real. None of that I'm-so-heavenly-bound-I'm-no-earthly-good stuff, or that I'm-so-o-o-o spiritual mentality; Carla was open and honest about her own past, which made it easy for her to sympathize and be nonjudgmental of others. Her Ladies First sessions were always overbooked.

"You're right, Carla," Vivian responded. "That is why I have a proposal that this next fellowship not be one Saturday, but a series of four Saturdays during the month of September." Vivian reached into her Gucci purse and pulled out some papers, passing them around before continuing. "Ladies First. The S.O.S. Summit" was in large, bold type across the top of the first page. "This series," Vivian continued, "would cover four specific areas, one per Saturday, following the "S" theme: Spiritually Speaking, Sacred Sex, Setting the Standard versus Society's Status Quo, and the Sanctity of Sisterhood." The ladies glanced through the outlines Vivian had distributed as she spoke.

Pat asked a question as she looked at her copy. "Why isn't there anything about men in here? When it comes to adultery, affairs, fornication, all of what we're discussing, they're just as much to blame as we are."

"True," Vivian answered quickly, having considered this herself. "But like I said earlier, this meeting isn't for or about men; it's about women. Let's let our husbands handle the brothers."

Rebecca signaled the waiter for more water, and asked, "Why are we calling this a summit instead of a conference?"

"Ooh, thanks, Rebecca," Vivian answered. "I meant to address that first. When God was speaking to me about this, He specifically said "summit" and not "conference." I was confused at first because when I looked this up in a meeting context it said 'a meeting between two heads of state.' However, when I researched the meaning further, I understood God's intent for this meeting. The summit is the apex, crown, head, height, peak, pinnacle, it's the very top. These words and other definitions are in your packets. God has said this is what we're reaching for in our relationship with Him and each other. And that we will be the 'heads of state' in the state of our womanhood, the state of our well-being and self-esteem, the state of our sexuality and spirituality. We will be the head and not the tail!"

"Well, God betta' talk about His daughters!" Carla crooned while swaying in her chair and patting her well-coiffed braids.

"What did you say? Apex? Crown? Top? If you don't know . . . you betta' axe somebody!" She high-fived Chanelle sitting beside her, and the others nodded their agreement and threw in their amens.

"You've got it, Carla." Vivian said. "That's where God wants us to be—at the summit of our lives in every way. And these are some of the ways we begin to get there. "First topic: Spiritually Speaking. Dealing with a woman's love for the God in her and therefore for herself. Of her body being a temple, that kind of thing. Looking at the necessity of loving oneself before love and respect can be given to others. Healing our spirits and reclaiming our souls. Next, Sacred Sex, and I think you'd be great here Carla. Dealing on a frank, in-your-face level about the very definite role sex plays in our lives."

"So, I'm the only one at this table getting any, is that what you're saying?" Carla asked with a smile.

"Now, you know that ain't true," Terri countered, patting her oh-so-pregnant stomach.

"I think all of our men are taking care of home," Vivian crooned easily as she eased back in her seat with a smile. "But your story, which you've shared before, your knowledge of what it's like to be single and horny, celibate and not, having a child out of wedlock and overcoming all of that to become one of God's leading first ladies is a special kind of testimony. That's what these ladies need today, real talk."

"I used to get so tired of going to those singles seminars," Pat began. "And hearing these women of God quaintly telling me to hold on, wait on God, get busy for the Lord, don't look, it will come when you least expect it, it's better being single because you can serve God more, and my favorite—marriage is hard, marriage isn't all you think it is! Stay single as long as you can, they'd encourage. Of course, they were all going home to husbands."

"Exactly," Vivian continued. "I've been married for fifteen years and was a workaholic before quitting my job to help Derrick, so even though I remember lonely nights, it's not the same as

Carla's story. Nor could I ever tell any story with your passion," she teased, lightly grabbing her friend's arm. "The point is, all of our stories are unique and they're all needed. There's a myriad of situations out there, where sex and relationships are concerned, that need to be addressed."

Vivian paused and took a sip of her tea before proceeding. "Setting the Standard versus Society's Status Quo deals with Godly values versus the world's values. I think we need to draw a more definite line about what's acceptable as a woman of God and what's not. I think we've all been guilty of not stressing that enough in today's lax society. It's like we see so much sex that we've become desensitized. Having a baby and not being married is no longer the exception in our neighborhood but the rule. Not enough of us are sending the message that while we all make mistakes and God forgives, this behavior is not okay. It is not in the best interest of the woman or baby, and it's not God's ideal family design." Vivian waited while the waiter poured more tea and continued. "And not having sex? That isn't even a serious consideration for many of our young women. Being a virgin is so rare that such an admission brings applause."

Rebecca looked up, her eyebrows raised. "Just because somebody is still a virgin?"

"Seriously," Vivian continued. "Derrick and I were at a Christian concert the other night, and one of the young female singers proudly stated she was twenty and still a virgin. The audience cheered. Now, I'm not saying the statement wasn't worthy of applause, but I do believe that reaction points to how unusual virginity is these days.

"The fourth and final Saturday would cover the summit theme, the Sanctity of Sisterhood. How can we be our sister's keeper? And should we? How can we care about each other the way we used to? Respect each other like we used to. Uphold each other like we used to. I don't want to over simplify these issues, but

SEX IN THE SANCTUARY

I believe there would be a lot less husbands stepping out if there weren't so many willing women to step out with, and more marriages if there weren't so much casual sex. That we as women would feel better about each other if we felt better about ourselves. I think it's time to really take up the cause for the Sanctity of Sisterhood and become the women who give honor to the glory of God as we set the standard for women all over the world to follow. It's time to be the head and not the tail—above only and not beneath!"

"Unless it's beneath our husbands," Carla murmured.

Rebecca rolled her eyes at Carla and patted Vivian's arm.

Vivian hadn't realized how vehement she'd become as she finished her summit descriptions. She hadn't noticed her eyes had become misty. The table was quiet. Chanelle folded and refolded her napkin. Ruth sat back and bowed her head as Pat looked out over the water. Carla leaned forward and spoke softly, gently teasing this time.

"And you say you can't be passionate."

Vivian wiped away a tear before it had the chance to run down her cheek and managed a weak smile. "I did say that, didn't I?" She looked out over the ocean, enjoying the April breeze and remembering the conversation she'd had with Tai a few weeks ago, when after Tai had initiated it, they'd discussed King's affair.

"I'm so sorry." Vivian wished Tai were there so she could give her a hug. "What are you going to do and how can I help?"

Tai was silent a moment before she responded.

"Tai, you still there?"

"Yeah, girl. I'm here. I'm thinking about your question, and I really, really don't know. I'm so tired of this, so tired of feeling hurt and unappreciated and . . ." Tai's voice trailed off into weary silence.

"Have you and King talked about it?"

"Not really. I asked him about Hope and he said nothing was going on."

"Who's Hope?"

"You remember her. She's the one who did the dramatic reading from the Book of Ruth when you guys were here, very active, talented. On fire for the Lord, or so I thought."

"Oh, yeah. Short, pretty girl? Lots of energy? Big smile?"

"Uh-huh."

"I remember her."

"Well, about a year ago she started a ministry within our church called KARE, Kingdom Arts Reaching Everybody, which emphasizes nontraditional ways for youth and young adults to serve God, like acting, dancing, sports and stuff. It's a very good program. I was excited about it and approved it wholeheartedly along with King. In fact, I don't doubt that she loves God."

Vivian had leaned back in her oversized lounge chair. She had taken the phone out on the patio and stared at the beauty of her flower garden situated just beyond their heart-shaped pool before closing her eyes and trying to hear with her inner as well as outer ear. "So what happened that has you now thinking her zeal is for *your* King and not *the* King?"

"It's not a specific incident; it's just a feeling I have," Tai responded. "She dresses differently, changed her hairstyle, seems to be more conspicuous, move lively in the services. I don't have any proof that they're having an affair, but I don't have any proof that they're not." Tai laughed nervously. "Do I sound paranoid?"

"Maybe, but you have your reasons. Have you asked her?"

"Believe me, I was going to. King made me promise I wouldn't."

"Is that a promise you can keep?"

"I don't know, girl, I just don't know. What I do know is that I'm not going to continue living my life like this. King is seeing somebody. He spends too much time away from home or in his office. We've drifted apart again. I'm tired of putting up with his shit. I'm tired period."

"Are you thinking about leaving King?" Vivian could barely hear her own question, she spoke so softly.

"I'm thinking about being at peace. The children love their father and he loves them. I'd never want to take that away from them. But at the same time, a woman can only take so much. You know this isn't his first time. Or the second. How can I be guaranteed it will be the last? It was supposed to be the last time the last time."

Vivian was quiet, praying silently in the spirit. "I just feel," she said finally, "I just feel you should really seek God on how He wants you to handle King, and this situation. Move with His spirit and not your emotions. I'm not getting a definite word on this Hope girl, but I'm not getting an all's clear either. I do know that whatever is going on, God is right there with you. He's in control, and whatever happens, you're going to be all right."

"I know I will," Tai said without conviction. "It just doesn't feel that way right now."

Vivian glanced at her watch, sitting up as she did so. "I've got to get to the Ladies First meeting. In fact, Tai, I need to talk to you about that later on. But right now, let's pray. Heavenly Father, we thank you, we bless your name . . ."

"Vivian, are you okay?" The words of concern from Carla snapped Vivian out of her reverie.

"I'm sorry, y'all. Yes, I'm okay—just a lot on my mind."

"Anything we can help you with, pray about?" Rebecca inquired softly.

"Thanks Rebecca but no, not at this time. I just ask that we all keep this summit lifted in prayer as I believe it will be life changing. I pray it will be life changing to all who attend."

Carla eyed her friend, feeling the turmoil that was going on inside her. She knew that a special prayer would be sent up for Viv and for whatever was bothering her during her prayer time later. "Well, if we're finished here," she began, breaking the silence. "I've got two nappy-head kids on their way home soon. Best get to steppin' so I can be there to greet them."

"Yes, ladies, we're finished," Vivian replied as the waiter placed the check on the table. "I'm really excited about this and appreciate all of your input. Any suggestions on where to have the next meeting?"

"You guys are welcome to have it at my place." Chanelle had just purchased a condo and was anxious to break it in. "I haven't had a lot of people over and would love to practice my hosting skills. I also ran across a vegetable quiche recipe that I'd love to try out."

"Oh, Lord, here we go being somebody's guinea pig." Carla, blunt as always, spoke what others were thinking, "Can you cook, girl?" Chanelle nodded a yes. "Humph. I better bring a pizza, y'all, just in case." They all laughed as Chanelle insisted no one would be poisoned or go hungry at her house, thanking Carla all the same for her generosity.

"Who wants to pray?" Vivian asked.

"I will!" Carla jumped in enthusiastically. "Lord knows we need to pray." They all grabbed hands and bowed their heads. "Father God," she began. "Please help Chanelle cook this food next week . . ." Everyone laughed in spite of themselves.

Girls and boys didn't look alike "down there"

Cy was still smiling as he curled himself into his new toy, a midnight blue Azure Bentley. He was leaving City National Bank where he'd just met with his friend and business associate, Todd Green, a company vice president. Todd was the one who'd suggested that Cy get into real estate after liquidating his Internet stock and becoming an instant multimillionaire. So it was only right that Todd be taken to lunch with some of the one-and-a-half-million-dollar profit Cy had received from his latest real estate transaction.

You could barely hear the mechanism that neatly folded the Azure's convertible top into its niche across the backseat. Cy hit the CD button, and the melodies of Boney James filled the air from a system whose sound was so pure it was as if Boney himself was playing his saxophone from the passenger seat. Cy leaned back as he smoothly navigated through afternoon traffic in Beverly Hills, turning west on Wilshire Blvd., and heading to his next meeting in Century City, another investment opportunity. Cy was mulling over this possibility as he pulled up to the traffic light and heard a horn honk. It sounded a second time and Cy looked around. Next to him was an attractive blonde in a black Jaguar convertible. She took off her sunglasses, flashed a come-hither smile and shouted,

"Hey! Love the car!" She then reached into her purse, pulled out a business card and, as the light was changing, tossed it onto his front seat, saying, "Call me. I'd love to buy you a drink." Cy glanced at the card before continuing through the light and smiled as he shook his head back and forth. Women, how they did come on. That was the story of his life from the time he was six years old and Gracie May had pulled her pants down when they decided to play doctor in an isolated corner of the playground at recess.

It was Cy's first look at the female anatomy and his first knowledge that girls and boys didn't look alike "down there." He remembered being embarrassed and astounded before shouting out, "Look, y'all. Gracie May ain't got no dingy!" That innocent admission had brought with it the attention of Mrs. Patterson, their first grade teacher, who marched over to the corner where they were "practicing" and asked the obvious, "What are you doing?" in a stern, commanding tone. By then Gracie May had pulled up her ruffled panties and tried to smooth her wrinkled skirt that had pieces of grass and a twig hanging on it from her lying on the ground. "Nothing," Gracie had replied hastily, her head down, eyes wide and close to tears. They had to spend the rest of recess inside with Cy writing "I will not say bad words" across the chalkboard and Gracie penning "Pulling my pants down is bad" in her Big Chief tablet. He hadn't realized that "dingy" was a bad word and thought belatedly that "thing" might have been a better choice.

Cy's cell phone rang as he neared the large business complex that housed the Morgan Group where his meeting would take place. He deftly navigated the crowded parking lot and slid the Azure effortlessly between two cars near the front of the building. He punched the speakerphone button as he turned off the CD. The world seemed almost silent with the absence of Boney's "Sweet Thing."

"Cy speaking."

"Hey, Mr. GQ. It's Pamela."

"Pamela! How are you?"

"Better now that I'm listening to that gorgeous voice of yours. Busy?"

"Yeah, heading into a meeting. Call you later?"

"You better."

"I will. Goodbye."

The top of the Bentley clicked quietly into place as Cy reached back for his briefcase. Pamela. He smiled at the thought of her. Pamela was a sweet lady, funny and ambitious. She wasn't bad to look at either. And most importantly, she wasn't a member of Kingdom Citizens'. That was a huge plus. Dealing with Millicent had taught Cy a valuable lesson in the art of dating as far as the Christian community was concerned—stay away from family. "Family" was how the members of Kingdom Citizens' referred to each other, and with good reason. Derrick and Vivian worked hard to maintain a close, friendly, family atmosphere in a church that was nearing five thousand members. Fellowshipping with family was one thing; dating family quite another. "Too close for comfort" took on new meaning when it came to a failed romance with a person you had to see every week and worse, even work with on occasion. Not that Millicent was unfriendly. No, she was kind and as efficient as always when they worked together. But Cy knew Millicent still carried a torch for him—well, everybody knew that—and it made him uncomfortable. He had told her in no uncertain terms after just a couple months of going out that while he found her to be a nice person and beautiful woman, she was not the woman for him. He knew she'd been hurt by that revelation, but Cy didn't want to lead anybody on and have her hoping for something that could never be. After that, even though he was propositioned weekly if not daily by women at the church, he decided to steer clear of that pasture and look for companionship in another field.

Not that his decision had stopped Millicent or other women

of Kingdom Citizens' and other churches from trying. Cy still received dozens of letters ranging from invitations for dinner to a
"word from the Lord" about his future wife, usually the writer of
the letter. One time it was a mother who'd written that she had
dreamed about him and her daughter marrying. Cy remembered
being tempted to reply to the mother and tell her to lay off the
Tabasco before going to bed, but finally decided to ignore it and
hope it and she would go away, along with the others. There had
been more than one pair of lacy panties and other sundry items
sent in packages to the church and more than one suggestive
photograph. These all came from God-fearing, tongue-talking,
bonafide daughters of the Kingdom. Then there was the photograph he'd taken innocently enough with a female member at a
church banquet. The picture had been copied onto a piece of
blank, lacy wedding stationery filled with flowers and bells and
framed with a caption reading "Mr. and Mrs. Cy Taylor" at the bottom and sent to him, along with a letter of undying love from the
woman in the picture who had knowledge from God Himself that
they were to be married. Why hadn't God told him? There'd been
tickets to concerts, plays, sporting events and ski trips. One lady
had gone so far as to purchase the plane tickets for a weekend in
the Bahamas she was sure he'd enjoy. She'd even assured him in the
letter that accompanied the ticket confirmation that he'd have his
own room. How generous! And Mother Moseley was always
bringing one nice lady after another up to him after church to
"just say a Sunday hello."

And then there was Millicent, always there, always trying to
help—looking at him, staring as if to read his very soul when she
thought he wasn't looking. He wished she didn't feel the way she
did about him. Most men would welcome the attention that being
Cy Taylor brought, and Cy would gladly give it to them if he
could. He'd much rather enjoy quiet anonymity in the background
with a lady intelligent enough to carry herself in a manner that invited being pursued. Being hunted brought Cy no pleasure, but

being the hunter, now, that was another story indeed! As if think-ing about her had conjured her up, Cy looked down at his caller ID and noticed Millicent's number. It had forwarded from the phone in his church office, and had a 911 after the number she'd entered. No, Cy didn't like being pursued at all.

Waiting on Jesus—
Your Mr. Right

The Jacuzzi's jets pounded against Millicent's back and leg muscles as she maneuvered herself into a position to better benefit from their rejuvenating force. This was her favorite part of the workout, the end. Aaron, her personal trainer, always laughed as she said this to him week after week while he guided her through the routine responsible for her slender thighs and tight abs, "My favorite part, the end!" She'd been adamant about not wanting to look like a weight lifter, just toned and healthy. She repositioned herself again and, with her long hair wrapped in a towel turban-style, slid down into the warm, bubbling water. She straightened her long legs out in front of her while holding on to the steel railings, causing her to float in the oversized pool. As always, her thoughts were on her husband, Cy Taylor. At least he would be her husband if she had anything to say about it!

Millicent, like most women, had fallen in lust with Cy the first time she saw him. Unlike most women, however, she obsessed over making this dream a reality. She'd pursued him with barely concealed zeal from the moment he became a member and was delighted when, after finding out about his investment background and asking him to look at her portfolio, he'd suggested they discuss it over lunch. By dessert, she'd decided. "I want this man." Millicent usually got what she wanted.

She pulled herself from the bliss of the Jacuzzi bath and dressed for her dinner date with friend and prayer partner, Alison Groves, an evening she was sure she'd enjoy. Not only was Alison fun and quick-witted, but she was also one of the most spiritual women Millicent had ever met. It was her spirit in fact that had drawn Millicent to her one year during a women's retreat in Palm Springs, headed by First Lady Vivian Montgomery. It was following a session Vivian had taught on "Waiting on Jesus—Your Mr. Right." Millicent had been quite moved with some of the points Vivian had so eloquently presented. Not that she'd agreed with all of them, particularly those that admonished her to be still and know that God was God. Millicent was tired of waiting for Cy to make a move. Where he was concerned, she much preferred the Scripture that said faith without works was dead.

After Vivian's presentation, Alison had seen tears in Millicent's eyes. She walked over to the chair where Millicent was sitting and asked simply, "Are you okay?" They hit it off instantly and went to a restaurant that night instead of enjoying the conference's buffet. They were best friends before dessert. Millicent even shared her dream of becoming Mrs. Cy Taylor with Alison. Alison listened intently and shared that she wasn't picking up Millicent and Cy getting married in her spirit, but that she would be praying for her nonetheless. Alison never judged Millicent for believing it, though—that Cy was her husband—never told Millicent she was crazy or trippin' or anything like her other friends had when she thought that Duane Lucas was her husband. She'd told everybody about that, in the manner of "name it, claim it," and had been thoroughly embarrassed when instead of her he'd married a plain Jane named Melissa. After that she'd vowed never to be put out on "front street" again. In fact, she'd vowed never to tell anyone the next time God showed her who her husband was, but the words just seemed to come out of their own volition as she and Alison talked that night. From then on Alison had been there to support her, to pray with her, to hand her a Kleenex when she needed one. She'd already asked Alison to be her maid of honor.

Glancing briefly at the mirrored wall before leaving the fitness center, Millicent looked at her watch and quickened her pace. She'd spent too much time in the Jacuzzi and would be cutting it close to get to Beverly Hills and Crustacean, the chic Asian-inspired seafood establishment, by eight o'clock. She could already hear Alison whining. Alison, who was never late for anything, hated waiting on those who were. Millicent was the epitome of class and success as she crossed the parking lot, her slender build complemented by the narrow, cream-colored skirt she wore just above the knee of her shapely, bare legs. She'd topped it with a cream angora springtime sweater from the Donna Karan collection and contrasted the ensemble with her bone-and-rust-colored sling-back, low-heeled pumps and matching purse designed to perfection in Calvin Klein's understated style. Her shoulder-length hair glistened against the setting sun, sans dye or weave, and was secured at the nape with a wide, bronze hair clip. She did a quick point and click, deactivating the alarm on her beige 2005 Infinity. Her cell phone rang as she opened the door, and she smiled, knowing it was Alison without glancing at the ID.

"I'm on my way," she said, laughing while starting the engine and pulling out of her space.

"On your way?" questioned the soothing, masculine voice on the other end.

Millicent's heart skipped a beat; the very person she'd been thinking about!

"Hello?"

"Cy?" Millicent didn't know she'd been holding her breath until she let it out.

"Yes, just finished a meeting and heard your message."

"Oh, right, I did call you earlier. How are you?"

"Besides this crazy traffic on the 405, I'm fine. You?"

"I'm fine, just finished another grueling workout with Aaron. You know how that brother can work you over."

Cy knew too well, from personal experience. Aaron was one of the most popular personal trainers in Los Angeles, and almost everyone knew firsthand or had heard of his infamous, individually crafted workout routines. But he didn't want to talk to Millicent about her physical fitness. He hadn't wanted to call her at all, but hadn't wanted to be rude either. After all, they were working on a committee together for one of the church's economic development projects. He'd missed the last meeting, and hoped the call was concerning that. Then again, maybe he was just too much of a nice guy.

"So what's going on?" Cy prompted, wanting to finish the conversation. "Do you have some information from the meeting at church?"

"No, well, yes actually, but that's not why I was calling. The meeting was brief, basically a reiteration of the things we'd discussed Sunday afternoon, just an update and confirmation of all the businesses participating in the job fair. We'll have over a hundred companies represented, and it looks like the classes will be fantastic, especially the introduction to computers course. The office has received a ton of calls concerning it. And your money management class is, as usual, one of the most requested in the lineup. Are you ready, instructor?"

Cy laughed. "For the class or the participants?"

"Both," Millicent responded, smiling at Cy's comment. She was glad he felt comfortable enough with her to admit his women woes. "But I'm sure you can never be quite ready for those participants. Such enthusiasm!"

"Yeah, right." Cy paused, noting she was the most enthusiastic of all. "So what else is going on?"

"Well, I got a call from Roland about my portfolio. He had some suggestions about diversifying and moving some of my more volatile stock into the safer mutual fund categories. I was hoping to run some of the details by you and get a second opinion."

"Well, I'd never second-guess the man; he's one of the best in the business." Cy had referred her to his friend and business partner shortly after their dating ceased and the phone calls with questions about her portfolio multiplied. "Roland is one of the reasons my portfolio is as strong as it is. He has an innate sense of timing when it comes to the stock market and the seemingly invisible mood swings of our nation's economy. I'd go with what he says."

Millicent was disappointed but didn't want to give up easily. "I was hoping I could fax a copy of the summary page to you and maybe discuss it over lunch tomorrow, my treat."

"I appreciate the invite, but that's not going to be possible." Cy decided to end the conversation before it became even more uncomfortable for him than it already was. "Like I said when I referred you to him, Roland really is the best person I know to guide you through the sometimes murky waters of stocks and bonds. Don't worry. He won't steer you wrong. Listen, Millicent, I've got to go—"

"Yes, of course. So I'll, uh, see you Sunday?"

"Sure," he said abruptly and silently added, *hopefully from a distance,* as he hung up the phone.

Millicent began to daydream after the call disconnected. Before she knew it, she'd driven several blocks past Crustacean. Her cell phone rang again as she got in the left-hand lane, made a U-turn and headed back down crowded Wilshire Blvd. She looked at her watch and at the ID. Yes, it was Alison and yes, she was late.

Sistah Almighty and Sistah Alrighty

Hope's mind was moving a mile a minute, and so was she as she rushed past the doors of the main edifice and headed for the walkway that would lead her to the side of the main building and the front of the multipurpose center that stood gleaming fresh and new, next door to the sanctuary. Among other things, the center housed the youth activities and was a jewel in the crown that was the church's renovation and expansion project.

Two church matrons, whom Hope had secretly named Sistah Almighty and Sistah Alrighty, exited the main building. "Praise the Lord, ladies!" she hollered cheerfully without breaking stride.

She didn't have to break stride or look back to imagine their reactions. Hope knew that Sistah Almighty thought the skirts she wore, only slightly above the knee, would send her straight to hell, and Sistah Alrighty was always glaring at her whenever she spoke to Pastor King, as if she were going to throw the man on the floor and accost him in the pulpit! *They're just jealous,* Hope thought as she neared the door of the youth center, already hearing a swirl of activity inside. And they weren't the only ones. Hope was aware of how some of the ladies in the church felt about her. They probably thought she was after the preacher. She'd been accused of that before. Well, she didn't care one iota what those biddies thought; she knew she was flowing in purpose and destiny, and as far as those women were concerned, well, they could just kiss her Bible!

"Hey, Hope, wuz up?"

"Ooh, Hope, I like your shoes!"

"Hope, are we going to finish the routine today?"

"Hope, Selena likes Terron and is trying to get him to go out with her."

"I'm not either!"

"You are, too."

"Unh-unh!"

"Uh-huh!"

"You a big fat lie!"

"Okay, okay, that's enough!" Hope said, grabbing both girls, pulling them under her arms and giving each a chin nuzzle. "Since you both have so much energy, I've got some work for you two." She stopped at the table in the foyer and opened her briefcase. Terron, the leader of the new dance troupe called Heaven's Hip-hoppers, swaggered around the corner, sixteen years and one hundred sixty-five pounds of testosterone chomping at the bit.

"Hey, Hope! I like that outfit. You're looking real nice today."

"Well, thanks, Terron. I hope that routine you're choreographing impresses me as much as I'm obviously impressing you."

"Oh, don't worry," Terron drawled while effortlessly executing an intricately woven series of hip-hop steps before gliding forward and spinning to a stop right in front of her. "It's gonna blow the roof off, 'cause it's off the ska-zizzy!" Hope didn't miss the quick glance toward the one he was really trying to impress, little Miss Leah, nor did she miss the pout on Selena's face. I guess there were two somebody's who liked Mr. T.

"Now, I need one of you to make, say, twenty copies of this and the other to put them inside these folders." Hope reached for the keys that were somehow buried at the bottom of her purse, even though she'd just thrown them in there. Pulling them out,

Hope turned to Leah. "Here's the key to the office. Be sure to turn the light off and lock the door when you're finished."

Leah and Selena started toward the office, their heads together in a Terron-induced conspiracy. "Thanks, girls. And hurry up! We've got a lot of ground to cover tonight."

Hope felt a bit stressed but pleased with how things were going so far. She had been able to contact Righteous Rebel's management, and they had worked out a midnight concert for the youth to be held in a city auditorium Friday night. In addition to the debut of Heaven's Hip-hoppers, Hope had lined up a gospel singing group called Yadah, which meant praise in Hebrew, comprised of three lovely and talented ladies from a church in Kansas City. She'd also confirmed the participation of Musical Messengers, the gospel jazz group. Rounding out the evening would be the Angels of Hope dance group, a popular and funny Christian comedian from Chicago with an award-winning monologue called "A Praying Woman," and Hope's own dramatic spoken word presentation she'd composed to kick off the evening and entitled "Joyful." It was inspired by the penned verses of her favorite biblical character David, with whom she felt much kinship, and his now famous Psalm 100. As if someone had turned on a tape player, the words began swirling in her head, and she bobbed slightly to the beat, even as she headed toward the group of girls sitting quietly in a circle near the middle of the basketball court:

God is awesome, in all of His ways,
For all of our days, we should give Him the praise
So every man and woman, all girls and boys
Make a joyful noise, make a joyful noise . . .

"What are you bobbing to, Miss Hope-a-letta?" That would be Miss Get-On-Your-Last-Nerve Carmelita Lopez, whose all-encompassing eyes didn't miss much. She had a mouth on her but was nevertheless a good kid from a not-always-so-good home. In fact, Carmelita had led her own mother to the Lord after she'd come to one of the Youth Night Holy Ghost parties a year ago. She'd given her life to God that very night, and the church had since become her second home. One Friday night several months later, her mom had come to find out what all the hoopla from her daughter was about. As they rode the bus home, Carmelita had asked her mother if she could lead her to the Lord.

"What will I have to do?" her mother had inquired in a hesitant, skeptical tone.

"Just repeat this prayer that we learned in class Wednesday night." Carmelita had proceeded to say the prayer taken from 1 John 10:9–10 that she'd learned in their youth Bible study. Her mom hadn't thought much about the exercise at the time, but the next day, she got a call from the IRS stating she'd been overcharged on her taxes two years prior and they were sending her a check, with interest. It was then Rosa felt there was a connection between her repeating the words with her daughter and the IRS admitting a mistake—a modern-day miracle. Then and there she decided to take a closer look at this "church thing" in which her daughter was so involved.

"That's for me to know and you to hear later," Hope answered in delayed reaction to Carmelita's question while easing down into the circle the girls had opened upon her arrival. "Have you guys prayed already?"

"Yes, we were just waiting on you so we could show you the dance we've put together for the last verse."

"Okay, ladies, show me what you've got." And with that the girls got up, the CD was turned on and the soul-soothing sounds of Nicole Muller's "Redeemed" filled the auditorium.

"Did you see how tight that girl's pants were? It's a shame before God." Margie Stokes, or Sistah Almighty, was clucking her

Was she being paranoid?

Only a married woman who'd walked in the shoes that Tai now wore would understand how she could feel so alone in a crowded, noisy room. Timothy and Tabitha were both talking a mile a minute about a science fair project their class was building. Princess was busy making sure the twins understood how unimportant their project was compared to her need for a new outfit for the upcoming Spring Fling Day that her class was spending at the local amusement park. *There must be some boy she's trying to impress,* Tai thought, almost amused that Princess could not fathom the notion that Tai had herself been fifteen once upon a time. Not so long ago that she'd forgotten what that age felt like.

"So what's his name?" she asked casually while scooping out a small helping of lasagna. Tai was determined not to regain the ten pounds she'd lost since she and Mama Max began exercising two months ago.

"Mom! Why do you always think boys are involved when I ask you for stuff?"

"Because you're fifteen. Boys are always involved when you're fifteen."

"I don't got time for none of these boys around here. They're stupid."

"*Have* time, not got time. How did you get a 'B' in English with that grammar?"

"Mom! We were right in the middle of telling you about our project," Tabitha whined with the practiced skill of the most seasoned actress.

"Yeah," Timothy piped in. "And that's way more important than Princess's boyfriends!"

The beginnings of World War III began to rumble at this last comment, and Tai was in the process of calming the soldiers on both sides when King walked in.

"Hey, hey, what's going on here?"

Immediately everything was quiet and in order, something that happened frequently when King entered a room.

"Hey, Daddy!" Princess sang, jumping up from her chair and hugging him tightly. No matter who may come afterward, King Wesley Brook was definitely her first love.

"Hey! How's my Princess?" No doubt, the love was mutual.

"You're home early," Tai stated, rising automatically to put another place setting at the table. She went into the kitchen, grabbed a glass from the cabinet, opened the refrigerator and poured a tall glass of tea, setting it down beside his plate. She also grabbed the ranch dressing, his favorite, and placed it on the table beside the low-cal Italian, not her favorite but her fate, and Russian, the children's choice.

"Yeah, we finished up early, so thankfully I am getting to spend the evening with some of my favorite people."

Princess sat back down at the table. King leaned down to rub and kiss the top of Timothy and Tabitha's heads respectively before he took his place at the head of the table. He didn't hug, kiss or rub Tai's head.

"So how's everything for the conference coming?" Tai asked, taking a small bite of lasagna.

"So smooth it's almost scary," King replied, heaping a huge

helping of his favorite Italian cuisine onto his plate. "Especially Youth Night, it's gonna be awesome."

Tai's fork stopped midair. Suddenly the lasagna noodles became thick in her mouth, and the cheese seemed to lodge itself in her throat. She took a huge gulp of tea and swallowed quickly and then a couple more sips before putting her glass down.

King noticed Tai's reaction and mentally kicked himself. How could he have slipped like that and brought up anything to do with Hope? Too late, though, the kids took the topic and ran with it.

"Ooh, Daddy, is Righteous Rebel gonna do the concert?" the twins implored.

"Is he going to sing 'Holy Ghost High' or 'Number One Lover'?" Princess turned to her mother, thinking of her own performance. "Mom, you're going to love the Heaven's Hip-hoppers. Our steps are tight!" Tai just smiled.

King smiled, too, proud of the way his children embraced God and how enthusiastic they were in their service to Him. He glanced at Tai before answering their question.

"Well, don't tell anybody," he started conspiratorially, buttering his third piece of Italian bread. "But . . . yes! Righteous Rebel is going to do the concert!"

The twins high-fived each other, and Princess grabbed her father's hand. "Oh, Daddy, I'm so excited, that's gonna be great!"

"I'm gonna be front row, center," Timothy proclaimed, as if there were any doubt as to where he as a child of the church's first family would sit on such a night.

"And that's not all," King continued as he stabbed a large chunk of lettuce, then a tomato and finally a piece of broccoli onto his fork and stuffed it in his mouth. "You guys remember that CD I brought home last week, the group that sounds a lot like Destiny's Child called Yadah?" And then to Tai, "This is good, baby."

"Don't tell me they're gonna be there," Princess moaned, all too aware of the female competition, even though those girls were almost out of high school and one was in her freshman year of college. "Mom, now I need to get two new outfits! Mom! Are you listening to me?"

Tai nodded in the affirmative, but in fact, she hadn't been listening. She'd been trying to reconcile her feelings of anger with the ones of happiness that were swirling around the table. Was she really just being paranoid and horribly unfair to this Hope girl? Her children obviously adored Hope, as did those in the youth and young adult groups she directed. Sistah Stokes had voiced some concerns when Hope first came to the church, but that may have been in part because Sistah Stokes remembered King's old flame Tootie and her cat suits. And how could King just sit there and go on and on about his love interest, or should she say lust interest, right in front of her and the children like that? Was she being paranoid? And if so, why couldn't she shake this feeling of doom that rested in the pit of her stomach, low and heavy like tonight's lasagna?

Tai continued to ruminate on these thoughts as she prepared for bed that evening. King had already showered and was in his office downstairs. Princess had cleaned the kitchen and was talking on the phone, her favorite pastime, and the twins were playing a video game. She sprayed on a generous amount of jasmine-scented body mist and sat on the commode seat, rubbing baby oil on her heels and toes. She tried to remember exactly when this feeling of imminent doom came to pay her a visit, like an unwelcome distant cousin, and refused to leave. She reached for her cotton nightgown hanging on the bathroom door, then opted for her black, floor-length negligee instead. What was she doing? Was she actually going to try and seduce her husband, a man she felt sure was cheating on her? And maybe with the youth's assistant director no less?

Tai carried the bottle of jasmine water from the bathroom to the bed and, pulling back the sheets, sprayed a liberal amount on them, including the pillows. She hit the nozzle a few more times as she turned the bottle once more on herself, one on both temple points, between the breasts and a quick hit between the legs before recapping the bottle and setting it on the table beside her. She reached behind her to the bed's headboard, turned on the radio and her favorite station, Oldies 91.5. Barry White's voice reached out seductively and promised Tai he couldn't get enough of her love. *From your lips to King's ears,* Tai longingly thought.

Tai lay down on crisp, scented sheets as a cool spring breeze blew through barely opened balcony doors. She reached over and stroked King's side of the bed. She still loved him, even after all she'd been through with him, unconditionally, like Christ. No wonder the cross was the symbol of ultimate sacrifice. Because to survive a marriage, one had better be willing to get crucified.

King sat silently reading the newspaper in his study. He'd come here as a means of escape; it was an unwritten rule that he not be bothered when he was in his office. Being around Tai and the kids was becoming more and more uncomfortable. He felt as guilty as he did out of control. The phone rang. It was Derrick.

"Hey, man," King answered cheerfully, thankful to be distracted from his thoughts. "What's up?"

"I was calling to ask you the same question," Derrick said meaningfully.

Dang, King thought with a frown. He wasn't going to get away from his thoughts after all. He tried to sound nonchalant. "Same ole, same ole. Everything's cool."

"Is it?"

"Look, man," King said, his body tensing. "If you called to make a point, get to it."

Derrick heard the tension in King's voice and knew things were definitely not cool. He could tell King didn't want to talk, had tried to throw up a wall of attitude. But he wasn't backing down. This was what friends did, looked out for each other—especially when one saw the other heading for a cliff, blindfolded. King was letting pussy blind him. Derrick wasn't going to let him go out like that.

"Look, dog," he said in a tone of camaraderie. "I'm on your side. And my point's been made. Me and Viv want it to be you and Tai; that position is not going to change. But I didn't call to lecture. I called because I care about you, man, you and your family. You know that."

King closed his eyes, relaxed. "I know, man, I appreciate it. It's crazy right now. I know I've got to handle this, eventually."

"You and Tai talk more about it?"

"We talk around it. She thinks it's this girl at church. I told her no."

"But she knows it's somebody."

"I haven't lied to her. She asked me if I was seeing the woman, sleeping with her. I told her I wasn't."

"Isn't that lying by omission?"

"Look, man, don't get technical. She asked a question, I answered it."

"What if she asks you point-blank if you're seeing somebody?"

"I'll tell her yeah. I've got eyes, I see everybody."

Derrick laughed. "She will not be amused."

King grinned, appreciating the levity. "You're probably right."

"You know I'm right. She's probably ready to kick serious butt as it is."

King's grin faded. "I deserve it."

They talked a bit further. King agreed to keep him posted on what was happening and thanked him for the call. He hung up the phone, stood and began slowly pacing the floor in his office, carelessly arranging and then rearranging the stacks of work on his desk. What was he going to do? How did he get into this situation in the first place?

He remembered the first time he saw his other woman, all cute and bubbly, full of energy and life. Their conversation had been innocent enough: How are you? Fine, and you? But the message in their eyes was unmistakable. She'd given him her number. He'd given her a business card. They'd talked on the phone a few times. Again, just general, getting-to-know-you stuff. She wanted to know all about him. Where are you from? Kansas, born and raised. How old are you? Forty-four. What type of music do you like? Gospel, jazz, '60s and '70s R&B. And then more talks on the phone. More questions, more shared information. What are your goals? To build a Kingdom enterprise. Where do you see yourself in five years? At the head of a ministerial campus, complete with schools, day care centers, business offices, restaurants. Has anybody ever told you how incredibly intelligent you are? Tai had but King didn't remember it, or if he did, he chose not to share the information. Then he'd asked her out to lunch. Hey, it was the middle of the day so how bad could it be? Pretty bad. They'd met at the Crown Center Shopping Complex. The one anchored by the Crown Center Hotel. Real bad, sinful even. She'd suggested they take a stroll after eating, to walk off their lunch. He was the one who noticed the suggestive teddies in the boutique window. She was the one who suggested that he buy her one and let her try it on in one of the rooms next door. He was the one who could have said no. She was the one who hoped he wouldn't. They made it to the room. He never saw her in the teddy.

They'd gotten together almost every week from that point on, and she'd even traveled with him on occasion, always discreetly of course. *It's harmless,* he thought at first, but he knew better seconds after that first thought. *As long as nobody knows,* he reasoned. *God knows,* he countered himself. *She makes me feel good,* he acknowledged.

She's not your wife, God said. And in the gloom of his darkened study, King knew God was right. This woman wasn't his wife, and the one who was didn't deserve his infidelities.

★ ★ ★

Tai closed the *Essence* magazine she'd been reading and looked at the clock. It was twelve-thirty and King was still in the study. "Thought the conference was so smooth it was scary," she said aloud, remembering King's words at dinner. Then why was he still in the study at midnight? She was tempted to tiptoe downstairs, open the study door and lean provocatively against the doorway. Maybe take one leg and hoist it up against the doorjamb, giving King a glimpse of her not so hidden treasures. Maybe grab a tub of whipped cream before opening the door. They'd had strawberry shortcake for dessert, so she knew there was whipped cream in the refrigerator. But she didn't do any of those things. Instead she looked over at the empty space beside her, rose, fluffed up the pillow behind her head and grabbed another one for her stomach, turned out the lights, closed her eyes and tried to sleep.

King glanced at the clock. It was late, and tomorrow was another busy day. He left his office and walked quietly through their sprawling, ranch-styled house, taking great pains not to awaken Tai as he opened the door. He crossed over to the bathroom, closed the door and prepared for bed. He undressed in the bathroom, taking off his clothes and placing them on top of the hamper before turning out the light. He walked over to the headboard on Tai's side where he turned off the Ojay's right in between "stairway to heaven" and "step by step." He walked over to his side of the bed and slid in, naked as always, between the sheets. The scent of jasmine greeted him warmly and caused him to look over at Tai's side of the bed. She was lying on her side, away from him. A stab of guilt hit him unexpectedly, and he reached out his hand, only to take it back before touching her arm. He sank down on his back, eyes wide and staring. Tai moaned softly, then turned over and threw a leg over his. She placed a tentative hand on his hair-lined chest and scooted closer.

"I thought you'd never come to bed," she whispered, laying her head against his solid, muscled arm.

"Yeah, I thought I'd never get finished," he eked out, clearing his throat as he did so and making a big deal about getting settled in for a good night's sleep, moving his arm away from Tai's head in the process.

Tai noticed, but pressed the issue. "It's been a while." She scooted closer and put her head against his arm again, using her hand to outline an oblong path from his belly button to nipples and back again. She reached up and kissed his cheek. Why did she feel as if she was begging? This was her husband for God's sake!

King turned toward her abruptly and kissed her as he would Sistah Wanthers or Sistah Stokes. "I'm tired, baby. I love you. Good night."

And then he turned over, away from her, and pretended to sleep. But he didn't. Neither did she. They were both awake for a long time.

I love you, baby . . . tore-up feet and all

His embrace tightened as Vivian tried to move out of it. Derrick's arms were wrapped firmly around her breasts, his heavy leg slung possessively over her thighs. Her head was in the crook of his neck, just under his chin, with one leg angled out in front of her. As she stirred, Derrick pulled her in tighter and began to stroke her breasts in slow, teasing circles. He nuzzled her head beneath his chin, slid her hair back from her neck and kissed the nape. Vivian cuddled up against him and smiled.

"It looks like Mister Big is getting bigger," she teased, turning over to kiss him, morning breath and all.

"Yeah, he wants to come visit Miss Kitty," was his throaty reply as he squeezed her booty before turning her over and under his body.

"You know I need to brush my teeth," she murmured.

"You started it," he whispered, showering her face with feathery kisses before moving south and down to other delectable pieces of chocolate for his enjoyment.

"Hmmmm, I love it when you won't take no for an answer." Vivian began her own journey of kisses—the eyes, the nose, mouth, neck. The nipples, the stomach, six-pack, seventh heaven.

"Whoa, baby, you're about to start something down there."

"Baby, this party is already in progress."

"Well, let the dancing begin."

Vivian couldn't imagine a better way to wake up.

It was two hours later that Derrick and Vivian emerged from their love nest. Vivian had called the children on their private line and threatened them with bodily harm if she or their father was disturbed. Instead, she'd let Anastacia handle the fairly easy chore of getting D-2 and Elisia off to school. Derrick called his secretary with instructions to reschedule his nine o'clock appointment and to tell his ten o'clock that he was running late. He was humming a melody of his own making as he headed out of their bedroom and down the steps toward the smell of turkey bacon, eggs and hash browns.

"Looks like somebody worked up an appetite," he murmured while giving Vivian yet another cheekful of kisses.

"Stop that now, or your food will burn!" She turned off the fire beneath the eggs and grabbed the orange juice out of the re- frigerator. "Do you want coffee or tea this morning?"

Derrick looked up and licked his lips invitingly. Vivian could feel herself getting wet and warm again, something she felt was ridiculous for someone who was almost forty, had known the cul- prit of such vibes for almost fifteen years and had just finished an intense lovemaking session that would have rivaled any twenty- year-old's by comparison.

"Isn't there a third choice on that list?" he questioned.

"Orange juice?" Vivian countered, lifting the pitcher.

Derrick laughed out loud. He loved Vivian's sense of humor and her sharp mind. Although there had been a couple of bumps in the road, okay, jagged trenches actually, both he and Vivian had honored their commitment to be faithful to each other, and he was proud that while he knew plenty before, he'd never touched an- other woman after Vivian became Mrs. Derrick Montgomery. Nor

had he needed to. Vivian was just what a man such as he needed, a
lady in the living room and, well, something else in the bedroom.
Something else indeed!

Vivian fixed Derrick's plate and set it beside him at the breakfast nook where he was sitting reading the sports page. She'd already decided on coffee for the both of them and poured them
each a cup before making her own plate and bringing it to the
table. Derrick was knee-deep in Laker territory. It was the playoffs.
And the Lakers were winning.

"You act like that's news to you," Vivian began as she poked at
the paper veiling the love of her life.

"Huh?"

"There's nothing in there you don't know. Weren't you at the
game last night?"

"Yeah, but I'm just reading the stats."

"Your eggs are getting cold."

"Okay, baby."

Derrick put the paper down and grabbed the jelly to spread on
his toast. He was feeling happier than he'd ever felt in his life, and
he didn't quite know why. Vivian was always exceptional in bed, a
great cook and a superb conversationalist. Those things were nothing new. But it was as if they could both sense their marriage going
to another level, through no attempt of their own, but more like
one of life's unexpected and unasked for gifts.

"So," he started after having quickly devoured half the food on
his plate, "another meeting with the ladies today?"

"Yep. We're working on our meeting coming up in September. Only this time, we're doing a four-week series, the whole
month. That is, if it doesn't conflict with your plans. I looked at our
calendar, and while it's already pretty full, the series is still doable."

"Why the whole month? You've been doing only four Saturdays a year."

"I know, but God has really been dealing with me on an issue

I believe is more important, more challenging and more complicated than one Saturday can adequately cover."

"Unh. Must be about us."

"Us?"

"Men."

"Ding-ding-ding. My hubby's so smart," Vivian said, feeding him a forkful of hash browns from her plate. "You got it right on the first guess."

"It's not hard. You women only talk about three things, men, men and men!"

"Ooh, no you don't! We talk about a lot more than men; don't give your admittedly ingenious species too much credit!"

"Baby, it doesn't matter where y'all start out in the conversation because men is where you end up."

"That may be true, but there's a lot of ground that we cover in the process. And while granted, this series will focus on relationships, we are going to deal more with the relationships of women amongst ourselves as opposed to relationships between the sexes."

"Sounds interesting," Derrick crooned. "And dangerous."

"Dangerous?"

"Uh-huh. You know if you women ever got on one accord in a show of unity, we men wouldn't stand a chance."

"Your perceptiveness again overwhelms me, love. And you're right. But we're hoping the things that will end as a result of our banding together will be things that shouldn't exist in the first place.

"Like . . . ?"

"Oh, you know: lying, cheating, adultery, just the small stuff."

"Oh, those pesky little creatures."

"Exactly. More coffee?"

"Thanks, baby, just top it off."

Derrick watched as Vivian refilled their cups, taking in her supple breasts peeking out from underneath her silk robe.

Vivian sipped her coffee, quiet a moment. "We're going to send out an S.O.S., remind ourselves about the Sanctity of Sisterhood."

"Anything in particular lead you to conduct this series?" Derrick asked gently.

Vivian knew where his thoughts were headed. King and Tai. Of course their problems added validity to the need for the series. She told Derrick that and added, "I'm hoping Tai will be one of the speakers."

"Ha! Good luck with getting Tai in front of an audience. You know that girl likes to be backfield in motion. Especially now . . ."

"So has King told you who she is yet?"

"Who?"

Vivian gave him a look and turned away.

"No," Derrick said, turning her back to face him. He knew how the situation upset her, and hugged her until she didn't know where she ended and he began. "Did I ever tell you how special you are to me?"

"Once or twice. But you can tell me again."

Derrick could always make Vivian feel better.

"Baby, if I did that, I'd miss my meeting. I'm tempted to clear the decks and lay with you in bed all day as it is."

"But then I'd miss *my* meetings, not to mention my mani/pedi."

"And risk your feet cutting my legs with some unattended toenails? Oh no, baby, we must postpone this little tryst for another time!"

"Forget you, Black man!" Vivian laughed as she threw a towel at his tall, lithe frame ducking around the corner. He stole a peek while she was still laughing, her body turned once again and shaking softly as she wiped the counter. Derrick groaned.

"But you know I love you, baby, tore-up feet and all."

Lonely—and alone—again

Hope didn't know what started it. It was a Friday night. She'd gotten off work and, like many other Friday nights when she had nothing to do, gone to Blockbuster and picked up some DVDS. She'd then gone to Chopstix, her favorite Chinese food restaurant, and ordered her favorites—Kung Pao chicken, vegetable fried rice, hot-and-sour soup and an order of egg rolls with lots of extra soy and sweet-and-sour sauce. She'd then swung into the mini-mart with the Baskin-Robbins ice cream shop and ordered a pint, no, make that a quart, of ice cream, half mint chocolate chip and half rocky road. She weaved in and out of traffic in her zeal to hit as many green lights as possible, while bobbing and snapping to the sounds of Kirk Franklin. She pulled into her parking space in the small and cozy apartment complex that was her home and trudged up the steps and through the doors with her comfort food. She'd dumped the DVDS in the living room on the way to the kitchen where she put down her containers. She went back into the living room and turned the TV on before continuing through the living room into the short hallway to her bedroom where she shed her work clothes and put on a pair of warm-ups and matching booties. She went into the bathroom, washed off her make-up and pulled her hair back into a single braid. She went back into the living room, checked her answering machine and played back the messages—a short, sassy one from her mother (that made her smile), a long, detailed one from Sistah McCormick with a mile-high list of things she needed to check for the conference (that made her frown), a funny, somewhat naughty message from Frieda talking about a blind date she was going on and leaving instructions for Hope to call her on her cell a couple of times during the evening just to make sure she was all right (that made her pray) and a telemarketing call, the recorded kind, from somebody selling life insurance (that made her glad she had an answering machine with a delete button). That was it. She opened the front door and got the mail out of the box and gave it a cursory glance before throwing it on the coffee table for later perusal. Picking up the phone, she called her mother's house and got the answering machine. *Don't tell me Mom has something to do on a Friday night,* she thought before leaving a quick message that ended with "I love you" and audible smooches. Then she plopped down on the couch and idly hit the channel button, not realizing until she'd gone through the entire number series twice that she wasn't really watching anything on TV. She grabbed a foreign film with English subtitles that she'd heard a lot about called *Amour,* and while the movie previews were showing, went into the kitchen to heat up dinner.

As always, the food was delicious and the movie was charming. It was about an Italian man in Russia who'd fallen in love with a diplomat's daughter and was trying to woo her in spite of an incredible language barrier. He spoke no Russian or English, and she, while smitten with his Svengali charm, spoke no Italian. Hope laughed aloud at the handsome guy's antics at trying to prove his love for her, his Russian princess, and impress her father. The movie was about halfway over and she was eating a spoon of rocky road ice cream mixed with the mint chocolate chip when it started. For seemingly no apparent reason at all. At first it was like a slight chill, one that started deep in the stomach and mushroomed like an atomic bomb up through her chest and over her head and sprinkled back down like a fine layer of snow on a Minnesota morning. The wetness wasn't snow, but tears cascading silently and continually down her cheeks. She closed her eyes and swallowed hard, willing herself to stop. She put down the ice cream, almost unable to swallow the bite that was in her mouth, and pressed her hands to her eyes. Hard. The little man on the screen (that was the other funny thing, the Russian woman was about six-two; he was five-four) was on his knees, asking for the woman's hand in marriage. Hope didn't hear the answer because, without warning, her sobs had become audible and had developed into a low wail, a wail that sounded as if it belonged to somebody else. *What is wrong with me?* She hit the pause button on the movie and continued to cry silently into her hands, now wet with a messy mixture of tears and snot and saliva, creating an unshaped blob in the palm of her hand, kind of like the mixture of loneliness and unhappiness and fear that created an unshaped blob in the depths of her heart. Although it hadn't happened in a while and had come on unexpectedly, Hope knew why she was crying. Because it was Friday night. And she was lonely. And alone. Again . . .

After grasping that reality, the words of Bishop T. D. Jakes, her favorite televangelist, arose in her mind. "You can be alone and not lonely!" Hope wondered how one did that. She knew God loved her. She knew He would never leave or forsake her. But the truth of the matter was, she was alone *and* lonely.

She hadn't always felt that way, especially right after her move from Tulsa. She'd been so enthralled with being in a new place, meeting new people, seeing new things. It all helped her keep Shawn out of her mind. Then she'd flung herself full force into her job at the newspaper, working long hours when she first got her assignments, not only to get her feet wet but also to establish a reputation. Furnishing her place took up a huge chunk of time in those first months. Hope had always prided herself on her interior decorating, and with the salary her job provided, she would shop all weekend, just to find the right knickknacks for the whatnots.

Although her basic living room furniture, including the couch and loveseat, had come from Levitz, she'd pored over magazines, browsed countless shops and attended more than one estate sale to artistically personalize her living space.

Then, of course, there was Mount Zion Progressive. She had jumped in with both feet and the fervor of a new convert. She was the single, unattached one who could always attend a meeting, pick up teenagers, handle administrative work, choreograph a routine, hold a twenty-four-hour prayer session, and participate in other areas of the church besides her youth group, including inner city missionaries and the prayer line.

There was also John Madden, a friend of a friend at the newspaper whom she'd dated about six months before he dumped her because she wouldn't let him go for the gold. Besides him, however, she'd been on her own for the two years she'd lived in Overland Park, and although there were occasions of affection here and there, none was lasting, none keeping her warm at night. She'd vowed to God that the next man she made love to would be her husband, and she had regular shouting matches with the Father, asking just where was her husband hiding? She used to threaten God with time frames and ultimatums such as "If I don't meet my husband this month, I'm gonna fornicate," but God had obviously remained totally unmoved as if to say, "If you feel froggy . . . leap!" The men at her church seemed either married, dogs, intimidated or gay. Oh, the homosexuals tried to keep it on the down low, this was the Midwest after all, but she knew that a couple of 'otha brotha's were among God's anointed at Mount Zion.

"What is wrong with me?" Hope pondered again as the television, having been on pause for so long, went to screen saver. She, like so many other single, lonely women, had done the self-survey under harsh, self-inflicted thousand-watt lights, and no matter the statistics, came up lacking. She was attractive, she thought, and fun and smart. A college grad, she held a good job with an upwardly mobile future. She was saved, sanctified and filled with the Holy

Ghost. She knew how to cook and clean and liked to keep a tidy house. Although it had been a while and she had only the experience with Shawn, she liked sex. A lot. She didn't have any bad habits to speak of, didn't drink, curse or do drugs. She could be a bit anal, she admitted, when it came to cleanliness and order. Someone had once told her she had a Type A personality. But she wasn't in debt, and although her credit had been ruined during her college years, she was working to get it reestablished. She had no children. She felt she was a good, decent, caring person who wanted to get married and who, she thought, would make someone a wonderful wife. "So why," said the devil on her shoulder, "since you're so good and decent and caring, are you all by yourself?" That was the million-dollar question for which she had no answer. So she sat in her nicely decorated living room with melting ice cream and hard fortune cookies. She sat with no one's arms but hers wrapped around her, balled into the corner of her off-white leather couch, wishing she could sink into the cushions, the springs, the floor, the earth. She sat and cried, lonely and alone on a Friday night. And she didn't know what had started it.

Hello, husband

It was a full five minutes before Cy realized he was no longer reading the report in front of him. It had become a blur of black and white against the backdrop of his thoughts, scattering first one way, then another like empty candy wrappers in the wind. He pushed back the report, leaned heavily against his plush, black leather office chair and began tapping his Waterman Edson Blue Sapphire fountain pen against the solid mass of his Plexiglas and chrome desktop.

Images began to play across his mind—images of different women and different times. First there was Stephanie, who'd helped him lose his virginity at the ripe old age of thirteen. She had been seventeen and a senior in high school. Always tall for his age and ahead of his classmates, Cy was a freshman at the time and had told Stephanie he was fifteen. He was a guard on the Cougar's varsity basketball squad, one of their major offensive weapons and the golden boy of his domain. She was a cheerleader at their arch rival school, all legs, breasts and pom-poms. Cy was smitten. Stephanie was in love. They dated her entire senior year, but the summer she left for Spelman College in Atlanta, a new girl, Tatiana, moved into the neighborhood, and well, out of sight, out of mind was the melody that Cy's adolescent body played after Stephanie had gone.

Then there was Jodie, the first White girl he slept with, and Eva, a hot little Hispanic number who could do the splits both horizontally and vertically. Cy warmed at the memory. She was also his first heartbreak because it was one of the few times he was dumped for another guy, Pedro, whom Eva met at her cousin's wedding. They later married and the last he'd heard had seven children. Throughout his high school years there were others whose faces he couldn't recall, names he couldn't remember. Every woman who met Cy wanted him, and in his early years, he tried to be most accommodating. Cy had been wild by his own admission. He wasn't proud of it, of the countless virginities he'd stolen and hearts he'd broken. It had been for him as it had for so many of his peers, a way of life.

Then came college and Trisha. A smart and sassy preacher's daughter from upstate New York, Trisha had given him a run for his money. He laughed aloud as he remembered their first encounter while standing in the lunch line at the school cafeteria.

"Who is this pretty young thing standing in front of me?"

"Who wants to know?" She hadn't even bothered to turn around.

"Turn around and see for yourself!" Cy responded with confidence.

"I don't need to turn around to know I'm not interested." But she did turn around. "You may think you're the 'meow' to all the 'pussies' on campus, but if you'll listen closely, you don't hear me purring." With that, she grabbed her tray and swished her big booty and short-cut curly 'fro across the room, settling down at a table full of her sorority sisters. Cy was stunned. And smitten. She had thrown down the gauntlet and the fight was on. Cy won.

★   ★   ★

Cy rose from his chair and went over to the window, taking in the nighttime cityscape glittering twenty-one floors below his penthouse view. Leaning against the marble column, Cy smiled at the memory, gently rubbing his chin as he did so. He said her name aloud as memories of their three and a half years together flitted through his mind. She was definitely his first true love, and may have been his only one had he not been so foolish as to chance a one-night fling with one of Trisha's friends and sorority sisters, Jeannetta.

The smile on his face faded slowly at that memory. Jeannetta Harris. Cute and cunning, she'd played him like a saxophone. Lured him into her apartment on the pretense of sharing her large and diversified music collection with him. But Cy wasn't stupid; he knew what was up. He could still see the barely there red negligee that draped Jeannetta's large, yet shapely body, could still see those huge mounds of flesh bulging over the top of the sleek, silk material and looking like chocolate-covered grapefruit. Maybe if she hadn't put on the Isley Brothers, there would have been a chance for logical thinking, but when Ron started crooning "groove with you" and Jeannetta asked for a dance, it was all over but the orgasm. It was what they'd both wanted.

He'd known Jeannetta had a thing for him. What he hadn't known was the ongoing competitiveness Jeannetta had with Trisha. Trisha was everything Jeannetta thought she wanted to be: petite and pretty, smart and loveable, daughter from a rich family. If Cy was the only part of Trisha that Jeannetta could grab, she was only too willing to do so. The candles had barely burned down before the news had filtered to Trisha that Jeannetta had been with her man. Things were never quite the same between them after that. Even though it was the only time he had been unfaithful, Trisha, whose mother had suffered years of her husband's infidelities, couldn't risk the prospect of a similar future. Three months later she ended the relationship and never looked back.

He'd done everything to try to reconcile with Trisha, but her fear of an adulterous future within their marriage extinguished her passion like water on fire. She carried a love for him until John Rhodes, her next boyfriend who became her husband, helped her to put Cy and the pain he'd caused behind her. Cy wondered about them and how their life was now. Had there been children? After college, he had lost contact with her, and no one, not even her close friends, could seem to answer his questions regarding her whereabouts. Those sistahs stuck together! Except for Jeannetta, that is. There was another rash of names and faces after Trisha as Cy vowed to never give his heart away again.

Guess he forgot to tell his heart that. Because something about Joan, the woman he'd lived with for five years before finding God, had him placing his heart on a silver platter and serving it to her with kid gloves before their second date. Joan was very different from Trisha but special in her own way. Where Trisha was sassy, Joan was subdued. Where Trisha was the life of the party, Joan was the flower on the wall. Joan was intelligent and comforting, a calming presence and quiet strength. Her father was British, and she had his dry, cutting sense of humor. Her spirit was a balm for Cy's soul.

He wasn't sure why they didn't marry right away. Of course, in hindsight, it was obviously not God's plan. But at the time, there was nothing to keep them from tying the knot. Joan's parents adored him, and his parents liked Joan as well. They had similar interests and enjoyed some of the same leisure activities. Joan was athletic and energetic and was one of the few who could give him stiff competition in a game of chess. Even her declaration that she didn't want to have children—Joan was definitely a career woman—didn't bother him. At first. Again, in hindsight, this gentle yet firm stance against a family was what eventually unraveled their otherwise happy union. And with each passing year, Cy wanted children more and more.

Remembering Joan made Cy think of Pamela. Like Joan, she was an aggressive career woman, one who'd worked hard to climb the corporate ladder of success. Now vice president in a highly respected public relations company, Pamela had broken through the glass ceiling and joined the ranks of her mostly White, mostly male counterparts. Her campaigns were some of the most successful in the field, and more than once she'd been courted by the competition in hopes of bringing her talent and skill into their corporation. But Pamela had plans of her own, and when the dust settled, it would be under a door reading "DuBoise & Associates," and she would be the "big ballah, shot callah" in the house!

Cy tried to imagine Pamela and motherhood in the same sentence and couldn't. His eyes narrowed as he replayed tapes of their conversations in his mind and tried to remember the mention of children. He did not. Yet, he wasn't sure. He made a mental note to approach that subject on their next date. As hard as it was for him to fathom, Cy was feeling the urge to settle down with a wife and family. Golden boy, sought-after man-about-town, Cy Taylor. Who woulda thunk it? *Millicent Sims* was the reply that popped into his head, and frowning, he picked up the phone to discuss with her the marketing plan for the church's latest venture. Despite her attempt to be "just friends," her desires for a deeper relationship left Cy wanting to keep a distance between them. But church business made for regular conversations, almost weekly. How could he manage this without hurting her feelings?

Millicent leaned back and closed her eyes as she inhaled the luscious scent of sandalwood rising with the steam from her bathwater. The scent mingled with that of the candles placed around her large Jacuzzi tub. It was moments like this that justified the hefty mortgage payment on her rather small condo. It wasn't always the quantity but the quality. And the amenities the complex offered, like her Jacuzzi tub, the marble floors and a surround sound audio system, in this gated neighborhood gave Millicent the feel of luxury she desired. After all, she worked hard and made a comfortable living as a marketing director for a large firm. She was worth it.

Lazily grabbing the remote, she turned up the volume of the classical radio station offering background ambience and slid even deeper into her aquatic cocoon. Quietly humming the familiar Brahms melody, Millicent took her finger and created a trail of soapy suds across her lithe form. *I didn't realize how much I needed this,* she thought as she adjusted the bath pillow behind her head and settled into it. She made a mental note to schedule an appointment at the day spa next week for a full body massage and seaweed wrap. She might even splurge, grab a girlfriend and take a trip to her favorite spa in Palm Springs, topping it off with a luscious dinner at her favorite French restaurant there. She was definitely feeling inclined to treat herself like the child of God she was. Even if she wasn't special to anyone else, she was special to God and that was enough. Well . . . almost.

Before the thought could complete its cycle, another one popped up. True as it may be about her being special in God's eyes, it would mean the world for her to be special in another's eyes: one Mr. Cy Taylor to be exact. She would do anything, anything to make that a reality.

Millicent reached up and turned on the pulse jets, then lay back and escaped into her favorite fantasy. It was a beautiful Saturday afternoon, and she was in the foyer of Kingdom Citizens' Christian Center. The church was full of witnesses and well-wishers to this, the most important day in her life. She was on her father's arm, resplendent in a form-fitting, Vera Wang wedding dress, complete with a twenty-foot train. Her bridesmaids were gliding down the aisle, one by one in their off-the-shoulder green and gold satin creations, accompanied by Cy's handsome groomsmen. The classical ballad she'd created and entitled "The Path To Love" was being played softly and brilliantly by the ten-piece orchestra she'd commissioned for the occasion. Finally Alison, her maid of honor, was in place, and the familiar strands of the "Wedding

March" began to play. It was as if the sea parted and the floor gave way as Millicent floated down the aisle. She must be walking on clouds because she could feel nothing beneath her feet and had to grab her father's arm with her other hand to reestablish connection with the earth. Her heart stopped beating, and everyone except Cy seemed to fade from her view. For a delicious, heart-stopping moment it was just she and he in a whirl of clouds and color and crescendos of melodies from every love song since the beginning of time.

Her father kissed her gently as he withdrew his arm and guided her to her place beside Cy, her husband. In only a few minutes, the dream of a lifetime would come true, and she would bear his name. She looked up into his eyes, and once again the world receded as she became lost in a sea of mahogany magic. She mechanically followed the words of Minister Montgomery, lifting her chin as she said, "I do," with a clear, convincing voice.

"And now Mr. Taylor, you may kiss your bride."

The persistent ringing of the telephone brought Millicent out of her dream. She blinked several times before realizing that she'd fallen asleep. The jets had turned off automatically and the water had cooled. Millicent rose and stepped out of the tub, grabbing a plush towel as she did so. After drying herself and spraying a body mist, she reached for her silk robe and stepped into satin slippers before heading out of the bathroom and to the phone on the nightstand next to her bed. She looked down at the ID and recognized the number immediately. A smile spread slowly across her face.

"Hello, husband," she said to herself as she picked up the phone and hit the callback button. Cy's phone began to ring right after he closed the door to his penthouse and headed toward the elevator.

Trying to separate the "two becoming one" into two again.

"Hallelujah! Ooh, that's good!" Vivian exclaimed softly as her eyes misted over and her hands lifted in praise at the revelations of God. Ever since He'd given her the foundation Scripture for the upcoming Sanctity of Sisterhood Summit, Hebrews 2:11 which declared the Sanctifier and the sanctified were one, Vivian had marveled at how each stone of the summit topics had been laid and how each verse in the Scripture text fit succinctly with the topics of her initial outline. "Praise you, Jesus!" she said aloud as she put down her pen. She stretched and yawned, looking at her watch, eyes widening. Where had the time gone? She couldn't believe she'd been in the study for four uninterrupted hours, yet looking at her desk and the masses of notes and outlines was evidence that she'd gotten a lot done. Vivian's stomach growled as she reached for the phone, a further testament to the singular focus since her early morning prayer time. She had gone straight into her study afterward, stopping only for a cup of herbal mint tea before typing out the things God had whispered during her quiet time with Him.

Those were the most exquisite moments of her day, those morning moments alone with God. After Derrick left for the office and the children had been dropped off at school, Vivian marked out an hour or so of time for meditation with "Daddy," and

He never failed to meet her with just the right nourishment for whatever diet her upcoming day prescribed.

Vivian could scarcely remember the fear that had almost overwhelmed her, right after she'd shared her summit idea with Ladies First. Just like the devil to get inside her head and try to convince her that what she'd envisioned was too much to undertake, impossible to pull off. Even with all the encouragement of her fellow first ladies, the loyal support of her church staff and Tai's agreeing to speak, Vivian had fasted and prayed continually to work through the fear of failure that plagued her days following their luncheon. Derrick had been a pillar of strength and support as usual, but with his increasingly busy schedule and mounting responsibilities, Vivian knew this summit would be successful only with God's conspicuous blessing and assistance.

Vivian sat back and picked up the phone. On second thought, she replaced the receiver, opting instead to head toward the kitchen and a much-needed lunch break. She paused for a moment at the window, taking in the beauty of the summer day before continuing down the stairs, into the kitchen. She pressed the speaker button on the kitchen wall phone and punched in the voice mail code for the office line before opening the refrigerator and getting a pitcher of fresh-squeezed orange juice and a large Tupperware container of tuna salad. She grabbed a plate from the cabinet and began scooping out chunks of tuna as the messages played. Derrick had called to ask her opinion on a business matter. Her mother had called just to say hi and to check on her favorite grandbabies. Vivian was constantly reminding her mother that Derrick and Elisia were her *only* grandbabies, but that didn't seem to keep them from being her favorites. Mother Moseley had phoned to see if she could stop by a little later on in the day. Knowing Vivian was working from home that day, her assistant, Tamika, had called to update Vivian's calendar of counseling and meetings.

Vivian had just taken a bite from a cracker when the last message played. It was a teary Tai asking in a voice filled with pain for Vivian to call her right away. The uneaten cracker lay like sawdust in her mouth as Vivian grabbed the glass of orange juice she'd just poured, placed the tuna plate in the refrigerator and headed for the comforts of her family room and the cordless phone there. Without asking or praying, Vivian knew she'd need all the comfort she could get for the conversation that lay ahead. She took a long drink of orange juice, finally ridding her mouth of the cracker she kept chewing but was suddenly unable to swallow. Folding her legs beneath her as she sank onto the couch, she said a simple prayer as she punched in the speed dial to Tai's home. "Help, Lord Jesus."

"I'm divorcing King."

Those words seeped out of Tai's mouth like blood from a fresh wound. Vivian closed her eyes and breathed deeply, silently reciting the Twenty-third Psalm as she struggled to maintain a calm demeanor.

"Viv, you there?" Tai asked in a quiet voice.

"I'm here," Vivian replied simply. She thought of a thousand different responses, but none of them seemed adequate enough to voice aloud.

"Well, aren't you going to say anything?" Tai asked, not knowing what words she wanted to hear.

"What happened?" Vivian said finally, deciding that the best place to start was at the beginning.

Tai spent the next thirty minutes detailing the blatant confirmation of King's affair and his stark confession following an emotionally brutal confrontation that morning.

The nightmare had started the day before, after Tai's thrice-weekly workout at the Full Workout Fitness Center. Feeling proud of herself and the newly rediscovered waistline beneath her recently shed twenty pounds, Tai decided to splurge and purchase a couple summer suits. Passing the usual shops and strip malls in her quiet suburb, Tai had hit I–35 and headed to Kansas City's upscale shopping and dining district, the Plaza. She'd felt good as she sipped her peach and passion fruit smoothie, turned up the sounds of Oldies 91.5 and chanted along with the soul-stirring sounds of the Pointer Sisters. *"I know we can make it, I know we can . . ."*

Tai bobbed her head and tapped the steering wheel as she cruised down a wide-open Midwest freeway. Mama Max had been right. Focusing on herself and not worrying so much about the so-called other woman in King's life was just the thing. Tai was feeling better than she had in years. She had more energy, more stamina and more confidence. Her children were pleased, and King had not only noticed, but had complimented her efforts, encouraging her to continue and thanking her for the more nutritious yet still delicious meals of baked chicken and fish, steamed vegetables and light pasta dishes that had begun to replace her former casserole fare.

Tai breathed deeply and sent a "Thank you, Jesus" up as she found a parking space near the entrance to the Bonwit Teller department store. She squelched the urge to shop the clearance rack and instead headed straight to the designer suit department. A friendly yet unobtrusive sales associate seemed to know exactly what Tai was looking for, and just a little over an hour later, Tai left three beautiful suits behind to be tailored and carried with her two pair of Bebe pumps and a bag filled with feel-good toiletries, including a large bottle of Sung, her favorite cologne.

On her way to the rest room on the third floor, Tai passed the beauty salon. She couldn't remember the last time anyone but Sue had done her hair. Feeling adventurous, she stepped through the door. She left with a short, curly carefree hairstyle. Subtle highlights had been added to her rich, auburn color. After generously tipping Nia, her new best friend, Tai almost skipped out of the salon, she was that happy; thought she looked great.

She headed for her car, placed her purchases in the trunk and was about to get in when she remembered the bagel she'd had for breakfast and the smoothie she'd enjoyed right after her workout were long gone. She looked at her watch, and with two hours left before having to pick up the children from school, she sidestepped her first choice, McDonalds, and decided to take a stroll down the boulevard to see if there was a nice little sandwich shop in the area.

She stepped out of the parking garage into the warmth of the sun. It was a perfect May day. She hadn't even realized she was humming to herself as she stopped to peek in first one shop window and then another. She caught her reflection in the mirror and smiled as she patted her flatter stomach, pulling down her long pullover and thanking God that there was less "back" in the back. She turned her head first one way, then the other, still appraising her new hairstyle.

"Don't worry, you look good."

Tai turned around and blushed at the innocent compliment the young businessman had thrown her way before continuing down the street, swinging his briefcase and leaving behind a smile and good feelings. "I *do* look good," Tai agreed. It had been a long time since she felt this way. She almost skipped like a schoolgirl again as she rounded the corner and noticed a deli across the street. She was about to cross when a little Italian bistro just ahead caught her eye. She hesitated for only a moment before deciding to continue her spending spree and actually enjoy a sit-down lunch that someone else had prepared for a change instead of a sandwich, her unimaginative first choice.

"Table for one?" the waiter asked as he grabbed a menu and led her down a quaint, walkway that wound around wrought-iron table and chair sets hosting red and black candles and white linen tablecloths. Tai admired the building's Italy inspired décor as she followed the waiter deeper inside the restaurant. She noticed as the waiter led the way that there were also tables set up outside and was just about to inquire about one's availability when she heard a familiar laugh. Thinking she was surely mistaken, she decided to follow the waiter on around the corner and into the area from where the laughter had come. She quickly looked around but saw no one she recognized. There were three booths set up along the walls, but the occupants were hidden behind the high backs of the mahogany enclosures. She'd just sat down and picked up the menu when she heard the laugh again. It was unmistakable this time. She got up slowly and without quite understanding why, felt just a hint of trepidation. Why shouldn't her husband be enjoying a nice business lunch in the Plaza? She was! She was being silly. She shook her head, ridding unwanted thoughts. *And I get to show off my new hairdo!* Thinking of sharing lunch with her husband, she walked over to the booth housing the sound of his voice.

"I thought I recognized that vo—" she began, but never finished the sentence. She wanted to finish the sentence, but her vocal chords had ceased to function. She wanted to believe the attractive brunette—all ninety-eight pounds of her—was a business associate, a journalist perhaps or someone from the local Christian radio or TV station. She wanted to formulate some excuse, any excuse as to why her husband would be dining with this gorgeous creature who looked all of nineteen in the middle of the day and twenty miles from his church office. She wanted to capture an explanation that would hold down the bile that was rising from her stomach, but could not. The faces of both her husband and the other woman told her all she needed to know. King recovered first.

"Tai! What are you doing here?"

Tai was staring at the woman sitting in the booth with her husband and couldn't say a word. The woman had big, bright green eyes, now wide with astonishment. Her thin mouth had formed a silent "O." She was wearing a thin silver chain around her neck, the neck that Tai was gauging at that very moment to determine whether it would take one hand or two to choke.

"Tai," King began again, reaching out to grab her arm. Tai flinched before stepping back, at the brink of losing control, every muscle in her newly toned body taut with the effort of maintaining control. In seconds she thought of a myriad of angry outbursts, played several scenes of violence in her head. Her hands actually twitched at the thought of grabbing and wiping the already clean floor up with this brunette Barbie. Mama Max's face swam before her eyes, and she thought of her mother-in-law's encounter years ago in the hall outside hotel room number 915. *I think you've got something that belongs to me!* And King? Tai was sure there was something sharp enough in the restaurant's kitchen to take care of him. If he was hell-bent on passing his dick around, and that was what the look of guilt on his face implied, she'd make it easier for him. And then a quieter voice: *Don't lose it, girl, vengeance is mine saith the Lord.* Mama Max's voice seemed to fill her head with words of warning, words of wisdom. Tai didn't realize it, but she had been holding her breath this entire time, a fact that caused her eyes to blur for just an instant before an eerie calm washed over her, causing her to recover at last. It could only have been the Holy Ghost.

"I don't believe we've met," she said calmly, firmly and with meaning. "I'm Tai Brook, King's wife."

The woman didn't move but stammered weakly, "I'm A-A-April." Then clearing her throat for more poise repeated, "April Summers."

With the same uncanny calmness she'd just used to address her husband's mistress, for there was no doubt in Tai's mind as to whom this woman was, she turned to King. Her eyes were clear, devoid of emotion, almost unseeing. She worked to focus on the face of the man she'd loved over half her life. "Enjoy your lunch," she said as she shot daggers at April before turning and quickly walking away.

"Tai, wait!" King spoke quickly, getting up to follow her. The few customers in the restaurant followed the action as well. King placed a hand on Tai's shoulder. She jerked it off.

"Don't touch me!" she hissed between a neat, white row of clenched teeth. "And save your explanation for my attorney." King took a step back, stunned. Tai turned, head high, shoulders back and walked with the dignity of a queen out of the restaurant. At that moment, she felt that dignity was all she had left. Lord knew her appetite was gone.

That dignity carried her down the sidewalk, helped her cross the street and walk into the underground parking lot. Dignity helped her place the keys in her now terribly trembling hand into the lock and open the door to her brand-new SUV. She sat in the seat and was rock still for what seemed an eternity. She stared straight ahead seeing nothing, feeling nothing. Finally, like an automaton, she placed the key in the ignition and started the engine. She put the car in reverse and began backing out. Only the sound of a loud horn from the car directly behind brought her back to reality. She slammed on the brakes as the car carrying the angry driver careened around her and turned the corner. Tai turned then, making sure there were no cars coming before she continued backing up and headed out of the parking lot and into the afternoon Plaza bustle. The sun was still shining brightly, but Tai didn't notice. Strains of an Earth, Wind and Fire classic encouraged her to keep her head to the sky, but she didn't hear. She was barely aware of any activity around her as she navigated the city streets and entered the freeway. Although she was crying inside, wailing even, dignity kept her face dry. It was as though the Holy Spirit had literally wrapped around her emotions, blanketing her with the calm she needed to make it to the suburbs and her children's school in one piece. A million thoughts ran haphazardly through her mind. Thoughts of commitment and betrayal. Of adultery and anguish. Of marriage and murder. Here she was, on the receiving end of King's infidelity again. Not Hope, but April—a White woman. She knew that logically the color of the other woman's skin shouldn't matter, that adultery was adultery, but logic aside, the woman's color added volumes to Tai's pain.

Tai pulled up to the curb of the school and waited for the twins. It was over an hour before they came out, but Tai barely no-

ticed the time. When the twins bounded out from a group of stu-
dents and piled in the car, Tai bravely donned a mask of normalcy
for their ride home. When the kids noticed her new hairstyle and
said how beautiful it made her look, Tai almost lost it. She got
through the front door, then informed her unsuspecting children
that she wasn't feeling well and was going to her room, not to be
disturbed unless there was an extreme emergency. The silent but
deadly tone of her voice brooked no argument. She went to her
room, lay down and finally allowed the tears to flow, onto the bed
that she and King had shared for nearly two decades.

Vivian was a sympathetic listener throughout Tai's recounting
of the previous twenty-four hour's tumultuous events. She rarely
spoke except to ask a question or two and add the sympathetic
"uh-huh" at the right moments. She knew Tai felt better after
telling the story out loud, however painful.

"You said the confrontation happened this morning?" Vivian
inquired. "What happened when King got home yesterday?"

"When he got home, I was gone. I knew I couldn't handle
even a conversation with him yesterday, so I asked Jan if she could
watch the children until he got home, and I went to a hotel for the
night. It took me all night just to gather the strength to face him.
But I didn't want to put off the inevitable, so as soon as I got home
this morning, after the children left for school, I confronted him
about the bitch at the restaurant. At first he tried to act like it was
a business luncheon, but after I demanded it, he told me the truth.
That he was seeing her and that they had been intimate. You would
think that since I suspected it anyway, the truth wouldn't hurt so
much. It hurts like hell. April is where he's been spending his time.
I went off, attacked him; called him every name but a child of
God. He left a few hours ago. I haven't talked to anyone since, not
even Mama Max."

"Do you think King has told her?"

"With his lying ass? I doubt it." The silence lengthened as each became absorbed in her own thoughts. Finally Vivian spoke.

"You know I'm here for you. Derrick and I are here for *both* of you."

"It's helping me a lot just to talk to you, girl. I know you're here for me." Several more moments of silence passed before either woman spoke again.

"What are you thinking?" Vivian finally asked gently, wiping her eyes.

"I'm thinking about me and King and our lives together. About how I've loved him so long and so completely that I don't know where he ends and I begin. I'm trying to separate the "two becoming one" into two again. How do I do that, Vivian? I was so sure God joined us together. How do I divorce him? How do I divorce myself? I don't remember the Twyla before King! Where is she?" Tai was crying openly now.

"We'll find her," Vivian stated resolutely, with more confidence than she felt. "I'll help you, and together—me, you and God— we'll find her."

. . . Getting ready to preach a revival when I need reviving the most

"Pastor, did you hear me?" Hope's brow creased as she cocked her head to the side, sensing her pastor's pain.

"Oh, uh, sorry, Hope. What were you saying?"

"I was saying that the concert's all set, that we got the signed contract back from Righteous's management. Charles and I are working with his management team to secure the other details and—Pastor? Are you all right?"

"What? Oh, sorry, Hope. Actually I do have a lot on my mind this morning." King noticed the look of concern in Hope's eyes and quickly added, "We're leaving today for that revival in Cleveland and, uh, a lot of stuff has come up."

"Oh, the revival at St. Stephens? Bishop Anderson's church?"

King nodded.

"Is there anything I can do to help? I don't have to be at work until this afternoon if there's anything—"

"No, Hope, but thanks for asking. Listen, just give the rest of the details to Joseph on your way out. I've got some pressing things I need to handle right now."

The quick dismissal was like a bee sting. She and Pastor King normally got along so well together, almost too well some members speculated. But God knew her heart. She got up quickly and quietly, knowing she should go, feeling she should stay. She hesitated for just a moment, and King looked up quickly, with just the hint of a scowl. That unlocked Hope's feet from their spot on the floor, and she found her voice. "Well, I'll, uh, I'll be praying for you, Pastor," she said quietly.

"Good, good," King replied quietly before leaning back and turning his chair to face the wall. Hope's dismissal was complete, and he barely heard the door as it clicked shut behind her.

King wiped his face a couple times with his hands, then drew a hard line across his brow with long, tapered fingers before they came to rest on the sides of his chin. He stroked his chin slowly, methodically, as the scenes from yesterday and this morning played in his head. He felt tired. Tired and old.

He laid his head back on the strong, wing chair and closed his eyes. Scenes of the earlier confrontation with Tai swam before his eyes. *How did I get here?* he asked himself over and over in his mind as if he didn't already know the answer. *What am I supposed to do?* It seemed that no matter how he looked at the situation, all he saw was pain. Even though he wasn't *in* love with Tai, he did love her as his companion of twenty years and the mother of his four children. The last thing he wanted to do was hurt her. She'd been a good wife over the years, loyal and loving. She was an excellent mother, a good daughter-in-law to his mother, Maxine. And she'd been trying so hard the past few months to make him happy, exercising, losing weight. *Then why am I dogging her?* King thought of the children then, Michael in college, Princess on her way. He thought of their faces, all innocence and trust. He sat up, swiveled around, placed his elbows on the desk and his head in his hands.

A family movie played out in his mind: Tai having their children, the children growing up. Birthdays and Thanksgiving dinners, mounds of presents in the living room at Christmas, colored eggs on Easter Sunday. Tai's ever-present face in the front row of almost every church in which he'd graced the pulpit, silently encouraging, shining with pride. What was he doing?

Then, almost like the imp on the other shoulder another face swam clearly into view. April. Willing, wonderful April. The woman who'd made him feel young again before he'd even realized he felt old. The woman who made him feel alive when he felt he was drowning in a sea of sameness, adrift without passion or tenderness. He'd called her his lifesaver and told her she tasted delicious. When laughingly asked what flavor, he'd told her he needed to conduct an extensive taste test to find out.

April was pleasant and persistent, there with open arms and an empty bed, ready to lend sympathetic, non-judging ears to the woes of his disintegrating marriage. She never prodded him to divorce his wife and had at times even offered suggestions on how the marriage could be saved. In a twisted way, that made King admire her more, she seemed so unselfish. That this seemingly unselfish female had another woman's husband in her bed did not enter his mind. *She cares about me,* he thought as he justified his transgression.

He remembered the first time he saw her, looking outrageously sexy in a skimpy halter top with faded, cutoff jean shorts. She'd flashed him a little cleavage, began to flirt. He'd told her that not only was he a married man with children but also a pastor. He'd invited her to church; they'd exchanged business cards. She'd called the office the next day. After a few conversations, he'd suggested an appointment. She suggested her apartment. They'd agreed on lunch at the Crown Center Hotel Complex. Now, six months later, it seemed she had provided him with more counseling than the other way around.

A light rap on the door announced Joseph's entry. King didn't even turn; he knew that Joseph would be the only one coming in because of explicit instructions that no one else enter.

"Hey, boss man," Joseph began quietly. "You all right?"

"I've been better."

"Anything I can do to help?"

"Not really."

"Well, it looks like everything is in place for your trip." Joseph waited for King to respond, but continued after an uncomfortable silence. "We should be leaving in the next thirty minutes."

The private line on King's phone rang. Both he and Joseph stared at the flashing button. "You gonna get that?" Joseph asked after a slight hesitation. King's continued silence was the only reply. He sat there unmoving, staring solemnly at the blinking red light.

"All right then, boss. Call me when you're ready to head to the airport." Joseph, an invaluable and loyal assistant who had learned much about his employer of five years, walked quietly to the door, pausing to contemplate his boss and mentor a moment more before opening it and silently stepping outside.

The little red light stopped blinking and then almost immediately began blinking again. King glanced at the phone before standing up, stretching wearily and walking over to the fully equipped bathroom in the corner of his office. He turned on the cold water full blast and, taking a large amount in cupped hands, splashed his face repeatedly. It did little good. He still felt tired and groggy. He grabbed a monogrammed towel from the rack and held it to his face, shaking his head in his hands. He straightened again, placed the towel on the rack and walked back into his office to the sounds of his cell phone beeping steadily. He reluctantly reached for the cell phone atop his briefcase and looked at the caller ID. April, just like he figured.

Of course she'd been upset at the unexpected run-in with Tai. She'd been even more upset when he left the restaurant to try and catch up with his wife. Needless to say, their lunch was over. April hoped their relationship would not follow the same route. She'd begged him to stay, for them to talk it out, but King couldn't handle her company. He wanted either to be with Tai and talk about this situation, or he didn't want to be with anyone. He was too upset. He had too many things to think about. He'd promised to call her and he had, briefly, after finding Tai gone when he got home. That had been several hours after he drove around aimlessly. When he found himself on I–435 heading toward St. Louis, he turned around and headed home. He wouldn't run away from his problem. His stomach was in knots as he punched the garage door opener, and he wasn't surprised when he didn't see the SUV. Once he was inside the house, the phone rang with their neighbor, Jan, saying the kids were on their way home. When he questioned her, she told him Tai had asked her to watch them and no, she hadn't said where she was going. King figured Tai would want to spend some time alone. Still, he was worried and called her cell phone number. Finally, after several pleadings that she at least let him know she was all right, she'd text messaged that she was as well as could be expected and that, in no uncertain terms, she had nothing to say to him.

All that changed when she returned home the next morning. Dark circles under her eyes had informed him of her lack of sleep. He understood. The oblivion of nocturnal escape had eluded him, too. She'd started off calm, cool and collected with one simple question, "So is that the whore you're sleeping with?"

He didn't know why he'd lied. That was the pull that had popped the cork on Tai's suppressed rage, delivering on him the blows he was sure were meant for both he and April. He'd finally told the truth, not the smartest move either. Why was he angry? She had every right to question him about April. He'd been cold and callous in his reply, compassion and sympathy going out the window along with his last shred of decency as he had walked out, slamming the door behind him.

"Five minutes, boss." Joseph opened the door just enough to deliver the message, then turned back to his desk, gathering day planner, cell phones and notepads.

What irony, King thought as he slipped on his suit jacket and closed his briefcase. *I'm getting ready to preach a revival when I need reviving the most.*

Just as he stepped to the door and turned out the office light, the red light of his private line began blinking ominously in the darkness. April. He hesitated a moment before walking away from the call. The next reasonable move would be to walk away from his mistress.

Lord, have mercy

Hope watched silently as the somber trio walked over to the Lincoln Towncar. She was still smarting from the pastor's summary dismissal of her earlier. *What was that about?* As she watched what for all intents and purposes looked like a funeral procession, she was sure something was going on, and she deduced it had more to do with Pastor and less to do with the revival at St. Stephens. Joseph walked to the passenger side, opening the front door for Pastor and then seating himself in the back. Minister Hobbs slid behind the driver's seat on the other side. Nobody talked. Nobody smiled. All three were dressed in black. Had somebody died? *Stop it, Hope, your imagination is running wild.* She shook her head and reached for her keys, her eyes still riveted on the Lincoln. She saw Pastor rub his temples wearily. Joseph reached over and slapped his shoulders in a gesture of support. *It's none of my business,* Hope thought as she started her MG.

She had just put her car in reverse and backed out when she saw a little white, sporty Honda buzz into the parking lot and pull up next to the Lincoln. The car parked haphazardly and had barely stopped when a petite, brunette, obviously upset woman hopped out of the driver's side and rushed over to the Lincoln. Joseph jumped out immediately and pulled her away from the car as she tried, without success, to open the door on Pastor's side. She was screaming through the window, but Hope couldn't make out her hysterical and garbled words. Something about phone calls, she surmised as the woman frantically waved a cell phone in Pastor's direction. She rolled down her window and began to inch her car forward, but before she'd gotten ten feet, two of pastor's assistants ran out of the church and helped Joseph subdue the lady and walk her back over to the Honda and away from Pastor, who though appearing calm, stared straight ahead. After speaking with the woman for a few moments, Joseph walked back to the Lincoln, got in, and not two seconds later the luxury car was pulling out of the parking lot.

What was that about? Hope reversed her car and pulled back into a parking spot. *It may not be my business, but this is church grounds, so it is now church business and I'm a member!*

The two assistants were still talking to the calmer yet still seething woman. Hope shook her head, wondering why women like that had to make such fools of themselves. She knew many women in the church had their eyes on Pastor, and the thought nauseated her. Hope stepped out of her car and walked toward the church, all the time eyeing the trio next to the Honda. The woman didn't look familiar. While Hope watched, the woman tossed her head haughtily, walked to the car door that had been opened for her by one of the assistants and got inside. The girl was upset. Hope was about to walk over and offer her counseling services when the woman started the car and gassed the engine. The car flew backward, running over a small shrub.

"Hey!" Hope shouted as she moved out of the way. The woman didn't even see her, just put the car in drive and tore out of the parking lot. An eerie silence remained.

Hope waited for the assistants to cross the parking lot. One of them, Drew, had pursued Hope when she first came to the church. She'd considered it briefly, before finding out he was also trying to talk to every other skirt in the building. He was a born flirt and cute in a Pillsbury Doughboy way. He was shaking his head as he crossed the pavement. Hope flashed a stop-and-talk-to-me-because-yes-I'm-in-somebody-else's-business-but-I-need-to-know" smile. He stopped.

"I was getting ready to come over and offer counseling," Hope began as she turned to match steps with Drew, who continued into the church. Hovering at the front door and talking in conspiratorial whispers were Sistahs Almighty and Alrighty. *Great,* Hope thought. *Now everybody's gonna know.*

Drew kept walking toward the classroom doors and, trying each knob, found one unlocked. He opened the door. Hope quickly looked around to make sure no one saw her and stepped inside.

"So how are you, Hope?" Drew asked quietly, leaning back against the door as she stepped across the room and sat in a chair.

"I should ask how you are! I thought you were going to have to call backup."

"Oh, that wasn't nothin'."

"Well, nothin'" almost ran me over. Who is she, another Mrs. Brook wannabe?"

"You know how it is." Drew was being pointedly evasive. Hope was not amused—or deterred.

"I haven't seen her around here."

"Me either."

"So who is she? Obviously somebody who knows about the church since she drove into the parking lot, and obviously somebody who knows Pastor since she almost attacked him!"

"Well," Drew began, walking over to take a chair next to Hope. "You know how many women throw themselves at Pastor. She just joined the crowd."

"So you've never seen her before either? You don't know who she is?"

"Naw. Never seen her before."

"So what was she saying to Pastor?"

"Something about him not returning her calls, blah, blah, blah." Drew tried to lighten the mood. "The woman is probably on crack!"

Probably not was what Hope thought. "Hummm," was all she said.

"So, pretty lady," Drew drawled, grabbing Hope's hand and raising it to his lips for a kiss. "When am I going to get that oh-so-elusive telephone number?"

Hope smiled as she gently pulled back her hand and stood up. "When you finish calling the ninety-nine numbers you've already gotten from all the other sistahs in our church family. God bless you, brotha!" When Hope opened the door, she looked both ways to make sure the coast was clear, then quietly closed the door behind her. It would do no good for Sistah Almighty or Alrighty to see her coming out of a church classroom with one of the menfolk.

As she stepped into the foyer from the hallway, she noticed the very occupiers of her thoughts coming through the front door. Knowing she was one of their least favorite people didn't stop her from greeting them. "Hey, Sistah Stokes. Sistah Wanthers."

"How do."

"Hello."

They both eyed her suspiciously. Hope lowered her voice and leaned forward. "Now, you ladies know we aren't supposed to gossip, but I know you saw what happened in the parking lot, and I know you'll agree we need to pray for Pastor King. That woman almost ran me over."

Sistah Stokes couldn't resist the dangling worm. "What?" she said aloud and then dropped her voice to a whisper. "Well, who was she?"

"Let's take this conversation outside, ladies," Sistah Wanthers interjected sternly. "It ain't right to have gossiping and such up in this here sanctuary." Then she almost ran over Hope trying to beat her through the door. Hope didn't know Sistah Alrighty could move so fast! They all headed for the exit doors and stepped outside, walking toward the edge of the building. "Now, what kinda nonsense was the girl saying? I don't hear as good as I used to," Sistah Wanthers said as she inched closer to Hope.

"Calm down, Elsie!" Sistah Stokes admonished. "Let the girl have her say."

Hope smiled. It was said that the act of war made strange bedfellows, and if there was someone out there trying to ruin their Pastor's marriage, the war was on.

"The lady was screaming she was in love with Pastor. Now, I know I haven't seen her at church before, so I don't know how she knows about him or the church. But we know how the enemy can cause delusions. Pastor might not even know that woman, and here she is causing a disturbance almost on the doorstep of God's house!"

"The devil is a lie!" Sistah Almighty bellowed. "*Ah shantae ee roe sandala ma shee key ah.*" It had taken this dyed-in-the-wool Baptist a while to surrender to the notion of speaking in tongues, the holy language, but this was a serious situation, and she needed to feel her help coming. She continued with unbridled zeal. "The blood of Jesus! *Ee roe a shanta my handalah roe hah!*"

Sistah Alrighty, who'd never yielded to the holy language, became impatient with her entreating friend. "Will you hush up?" she hissed, then softened a bit at the thought of telling someone not to pray. "What I mean is, we need to pray, but, uh, we first got to know just what to pray about!" Then she turned to Hope. "What else did she say?"

Hope raised her hand to hide a smile, coughing quickly instead. "I don't know, but she was hysterical. And then Joseph grabbed her and pulled her away from Pastor's car. I think we've just got to pray a hedge of protection around Pastor Brook to keep him from the traps of the devil." Hope looked at her watch again. It was obvious there was no information here. "Well, I've got to go to work, ladies. Be blessed."

"Uh-huh."

"You, too."

Sistahs Almighty and Alrighty watched quietly as Hope crossed the parking lot in her stylish, snug black suit. They weren't aware that they were frowning as she opened the door to her car and got inside. Hope fastened her seat belt, adjusted the mirror, put the car in gear and took off slowly, waving to the sisters as she passed them. They waved back, smiling, watching the car until it disappeared around the corner. Then they slowly turned to face each other, the smiles turning upside down.

"Are you thinking what I'm thinking?" Sistah Almighty asked with a raised eyebrow.

"Sho' is," Sistah Alrighty countered, pausing for effect. "That the pot bet not call the kettle black. She betta pray, all right."

"Unh, unh, unh. Sho'nuff. Best she prays for herself before she prays about somebody else."

"Lord have mercy."

"*Ee roe shantalah my hayah dah ee tah,*" Sistah Almighty began again. This time Sistah Alrighty bowed her head, beginning her own intercession with God as they both turned toward the church and began walking inside. Prayer, after all, was something that *could* be done in the house of the Lord.

God was with her and she was going to be okay

"White woman! Did I hear you say . . . White woman!" Sistah Maxine was wearing out a trail in the living room carpet, from the fireplace to the window and back to the couch. "Don't tell me my son was wallowing in some peepee!"

Tai's head shot up. Mama Max was always hard to follow when she was angry. And Tai hadn't seen her this angry in quite some time. She'd waited a week to tell her what happened, until she herself had calmed down enough to get the words out without choking.

"Peepee?" Tai asked, a quizzical look accompanying the question.

"Yes. Pee. Pee. Pink pussy."

"Mama Max!"

"Yes, I said it. Those hussies are always after our Black men. They got everything else, now they want them, too!" Mama Max sat down on the couch briefly, only to jump back up and start pacing again. "Triflin' heifa! I bet she looks like a mangy dog!"

"No, Mama, she's actually very attractive," Tai stated matter-of-factly. "You know King only likes the best."

"Humph," Mama Max said, crossing the floor and sitting down with a thud. "Attractive. Yeah, like the AIDS virus." Both ladies became silent, deep in their own worlds, their own thoughts. After several moments, Tai stood up.

"You know, this isn't King's first affair. And all of the other women were Black. I admit, at first it really bothered me, too, that she was White. But wrong is wrong, no matter what the color. I'm not pissed anymore because the woman is White. I'm pissed because she's with my husband." Tai paused, scowled. "And he's with her." She headed to the kitchen. "You want some coffee, Mama Max?"

"Yeah, baby," Mama said distractedly. "With a shot of hundred proof!" she added, smiling.

"I do have some Bailey's if you want."

"Bailey? Who's that?"

"It's a liqueur that tastes like that Irish-flavored creamer you like so much. I'll let you try some of mine and see if you like it."

Mama Max said nothing as she sat staring into space, squinting her eyes as she peered far beyond the natural realm. Tai went to the kitchen and returned carrying a tray with a coffee urn, two cups, a bottle of Bailey's Irish Cream and a few mini-croissants. She eyed Mama Max as she set the tray down and began pouring the coffee. Mama Max had not changed positions.

"What are you thinking, Mama?" Tai asked quietly, placing a croissant in front of her mother-in-law and friend. She opened the Bailey's and poured a generous amount into one of the steaming cups, then grabbed a spoon and stirred slowly, still looking at a frowning Maxine. "Here, taste this."

"What? Oh, uh, thank you, baby." Mama Max reached for the cup, smelling the contents. "Hum, it smells good." She took a tentative taste, blowing on the coffee as she did so. She swallowed, pondered the taste and took another sip, a bit larger this time. "Ooh, yes, this is delicious! What did you say it is?" she asked, reaching for the bottle.

"Bailey's Irish Cream," Tai said, pouring another cup of the mixture and grabbing a croissant before seating herself on the couch next to Mama Max. "Sandy, a friend from my Sprint days, introduced me to it. I wonder what she's doing these days?"

"It ain't gon' happen," Mama Max stated quietly. She hadn't even heard Tai's last comment.

"What ain't gonna happen?"

"This little peepee thinking she's gon' ruin your marriage." Mama Max looked at Tai with narrowed eyes. "Ain't gon' happen."

"Oh, Mama Max," Tai began, and now it was her turn to pace. "She may not have been the only one, just the one I know about. This marriage was in trouble before she came along."

Mama Max was silent.

"It's not just King, Mama. I don't know if *I* want to go on anymore with this life, this marriage. I don't know if I have the energy to forgive and forget, to put yet another woman behind us and be the strong, supportive wife. This affair has destroyed every ounce of trust I'd built back up from the last affair, the last one I've known about, that is. You know I've had nagging feelings about King's fidelity for a while now. I didn't have proof, but these feelings have been here for a long time.

"I'm tired," Tai continued, returning to the couch and pouring herself another coffee with a liberal dose of Bailey's. "I want out."

Mama Max looked at her, but didn't reply immediately. Finally she grabbed Tai's hand and stroked it gently. "I know you're tired, baby." Tai began to cry. Mama Max spoke again, softer this time. "I'd be tired, too." She reached over to refill her cup, then put it down instead and looked out the window.

"I don't know what my son is thinking. He's got a great wife, wonderful children, this beautiful home and a church that's boomin'. I can't even believe he's risking the loss of everything behind some little hussy who probably can't even spell first lady, let alone be one."

Tai finished her croissant and reached for a napkin. "Nobody said adultery made sense."

Mama Max continued. "You've been with him since the beginning, taken his crap, covered his sins while he acted like a plum fool."

Tai got ready to interject. Mama Max raised her hand.

"No, no, you know I'm speaking the truth. Now, he's my son and I love him, but wrong is wrong. God don't like ugly and neither do I, and I'm going to tell him so just as soon as he gets home!"

"Mama, I don't even know what good talking will do at this point."

"Well, I know what it will do. Bring my blood pressure down for one thang. I've got some thangs on my chest and I'ma get 'em off! Ain't no son of mine gon' disgrace his family like this. And with a White girl, too?" Mama Max crossed her arms, rocking back and forth. "Not on my watch!"

"Mama, adultery is adultery. Like I said, the color of her skin doesn't matter."

"It *does* in my book," Mama Max insisted. "What is that saying about me as a Black woman? No, honey, I didn't raise my son like this, and if he think he's just gon' ride off in the sunset with his little cracka' and not think his mother is gon' have anything to say, then he's got another think coming!"

Tai appreciated her mother-in-law's indignation, but offered her own perspective. "Before, no matter how hurt I felt at King's betrayals, there was always a part of me that believed in him and his love for me. I couldn't imagine life without him, without the church, our family being together." She paused. "Well, I'm beginning to imagine it now. And it doesn't look as scary or feel as bad as I thought it would." She placed her coffee cup down as the phone rang. Reaching for the cordless, she looked at the caller ID and pushed the talk button.

"Hey, neighbor."

"Hey, Tai, how are you?"

"Okay."

"Well, I just called to tell you I could pick up your kids when I pick up Brandon if you'd like. I saw your mother-in-law's car in the driveway and thought you might be busy."

"That would be nice, Jan. And it would give Mama Max and me time to finish our discussion."

"Would you mind if I took the kids to the mall with me? I was planning on getting something for my little one. And you won't have to worry about their dinner 'cause we'll grab something to eat, too."

Tai whispered a silent prayer to God for His act of kindness. She knew how perceptive the twins were, and today she didn't have the energy to put on a happy face. "That would be wonderful. You're a blessing, Jan."

"That's what neighbors are for," Jan said cheerfully, and then added a bit more somberly, "Are you sure you're all right? I don't mean to pry, but I've been worried about you."

Tai smiled again. This was just like Jan. She probed enough to let Tai know she cared, but not enough to be too nosy. The fact that Jan was White underscored her reasoning in not placing undue emphasis on the color of King's latest conquest. Women, Black or White, weren't all alike. "I'm a bit tired. Just pray for me, okay?"

"Well, if I can help in any way, with the kids or anything, just let me know."

"I'll do that, thanks again. Oh, wait! Let me bring over some money for the twins."

"Don't you dare!"

"Are you sure?"

"Look, Tai, I clip coupons. I think I can handle an evening at the mall, okay?"

"Okay," Tai said, laughing out loud. Maybe she would talk to Jan. Get a White woman's perspective on King's White woman. "Thanks again."

Having cleared the tray and other items from the coffee table, Mama Max returned to the couch. "Anybody important?" she asked.

"Just my neighbor, Jan, volunteering to pick up the kids. She's gonna take them to the mall. Bless her heart."

"You talking about that woman next door in the brick house?" Mama Max asked with thinly veiled suspicion.

"Oh, come on, Mama Max, Jan is a wonderful person who has no interest in my husband. I trust her."

"Uh-huh, I trust her, too," Mama Max countered smoothly. "As far as I can throw her."

Tai was about to reply when the phone rang again. She picked it up and looked at the ID. It was Vivian.

"Hey, girl."

"Hey, yourself. I'm just checking in. How are you?"

"I'm okay. Mama Max is here."

Vivian relaxed immediately. "Ooh, that's good. What about King?"

"Gone to a revival in Cleveland. Talk about God's timing."

"What? You wish he hadn't left?"

"Oh, no, this is a blessing. I probably would have killed him had he stayed."

Vivian smiled, and you could hear it in her voice. "Great. Anger. That's a good sign."

"Whatever. I'll call you later, okay?"

"Sure, girl. I love you."

"I love you, too." Tai punched the off button and threw the phone on the couch between her and Mama Max. "That was Vivian."

"Hum. What are her feelings on the matter?"

"You know Vivian, the pillar of support. She said she was with me no matter what happens. You know how close all of us are. Both she and Derrick are praying for us."

"I wonder if Derrick is faithful," Mama Max queried.

"As far as I know," Tai replied. "Not that Vivian hasn't had to do major battles with women all too eager to unseat her from her position as Mrs. Montgomery. But Derrick is totally committed to their marriage, always has been.

"I remember this one story she told me about this woman who was after Derrick, practically stalking him. She was at the church whenever the doors opened, just blatant. Derrick had told Vivian immediately, which was good since Vivian had peeped girlfriend's hand from the moment she stepped foot in the church. Finally she and Derrick came up with a plan."

"What was that?" Mama asked.

"Well, the woman had been calling the church almost every day insisting on a counseling session with Derrick. Although they tried to set her up with one of the associate ministers, she adamantly refused to see anyone but him. So he finally agreed to see her."

"Umph, just like a man. The dog."

Tai, sensing Mama Max getting ready to add Derrick to her you-know-what list, hurried on. "Let me finish. When she got to the church and was ushered into Derrick's office, who do you think was waiting there?"

"Who? Oh, I see . . . Vivian," Mama Max exclaimed, mentally putting Derrick back in her good graces.

"You got it, and if you think the woman was surprised to see Vivian, imagine Vivian's surprise when after grabbing the woman to prevent her from running out the door like she tried to, she discovered the woman was buck naked underneath her all-weather coat."

"No!"

"Yes!"

"That no-good hussy! Women will do anything!"

"Vivian had the last laugh. She called the police and had the woman arrested for indecent exposure."

"Good for her."

"Well, the charges were dropped because Vivian didn't pursue it, but the woman got the message and never showed her face at the church again."

"I can't believe the trollop had that much decency."

"Well, she had a little help. Before the police arrived, Vivian led the woman to believe there were security cameras in the office and hinted that these telling pictures might get accidentally handed out to the congregation if the woman didn't find another church home."

Mama Max howled. Soon Tai joined in. The laughter felt good to Tai. She'd been doing entirely too little of it lately.

By the time Mama Max left a couple hours later, Tai felt better. Better and stronger. She was determined not to be a victim. For the first time since she said, "I do," she decided to get in the driver's seat where her marriage was concerned. In the ensuing quiet surrounding her with Mama and the children gone, she made some clear decisions. The first was to move out of the master bedroom and into the guest room immediately. She'd wanted to move out of the house, but that would have been too disruptive for the children. As it was, they were bound to be curious about the new living arrangements, but she'd think of something. One thing was for sure—she wouldn't keep sleeping with the enemy.

Second, she decided to get a life. She would call Vivian and become more involved and active with the upcoming S.O.S. Summit. Although she wasn't much of a speaker, she felt there was something she could impart to the women in the body of Christ. The more she thought of it, the better she liked the idea. It would be therapeutic, a catharsis. She hoped it wasn't too late to add another topic to the agenda. That naturally led to another idea she'd thought of a couple months ago. She would take a computer class at the local community college and brush up on her skills. A life without King may mean a return to the workplace, and while she didn't relish the thought of not being able to be as hands-on with her children, she felt the sacrifice would be worth it to have peace of mind.

Third, and she didn't know how she was going to do this, but she could no longer support King in the ministry. True, she loved Mount Zion Progressive and considered the members to be like family, but she could no longer live a lie. She would continue most of her first lady responsibilities, including presiding over the women's fellowship and the program for unwed mothers. And she would continue the traveling prayer ministry for the sick and shut-in. But she wouldn't be standing by King's side every time he mounted the pulpit. She'd do it on Sundays for appearances, but that was all. And she wouldn't travel with him when he was invited to other churches. From this day forward, Tai vowed to be first lady in the eyes of God only, and not in the eyes of King. With that in mind she reached for her Amplified Bible, turned to Isaiah 54 and began to read aloud: "*For the Maker is thine Husband, the Lord of hosts . . . I will have compassion and mercy on you, says the Lord your Redeemer . . .*"

As God's promise to have mercy on Tai with everlasting kindness resonated, joy replaced her anger. The tears fell, but they were ones of hope, not despair. God was with her and she was going to be okay. She knelt in prayer and much to her surprise began praying for King and the other woman. She prayed for women all over the world, women who were married to philandering men—women like her. She prayed for the ministry and for ministers everywhere—ministers like King. She prayed for first ladies, deacons' wives, trustees' wives, men's wives. She prayed for the single women so desperate for companionship and starved for love that they turned to other women's husbands with no thought of shame or responsibility. She prayed for her children's well-being during this strenuous time. She prayed for the right way to handle them, and for their emotional well-being. She prayed for children of divorced and separated parents everywhere. Children caught in the crossfire—children like hers. She was just getting off her knees as she heard the front door open. When she went down to greet the children her hugs were sincere and her smile was genuine. God was with her and she was going to be okay.

Thou shall not kill

Vivian was taking the casserole out of the oven as she heard the front door close. Derrick was back from his week-long revival in Canada. "Perfect timing!" she called out to him.

He came into the kitchen with a smile that said, *I-miss-you-and-I-love-you-and-I-want-to-do-it-to-you-right-now-on-the-kitchen-floor!*

"What's that?" Vivian crooned, trying to peek behind Derrick's back to see what he was holding. He pulled out an exotic bouquet of orchids and birds of paradise.

"Exotic flowers for an exotic lady. My erotic—I mean, exotic queen!"

Vivian laughed and swatted at him playfully. "You were right on both counts. Exotic *and* erotic! I'm just glad you didn't say neurotic!" They both laughed.

"These flowers are lovely, boo, to what do I owe the pleasure?" She opened a cabinet and took out a crystal vase, filled it with water and began arranging the bouquet carefully.

"To the fact that I love you, I need you and I can't live without you."

"Well, that makes two of us." Vivian placed the last flower in the vase and walked over to her husband. She wrapped her arms around his neck and brushed her lips lazily over his.

"Don't tease me, woman," Derrick murmured, pulling her into a lingering kiss and tight embrace.

Vivian gave as good as she got. She broke the kiss, only to plant tiny smooches all over his face. She outlined his ear with her tongue and traced a moist path back down to his full mouth, reclaiming once again what she thanked God for every day. After a moment, she stepped back, smiling playfully. "Feels like you bought me a large cucumber, too. Did you want a salad?"

Derrick's reply was interrupted by the sound of feet on the staircase and the squeal of a baby girl excited to see her dad. "Daddy!" Elisia shouted, running into the kitchen. D-2 followed in a more subdued manner. He considered screaming and running to one's parents acting like a baby. He was much too cool for that. Still, he was glad to see his dad. Seeing their parents embrace was a common occurrence, so they were not surprised or embarrassed. Elisia tried to scoot in and make the embrace a threesome. Daddy, however, was trying to hide his "cucumber" and was in no position to break the now strategically necessary cuddle. Still holding Vivian with one arm he leaned down and kissed his daughter, acknowledging his son over her head. "Hey, son, hey, baby! How's Daddy's other girl today?"

"I'm fine, Daddy! Hey, can you come to my room and see the drawing I did today at school? Mrs. Nelson said it was beautiful!"

"I'm sure it is, darling. I tell you what. You go on up and get it ready and I'll be up in a little bit. As soon as I finish talking to your mother."

"Y'all weren't talking, y'all were kissing!"

"Whatever we were doing, we're not finished!" Vivian countered, smiling down at her daughter. "Your father is busy and will be up in a moment. I get him first, remember?"

"Yes, ma'am," Elisia said, smiling. "But you'll come up soon, right, Daddy?"

"I'm already up," he whispered in Vivian's ear, and then to his daughter, "Yes, sweetheart, I'll be up soon." They both smiled as their daughter skipped out of the kitchen and headed upstairs. D-2 had already left to spend time with one of his best friends and their favorite pastime—basketball.

"You're incorrigible," Vivian continued as she resumed her husband's seduction, loosening his tie and beginning to unbutton his shirt. "Just like I like you."

"I better stop while I still can," Derrick whispered, gently breaking away from Vivian with a final kiss on the cheek and pinch on the behind. "Something smells good."

"Everybody knows the smell of tuna casserole; you're changing the subject."

"I'm postponing the subject, but believe me this is a topic I do intend to take back up with you later tonight."

"Ooh, is that a promise?"

"Cross my heart."

"Then go on up and change and I'll bring you a cup of tea. Would you like that? I need to talk to you about something." Vivian's mood turned serious, and Derrick noticed immediately.

"Is this what you alluded to on the phone that you said I had to hear in person?"

"King and Tai."

Derrick rubbed his chin thoughtfully. "So that's what King wanted."

"He called you?"

"Left a message. I never got a chance to call him back."

"You need to, it's pretty serious. But go on up and I'll get your tea. I wouldn't want this discussion overheard."

Vivian poured water into the teakettle and turned the burner on. Then she grabbed lettuce, tomato and a cucumber out of the refrigerator to make a quick salad. By the time she sliced the last of the cucumber, smiling as she did so, the kettle was whistling. She poured the hot water over the teabags, and the smell of chamomile wafted up from the steaming cups. She grabbed a lemon out of the refrigerator, sliced it and placed it, the honey, a bowl of nuts and the two mugs on a tray, heading for the bedroom. Derrick was lying on the bed, his arms behind his head, when she opened the door. She smiled, closing the door with her foot.

"You're distracting," she said, coming over to Derrick's side of the bed and placing the tray down on his nightstand. Derrick was clad only in silver silk boxers and black socks. "You'd better put a robe on if you expect me to remember what I want to talk to you about."

Derrick swung his legs over the side of the bed, sitting up languidly. He made a reach for the tea but turned, grabbing Vivian instead, and pulled her down on top of him in the middle of their king-sized paradise.

"Maybe I don't want to talk," Derrick cooed as he reached under Vivian's tank top and grabbed a handful of her firm, lush breasts. "Maybe I want to do . . . other things."

Vivian rolled over and sat up, scooting to the end of the bed and reaching for his tea mug. "All in good time, my pretty," she droned. "All in good time."

Derrick sat up. He reached out for the mug that Vivian held out to him and grabbed a handful of nuts. Sitting back against the headboard, he looked at her intently. "So how bad is the damage this time?" he began while taking a sip of tea. He reached over for the honey and added another huge dollop to the steamy concoction.

"Tai wants a divorce."

"She said that?"

"She said it, and Derrick, this time I think she means it. She met King's—how should I say this nicely—'ho.'"

Derrick almost spilled his tea. "What?" He set down the mug. "When?"

"By accident, a week ago," Vivian answered, reaching for the nuts herself. She then proceeded to tell Derrick about her conversation with Tai and Tai's unplanned run-in with King and his mistress. By the time she finished the mini-version of this real-life mini-series, Elisia was knocking on the door. "Daddy, you promised!" she yelled from outside. Derrick had forgotten all about Elisia and her artwork.

Vivian stood up and walked toward the door. "Go on, honey, I'll set the table. Dinner will be waiting when you two come down." She opened the door and spoke to Elisia. "Where's your brother?"

"Outside. He's still playing basketball with Chris."

Vivian walked down the stairs, through the living room to the front door. She walked out onto the sidewalk, glancing two doors down to where Chris and his family lived. All she saw was an empty driveway with an abandoned basketball resting on top of their perfectly trimmed hedges. "I'm sure his mother will love that," Vivian mused as she scanned the block for her son. She then did what was done to her when she was his age; something that she was sure embarrassed him immensely as it had her in her youth. She bellowed.

"DERRICK!!!!" Almost instantly, Derrick appeared from the Winters' backyard.

"Aw, Mom, do you have to yell?" he whined, grabbing his shirt and heading over the grass toward his house.

"It worked, didn't it?" Vivian replied with a kiss to D-2's cheek, causing further chagrin since he thought Chris might be watching. "Now, hurry up and shower. Dinner's ready." She held him in a hug, and he tried to break away as they walked through the front door.

Vivian laughed as D-2 bounded up the steps two at a time and she headed to the kitchen. Humming quietly, she took out the necessary dishes and silverware for the table setting. She grabbed napkins and glasses and headed for the dining room. After setting the table quickly, she returned to the kitchen for the bowl of salad and basket of rolls. She then went back for the casserole dish. She smiled, relishing the simple acts of motherhood and married life. She again thought of Tai, and her smile faded. Her heart went out to the woman, who was like a sister to her. She couldn't possibly imagine the depths of Tai's pain. Going back into the kitchen for the pitcher of tea, Vivian tried to. Imagine Tai's pain. Imagine how she'd feel knowing that Derrick was cheating on her. She grabbed the vase of flowers and placed them on the buffet in the dining room as she pondered her possible reaction to finding out someone else was in bed with her husband. Then she tried to figure out how long it would take her to adjust to prison life, because that was where she'd be headed after she'd killed them both!

"Dinner's ready," she called from the foot of the stairs. "Yes, I would kill," Vivian whispered with quiet certainty as she leaned against the stair rail and pondered that thought until she heard her family coming down to meet her. *Thou shall not kill,* she heard in her conscience. "I know you're right, Father," she said aloud, moving from the stairway to the dining room, grabbing the butter from the kitchen on the way. "So I might as well ask for your forgiveness now because should something like that happen to me, I'm going to need it."

A good man

Her ebony skin glistened in the moonlight. Cy moaned as he pulled her to him, planting kisses from the top of her head to the soles of her feet. The night was balmy, but splashes of a cool breeze wisped against their bodies. She was the Eve to his Adam, and he indeed felt as if he were in paradise. He rolled over in the sand, pulling her with him, so that now she was on top. She sat up then, body erect (as was his), head thrown back, eyes closed, lips slightly parted. She licked them, enjoying her own mental imaging as she played a finger melody upon his ridged stomach and massive chest. Slowly she opened her eyes and looked at him. Her lips parted into a smile that could light all darkness. She began to purr, bending over to kiss his eyes, his nose. He reached up and grabbed her breasts, taking first one and then the other into his mouth. He could have sworn he tasted chocolate. She purred louder with each tug of her nipple, felt a cord rippling through her entire insides. They kissed again, slowly, leisurely. She reached down between his legs and grabbed his dick, her exploration continuing. Cy groaned, burying his head between her breasts, his breath coming in short, quick gasps. Slowly, reverently almost, she rose up with his manhood still in her hand and positioned herself over its huge, throbbing tip. Cy held his breath, the wonder of their imminent joining almost too awesome to comprehend. He'd waited a lifetime for her. She sank down on his shaft, slowly. Somewhere in the distance a ringing sounded, then got louder and louder as he sank deeper and deeper into her tight, wet pussy. Cy tried to shut out the noise and concentrate on this tender morsel surrounding him, but the clanging bell would not be denied.

He reached out blindly, searching for her, longing for the feel of her warm, soft body next to his. He touched a book first, the book he'd been reading before he fell asleep the night before, and then a pillow. He jerked his head up suddenly then, feeling disoriented and bereft of spirit. Like he'd found his greatest pleasure only to lose it again. He shook his head, sitting up and rubbing his eyes. He reached over absentmindedly and turned off the alarm without looking, his mind still on a woman on a beach on an island in another place and time. His brows creased. Could that have really been just a dream? It seemed so real. *She* seemed so real.

Cy Taylor, it's time to get married, he thought as he dragged himself off the bed and headed for the shower. His manhood marched before him. Cy stepped into the shower, the cold water flow at full blast. He massaged his shaft until he found release, then increased the temperature until steam began to rise above his shower stall, coating the glass and the chrome and the mirrors. He was hardly aware that the entire time in the shower was spent thinking about a nameless ebony princess whom he'd held in his arms all night long, and whom he wanted to hold again.

Cy dressed casually in a pair of Armani slacks and a Dawson Forte pullover. He grabbed his blackberry from the nightstand and headed downstairs to the kitchen. Still feeling a bit out of sorts, he poured himself a glass of apple juice and was about to grab a bagel when he changed his mind and decided what he needed was a full-course meal. He thought of a couple of restaurant options and looked at his watch. Great. There was plenty of time to eat a good breakfast and make a couple calls before his meeting with Derrick later that morning. That decision made, he strolled into his office, glancing briefly at his desk before walking past it to the window and a view that spread from the marina to the ocean with a crop of high-rises and office buildings glittering in the distance against the early morning sun. He rubbed his neck, feeling a bit tight, a bit wound up. His message light was blinking, but he didn't feel like checking it. He didn't feel like being in his office, any office really. Try as he might to shake it, he felt like being on a beach, feeling the sand between his toes and a beautiful woman between his . . . "Damn!" Cy said aloud, grabbing his briefcase and heading toward the door. The knob was turning as he reached for it, and Maria, his housekeeper, hustled inside.

"Good morning, Mr. Taylor!" she offered cheerfully. "It is a beautiful day!" Her sparkling, always optimistic personality was one of the reasons he'd hired Maria Garcia. She was a vibrant woman, still beautiful after twenty years of marriage and five children. Her long, thick black hair was streaked with the smallest hints of gray, and her large brown eyes peeked out from under long, curly eyelashes. Her buxom frame exuded the warmth he knew could make any child feel better. Cy wished he could be that child as he smiled back at her warmly and said, "Good morning, Maria," before walking through the door and closing it behind him.

Cy sat back and sipped his coffee, looking around his environment, looking for *her*. His physical body felt better, having been fed a king's breakfast of eggs, ham, pancakes, hash browns and as if to show that he wasn't totally ignorant of the value of health and nutrition, a bowl of fruit. His emotional well-being was another story. His reading of the morning paper was constantly interrupted with thoughts of the no-named woman in his dream. And for the first time since deciding to become celibate, he was close to losing control, as horny as a prepubescent teenager with a *Playboy* magazine. He had to get a hold of himself.

He thought about Millicent. Now, where did that thought

come from? Yet, there it was, and he pondered it as he finished his coffee and sat back to let his food settle a bit. No, she was definitely not the one. He had always thought her attractive, at least before the dream last night. Now he thought she was too tall and too thin with not enough coffee in her cream. He thought about Pamela with her corporate concentration and endless ambition. For some reason he couldn't see her rolling in the sand on a moonlit night, glistening from the sweat of their lovemaking. He thought of countless others who'd approached him in the last year, scores from the church alone, and all the letters with pictures enclosed and questions asked and promises made. And, suddenly, none seemed to satisfy him. His cell phone rang and startled him out of his reverie. It was Derrick.

"Minister Montgomery," he began formally.

"Cy, my man! Mr. Big."

Right now Cy didn't feel all that big. He signaled the waitress as he continued to listen to Derrick on the line.

"So listen, I just got a call from King, about his conference next month."

Cy nodded, as if that could translate through the digital system.

"Cy, you there?"

"I'm listening."

"Well, anyway, one of the speakers, Dr. Hayden, a financial expert, has had a tragedy strike his family. His mother-in-law passed away."

"Oh, no."

"Yes, and understandably his wife is taking it hard. I guess on top of the loss itself is a lot of family infighting—it seems there are some people who are contesting the will. It's taking a toll on their whole family, and the doc has cancelled all speaking engagements for the next two months so that he can give this situation his undivided attention."

"Well, I can understand that." Cy signed the bill the waitress brought over and headed to his car. He slid behind the wheel, set his phone on the hands-free module, started the engine and eased into traffic, heading for his business appointment and then to Kingdom Citizens'.

"So, anyway, that's why I'm calling," Derrick continued. "They are looking for someone to handle that part of the conference, and I thought about you."

"Me? You know public speaking isn't really my thing. I'm much better in a one-on-one, consultation-type setting."

"I know that, but you're the money man, and I know, can't no-body handle money like you can. If you don't have the answer, you know where to find it, and I have the bank account to prove it! I think King's members would benefit from somebody like you. Not a preacher preaching to them about prosperity and God's promises and naming and claiming and believing and receiving and all of that, even though all of that has its place, but a businessman teaching them simply and specifically how to turn their finances around and in doing so turn their lives around. I can't think of anyone who could do that better than you."

"Hum. When is the conference again?"

"Next month. I can give you the details when we meet, but I wanted to put it on your mind right away. I know how you have to digest everything."

"And I'll do that. I have an appointment here in the marina that should be fairly quick and then I'm there."

"See you then."

Cy punched the speaker button disconnecting the phone and sat back. He didn't relish speaking in front of a crowd, even though he'd grown comfortable teaching the Kingdom family. He'd always been a better behind-the-scenes type of guy. But this might not be so bad. He thought about a business partner in Chicago and de-cided he could pay him a visit while he was in the Midwest. Come to think of it, it probably was time for him to get away. He'd been putting in so many hours at the church, and in managing his various business interests, that he'd hardly had time to relax.

Yes, that's it, he thought as he punched in a jazz CD on his computer system. Maybe he'd talk to his travel agent once he returned from Kansas, have her look up some island destinations. Maybe that was what the dream meant. That it was time for him to get a little fun in the sun. Whatever it meant, he knew it was time for him to get a little something.

Marriage. The idea was becoming more and more palatable to him, more and more appealing. Some sweet little thing to cook his meals and wash his clothes and warm his bed and have his children. He smiled at what would certainly be considered a chauvinistic attitude in today's society. But he thought back to his mother and how happy she'd been doing precisely that for his father. He recalled vividly how her eyes would light up whenever his dad entered the room. He remembered the warmth and affection with which his dad treated his mother, making her feel like a queen. He remembered when his mother wanted to start her own business making "hospitality baskets" that were filled with homey goodies like fresh jam and baked bread, quilted blankets and handmade shawls, booties, hats and mittens. He remembered how his father supported her decision and turned half of the garage into her working domain, complete with shelves for the baskets and drawers for the items she created. They were quite a team, those two. You could feel the passion in their marriage, the love. Cy wanted his marriage to feel just like that.

These were his thoughts as he stepped into the tropically decorated office building lobby for his business appointment. And these thoughts continued as he stepped into the elevator and pushed the button to the tenth floor. Thoughts of marriage and teamwork, passion and love. And just as the bell sounded and the doors opened, thoughts of an ebony goddess with shimmering skin whose eyes sparked fire in the moonlight.

A couple hours later, Cy arrived at Kingdom Citizens' for the meeting with Derrick. They discussed the building expansion at KCCC and the upcoming conference at Mount Zion Progressive. But Derrick could see that Cy's mind was elsewhere.

"I'd say a penny for your thoughts, but I think they're worth a whole lot more." Derrick sat back on the leather sofa in the pastor's office and eyed his friend speculatively. "Was your prior appointment that intense?"

"I'm cool, Dee. Just a bit distracted, I guess. I didn't get much sleep last night."

Derrick just raised his eyebrows.

"Please, it's not even like that, although, truthfully, I wish it were." Then Cy changed the subject. "How do you like married life, Derrick?"

Derrick's curiosity registered all over his face. "Hum, interesting question. What brought that on?"

"Just curious, I guess. You know, I'm not getting any younger, and this celibate thing, well, it's not for me. I'm starting to climb the walls, and I don't like climbing, if you know what I mean."

"I hear you, brother, I don't envy you single men at all. God must know me very well because he sent Vivian along before I really even got started in the ministry. Guess he knew I'd have to be, uh, satisfied in order to do what it is He's called me to do."

Cy smiled at his pastor's explanation. "Well, Vivian is a blessing, everybody knows that."

Now it was Derrick's turn to smile. "Not like I do, brother, not like I do." He decided to pass the ball back to Cy's court. "So what's her name?"

"Who?"

"You're thinking about marriage; you must have someone in mind."

"No, not really."

"You know Millicent worships the ground you walk on. I

know y'all had something going a while back. She seems like a good woman."

"Yes, she's a good woman, and no, there's nothing still going on with her. She's just my sister in the Lord, Dee, a friend."

"The look I see in her eyes when she's looking at you goes a little farther than friendship, my man." Derrick cocked his head to view his friend more intently. "So are you telling me that out of all the fine women in Kingdom Citizens', *nobody* is in the running, standing out from the crowd? 'Cause you can't tell me there isn't a crowd."

They both laughed at that. Cy gave his friend an abbreviated rundown of some of the women he'd pondered over breakfast a few hours earlier. Pamela still came out as the strongest possibility, but there was something missing. Yes, he had deep feelings for her, and yes, she was fine. He didn't doubt she'd satisfy him in the bedroom, and he knew she had an intelligent head on her shoulders. Still, he didn't know if she was someone he wanted to spend the rest of his life with. Because that was the other thing—he didn't care about the statistics. He wanted to do this marriage thing only one time. He told Derrick all that, too. But he didn't tell him about the dream.

"So how did you know Vivian was the one?" he asked instead.

Derrick thought a while before speaking. "From the moment I saw her, I think. We were back in the Midwest at a convention, and I caught a glimpse of her as I was walking up to the pulpit. She had this energy that was palpable and a body that wouldn't quit. I couldn't take my eyes off her."

"So how did you two meet?"

"That was the easy part. She was King's wife's best friend. They're still best friends. Anyway, we all went out after church, and it was pretty much on from there. She gave me a little run for my money for a minute. She never wanted to be a preacher's wife." Derrick smiled at memories he was obviously unwilling to share.

"But who could resist the Reverend Derrick Montgomery, right?" Cy asked, smiling.

"Exactly," Derrick responded, reaching for a folder as he did so. "No, really, it was 'who could resist God's will.?' She knew I was the one for her; she'd gotten confirmation before I asked her."

"Confirmation? What was the sign?"

"She had a dream that I was going to pop the question a couple days before I actually did it. So she wasn't surprised. She knew I was the only one."

Cy's attention focused on Vivian's dream. He was getting ready to question his friend further when Derrick's intercom sounded. It was Sean, one of Derrick's assistants.

"Pastor?"

"Yes, Sean."

"Mr. Roberts is here."

"Okay, send him in in five minutes. See if there's anything he needs." Derrick turned to Cy, who was already gathering the paperwork on the coffee table and placing it in his briefcase. "Did we cover everything?"

"Yep. Looks like we're all set. I'd say Kingdom Citizens' Shopping Center will be up and operational in just over two years. I've pulled a committee together to look over the list of potential tenants aside from the bookstore, restaurant and business offices we've already okay'd. Don't worry, Derrick. Everything is moving ahead smoothly. God's hand is definitely on this venture." Both men stood.

"You're a good man, Cy Taylor. And Vivian and I will be praying for God to send you a good woman. You deserve it."

"Will you tell him to put a rush on it?" Cy said, laughing, a laughter that didn't quite reach his eyes. His eyes said that he was dead serious.

"He may not come when you want Him," Derrick answered as Cy neared the door, "but He'll be right on time."

If this isn't God . . .
I don't know what is

Millicent was just reaching for the office door when the man of her dreams opened it. Cy Taylor. *This has to be God*, she thought, offering up her most dazzling smile. It had to be God. Why else had she felt an unexplainable urge to come over to the church on her lunch hour? Sure, she did have some things to handle regarding the Ladies First meeting, but she could have stopped by after work. No, this was just another sign that before the dust settled, she would be Mrs. Millicent Taylor.

"Well, aren't you a sight for sore eyes!"

"Hello, Millicent." Millicent was about the last person Cy wanted to talk to right now. He tried to keep moving, but could see that he wasn't going to get away without a conversation. Millicent just turned to fall in step with him. He stopped.

"How are you?" Millicent thought Cy looked a bit distracted.

"I'm okay."

"Good." She wasn't convinced but decided not to push. "I left a message for you earlier."

"Oh? I haven't checked."

"Well, see how God works? He wanted me to be able to talk to you in person. And you know I'm okay with that." She took a step closer. Cy took a step back.

"What did you need to talk to me about?"

Millicent looked at her watch. She still had forty-five minutes and could even squeeze out a few more if need be. "Why don't we discuss it over lunch? I'm starved and I only have an hour."

"I've got a business appointment. I'm on my way now." Cy didn't feel good about lying, but sometimes it was just easier. This was one of those times.

Millicent didn't try to hide her disappointment. "You can't reschedule? I haven't had a chance to really talk to you in weeks. If I didn't know better, I'd think you were avoiding me."

I am, he thought. "Now, why would I want to do that?" he said.

Millicent smiled again as Cy visibly relaxed. "Maybe because you know how I feel about you and that makes you uncomfortable."

Her honesty caught him off guard. Cy was silent for a moment, sure that whatever he said wouldn't be the right thing. "And you know how I feel about you," he said finally.

"Feelings can change, you know. With God, all things are possible."

Why did she have to go there and bring God into it? Cy was not in the mood for Millicent today. He looked at his watch. "I gotta get going." He started to walk away, but Millicent grabbed his arm.

"Cy? Can we please get together for dinner tonight? I really do need your opinion on a few things. And I have the budget for Ladies First."

Why did she have to beg? He hated to hear a woman begging, whining as if she were a dog and he was the bone. *As a matter of fact* . . . Cy had to squelch a smile before responding. "I can't do dinner tonight but I will call. See you later."

You will most definitely see me. Millicent smiled to herself as she headed for the office. She was more convinced than ever that Cy Taylor was her man. She counted off the reasons in her mind, reasons she'd created and collected. The first was the fact that they had dated, however briefly. She recalled their first date, lunch and an art gallery visit, as she waved at Stacy and Tanya sitting in the youth ministry office. She continued down the hall and turned into the break room, pouring herself a cup of coffee. She then proceeded down to the smaller conference room, setting her stack of files in front of her but not bothering to open them. Instead, she kept convincing herself that she was Mrs. Cy Taylor.

She flipped through her mental memories to their last date and the last kiss. They had been outside of Millicent's condo, and even though she'd pleaded and pleaded, Cy had refused to come inside for coffee. He'd bent down then to plant a kiss on her cheek. Millicent had turned her face and met his mouth with her own. She'd deepened the kiss and pressed herself full against him. He'd instinctively reached around and grabbed her waist. She'd stood on tiptoe and placed both arms around his neck before letting one arm slide down his arm and across his back, stroking firmly, yet gently. That was when she'd felt the rise of his passion against her. She'd rubbed against it then, her eyes opening briefly as she noticed the size of it, evident even with all the layers of clothing. She'd moaned then, and that moan had brought Cy back from wherever he was because he'd broken the kiss abruptly and stepped back, breathing deeply, his eyes hooded and glazed. Millicent sat back smiling, sipping the coffee slowly. Oh, yes, he'd wanted her at one time.

Millicent was used to men wanting her. She'd attracted them like flies her whole life. And once the sex started? They were hooked. She knew what she had and knew how to work it. Most of the time, she'd get bored after a couple of months and move on. There was little thought given to the trail of broken hearts left in her wake. But that was before Cy. No one had interested her since he'd come along. And she knew that if she could get him between the sheets for one night, it would be over. He would be hers.

Millicent's eyes narrowed as she plotted her strategy. Yes, she wanted him. "It's God's will," she said aloud.

She thought of all the times they had worked together on first one project, then the next. Church activity made it easy to stay close to him, stay involved in his life. She wasn't happy about his having referred her to one of his former partners regarding her investments, but that was just temporary, she assured herself. She'd seen him looking at her when he thought she wasn't watching and was convinced that all he needed was a little prod here and a poke there; men could be such scaredy cats when it came to commitment.

Millicent was getting closer to Vivian. Maybe she would confide in the first lady, seek her advice on how to proceed. After all, a woman who'd been able to hang on to a man like Derrick Montgomery all these years had to know a thing or two.

"Hey, Mill, what are you doing here?" Vivian's question interrupted Millicent's daydream, and she jumped at the intrusion.

"Oh, Sister Vivian, why, I was just thinking about you! Do you have a moment?"

Vivian looked at her watch. "Just a moment, I'm meeting my husband for lunch. Is everything okay?" She motioned toward the folders. "You've got a lot of work there."

"Oh, it looks worse than it is. Actually, things are rolling along like a well-oiled machine. I was going to call you later after talking with Cy. I have the budget ready for the Ladies First summit."

"That's great, Millicent! You are truly a woman of God. He's going to bless you for all you do in this ministry."

"I sure hope so," Millicent said quietly.

"Well, sistah, you can *know* so! You know what the Word says, *'Delight yourself in the Lord and He will give you the desires of your heart.'*"

"That's one of the things I want to talk to you about, Sister Vivian."

Vivian looked at her watch again. "I tell you what. Call Tamika in the morning and have her schedule an appointment for us. As soon as possible. If you want, we can make it a lunch. Someplace nice. Give ourselves a treat."

"What about Gladstones in Malibu?" Millicent asked, standing and gathering the folders together. She grabbed the empty coffee cup and threw it in the trash.

"I haven't been there in a while. That sounds great," Vivian replied, heading toward the door. "You just keep believing. God's going to work it out."

Millicent stared after Vivian, not moving. God was indeed going to work it out. Vivian's words were just another confirmation. She'd been getting them all day. First, God directed her to the church. Then she ran into Cy. Then she saw Vivian within seconds of thinking about her. "If this isn't God," she said aloud, "I don't know what is." She looked down at her ring finger, smiling softly, before opening the top folder and looking down at a paper she'd been doodling on before Vivian came. She'd filled up the page, repeatedly writing four words: "Cy and Millicent Taylor."

Some good news

More than a month had passed since Tai had caught King with April. She had settled into a new yet strangely comfortable routine. With school out, she'd asked Anna to assist more with the children, including taking them to and sometimes picking them up from their summer sports and other activities. At least on the three days a week she went to the six-week computer class that had just started at the local junior college.

She loved being back in school. It made her feel young and fresh again. And she wasn't half mad at herself when she looked at the little teenyboppers and twenty-somethings that rushed around in their youthful glory. *Y'all don't have a thing on me*, she'd thought that first day. And, as if to prove the point, she'd been approached by more than one man young enough to be her son. Yes, school had definitely been a good idea. She loved it so much that she was even considering continuing on toward a degree. She'd seen a commercial on television a few nights ago that spoke of a program where one could earn their degree in as little as eighteen months. A college-educated woman after all these years? She smiled at the thought.

After her computer class, she usually went to work out. She was still losing weight and had more energy. Sometimes she'd stop to pick up Mama Max; sometimes Mama would meet her at the fitness center. Those were always good times. Mama Max had lost ten pounds and didn't tire out as easily as she used to either. Maxine Brook was not only her mother-in-law, but her friend, and she'd never be able to thank her enough for all she'd done. Her own mother, Mrs. Williams, would never understand what Tai was feeling. That was why Tai hadn't told her about April, had just mentioned "marital problems."

Her mother had responded, "Everyone has problems, dear, but none that the two of you and the good Lord can't handle." She'd then changed the subject and started talking about a recipe she'd gotten for homemade noodles and how excited she was to try it for Dad's favorite "feel-good meal," homemade chicken and noodle soup. No, it was best to keep quiet for now, until it was necessary to tell her parents what was *really* going on.

Her mother, so prim and proper, a direct and startling contrast to Harold, her boisterous, extroverted father. Tai tried to picture her father being unfaithful, but the image could not be formed in her mind. She tried to picture her mother's reaction if her father was unfaithful, but that picture eluded her as well. She thought back then, back to and through her childhood. She tried to remember any times she felt discomfort from either parent and couldn't recall a memory. To this day, they seemed to have eyes for only each other. How she wished she and King could be like that.

During most afternoons, Tai worked on things for the church or with Vivian on S.O.S. Since purchasing a computer, she and Vivian were once again pen pals, via e-mail, and more than once they'd laughed at how the letters had changed from the ones of their teenage years. Tai was still toying with the idea that God had placed on her heart concerning the summit. It hadn't taken full shape yet, but somehow she knew she had something to offer the women who would be gathered there. She just didn't quite know what that something was . . . yet.

Evenings were spent with the children. On the rare occasion

that King came home early, they'd have dinner with both of them talking to the children and seldom to each other. She hardly saw King anymore, and they spoke only out of necessity. King had been jolted when he returned from the revival and found his wife moved into the guest room. He'd asked what the move meant. She'd said she didn't know. End of conversation. Tai knew she couldn't go on living like this forever, but she was only trying to get through one day at a time. She figured she'd get through their conference in July, get the children all set for the upcoming school year and then head to Los Angeles and the Ladies First S.O.S. Summit in September. She was really looking forward to getting away and realized with mild surprise that she hadn't been away, without children or family, in her adult life. *It's time for a change,* she thought, and wondered if getting away for a while was the only change she was talking about. It wasn't.

Tai's body was on autopilot as she moved from the children's rooms to the laundry room downstairs. Her mind was whirling with thoughts of what to do. She thought of King then and wished that at some point his mind had focused on what *not* to do. Like how not to have yet another affair and risk his marriage and put his wife and subsequently his children in such a predicament. She methodically separated the clothing by color, placing whites together, then colors and permanent press. She twisted the dial, grabbed the detergent, poured it in and waited for the water to start filling the machine. She leaned back, and an unwanted image floated to the surface of her mind's eye—an attractive woman with brunette hair and piercing green eyes. She remembered the fear that crossed April's face for an instant, before being replaced with an attempted look of innocence as she stared into the eyes of her lover's wife.

Tai began shoving the towels, underwear and other whites into the machine with a vengeance. King still hadn't apologized. Aside from the blowout argument they'd had the day after she'd seen King and April together at the restaurant, he'd offered no explanations. Of course, she hadn't made herself available for conversation. So what? He was the one at fault. It was his responsibility, no, *obligation* to seek her out. She was the one who'd been wronged, the one who'd been dogged. She'd been in this position too many times and would be damned if she was going to go to him and ask him anything about him and his slut. Hell would freeze over first, and she didn't think that would happen any time soon because the Midwest was experiencing its biggest heat wave in fifty-five years.

Tai left the coolness of the laundry room and crossed the family room, opening the door leading to the backyard and outside. The heat rushed up to meet her, and she thought twice before remaining in the yard. The huge oak tree looked inviting, though, and she felt the need to breathe fresh, natural air. She walked over to the jungle gym and swing set, idly pushing the seat as it swung back and forth. She walked to the back of the house and grabbed the hose, turning on the water and sliding the hose across the yard toward the wilting flowers. She placed her thumb over the end of the hose then, causing a spray of water to shoot forth and cover the entire flowerbed. After a moment, she reached down, pulling some of the weeds out that had surrounded the base of the summer zinnias that had replaced the spring tulips. She wondered if getting April out of King's life would be as easy as pulling up these weeds. A laugh that sounded more like a snort sprung out of her mouth. "I doubt it," she said to the blooms waving under the pressure of the cool water. She stopped then, walking back to the water spout and turning it off. She walked back to the big oak tree and then over to the swings. *Hum*, she thought as she sat down on one of the brightly colored plastic boards. *My booty isn't as tight in this thing as it used to be.* She smiled at that thought, but the smile was quickly erased when an image of April once again flashed through her mind. A woman who looked as though she weighed a hundred pounds sopping wet and who could probably fit two booties into this seat. April. "April Summers," Tai said out loud.

Tai began a slow swing back and forth, back and forth. She

tried to imagine life without King. What would she do? Where would she go? She'd have to leave the church, of course, and having formed many deep friendships while being first lady of Mt. Zion, she knew that wouldn't be easy. Would she stay here, in this city? Probably not, she decided. It would be hard enough trying to make a new life for herself without the thought of running into him or Mt. Zion members every day. *Where could I go?* Tiny beads of perspiration gathered around her neck before trickling down her back. That was all the encouragement Tai needed to go back inside. She stood up then and looked around. She could almost hear the sound of the children, especially the twins who had practically grown up in this very yard. She thought then about the children—the twins, Michael and Princess. How would they feel about their parents' divorce? She'd always tried so hard to keep the bad parts of her marriage away from the children and was almost certain they had no idea how close they were to becoming part of a single-parent household. When asked about the new sleeping arrangements, she'd simply said that like Timothy and Tabitha the year before, she and their dad now needed their own rooms. The twins were "too near her not to hear her." They had shared a room until they turned twelve and accepted the explanation without question. Michael was doing very well at Northwest University, and Princess had accepted Tai's explanation that she and King were having a major disagreement and needed space between them. All the children had such bright futures ahead of them, such promising paths. She wondered how filing for divorce would affect them, how it would change their lives.

Her main concern was for the twins, both of whom worshipped their father. They had good reason. No matter how King behaved as a husband, he was always an exemplary dad. She wouldn't do anything to color the children's image of their father. They'd find out soon enough about his character flaws. Timothy was especially close to both King and his grandfather, the only child out of the four she could see following in her husband's footsteps of min-

istry. He'd take it hard, Tai decided, but Tabitha would be there to
help him through it. The twins, as most twins were, had always
been extremely close. Tabitha was the rational one among her children, all logic and wisdom with a just-the-facts-ma'am mentality.
Tai smiled as she thought of her studious young daughter, glasses
pushed low, brows drawn together as she tried to dissect and figure
out the problems of the universe. Truth of the matter was, she figured them out better than some adults most of the time. Tabitha
would be okay, Tai concluded. And, so would Michael. Princess
would be very disappointed and would probably blame her. She'd
always been a daddy's girl. And, Timothy, well, he was at the age
that if he wanted to stay with his father, that would be okay.

Tai was confused. Was divorce what she really wanted? On
Mondays, Wednesdays and Fridays, she knew for sure she'd leave.
On Tuesdays and Thursdays, she changed her mind and decided
the marriage could survive. On Saturdays she tried not to think
about it, and on Sundays she almost succeeded. She still hadn't of-
ficially mouthed the words "I want a divorce" to King. So did she
want the divorce? Or did she want the marriage? Today, Tai didn't
know what she wanted.

She headed for the kitchen and a large glass of water. That was
one of the nutritionist's suggestions that she'd taken to heart and
felt better because of it, to drink more water. She filled her glass
and leaned back against the counter, still deep in thought. It
floored her how she was standing here, calmly entertaining the
thought of a life without King. If anyone had told her she'd have
such thoughts, even a year ago, she'd have laughed in their face and
called them a fool.

Tai reflected back over the last six months and tried to envi-
sion when King could have been meeting April. Most evenings, at
that time, he'd been home. Of course, that just gave him all day. Tai
had no idea what the other woman did for a living, or if she
worked at all. Suddenly Tai stood straight up. Money! Was King
giving this bitch money? Was he supporting her? Tai hadn't even

thought about the financial repercussions of what all this meant. She'd never concerned herself too much with the finances. King and their accountant handled the money. That was going to have to change. It was time to find out just where everything stood, including their financial situation.

The thought of Miss Thing getting a penny of what should have been her and the kid's money sent her blood boiling. The thought of King giving her their money sent her pressure even higher. Tai thought about the fancy little bistro in Kansas City's elite shopping district, where she'd busted King and his little paramour tramp. She thought of all the shops surrounding that area and the price tags on the merchandise in those shops. Her imagination began conjuring up all sorts of scenarios, none of them pleasant. She saw King buying the other woman gifts, maybe even meeting her for private getaways at a luxurious hotel. Where had they been meeting? Not at the church, she would have heard about that, just like she heard about last month's visit to the church parking lot.

Tai put her head in her hands, but straightened as she heard Mama Max and the kids coming through the front door. A welcome reprieve; the situation was too much to think about, too much to consider. All she knew was that she was sick and tired of being sick and tired. And she was tired of thinking about the marriage mess. So she joined everyone in the family room and turned on the stereo—loud. Before long she, the twins and Mama Max were all praise dancing, the adults trying to mimic the kid's moves. Nothing could lighten one's mood faster than a good dose of gospel music. With all that was going on, Tai needed as much "good news" as she could get.

Everything is not all right

King looked around inconspicuously as he left April's condo. Not that he thought he'd see anyone he knew; April lived in a very suburban area. He felt certain few if any from the church even knew of the complex's existence.

He hit the car alarm/unlock mechanism on his key chain and opened the door, pulling off his suit coat before getting inside. He was tired, yet rejuvenated. This was his first time being with April in almost a month, and she'd let him know in no uncertain terms how much she'd missed him. That made him smile. One thing about April, she turned him on in every possible way and would do anything he asked to please him. Anything.

Some of the things she'd done occupied his mind as he turned onto the boulevard and headed for the freeway. April had been a roaring flame that could not be doused. She'd literally begged him to stay the night, although he'd explained to her that that would never be possible. *Not yet anyway.* And just what did he mean by that? King pondered the thought for a moment. Could he really see himself with April on a more permanent basis? He thought of her walking in as first lady of Mt. Zion and of the probable looks on some of the members' faces, such as Sistah Stokes and Sistah Wanthers, and laughed out loud. *I'd really get a chance to see them prove their unconditional, Christian love.* He laughed again. No, he honestly couldn't say that he loved April that way. He admitted to a deep, deep affection and immense attraction, but to divorce Tai and marry her? Granted, she moved him in a way he hadn't been moved in a long time, but there were more things to consider than his physical pleasure. But was it just sex? He thought about the conversations he and April had, about life and the world, society and finance. April was very bright, the daughter of a banking executive, and she'd grown up having and knowing how to handle money. She'd also traveled extensively and seemed well informed on societal issues. No, it wasn't just a physical thing; April stimulated both heads.

So what was it, then? Why could he not see himself going to the next level with her by his side? Well, for one thing, April was totally ignorant of church matters in general and the Black church in particular. True, he'd been sharing parts of that aspect of his life in the months they'd been seeing each other, but he dared not invite her to the church. And with good reason—as thoughts of the Italian bistro confrontation flashed into his mind. At least he had that much sense. He didn't want his woman and his wife in the same church at the same time. By his invitation, no less. But somehow, April did need the benefits of a church setting, fellowship with other believers. Was it really fair of him to deny that part of God to someone he loved? *Loved?* Where had that come from? Did he really love April? He deliberated on that thought for a moment and, drawing no concrete conclusions, moved on to other thoughts, like his mama. She'd demanded he end the affair. He'd refused, told her it was his life.

Besides, she hadn't said anything that he didn't already know. He knew how Tai loved him. He knew how hard a divorce would be on the kids. He knew the ministry might suffer if he started openly seeing April, even after a divorce. "What are you thinking?" she'd barked at him. Her words played in his head like a song he couldn't forget. *I raised you better than that, and Negro, as long as you*

Black, you bet not think of bringing this kind of shame on the family! I didn't raise no fool, so for the love of God, stop acting like one! That was when he'd walked out of the room, not stopping until he was in his car and heading down the drive. They'd spoken little since.

His thoughts turned to Tai. She'd moved out of the master bedroom, and he wasn't surprised. At least this time it was just out of the bedroom; the times with Tootie and Karen one of them had left the house. He felt too guilty to take the lead and encourage the candid conversation that was needed between them. What was there to say except, "I'm sorry, I'll stop." He knew that was the right thing to do. At times he felt horrible about being with April. He still loved Tai. He'd known her more than half his life, how could he not? They'd been through a lot together, built a life together. But he was cheating on her. Why? Because April brought an excitement, an edge, to his life. Something had been missing, and she filled it. April made him feel good.

King didn't know what to do. Was it better to let things ride and hope that one day Tai would get over it and forgive him? Forget April ever happened? Put the past behind her like she had before? No, for some reason, this time felt different. Tai was different these days, more confident, more sure of herself. These were things that should have made King proud, but they served only to make him more uneasy. He wondered what she was really thinking, but at the same time was almost afraid to find out.

King thought of April again. He'd reprimanded her fiercely for making the scene at the church before he went to Cleveland, and his not seeing her for almost a month was her punishment, even though he, too, had felt the emptiness of her absence. She seemed to have gotten the message. She'd tried to justify her behavior but eventually became contrite; assuring him that it had been only her frustration at his not returning her phone calls that had led to such drastic measures. She knew he was married and not always available. Things would have to be on his terms or on no terms at all. She promised never to do anything so foolish again. Then she'd ducked down beneath the sheets and made him forget that he was ever angry with her, using her mouth to say things that words could never convey.

King exited the freeway and entered the subdivision where he and Tai had lived for almost ten years. He decided that after this two-month stalemate, it was time for a real conversation. He was the man of the house, and he couldn't let things continue the way they'd been going indefinitely. He needed to know where her head was, what she was thinking. Shoot, he didn't even know what *he* was thinking. How could he be sure what was on *her* mind? At any rate, they needed to talk—she was his wife after all. And even with all that was going on, he couldn't imagine a life without her in it.

"Maybe tonight," he said aloud as he turned down his street. Without warning, a picture of April, all sexy and spicy in the black lace teddy he'd purchased, along with garter belt and hose, swam before his eyes. "No, my mind is too distracted," he decided with a grim smile. "I dealt with April tonight; I'll deal with Tai tomorrow." He punched the garage door opener and saw that the choice might not be his to make. Tai's SUV was nowhere in sight. *Tai knows she should be at home!* King frowned, totally forgetting that he himself was just pulling in the driveway. He muttered indignantly as he reached for his briefcase before closing the door. *Tai needs to remember that she's a wife and mother first, that nothing is more important than that.*

King's anger continued as he opened the door and felt rather than heard the driving drumbeats of hip-hop music. Lights were on everywhere. He walked through the kitchen and into the den where Timothy and Tabitha were playing videos.

"Go tell Princess to turn that music off . . . NOW!" King's uncharacteristic bellow caused both kids to jump.

"Ooh, Daddy, you scared me," Tabitha said as Timothy flew by her and bounded up the stairs to happily deliver his father's command. "What's the matter?"

King took a deep breath, tossing his briefcase on the well-worn couch and taking off his jacket. "Where's your mother?" He answered Tabitha's question with one of his own. The booming bass stopped suddenly, and the house once again stood still.

"She left."

King's heart stopped. Just quit beating. Anger quickly turned into something else. His worst fear was being realized—and he hadn't even known it was his worst fear. "What do you mean, left?"

"She said she needed some time to herself and to call Jan if there was an emergency. She said we had to go to bed at ten 'cuz she might be out late."

King's heart started beating again—even as he thought about what Tabitha just said. *Call Jan in case of an emergency? Not me? Not their dad?* Fear turned back to anger.

"Why does Mama need time to herself, Daddy?" Tabitha turned large, probing eyes on him, her head cocked slightly to the left. Suddenly she looked older than her years, and King felt older than his.

"I don't know, baby." King searched his mind for a logical explanation, knowing that that was the only kind that would fly with Tabitha. "Maybe so she could hear herself think over that loud music."

"The music wasn't on when she left, Daddy," Princess said as she and Timothy bounded down the steps. She leaned down to give King a kiss before heading into the kitchen.

"That music was way too loud, Princess. I don't want to come in here and hear it at that volume again. Do you understand me?"

Princess poked her head out the kitchen door. She wasn't used to her father speaking to her harshly. "Yes, sir."

"Why you mad, Dad?" Timothy sat down next to his father. Tabitha gave an I-told-you-that-you-were-mad look to King before turning back to the television.

King had had enough. Yes, he was mad, and no, he wouldn't discuss it. So he shifted the focus to Tai. "Where'd your mama go? She knows better than to walk off and leave you guys by yourself."

"We're not babies, Daddy," Princess said as she reentered the room with a soda and bag of chips. "Besides, Mama never goes out. She looked good, too—new outfit and everything."

Now, where in the hell did she go all dressed up? King grabbed his briefcase and jacket and headed toward the stairs. As he trudged up, he erased the instant images of Tai out with another man. Even as they ran across his mind, he felt a pang of guilt that he, someone who had just left his mistress's house in general, and bed in particular, could even think to question Tai's whereabouts. She was probably just visiting some sick and shut-in church member, or over to his mother's.

Tai laughed so hard her sides hurt. She grabbed another handful of popcorn and followed it with a long swig of Coke. She looked over at Sandy, who was laughing, almost crying, while eyeing Tai with a satisfied gleam in her eye. "It's good to hear your laugh again, woman!" she said between chuckles.

"It's good to laugh," Tai said as the crowd roared their approval of the Clean Comedy Monday stand-up comedian. "You don't know the half."

"Well, like I said, you ran across my mind today," Sandy continued, both of them enjoying the reprieve as one comedian left and pop music filled the room until the next performer took the stage. "I haven't talked to you in forever, but we had some good times when you were at Sprint. I can't believe we haven't stayed in better touch. But then I knew you were busy, with the church and your family and everything."

"Well, let me just tell you. I'm glad you thought of me, delighted you called and thrilled to be sitting here. I didn't even know they had clean comedians like this. I mean, I always loved

Sinbad, but I haven't heard him doing comedy in a while. Other than him, I didn't know there were a whole group of comedians out that had acts without all the profanity and sex-filled punch lines. All I'd heard of was Def Comedy Jam, and you know I can't handle that."

"Well, I will say you look much better now than when you first arrived. Are you sure everything's all right?"

"No, Sandy, everything is not all right," Tai said, taking a sip of Coke and still smiling. "But it's gonna be."

Before she could ask any more questions, the MC introduced the next comedian, and before long Tai and Sandy were howling again.

A church girl

Hope sat back, determined to savor the soothing sounds of jazz guitarist Norman Brown. He was one of Kansas City's own, and the crowd was especially enthusiastic. The musician's playing was flawless. It had been so long since Hope had gone to anything other than a gospel concert that she almost forgot how to act. But she was glad to be out. Glad she'd accepted Frieda's invite to double with her and her latest love interest and do something besides watch videos on a Friday night.

She bobbed her head to the left and the right, taking a moment to slyly check out her date, Rashiid. She had to admit the brother was fine, although with Frieda she'd expected no less. Frieda believed that there were just as many good men in fine packages as in ugly ones, and she always insisted on unwrapping the fine men first. Rashiid seemed to be enjoying himself, laid back in his seat, his shoulder rubbing against hers as he, too, bobbed his head to the beat. He glanced over and caught her gaze. She averted her eyes, but not before she saw the dazzling smile that eased from his mouth as he noticed her stare. He reached over then and put his arm around her, not possessively, but protectively—as if to say, "Check me out, baby, it's okay."

Hope tried to relax further, taking a sip of her Perrier with lemon and focusing once more on the sounds coming from the stage. Each musician was now taking his individual turn in the spotlight with rousing solos, and the crowd shouted and applauded their pleasure at each performer's expertise. Hope joined in because as a performer, she understood how the energy from the audience only enhanced an artist's performance. Not only that, but she was truly enjoying herself. She vowed to do this more often and, chancing another peek, thought she might like to do it more often with Rashiid.

"I told you they were off the chain!" Frieda whispered loudly into Hope's ear, grabbing her arm as she did so. "I'm so glad you came."

"Me, too." Hope replied, and she really meant it.

Frieda dropped her voice to a lower octave. "So what do you think about . . . ?" She didn't finish the sentence but rather cocked her head in the general direction of Hope's new friend.

"Woodeewoo!" Hope yelled, seemingly at the latest song's flourishing finish, but knowing Frieda caught the gist of her yell's real intent. Frieda laughed her agreement.

"I thought this one might pull you out of that church pew, for a minute anyway."

"Well, I don't know about that, but I am enjoying the evening."

"Good," Frieda said before she turned her attention once more to Norman Brown and company, who were executing a masterful rendition of the Luther Vandross hit, "Any Love."

Hope smiled as she floated away on their soothing, musical carpet ride. She closed her eyes, and for no reason that she could fathom, Sistahs Almighty and Alrighty came to mind. She almost laughed out loud—picturing the frowning countenance she was sure they'd have to discover she was enjoying "the devil's music." *Well, let them frown,* she thought as she began snapping her fingers quietly to the beat. *Unlike them, I do not intend on ending up like a shriveled raisin in the sun. Unh-unh, darlin', I see a husband-and-babies package with my name on it.* She looked at Rashiid again, openly this time, and he smiled back, squeezing her shoulder as he did so. She wondered if he went to church. Or if he even knew God. What if he wasn't Christian? With a name like Rashiid, he could be Muslim. Oh, no, there'd be no *"asalum alaikum"* in her house! Not that his name alone told her anything. Besides, it was just her first date with the man. He may not even like her. What would she think about that? She decided to just enjoy the band, the man and the evening and let the chips fall where they may.

An hour and a half later the couples sat high above the city in Skies, the swanky revolving restaurant atop the Hyatt Regency Hotel. Both Rashiid and Frieda's date, Damon, were sipping Courvoisier. Frieda nursed a strawberry daiquiri while Hope thoroughly enjoyed a cappuccino piled high with whipped cream and brushed with shaved cinnamon. While nibbling on a variety of appetizers, the couples enjoyed the view and recounted the concert highlights. Hope again thought about how good she felt and how long it had been since she'd actually been on a date. She thought about the men at her church and couldn't imagine being here with any one of them. Then she looked over at Rashiid and couldn't imagine being here with anyone else. As Frieda and Damon flirted with each other, Hope turned to Rashiid and smiled.

"So," she began, taking a sip of her steamy brew, "I take it you're a jazz connoisseur. I'd not heard of the band before. They were excellent."

"Yeah, I like jazz. But I like all kinds of music. R&B, hip-hop, all of it."

"Do you get into gospel music?"

Rashiid turned to look at Hope more fully. "I haven't gotten into too much of that, but I do like Kirk Franklin, and who's that one chick, the tall one who looks like a fashion model?"

"Yolanda Adams?"

"Yeah, that's her. That sistah can blow! I saw her on the BET Awards and was like . . . who is that?"

"Yeah, she's one of my favorites. But I like all the contemporary artists, Trinitee 5:7, Fred Hammond, Nicole Muller, the Gospel Gangstas, Tonex . . ."

"The Gospel Gangstas," Rashiid repeated with skepticism.

Hope nodded.

"I haven't heard of them. Maybe you can let me hear your music sometime."

"I'd like that. I have some really great stuff."

"Yeah, I just bet you do," Rashiid responded with a gleam in his eye. "Frieda says you're a church girl."

"I go to church, so I guess you could call me that."

"My mother used to play this song by Marvin Gaye called 'Sanctified Lady.' Could I call you that?" Rashiid was grinning; he was obviously enjoying himself.

"Yes." Hope was enjoying him, too.

Rashiid moaned under his breath. "Have mercy," was all he said. He took another drink of Courvoisier.

"Maybe you'd like to come to my church one day."

"I might, if you issue me a personal invitation."

"Consider it done. We've got a concert coming up in a couple weeks with the hip-hop artist Righteous Rebel. Only he's God's man now. He only does things that glorify Him."

"Ah, yeah? I remember reading about that. I like Righteous's music. "Holy Ghost High" is tight! I just might come check it out."

"I thought you didn't listen to gospel music?"

"That ain't gospel, that's hip-hop!" Hope and Rashiid continued to talk comfortably, learning more about each other. She learned he was the oldest of three boys, had lived in Kansas City all his life and worked as a foreman at a construction site. He'd gone to church with his grandmother as a boy, still got there on some Christmases or Easter Sundays until he was sixteen, but hadn't stepped in one much except for a funeral service or wedding ceremony since he graduated from the local community college. He believed in God but spurned religion, believing that all ministers were just pimping the congregation for money. His father, who left his mother when Rashiid was five, was the one who named him. He had a three-year-old daughter, Rasheda, was on good terms with the mother and paid child support. He beamed with pride as he talked of his daughter, and Hope could see the love he had for the little girl. She couldn't help but think, however, of the long-term, and how that little girl and her mother would be a part of her life as well should anything develop between her and Rashiid. It wasn't as if she'd already imagined herself walking down the aisle or anything, but she knew that there was no desire to simply date; she was dating only with an eye toward marriage. To that end, these things had to be considered with every potential candidate.

Before Rashiid dropped her off in his shiny, new BMW, she'd given him her cell and home numbers. He'd given her his number as well—his home number, always a good sign. She'd already decided to go out with him again, and he was actually looking forward to the Midnight Musical. Maybe she needed to look outside the box, she decided as they said their goodbyes and he gave her a big hug and a kiss on the cheek. He seemed smart, kind and affectionate. And she hadn't missed the hardness of that massive chest as he'd hugged her. Not that she was thinking of anything physical mind you, it was just an innocent observation. Still, in the middle of a Midwest heat wave, a shiver went down her back so hard it made her booty wiggle.

Are you sure she's not bucking for First Lady?

The clink of metal on china was the only sound heard in Carla's massive dining room. She smiled, noticing that conversation had all but ceased as the committee of Ladies First enjoyed her culinary skills. Carla loved to cook, always had, and the biggest thanks she could receive were the sounds she now heard.

"Girl, this is delicious!" Vivian declared, taking a break from eating only long enough to wipe her mouth with a napkin and take a sip of tea. "I think this is the best salmon I've ever tasted."

"I second that emotion," Terri added. "I would ask you how you made it, but I'm sure it's another of your secret recipes that cannot be divulged."

"You got that right!" Carla grinned, taking another helping of spicy rice. "Besides, if I told you how I cooked it, you could then make it yourself and may be inclined to no longer grace my dining room with your lovely presence."

"Oh, so that's how you keep your friends," Minister Rebecca teased.

"That and my winning personality!" Carla didn't miss a bite or a beat.

Later, as the women settled into Carla and her husband Stanley's comfortable family room amid slices of peach cobbler and cups of coffee and tea, Vivian gave her update on the S.O.S. Summit. She lauded the invaluable assistance of Millicent Sims, who had become her special assistant on the project. Vivian admitted that much of the schedule's smooth coming together was in no small part due to Millicent's efficiency and enthusiasm.

"Are you sure she's not bucking for first lady herself?" Carla asked after Vivian once again extolled her praises.

Vivian thought about the meeting she'd had with Millicent. When Millicent had admitted to her that she was in love and that she believed the man was her future husband. She didn't offer the man's name and Vivian didn't press. She did say he was a member of the church. Vivian hoped she wasn't talking about Cy Taylor because he'd clearly stated that he wasn't interested. Still, they spent a lot of time together working on various projects. Vivian had admonished her to stay prayerful, and to make sure she was hearing from God. Millicent believed she'd already received signs of confirmation that this was indeed the man that God chose for her before the foundations of the world were laid. Vivian was all too familiar with the dreamy look in Millicent's eyes as she talked about her future husband and the desired role that they, as a couple, would play in the ministry. Again, Vivian admonished her not to put the cart before the horse, but to make sure she was clear on God's desire versus her own. After all, everyone and their mama wanted to be Cy's wife.

"Earth to Vivian, come in please!" Carla implored dramatically.

Vivian wasn't aware that she'd been deep in thought and hadn't answered her friend's question. She decided to be tactful and keep Millicent's aspirations and her thoughts of said aspirations to herself.

"I believe every woman wants a Godly man, and no, that doesn't mean my husband," she began carefully. "However, I think Millicent would make a wonderful preacher's wife. I'm sure you'll all get to know her better as the summit nears, since she'll be overseeing the administrative responsibilities."

The women continued giving their updates and solidifying the flow of topics. Everyone had been thorough and presented outlines that not only impressed Vivian, but excited her. These women were as committed to S.O.S. as she was, and their sincerity showed in the quality of their work. Vivian felt this was the start of something good, something better than she'd imagined. Minister Rebecca and Terri McDaniels were presiding over the Spiritually Speaking segments, Pat and Chanelle were handling Setting the Standard versus society's Status Quo, Vivian and Ruth were covering the topic of the Sanctity of Sisterhood and Carla, along with Tai, would lead the way on Sacred Sex.

Carla was excited about working with Tai, whom she'd met a couple years ago during a Brook family visit to California. She didn't know her well, but Carla sensed a depth to Tai that was rarely seen in others. She also felt Tai was suffering, that something somewhere wasn't right. At first, Carla had questioned whether the particular section regarding sex was the best place for Tai to participate, but when Vivian told her she'd heard God on the matter, the subject was closed.

Carla had spoken with Tai at least once a week since then, and now understood Vivian's confidence. Tai was open and honest, another "real" sistah. Yes, there was definitely more there than met the eye. Without anything to confirm it, Carla also suspected trouble in Tai's marriage. Tai hadn't offered and Carla hadn't asked, but it was the things not said that caused Carla to draw this conclusion. She looked at Vivian and wondered if she should say anything. She knew Vivian was tighter than a steel drum when it came to keeping a confidence. No, it would be better for Carla to "watch and pray," knowing that if she was to know more, the information would come when the time was right.

Vivian wrapped up the meeting with what she thought was exciting news. Iyanla Vanzant was to be their luncheon speaker. Vivian's respect for these, her Ladies First comrades, had risen to new heights when she suggested this non-Christian choice and received open attitudes, intelligent discussion and, finally, agreement. Vivian always had her own mind and views on what and who were acceptable to God, and often thought outside the typical Christian box. She'd been given a copy of Iyanla's *Acts of Faith* several years ago and read other books that she'd written since then. Being a Yoruban priestess discounted her from most Christian circles. Vivian understood, but this summit wasn't just for Christian women, it was for hurting women, and she felt Iyanla's own experience afforded her the compassion and understanding necessary to reach beyond religious, cultural and racial lines and soothe bruised hearts with words of wisdom.

Minister Rebecca dismissed them in prayer. The ladies parted, full of excitement and anticipation for what was quickly becoming the meeting of the season, one not to be missed.

Put feet to your faith

The soothing sounds of instrumental music greeted Millicent as she opened the door to Beverly Hills Bridal Boutique. She smiled. Almost immediately she was transported into the world of fairy princesses and knights in shining armor. For this shop surely held every woman's fantasy and a pivotal part of Millicent's future.

She reached out to touch the varying styles of satins and silks, her hands tracing the intricate workings of beads and lace. She fingered the sheer veil nettings and allowed the wispy yards of fabric to drape her skin.

"That is one of our loveliest designs," the saleswoman said, smiling brightly as she joined Millicent next to the silk and pearl garment. "It's a Vera Wang."

"It's absolutely breathtaking," Millicent responded.

"With your slender figure, you'd look amazing. When is the big day?"

When is the big day? Wasn't that the question of the century? Millicent wasn't sure *when* she'd marry Cy; she was only sure that she *would* marry him. "We're still working out the details," she responded casually. "But one can never start shopping too soon, right?"

"Absolutely," the saleswoman countered. She walked with

Millicent, who'd moved on from the Vera Wang dress and stood next to an equally gorgeous Oscar de la Renta design. "Do you have a particular style in mind?"

"I've been looking through bridal magazines and have some definite thoughts. I think I'll just browse a while and see if anything catches my fancy."

"Well, we've got some of the best designs in the country. My name is Shannon. Call me when you're ready to try one on or need further assistance. I'll be glad to answer any questions you have."

Millicent thanked her and continued looking. Her thoughts were a whirlwind, jumping from Cy to her wedding day, to her conversation with Sister Vivian and finally to the prophetess whom she'd seen a few days ago.

It was at a small Pentecostal church in south central Los Angeles. Usually, Millicent shunned these small, nondescript "holy roller" congregations. But she'd been listening to an AM radio station, a Christian channel that broadcast a variety of ministers and their sermons. It wasn't a station she listened to often, but on this particular day she'd been scanning the dial when Prophetess Clare Baldwin from Jackson, Mississippi, came on and issued the word of the Lord, prophesying to callers on matters from men to marriage, children to jobs. A force outside her seemed to draw Millicent to the woman's fiery delivery and incantations. She'd tried to call in using her cell phone, but the station's line stayed busy throughout the broadcast. Then the announcer mentioned that Prophetess Baldwin would be at God's Temple Pentecostal Church that evening and would be coming with the word of the Lord. Millicent pulled over and wrote the address down.

She'd felt a bit apprehensive and more than a little out of place as she'd entered the small, shabby sanctuary. The benches were old and worn, some covered with marks and scratches made years ago by bored, restless children. The carpet on the floor was a dingy blue, almost gray, with unraveling threads and worn spots from years of high heels and shoutin' shoes. The walls had been white once upon a time, but now were a combination of faded yellows and muted ivory, darkened by the sun and a painter's neglect. A large brown stain snaked down one wall, evidence that not only the sanctuary but also the roof was in need of repair. There was an upright piano on the left side of a raised pulpit, looking shiny, new and out of place amid the dreary surroundings. A Hammond organ was on the other side, the red upholstery on the bench worn and faded. There was a tiny choir loft behind the pulpit and a faux stained-glass window in the center, with part of the "stained-glass" peeling off. On the right side of the window was a large cross, on the left side a hand-painted sign that read "Jesus Saves," a poorly drawn dove with an olive branch under the lettering.

A front-row saint by her own admission, Millicent had taken a tentative seat in the next to last row of the tiny edifice. She estimated it could probably seat a hundred, maybe a hundred and fifty on a good day. There were about ten people sitting in the sanctuary when she arrived, and if she wasn't so determined to get a word from the Lord concerning Cy, she would have tucked tail and run the moment she'd stepped inside. In fact, she was thinking about doing so when a lady came up behind her and said, "Praise the Lord!" in a voice that would have awakened the dead. Millicent jumped, then turned and looked into the kind, grandmotherly eyes of one of the church mothers, so assumed because of the white dress and lace hanky almost entirely covering the woman's gray hair. The woman laid a hand on Millicent's shoulder, giving her a couple of pats, and with a nod of her head walked around Millicent down to the first row, greeting all of those sitting in the pews by name and then getting on her knees and saying a quick prayer before she dropped her purse, took off her jacket and eased onto the hard wood pew, where she began humming to herself and rocking side to side.

Millicent had been sitting almost an hour before a young man, twenty-ish, walked to the piano. She silently thanked God for her church's timeliness. For a service to start an hour later than scheduled was unthinkable at Kingdom Citizens', and as the church filled up, Millicent realized that evidently these members knew their church was on CP time. The pianist began playing an instrumental piece that Millicent didn't recognize. She did recognize his wonderful playing ability, though, and closed her eyes to focus on the music. After several minutes he began to play "My Soul Loves Jesus," and Millicent could finally sing along.

They sang and played and prayed for another hour before Prophetess Clare mounted the pulpit along with a large, severe-looking woman and a man who Millicent correctly assumed was the pastor. Clare appeared younger than Millicent had imagined and was attractive in her own simple, plain way. Her jet-black hair was pulled back into a tight bun, no bangs, wisps or tendrils escaping. Her face was devoid of make-up. The prophetess also dropped to her knees as she entered the pulpit, staying there quite a while before getting up and sitting in the second of the three pulpit chairs. She sat quietly and solemnly, her eyes closed, elbows resting on the chair arms and hands clasped in prayerlike fashion as she swayed softly to the sounds of worship.

For two more hours, Prophetess Clare preached, prayed and prophesied over those in the audience, as God led her. Millicent prayed each time the prophetess finished with one person that she would be next, but it seemed that the prophetess was going everywhere except in her direction. She had almost given up when the prophetess came from behind her and said, "You! Stand up and hear the word of the Lord!"

Millicent's legs began to tremble as she looked into the eyes of this woman who looked young but seemed old. Her eyes were black and seemed endless—and even if you wanted to, you couldn't look too long. Following the example others had set, Millicent bowed her head, closed her eyes and waited for the prophetess to continue.

"You are searching," the prophetess began. "Searching for answers, searching for love." Millicent's heart skipped a beat.

"You've been asking God a question and demanding a sign. But the word of the Lord says there will be no sign. Listen to His instructions, believe what He says and put feet to your faith. If you trust and obey, you will find the path that God has ordained." She went on saying that Millicent was a chosen woman of God and would mentor young women as she led them to Christ. She would try to remember later what else she'd said because the only thing that kept replaying over and over in her mind were the words "put feet to your faith, put feet to your faith, put feet to your faith . . ." Millicent was so grateful for the word she received that she'd put a hundred dollars in the offering plate.

The next day Millicent had had a meeting with Sister Vivian, but chose not to confide in her, at least not to the point of revealing Cy's name. Instead, she'd bought fifty dollars' worth of bridal magazines to plan her wedding and travel magazines to choose the perfect honeymoon locale. She'd already begun making lists of potential bridesmaids, flower girls and musical selections. For the rest of the week she daydreamed constantly, seeing herself at the altar, amid an adoring crowd at Kingdom Citizens'. Pastor Montgomery in front of them and Cy at her side. *Put feet to your faith,* she heard over and over like a litany in her mind. It was this litany that propelled every other action, including her standing in this bridal shop at this very moment. This litany that motivated her as she lovingly fingered the dress in front of her, endless yards of silk and crepe de chine fashioned in an off-the-shoulder design. The cinched waist flared out into a wide princess-style skirt. The detachable train was almost twenty feet long. The veil was attached to a tiaralike crown, inlaid with cut glass that sparkled like diamonds and surrounded a single pearl in the center of its headband. Millicent smiled. "I'll try this one," she breathed to the saleswoman, who was immediately by her side.

"This one will be perfect," Shannon volunteered happily.

"Yes, perfect," Millicent responded. And she sounded totally convinced.

When the last time you had some, baby

"Oh, Father, give me strength," Hope prayed silently as she pulled herself out of the little MG and headed for her apartment. She was exhausted, and the soaring July heat didn't help. This was the second day of "Leading Us Back to Our Future," the leadership conference that had taken months to plan and execute. If the registrations and yesterday's crowd were any indication, the conference was a huge success already. Not to mention Dr. Myles Monroe was closing out the conference. She'd read his books on potential and knew his message would inspire.

Unfortunately, Hope was in no shape to appreciate it. The last two weeks had been an endless flurry of meetings, rehearsals, meetings, phone calling, rehearsals, work, meetings, church, more rehearsals and more meetings. Sleep had taken a distant second to everything else, and her body was feeling it.

She opened the door and headed straight for her bedroom, stopping only long enough to kick off her pumps before falling across the bed. For one quick second, she thought about not attending the afternoon sessions, then remembered her promise to help one of the coordinators put together some last minute additional materials. That promise and another Angels of Hope rehearsal following the afternoon sessions convinced her to go. She turned on her side and grabbed a pillow, cushioning herself more deeply into the nest of her down-filled comforter. She wondered if a cup of coffee would do the trick. Groaning, she sat up and instantly regretted having gotten into bed in her suit. The linen skirt, already wrinkle prone, was now wrinkle filled. *Might as well change into something that can carry over through tonight*, she thought, opening the closet. She wanted to pay special attention to how she dressed just in case Rashiid accepted her invitation to come hear Pastor Montgomery speak.

Rashiid was handsome and entertaining. But as much as she hated to admit it, she knew he was not her future husband. If she were honest with herself, she'd known this after their second date. Actually, she'd known it by the first half of their second date. When, laying her cards on the table up front, she'd told Rashiid that she was celibate. He'd looked at her as though she'd grown an extra head.

"When the last time you had some, baby?" he'd asked with such sympathy you'd think it was food, not sex she'd gone without.

"A long, long time," she'd responded. *So long that at times I feel I wouldn't know an orgasm if it came up to me in broad daylight and shook my hand.* From that moment, she became a challenge to his male ego. Would he be the one who could end her self-imposed celibacy streak? But for the grace of God, he wouldn't have had to try very hard. Sometimes Hope was so sex starved she didn't think she'd make another day without an avenue for physical release. Just last weekend, she'd almost seduced the pizza delivery man, actually asking if he wanted to come in and share a slice. And pizza was *not* what she had in mind. Yes, he'd laughed, thinking she was joking. She was not. After two years of abstinence, Rashiid didn't know how hot the fire was and that if there ever was a moment of weakness, he, not she, would feel like the sacrificial lamb.

Rashiid made it clear that he wasn't looking to marry anytime soon. He'd also voiced a general distrust of women after the mother of his child got pregnant while swearing to be on birth control. Funny how this distrust hadn't prevented him from trying to get into Hope's panties. He believed that one didn't have to be married to be committed to another, and that one didn't have to be committed to another to have sex. He assured her that she wouldn't be sorry if she let him satisfy her, that every woman needed a man in her life. Of this, Hope had no doubt. But what Rashiid didn't understand was that sex alone would never be enough for her. He'd never understand that the man she'd follow after would have to be following God. Hope wanted all or nothing, no compromise. And as much as she didn't want to, she was willing to wait until her "all" came along.

Not that waiting was easy. Just last month, she'd threatened God with another fornicate-by-Friday ultimatum, vowing that if she didn't meet her husband by the weekend, it would be God's fault if she "fell from grace." She'd assured Him that she couldn't wait any longer, and she had decided that Paul, her friend and coworker from the paper, would be more than happy to oblige her in helping her carry out this threat to God. Well. God didn't answer her by sending a husband to her doorstep, but Paul also didn't come to work that Friday. She found out the following Monday that he was invited at the last minute to go to Vegas for a three-day weekend. Guess God showed her, huh?

Despite Hope's declared motto of "no ring, no thing," Rashiid kept calling. And in spite of the fact that Hope knew there was no future with him, she continued to take his calls. Call it loneliness, boredom, desperation, whatever, something about Rashiid's desire to make her his, no matter how carnal, made her feel like a woman, made her feel special.

Hope's thoughts wandered to the man who would lead that afternoon's finance seminar, Mr. Cy Taylor. Almost as quickly as it came, she pushed the thought aside. No! She wouldn't *even* go down that road hoping he was her future husband. She was sure it was like the road to hell, awfully crowded! Yes, he was fine. Yes, he was a man of God. All right, already! He was everything she could ever hope for, dream about, pray for! He was also a heartbreak waiting to happen—a man who probably had more women than the desert had sand. The last thing he needed was another woman with stars in her eyes panting after him like a dog in heat. No, she wouldn't even allow her thoughts to begin to go in that direction. There was no way someone like him could be interested in someone like her.

Without warning, her eyes clouded over and the tears began to fall. How much longer would she have to wait? What was wrong with her that the thing she wanted most, to be married and have a family, continued to elude her? Wasn't she trying to live right, work in the Kingdom, obey the Word? Why did God continue to make her suffer when everyone else was getting married? She'd even read an article that said Elizabeth Taylor was thinking of marrying again. How could God let Elizabeth have a zillion husbands before Hope had one? She had done everything: fasted, prayed, professed, confessed, visualized, prophesied, believed, received, tithed, cried, begged, bartered and nothing, *nothing,* seemed to work. She was still single, still lonely and still hornier than a brass band.

Hope angrily brushed away her tears and straightened her shoulders. She would not have a pity party today. Absolutely not! Forget Rashiid, forget Cy Taylor, forget men period and forget marriage. She didn't care anymore. She couldn't care. She'd get dressed up and look good for her own datgum self and let her own self-approval be enough. She'd rehearse the Angels of Hope to perfection and release her energy by dancing with all her might before the Lord. She'd finish this conference and then take a vacation. Maybe she'd go to Boston and run the marathon, climb Mt. Everest or take up kickboxing. She'd do something to get rid of all this pent-up sexual energy. Maybe it wasn't in God's plan at all for her to get married. But didn't Paul say it was better to marry than to burn?

Still looking through her closet, Hope's hands stopped at the raw silk tailored suit she'd splurged on five months ago and was still paying for thanks to her Dillard's charge card. The golden material highlighted her toasty skin color, the short waist jacket with flared bottom accenting her small waist and womanly curves below. The craftily pleated skirt poured over her ample hips and molded to her bubbled derriere with just enough slack to not be sinful before tapering to a finish a couple inches above her knee. Hope moved to her chest of drawers and pulled out a colorful silk scarf filled with bold geometric designs in rust, burgundy and brown earth tones, flecked with gold threads. That accessory, artfully arranged around the jacket's low neckline would ensure modesty as well as provide a splash of color to the ensemble. She grabbed some rehearsal clothes and a change of shoes before heading to the kitchen for a much needed caffeine pick-me-up and quick sandwich.

Millicent navigated the unfamiliar streets with a level of comfort. She mentally thanked the cheery car rental agent who'd drawn a flawless map directing her to Mt. Zion Progressive Baptist Church in Overland Park. Millicent was familiar with the Midwest, she'd attended business seminars in Chicago, but this was her first time in Kansas. Her ride from the airport down I–35 to Overland Park had been uneventful, the unfamiliar territory rushing by in a mesh of office buildings, gas and food stops and flat green and brown terrain. Her mind was only peripherally aware of the highway signs as she cruised down the freeway. The rest of it was filled with prayers of thanks that she'd found out about Cy speaking at this out-of-town conference. Maybe Cy would be more open to spending quality time with her away from L.A. and Kingdom Citizens'.

Millicent eased the Ford Taurus to the corner and turned right onto a street of well-preserved homes and manicured lawns. The church on the next corner stood out even from a distance, sparkling white against the Kansas summer sun. A majestic steeple jutted into the sky, housing a gleaming gold bell. The L-shaped layout stretched the entire block with what looked to be offices and classrooms. Cars lined the street on both sides in each direction. Millicent saw a handsome young man in a sharp, black suit and pulled over.

"Excuse me, I'm Minister Cy Taylor's guest. Where should I park?"

The young man leaned down to the car window, his sweeping gaze giving Millicent the once-over. He smiled appreciatively. "Follow me," he said with a smile before going across the street and moving aside a bright red cone from one of the reserved spaces. He directed Millicent to the spot and waited for her to park and turn off the engine. Instantly, he was at her door, opening it for her and eagerly awaiting her exit. He was not disappointed when he did so and Millicent returned his approving smile.

"So you're from L.A.?" he asked, falling into step with her as she crossed the street.

"Yes."

"Are all the women out there as fine as you?" he asked, grabbing her arm and gently guiding her past the sanctuary and down a sidewalk to what were apparently the executive offices.

"Not all of them," Millicent replied to the open flirtation with a smile.

"You married?" he continued as he opened the door to the offices and stepped back to let Millicent precede him inside. She felt his eyes on her back as she entered. She ignored the question and instead asked her own.

"What time does the afternoon session begin?"

Her admirer got the message, or so she thought, because he lost the smile and became more businesslike. "In about thirty minutes. Here is the hospitality room. There's coffee and hot water for tea, along with some snacks if you're hungry. Make yourself comfortable and I'll let the office know you're here. What's your name?"

"Millicent Sims."

"Millicent, I'm Tony." He held out his hand and clasped hers firmly when offered.

"Nice to meet you, Tony." She hesitated a moment before pulling back slightly, disengaging her hand.

He turned to leave and was at the door when he stopped and turned around. "So did you say yes or no to the marriage question?"

Millicent smiled. "I didn't say."

Tony persisted. "Guess that means you're available."

Millicent walked over to the coffee and poured a cup. "Thanks for your help, Tony. Please let Mr. Taylor know I'm here." She turned around and reached for the cream, her back being his cue that the conversation was over and he was dismissed.

A cool glass of water in the Holy Land

Cy leaned back, laughing at King's commentary on "church folk." It was easy to see why this was one of Derrick's best friends. He was very charismatic, intelligent, passionate and shrewd in business. They'd talked only briefly during King's trips to Los Angeles, but after last evening, with a competitive game of tennis and a late dinner that went past midnight, Cy felt he was hanging with an old friend. The topic switched from members to finances as the diners enjoyed a sumptuous lunch of fried chicken, greens, garlic mashed potatoes and macaroni and cheese. Within the topic of finance, the focus shifted from fund-raising to community development to tithing.

"I don't know why folks are so tight," one minister voiced while cleaning a wing to the bone. "You can't take it with you."

"That's not what Brother Johnson thought," countered Bishop Anderson from St. Stephens in Ohio. "You heard what happened to him, didn't ya?"

Men around the table shook their heads in the negative.

"Well," Bishop Anderson continued, leaning back in his chair and grabbing a toothpick. "Old Mr. Johnson was tighter than a fat woman's girdle, shrewd as a snake and nobody worked harder. By the time the old man became ill, he was worth about a million bucks. Well, the time arrived when it became obvious that Mr. Johnson was not going to recover from this illness, and he began taking care of business and making peace with the Lord.

"He worried nonstop about the large sum of cash sitting in his various bank accounts. He'd never married or had children and couldn't think of one solitary person he wanted to have the money. He wasn't involved in any charities and, because he didn't like some of the church members, didn't want to leave a large lump sum to the house of God. Finally, he decided if he couldn't spend the money, nobody would. He called his pastor to explain his dying wishes.

"'Now, Pastor,' he began. 'I have called the bank and made it possible for you to withdraw all of my money after I'm gone. Here's what I want you to do. I want you to put the money in the large suitcase in my bedroom back home. Then I want you to bring that suitcase to the funeral, and I want you to put that suitcase on top of my casket after they lower my body down. They say you can't take it with you, but with your help, I'm going to do just that. I know that as a preacher and all, I can trust you to take care of this last request.'

"'The Lord will make a way,' the preacher solemnly replied.

"It was just a couple days later that old Brother Johnson breathed his last. As per his instructions, the preacher went to the bank, drew out the money, retrieved the suitcase from Mr. Johnson's home and put the money inside. After the funeral service was over, the small gathering of people drove to the gravesite. The preacher spoke a few more words, and then the graveyard workers began lowering the casket into the ground. As soon as they and the scant crowd had departed, the preacher walked over to the grave. Kneeling down he began to speak.

"'I went and got your money just like you asked. And, true to your wishes, here's one million dollars.' The preacher then pulled an envelope out of his coat pocket and let it float silently into the open grave. He paused a moment, then continued. 'You've always been a smart man, Brotha Johnson. And since you knew where you'd spend the money, I'm sure you'll know where to cash this check.'"

Bishop Anderson let out a loud guffaw after the punch line. The other ministers reacted with equal amounts of laughter and groans. It was apparent that Bishop Anderson, taking off his glasses and wiping his eyes, had enjoyed his own joke the most. King looked at his watch just as Bishop McKinney was warming up for one of his long-winded stories.

"Well, I got one better than that for you," he began in his most prolific preacher's voice.

King pushed back from the table. "I'm afraid it's going to have to wait," he said with a smile. "Duty calls."

As the men began moving there was a knock at the door. Tony entered and looked around the table for Cy. "Uh, Mr. Taylor, your guest has arrived."

"My guest?"

"Yes, a Ms. Sims? Millicent Sims?"

"Oh, right."

"Should I bring her back to join the pastor's wives?"

"No, just, uh, make sure she gets seated out front, will you?"

"Sure, sir, I'll take care of it, Mr. Taylor."

The frown on Cy's face lasted but a moment and then was gone, but not before King noticed it. He waited until the other ministers had filed out before him and then asked Cy, "Everything okay?" He fully expected the typical Christian all's-right-with-the-world-I'm-fine-just-blessed response and was taken slightly aback when Cy responded, "Not really."

"You want to talk about it?" King asked before remembering that at present, he was the last person to give advice on relationships, but also remembering more than one tongue-talking female stalker he'd endured over the years.

Cy paused. "Naw, brotha, it's just one of those things."

King didn't press. He was having "one of those things" with a woman himself. Both men were silent as they walked down the hall toward the main sanctuary.

Tai looked around her as she entered the sanctuary. The place was almost full, even for the afternoon session. Not surprisingly, there were a disproportionate number of females in attendance. Cy Taylor's pedigree must have preceded him, she thought sarcastically. Yes, she was seeing some members she hadn't seen in a while.

She continued down the aisle, smiling at some, waving at others. No matter what was going on with her and King, this was still her church, these were her friends as well as members and she loved them. She spotted Sistah Wanthers and Sistah Stokes sitting on the second pew to her right. She hugged both ladies warmly.

"Sistah Stokes, you're looking good. Is that a new suit?"

Sistah Stokes preened like a peacock in full feather. "This old thing? I've had this suit forever, just ain't worn it much. It's probably my new scarf that makes the difference."

"Well, whatever it is, you look lovely." Tai moved quickly to Sistah Wanthers, lest she feel she was being left out. "Now, I *know* I haven't seen that hat before! Sistah Wanthers, nobody can wear a hat like you."

"Ah, go on, Queen Bee," Sistah Wanthers replied, reaching up and lovingly patting the wide-brimmed hat decorated with leaves and flowers. "My niece got it for me, wasn't that nice?"

"It sure was. You ladies are going to make it hard for Minister Taylor to concentrate on his topic." Tai winked conspiratorially.

Sistah Wanthers gasped, pinched back a smile and put a hand to her mouth while Sistah Stokes blushed and began to fan herself with a program. "Now, you just go on, Queen Bee. Everybody knows you're the finest thing in here! And you're losing weight, aren't you? You must be, 'cause that suit sure looks good on you. Sure looks good. I think I'm seeing some curves I ain't seen in a while." Now it was Sistah Wanthers turn to wink.

Tai thanked them and moved on, smiling and making small talk with a few more members, inquiring about family and other situations she knew of through counseling sessions and calls to the house. She asked Mother Bailey about the hip that had been bothering her recently, thanked Sistah McCormick for all her hard work on the conference and blew a kiss to Sistah Stronghart. She reached the front row and looked back to see her mother-in-law coming down the aisle, dressed to the nines in a navy blue suit with matching hat, purse and shoes. She had just sat down next to Vivian and two rows in front of Millicent, when the side door opened and the ministers entered. No one could have been more surprised than Tai at her reaction to seeing Cy Taylor. The room got quiet and the earth stood still. Tai's eyes followed him up the steps, across the platform and down into his seat. It wasn't until Mama Max tapped her that she realized she'd been staring.

"Now, that's a sight for sore eyes," her mother-in-law whispered.

Tai swallowed and nodded, but couldn't respond. She missed the quick look Mama Max gave her and the slight frown that wrinkled her brow. Tai casually looked around and saw her feelings reflected in the other women's faces. It was as if the sun and the moon had left their heavenly orbit and come inside the church for a visit. A smile tugged at the corner of her mouth as she saw Sistah Stokes adjust her scarf and Sistah Wanthers rearrange the veil on her hat. Denise Williams, the administrative assistant, was sitting as still as a statue, her eyes drinking in Mr. Taylor as if he were a cool glass of water in the deserts of the Holy Land. Kimberly Stevens, the director of public relations for the church, suddenly had business with Minister Hays and slithered and swayed down the aisle to conduct it as Lisa, King's personal secretary, gazed at Cy with undisguised lust. Her eyes were shining and bright, her lips were parted slightly and her body was literally raised off the pew to get a better view of the afternoon's guest speaker as he sat down.

Tai admonished herself to calm down, even as she admitted it

had been forever and a day since her heart had raced like that at
the sight of a man. She relished it even as she questioned the fact.
It wasn't as though she hadn't seen him before; in fact, she'd eaten
dinner with him at Vivian's house during their last visit. Maybe it
was the way he wore that suit, like a second skin. And was his hair
longer? It looked as though he'd let it grow out some, giving him
an untamed, roguish look. Maybe it was the fact that she and King
hadn't made love in months. Whatever it was that was causing
these feelings, she was going to rein it in, tie it up and put a lid on
it. She was a married, virtuous woman of God, and she would not
let her thoughts stray. She looked up and followed, as if mesmerized, Cy's hand as he slowly rubbed his mustache while listening to
something King was saying to him. *Satan, get behind me!* She would
not let her thoughts stray. She would not! But the more she
looked, the more her thoughts strayed, as if will had nothing at all
to do with it.

Hope waved in what she hoped was a discreet gesture, trying
to get Louis, the head usher's, attention. She hadn't expected to see
so many cars for the afternoon session and was grateful there'd
been a parking space left for her in the reserved section, although
she thought that Tony Williams' attraction for her may have had
something to do with that. He was always trying to get his flirt on.
Well, no use looking a gift horse in the mouth! She was now glaring at Louis, willing him to look at her. She'd purposely waited
until offering so she could walk in unobtrusively. The sanctuary
was almost full. Some of the members of her dance troupe saw her
and waved. She waved back. One of them rushed over to ask her a
question, which she answered before shooing the excited teenager
away. She saw another getting ready to approach and held up her
hand. If she didn't stop the madness, the whole squad would be
back by the door, vying for attention. She wanted to scream at
Louis, who seemed to see nothing past the next row he was direct-

ing to stand and walk around the offering table. Finally Hope gave up and squeezed into the line, coming up the right aisle of the church directly into Louis's path.

"Hey, Louis, any seats left up here?"

Louis frowned. For some reason that she could not fathom, Louis disliked her. "I don't know, Hope, it's kinda tight already."

Hope looked around. It was tight. She glanced over to the other side of the church. There were several places left over there, but Holy Jesus and Heavenly Father, the ushers would probably have a cow if she attempted to sit in the area reserved for pastors', deacons' and trustees' wives. "What about up there, next to Sistah Wanthers?"

Louis sighed audibly. "Come on."

Hope was itching to give an impromptu sermon on the virtue of good manners and brotherly love, but she figured it would be wasted breath. Louis approached the second row and held out his hand stiffly, the motion for her to enter the pew. She ignored the hostile eyes that glanced up at her as she excuse me'd down the row. She almost laughed out loud as she glimpsed the look of disdain on Sistah Wanthers's face as she sat down beside her. Sistah Stokes looked at Hope from the top of her sleek hairdo to the soles of her pumps. Her eyes followed as Hope sat and widened with such horror you would have thought it was Hope's vagina and not knees that showed beneath the hem of her skirt. The drama never ended. God had made her like a Coca-Cola bottle, and she wasn't going to dress as if she were a Cola can. She met Sistah Stokes's eyes and smiled indulgently.

"Hello, Sistah Wanthers. That's a beautiful hat you're wearing."

Mrs. Wanthers attempted to change her smirk into a smile but was only half successful. "Your skirt's a little short. Do you have something to cover yourself?"

"No, ma'am, but I think I'll be fine. I'll just, uh, lay my Bible on my lap. Cover myself with the Word of God, hallelujah?" Hope barely managed to bite back a chuckle as she acquiesced to the older woman's displeasure and placed her Bible at a strategic angle on her lap. "Is this better?"

Sistah Wanthers only grunted before turning to the other side and speaking to Sistah Stokes. Sistah Stokes peeked over, frowned and began fanning furiously with her program while muttering, "Mercy, Lord, mercy!"

Hope hid her annoyance behind a smile. This respecting your elders bit sometimes was a hard pill to swallow. Her kneecaps were barely showing! She spoke to Sistah Stronghart, who was seated on the other side of her. Sistah Stronghart complimented her on her new outfit. "That's a gorgeous suit, Hope. You look beautiful," she whispered sincerely.

"Thank you," Hope responded. Beauty was definitely in the eye of the beholder, and what was sinful to one person was sanctified to another. *Whatever.* Hope opened her program and began reading the afternoon's topics. She'd been so engrossed in trying to find a seat and then trying to pacify Sistah Wanthers and Sistah Stokes that she wasn't aware of the pair of golden brown eyes that had watched her ever since she'd entered the sanctuary.

Two things happened that had never happened before when Cy saw Hope for the first time. One, she literally took his breath away, and two, he got an erection. Immediately. In the house of God, in the pulpit, in broad open daylight no less. *My God! Who is this woman?* he thought.

It was as if he felt her before he saw her. That could be the only explanation he could give to why his head had come up just as she stepped through the doors. He'd taken her in all at once. The beautifully sculpted, heart-shaped face, the large, bright eyes and dazzling smile and a body that would stop traffic. He'd devoured her profile as she turned and talked with a kid who ran up to her. Her breasts tugged invitingly at the suit's enclosure. His hands actually itched, and he swallowed as she turned, revealing a lush, plump booty, only partially concealed by her suit jacket. Cy thought of basketballs and pumpkins and suddenly wished he were a piece of silk so as to have an excuse to wrap himself around that booty and hug it ever so tightly. The picture of a sand-strewn beach wafted up in front of his mind's eye, of him and an ebony goddess rolling languidly over the sand. That was where he'd seen her before! In his dream. Cy shook his head slightly and lowered his eyes, willing himself to lower his libido as well.

But he couldn't keep his eyes off her. He watched, fascinated, as she tried to get someone's attention. Who? Oh, the usher. She looked around, licked her lips and tried again. Cy watched her tongue as it darted in and out of her mouth, and before he could banish the thought, he imagined that tongue darting in and out of *his* mouth. He squirmed uncomfortably in his chair and once again looked down at his notes. He willed the discipline that helped him excel at just about everything he did to take over, but his body and mind betrayed him. The next time he glanced up, she was walking down the aisle, the suit's shimmer accenting each captivating step. He prayed to see her smile again and was instantly rewarded as she turned to greet the woman next to her as she sat down. The woman stared down her nose at Hope and spoke to her briefly before whispering to the lady on the other side. Cy smiled. *Jealousy will get you nowhere, you old coot.* Then he censured himself at the thought. What *was* he thinking? And why did he feel so protective over a woman he didn't even know? Cy watched as her hair gently framed her face as she bowed her head and pored over the program. He continued to stare, hoping she'd look up again, so that he could catch her eye. And do what? Wink? Blow her a kiss? Shout out from the pulpit and ask for her phone number? Blatantly inquire if fries went with that shake? Lord, he was acting like a pimply-faced teenager. Shoot, he felt like a pimply-faced teenager, especially as he fought to cool down his body and lose the telltale bulge in the front of his pants. For the love of all things holy, it was actually throbbing! Dang! Would his jacket cover it? "Stop!" he whispered aloud. King looked over questioningly, but Cy refused to meet his gaze. Had he said that loud enough for King to hear? *Lord, I've got to get a grip.* He looked down at his notes again, then closed his eyes and started reciting the Lord's Prayer. Finally, he and all parts of him began to relax. The afternoon session could now begin.

The marriage bed is undefiled

Vivian smiled warmly as she looked at her friend of over twenty years. Tai still looked good, but to Vivian's observing eye, the strains of an unhappy marriage were beginning to show. There was a tension in Tai's face that wasn't there before, crinkles around and slight bags under her eyes that Vivian didn't remember being there last summer. She reached out her hand and grasped Tai's arm. "It's good to be able to hang out with you again," she said sincerely. "The workouts agree with you, too. You look good, girl."

Tai smiled appreciatively at her friend and replied, "Thanks, Viv, it's good to see you, too."

They were both quiet as Tai maneuvered her Lincoln SUV around the hotel's driveway and turned onto the boulevard. Vivian glanced at her a time or two and thought she noticed a glistening in Tai's eyes. Tai still didn't speak, although Vivian knew there was a lot on her mind. She decided to let her friend take the lead. When Tai was ready to talk, she would.

Tai leaned over and switched the radio from a gospel station to her favorite oldies channel. She still thought part of her love affair with these classic R&B tunes stemmed from rebellion at her father's not allowing the music in their home when she was young.

The soothing sounds of the Spinners talking about a rubberband man lightened the mood.

"I haven't heard that song in years!" Vivian sat back and bobbed her head slightly. "This reminds me of Charlotte when she was in love with Danny 'Heartthrob' Jenkins."

"How is Charlotte?" Tai didn't know Vivian's older sister that well, but she'd seemed pleasant and down-to-earth the few times they'd met.

"Charlotte's doing well, finally getting over the divorce and moving on with her life."

"How long has it been now?"

"Five years already. Can you believe it? She's actually seeing someone, a man she met at a job fair two years ago."

"How are the kids doing?"

"They're adjusting. Brent has had a harder time with it than Darrin. He really acted out when they first separated, skipping classes, fighting in school. But since they've started spending the summers with their father, things seem to have calmed down."

"And he's remarried, right?"

"Yeah." Vivian couldn't keep the irritation out of her voice.

"You still don't like her, do you?"

"I guess not, although it's not really fair. She didn't have anything to do with Charlotte and Danny's marriage failing. I guess seeing any woman with him other than my sister gets on my nerves. Let me rephrase that, seeing *him* gets on my nerves. He caused Charlotte so much pain. I only see them at family reunions. And try to have as little to do with them as possible. I can't believe Charlotte even invites him, but she insists it's best for the kids. According to her, he's still part of the family. And then he insists on bringing *her*. He's still a dog."

Tai smiled. "You know we have to love one another, sistah."

"I know," Vivian continued, groaning. "But we don't have to *like* them, do we?"

Tai chuckled. "Hell no."

"I guess," Vivian continued, "a man's going to always have somebody, no matter how he acts. What are the statistics now, like ten women to every man? The men sure take advantage of that, don't they? They can always get somebody." She looked at Tai.

Tai nodded, but kept her eyes on the road. "Speaking of men having somebody," Tai said, changing the subject, "I bet you could start a choir with the women trying to climb into Cy Taylor's bed."

"A mass choir, girlfriend, one thousand voices strong!"

"I can imagine. His seminar was exceptional, and I hear his tapes sold out. Is it true he's a millionaire?"

"Many times over. He's had uncanny success in the stock market. Must be the anointing."

"Millicent's a blessed woman."

"Millicent?"

"Isn't she his lady friend?"

"She'd like to be, but no. Cy has made it clear that he doesn't believe she's his future wife."

"It's clear to her all right. Clear as mud. She led me to believe they've all but set the date."

Vivian looked at her friend before replying. "Between you and me, I'm rather concerned about Millicent. We had a conversation last month, and I think that she thinks that he's her future husband. My spirit tells me she's in for a rude awakening."

"Didn't Cy invite her to the conference?"

Vivian thought for a moment. "More likely she invited herself. I mentioned Derrick's participation just last week and she said nothing of coming. My guess is she found out Cy was conducting a seminar and that's what prompted her being an attendee."

"She and hundreds of others. We put an insert with his picture on it in the brochure, you know. Word must have gotten around. You would have thought there was a rock star in the building with all the females who converged on him after service. I'm surprised I didn't see Hope at the front of the line. I did notice she had on a new suit for the occasion. And I did see her finally finagle her way to his side in the reception room last night."

"Well, I think it's wonderful that women are so concerned with getting a handle on their finances," Vivian stated with a smile in her voice.

"Right, on the man who *has* the finances more likely. Can't say I blame them, though; the man even made my kundalini tingle!" "Kundalini" was a reference to the seventh chakra, the area of the body that supposedly housed sexual energy, according to her former New Age coworker Chandra, whom Tai had tried unsuccessfully to convert to Christianity. Publicly, she shunned Chandra's New Age sayings. Privately, however, Tai had humorously adopted this particular word and in better times between she and King had often invited him to "stir her kundalini with his ding-a-lingy."

"Girl, shut up!" Vivian laughed at this remark, remembering when Tai had first told her about this new addition to her vocabulary.

"Tell the truth, shame the devil."

Vivian laughed again at the forthrightness of this first lady. "Tai Brook, you have no sense."

"Baby, I've got five senses, and they were all working overtime with that man in the room. God forgive me, but I must admit that when I looked at him, *baby*!! Some thoughts ran through my mind, and not all of them were holy!"

"Girl, you a mess!"

They were silent for the remainder of the journey, each woman deep in her own thoughts. Before long, they'd reached their destination, Gates Bar-BQ. Tai and Vivian bowed their heads briefly before plowing into the succulent meat. It was one of the few times Vivian suspended her self-imposed "fish only" meat diet and ate a piece of chicken. If there was ever a place that made eating chicken a worthy event, it was Gate's. She grabbed one from a stack of napkins and wiped her already greasy mouth and fingers.

"Ooh, I'd forgotten how good this was. And the sauce? Unh, unh, unh!" Vivian grabbed a long, thick fry and dipped it generously into the tangy, spicy barbeque sauce before taking a large bite. "Remind me to buy a couple bottles of this before we leave."

Tai smiled at her friend's pleasure. She wasn't the only one who thought that Gate's made the best barbeque sauce in the world. She pulled apart a piece from the pork slab she'd purchased. "Sure you don't want a rib?"

Vivian's stomach recoiled at the thought of eating pork, and she just looked at Tai and rolled her eyes before Tai continued. "Some of this nice, juicy pork, girl, it's good for what ails you!"

"More likely, it will *be* what ails me!"

Both women laughed before Tai looked up and caught her breath, her eyes widening and then narrowing in a single motion. Vivian turned to see what had caught Tai's attention and saw a petite woman with shoulder-length, brunette hair standing in line. She turned back around, giving Tai a questioning look. Tai sat back in her seat, took a sip of soda and visibly relaxed.

"Is that her?" Vivian asked quietly and cautiously.

"I thought it was," Tai replied. Her shoulders slumped at the thought of her husband's mistress, and suddenly the sauce-slathered ribs didn't taste so good. "She looks enough like her to be her sister."

Vivian turned again to get a better look. When she turned back around to gaze at her friend, there was compassion in her eyes. "So it's still going on, huh?"

"The affair? Oh, yeah. King tries to be discreet and act like nothing's happening, but I know."

"So you two aren't—"

"Please. And it's going to stay that way. As long as his no-good ass is fuckin' someone else, he won't be fuckin' me!" Tai reached down, grabbing another rib, and bit into it ferociously.

Vivian inwardly winced at Tai's verbal bluntness but did not censure her friend. She couldn't imagine how she'd feel or what she'd do if she found out Derrick was having an affair. She could only sympathize with Tai, knowing that there wasn't enough mercy in the Bible to keep her in an adulterous marriage. Still, Vivian was in no position to judge what was and was not the right reaction where Tai and her marriage were concerned. She knew only that whatever happened, she would be there for her friend. Vivian continued after a long silence. "So what are you going to do? It's been two months now. Things can't keep going the way they are."

"That's just it, Viv, I don't know what to do. As crazy as it sounds, a part of me still loves King. I thought I had my mind made up to leave him. But during the conference I was acutely aware of my church family, how much I love them and how much they mean to me. What would happen to that if I divorced the pastor? Where would I go? What would I do? And why should I be the one to give up the things and people I love when I feel I played an equal, albeit different role in Mt. Zion being the church it is today? I mean, really, do you think there would be a spot in the pews for an ex-first lady?

"I've thought about relocating because I know this city wouldn't be big enough for both of us. Maybe I could go back to my family in Chicago or maybe to my relatives down south. But how would that affect the kids? You know with the twins, the sun rises and sets on their father. How could he continue to play an active role if I move away? But how could I keep from killing his ass if I stayed in the same town?"

Vivian's eyes widened, a look of genuine concern on her face.

Tai laughed out loud. "Oh, I'm just kidding, girl. King may be worth a lot, but he's not worth a prison sentence with somebody else raising my kids."

Vivian laughed as she took a sip of soda. She was thankful for the lightened moment. "I was getting ready to ask you, is you crazy or is you just lost your mind?"

"Yes to both those questions," Tai said, smiling. Then the young brunette walked by, and the smile quickly faded from her face. "Right now, I'm taking it one day at a time. King and I are more like roommates than a married couple. I do my thing, he does his. We only talk when necessary and are civil for the sake of the children. I know about April, he knows I know and he's still seeing her. Mama Max has talked to him. He keeps telling all of us that it's over, but that's a lie. Every time he comes home after being with her, no matter how he tries to hide it, it's written all over his face. Those are the nights when I'm sure I'll leave." Tai took a deep breath as she sat back and stared out the window, trying to catch a glimpse of King anywhere in her future.

Vivian watched as the weight of the decision to divorce or not divorce King settled around Tai's shoulders. She thought back to how sure she herself had felt moments before as to how she'd handle an affair in her marriage. But would it be an easy, cut-and-dried decision? Just like that, it's over, bye? Much easier to say when the situation was hypothetical; much harder with the reality of twenty years, four children, two thousand members and one soulmate.

When Tai came home after dropping Vivian off at the hotel, the house was quiet. The twins were at the movies with her neighbor. King was, well, King was wherever he was, with April no doubt. Tai kicked off her heels and then grabbed them as she made her way through the living room and up the steps toward the guest room that was now her personal, private abode. She felt totally weary as she undressed, her conversation with Vivian weighing heavily on her mind. Thank God for Vivian. Though talking about it was painful, it had felt therapeutic to talk about King and their marriage, a conversation she knew would go no farther. With Vivian, Tai could be herself and not be judged, criticized or reminded that she should feel a certain way or speak a certain way or act a certain way because she was a pastor's wife.

Tai stepped naked in front of the mirror. She eyed herself critically from first one angle, then another. She smiled triumphantly at her small bulge of a stomach. *Another six months and that baby will almost be flat again.* She cupped her breasts in her hands and pushed them upward and inward. They didn't sag quite as much. She'd now lost twenty-five pounds. No, the breasts were passable, though after four children, the word "firm" would never be used to describe them again. She turned to the back and frowned deeply. No matter how many leg lifts and butt tucks she did, her booty was still feeling the pull of gravity. And what did she have to do to get that cellulite to go away?

She slipped into a bulky, terry cloth robe and headed for the kitchen. She stood at the cabinet, deciding between a glass of water, soda, juice or wine. She opted for Princess's favorite which she now also loved, peach sparkling water. She grabbed a bag of popcorn and, putting it in the microwave, leaned back on the counter as it began to pop. She thought again about Vivian and their conversation. She smiled, thinking of the Sanctity of Sisterhood convention, the topic that she and Vivian had talked about excitedly and continuously after the subject of King and her failing marriage was exhausted.

She enjoyed working with Carla on the segment entitled Sacred Sex. Tai laughed at the irony of her speaking on this particular topic. She hadn't questioned when Vivian had suggested it, although Tai thought God must indeed have a sense of humor.

Tai poured the popcorn into a bowl, then grabbed it and the sparkling water and headed upstairs. She was still thinking about the various sessions for the summit when a Scripture popped into her head. Setting the popcorn and water down, she hurried over to the bookshelf and grabbed her concordance. Thumbing quickly, she found the passage almost immediately, Hebrews 13:3–4. . . . *Marriage is honorable in all and the bed undefiled; but whoremongers and adulterers God will judge.* Tai sat back and reflected on those Scriptures. "The marriage bed is undefiled," she whispered aloud. Tai glanced up at the clock on the dresser and reached for the phone, even as ideas continued to root and take shape in her mind. It was still early enough to call Carla. Tai hoped she was home.

King moaned and grabbed April's silky tresses as she swirled her tongue around his sensitive nipple, then suckled first one and then the other. She followed his kinky hair trail with her tongue, moving lower and lower until King's groan became a growl that he could not contain. He grabbed her roughly and rolled her over, pinning her beneath his massive bulk. He began the same assault on her that she'd done on him, now sending his senses roiling. He caressed and kissed and licked her before entering her fiercely, swiftly, pounding into her over and again. She moaned and writhed and whispered in his ear, "Ooh, yes, do it, baby. That feels so good, so good." Her words sent him spiralling, pumping harder, faster until they both exploded with mind-boggling releases that left them panting and sweating.

King gave April a peck before rolling off her and falling heavily against the mattress. He'd never had sex like this in his whole life. Had never met a woman who made him feel the way April did.

"I love you, King," she whispered, turning toward him and snuggling under his arm. She began kissing him again, first his mouth, then his neck, then sliding down to continue her oral assault.

"Whoa, whoa, baby, you're gonna kill me," King teased. "Let a brother catch his breath."

"I just can't get enough of you, you know that," April purred as she grabbed part of the sheet and began wiping the sweat from King's body. "You are without a doubt the hottest, most talented lover in the world. Thank you."

"Thank you?"

"Yes. Thank you for coming to me, being with me. You're my most prized possession."

"Oh, so I'm a possession now." King turned to face her, tenderly wiping strands of dampened hair from her face.

"You know what I mean. Not that I own you, but that you're my world. You're what matters to me."

King rolled back over and stared at the ceiling. He didn't like it when she talked like that, like he was her everything. He didn't, couldn't, belong to her. Someone named Tai was in the way. He rolled out of bed and headed toward the shower.

"Don't leave yet," April whispered. The words were spoken before she could stop them. She was a strong, astute woman and knew that with a married man she'd get only bits and pieces. Still, she wasn't ready for him to go.

King felt guilty enough when he left Tai at home. Now he was going to feel guilty when he left April? "You know how heavy my Sundays are. You know I can't stay." King looked at her as he turned on the bathroom light. She looked ravishing, sitting perfectly still in the middle of the bed, her hair cascading over her shoulders and down her back, lips slightly swollen, eyes boring into his. He let his gaze continue downward, firm, large breasts made even more voluptuous by a skilled surgeon's hand, nice, tight stomach, hot, moist . . .

King turned away quickly and walked into the bathroom, turning the water on full blast. He'd barely begun soaping himself before he heard the shower door open and felt her body press up against him before she reached around and grabbed the soap. "Here," she murmured, taking the bar and moving it sensuously in circles across his shoulders and down his back. "Allow me." April soaped her own body and then used her flesh to continue to soap King's. He stared down at her as she dropped to her knees to soap his legs and calves and to carefully wash his feet. His eyes glazed as his penis began to harden and throb from her expert ministrations. He grabbed her head, pulling her toward him. King didn't leave her house for a long time.

The spirit of seduction

Millicent was livid. She had simmered slowly since the last "amen" of Mt. Zion's leadership conference. She seethed with anger during the three-and-a-half hour flight home. Now her rage was in full boil. In her mind, Cy had not treated her at all appropriately. Didn't he know that she was his future wife!

The voice of God filled her mind. *No, he doesn't.*

"Well, he's gonna know it!" Millicent spouted angrily as she paced back and forth in her condo. She picked up a glass figurine and hurled it across the room. The impact left a dent in the wall and broke the carefully sculpted angel into several pieces.

She barely noticed, sitting down on the couch, breathing heavily, and shaking her leg up and down in a nervous patter. She thought back again to how the events unfolded in Kansas and became even angrier at each distorted memory.

First, there was the fact that Cy didn't come out to greet her personally when she arrived at the church, but rather had her escorted directly to the sanctuary. The hospitality suite didn't count; after all, *everybody* and anybody could come in there. She hadn't recognized one first lady or pastor in that room, not one! Wherever they were, that was where she was supposed to be. But after she was seated on the third row amidst the pastors' and deacons' wives

in the sanctuary, she felt less offended. And then when Mrs. Brook
had entered the main edifice with Millicent's very own first lady,
one Mrs. Vivian Montgomery, in tow, she knew her access to the
inner sanctum of conference attendees, and thus close proximity to
Cy, was basically assured. Relaxing with that thought, Millicent
had allowed her mind to create the probable scene of why Cy had-
n't asked to see her as soon as she'd arrived. Of course, he was
probably preparing for his session. She even remembered smiling at
the thought of his sermon preparations in their future. *Guess I
should get used to that,* she had mused. *My future husband will need his
solitude in those moments.* She'd imagined him holed up in the pastors' study, in deep thought, no, on his knees in prayer, seeking His
guidance from on high on how best to lead His children out of the
bondage of poverty into the promised land of prosperity. Had she
seen him laughing heartily at Bishop Anderson's jokes and thoroughly enjoying the kingly feast that was the pastors' private lunch,
and had she witnessed the adjoining room filled with first ladies
and other distinguished female guests, she would *not* have been
amused.

Her ruffled feathers were further calmed when, after Cy's illustrious and thoroughly informing conference seminar, she had been
escorted, along with Cy, Tai and Vivian, to the pastors' personal reception area and again introduced to Pastor King and his wife. She
felt right at home as they sat chatting amicably over coffee and appetizers, just the six of them, before being joined by a few other
ministers and their wives for a dinner in the private dining room.
The pastors' private dining room!

The Voice continued. *But that was only after you played the pity
card with Vivian, taking advantage of your relationship with her to be near
Cy.*

"I knew he wanted me to stay with him, but he couldn't ask
directly!" she countered.

I see.

She was not going to listen to the logic of her conscience.

"Satan, I rebuke you! Cy is my future husband and my place is by his side!"

I'm not Satan, stop rebuking Me.

Millicent jumped up and began pacing again. The dinner had been lovely; even Mrs. Brook, or Queen Bee as all her members called her, seemed to warm up to her. Tai was so excited about the S.O.S. Summit that her eyes fairly glistened while listening to all the updated information Vivian and Millicent were able to provide. Millicent had felt like one of the family. She felt like a pastor's wife, like Cy's wife. She smiled, remembering that feeling, and couldn't help smiling as she relived the utter rapture of sitting next to Vivian during the evening service, in the front row. Millicent tried to involve God in her illusion.

"Since it's Your will, it is only good practice for me to play the role of Cy's wife."

You're playing a role, all right.

Millicent would not be swayed. "I'm just speaking those things that are not as though they were!"

No, you're just speaking the things that you want and trying to convince yourself that it's Me talking.

That was enough. Millicent wouldn't stand around and listen to this garbage another minute. She ran into her bedroom, peeled off her clothes and donned a pair of shorts. She quickly pulled on a pair of cotton socks and grabbed her Air Jordans from the closet. She stopped by the bathroom and got a scrunchie to tie back her hair. She grabbed her jogging pouch and placed her keys, cell phone and a five-dollar bill inside. Without stopping to turn off lights or the radio, she headed for the door and sprinted outside, running swiftly and steadily until the only sounds she heard were her escalating heartbeat, her labored breathing and the sound of rubber meeting pavement in the quiet suburban streets.

Forty-five minutes later, Millicent sat tired and sweaty outside the local Jamba Juice Bar. She gingerly nursed a Tropical Paradise smoothie, a delectable blend of pineapple, papaya, banana, mango, orange juice, vanilla yogurt and crushed ice. It tasted heavenly and was especially refreshing after Millicent's hard run. The run had done her mind good as well as her body, had chased away the voice of the enemy that badgered her in her condo and allowed her to think of Cy in the husbandly terms that God had ordained.

Sitting back, she allowed herself to continue her thoughts of what had happened in Kansas. She was able to think clearer now, with less fury and more focus. Things worth having were worth fighting for, and where Cy was concerned, Millicent would fight every woman in the universe. And she would win.

That thought led to images of *her.* Hope something or other. Millicent had known she was trouble from the time she first spotted her the day of Cy's seminar. She didn't know what kind of trick she'd used, what lewd promise she'd given, but she'd seen how Cy's eyes seemed to follow her as she left the sanctuary and headed toward the offices. Millicent knew that game. Playing hard to get, acting as if she had no interest at all in speaking with Cy when Millicent knew that was exactly what she wanted to do. What woman didn't? God knew ninety-nine percent of the other women had made a beeline to his side as soon as the benediction ended. That sneaky she-devil was the number one reason Millicent had been so determined to stay by Cy's side. *Guess this is something else I'm going to have to learn how to handle, women always trying to get my man.* She remembered how the woman had shamelessly brought attention to herself during that night's services. How she had acted so into the worship, standing and lifting her hands and eyes to God as if He were really on her mind. Only a fool wouldn't recognize that she was only flaunting her body in that shimmering suit. Millicent loved God just as much as she did and was sure it didn't take all that!

She finished her smoothie and tossed the cup in the trash, heading back to her condo at a leisurely pace. She remembered how Cy's eyes had seemed to stay on Miss Thang, so much so that when the last worship song played, Millicent made sure she stood up first, just to make sure that this little biddy wouldn't be the only one reverencing God. *Reverencing my foot, advertising her availability is more like it.* Still, when the services were over and the special guests had retired to the pastors' reception area, Miss Thang was nowhere in sight. Thank goodness!

Millicent was only slightly rebuffed when Cy turned down her offer to drive into Kansas City and visit a jazz club Millicent had spotted in her hotel's "Things To Do" guide. Of course he would be exhausted; he'd stood in the sanctuary for almost two hours after his seminar, fielding questions and fighting off Mrs. Taylor wannabes. But Millicent hadn't left his side, handing out pamphlets and pretyped seminar notes, getting him water, arranging the sale of his tapes in the church bookstore, you know, things a wife would do. After all, hadn't he agreed to have breakfast with her the following morning? The fact that he hadn't come alone, but had shown up with two matrons from Mt. Zion, a Mrs. Stokes and a Mrs. Waters, or Winters or something or other, just underscored the fact that he wanted others to know they were an item, a couple, a pair. Further, his attention to these old ladies simply confirmed his sensitive, compassionate side and probably gave the elderly, apparently lonely women something to talk about for months to come.

Millicent knew for a fact that Cy hadn't attended the next morning's sessions because of a leaders' meeting held by Pastor Brook for a few, select visiting ministers. Millicent had used this time to try and locate which hotel Cy was staying at, to no avail. She'd called all of the places that she could think of that would suit his fancy—the Sheraton, Hyatt, Hilton, Crown Center and a few more upscale hotels the concierge had suggested, but one Mr. Cy Taylor was not registered at any of them. She'd checked hotels in Overland Park and Kansas City with no luck. Had she been able to find him, she would have been able to watch, or rather guard him more closely and make sure that some floozy didn't try and stalk him, try and finagle her way into his hotel suite! Millicent had pleaded the blood of Jesus at the very thought!

She'd breathed an audible sigh of relief when after looking around she discovered that Hope was not in attendance at the afternoon session. She'd probably poked her head into the morning one and, after not seeing Cy, figured she should take her manhunt elsewhere. That was the best thing she could do, because if Cy was the game she was hunting, he'd already been snagged. Her tension mounted slightly, however, when Cy was a no-show at the afternoon session as well. She'd made subtle inquiries until she ascertained that Cy had left with a few of the other ministers for a trip to Kansas City. This didn't make Millicent feel totally comfortable, but at least he was with men of God. Sister Vivian and Queen Bee hadn't been there either, but after all, they were close friends and had probably taken the opportunity to catch up on each other's lives.

No, her dander hadn't risen fully until the evening services when Miss Thang came waltzing in wearing a gaudy, loud, lime green dress that fit her body like the peel on a banana and, gasp and sputter, showed the imprint of her disgustingly large rear end for all the world to see! A true woman of God would never be seen in such a revealing design; only hoochies dressed like that. Millicent knew that this outfit was part of Hope's arsenal and that Cy was her target. When they were introduced at the reception, Millicent made sure Hope got the message, that she was no threat to Millicent's future. Long after Cy was gone from Kansas and Hope was forgotten, Millicent would be with him in L.A., at his church and in his home. After all, Millicent had his home *and* cell phone numbers. She knew him intimately. They had kissed, passionately, and Millicent knew that but for his Godly restraint, he would have gladly done more, much more. It was obvious that he'd wanted to. No, Millicent would not be intimidated by this woman. In a few hours, Cy would be on a plane headed to Chicago and, in a few days, would be headed back home to California, back to her.

Millicent held on to those comforting thoughts throughout the Midnight Musical and the Angels of Hope performance. Again, she watched as Cy gazed at Hope, as if transfixed by something more powerful than he could control. The woman was probably into witchcraft. The spirit of seduction. Millicent had quietly spoken in tongues during the entire performance, binding the enemy and breaking her curses. She was sure it worked because after the musical, little Miss Slime in Lime was nowhere to be seen, and it was Millicent who sipped coffee with Sister Vivian and the first lady even after Cy, citing fatigue and an early rising the next morning, had left the hall to return to his hotel. Millicent assumed his was an early flight to Chicago and since her own flight left at eight A.M., she'd left shortly afterward and returned to her hotel to pack.

Millicent let herself into her condo and turned to lock the door, leaning back against it. A small smile tugged at the corners of her mouth as she again placed the events of this weekend in their proper perspective.

She knew that she was destined to be Cy's wife. She knew that she was the one who sat at his side and dined with Pastor King, Queen Bee and the Montgomerys. She knew that she was the one who'd sat in the rows reserved for pastors' wives, the first row. She knew that she was the one who assisted him after his seminar, easing his burden by overseeing the selling of his tapes. She knew that she was the one who hugged him tightly, in front of everyone in the reception room, as he left to get ready for his early morning flight.

As she opened her closet to put away her tennis shoes, Millicent's eyes rested on the large garment bag hanging at the far end of the enclosure. She reached over and caressed the bag before unzipping it and opening it up. Soft swirls of silk met her hand as she gingerly fingered the intricate stitching, grasping and releasing the myriad beads across the bodice. Her eyes watered at the thought of donning this beautiful gown to walk down the aisle into the arms of her future, Cy Taylor. Millicent knew it was just a matter of time before this promise of God's came to pass. After all, she had put feet to her faith!

Millicent may have known many things. But what she didn't know was that Cy's early rising had nothing to do with a flight to Chicago. That after seeing Hope, he decided to leave for the Windy City at a later time. That he'd awakened early not to catch an early flight, but to have an early breakfast with the woman who'd captured his attention from the moment she'd entered the room. The woman who looked gorgeous in gold and glamorous in green. That after breakfast, he'd persuaded this woman to give him a tour of the city and to show this ordinarily busy man who now acted as if he had nothing but time on his hands what one did for fun in the Midwest. Millicent didn't know what Cy knew, that as surely as the sun shone and the moon glowed, he would see this woman again, get to know as much as he could about her. What Millicent didn't know was that Cy had fallen in love with Hope Jones as he glimpsed that first smile and had unconsciously pledged his eternal devotion to her as he watched her dance with unabashed reverence and adoration before the Lord.

She felt like Cinderella

"You know what they say. If something looks too good to be true, it probably is." Hope and her cousin, Frieda, were browsing in the suburban shopping center of Oak Park Mall, doing more talking and window-shopping than actual purchasing. The air-conditioned stores provided welcome relief from the August heat, reason enough to linger.

"Girl, I don't understand your butt at all."

"What do you mean?"

"I mean, isn't this what you've been waiting for, praying for? Haven't you been harping to me for two years about wanting God to send you the right man? About believing in miracles and God being able to do anything? Now you're telling me you've met somebody who to hear you tell it is all that and a bag of flaming hot chips, which my friend Rashiid obviously wasn't, I might add, and you *still* trippin'. You pitiful." A miniskirt with matching halter top caught Frieda's eye. "Ooh, girl, look at that outfit! It's calling my name." Frieda was already rounding the corner to enter the shop.

"Go on, Frieda, I'll wait for you out here." Hope walked over to the bench nestled between two large, lush-looking plants. She placed her bags beside her and eased her aching feet out of the low-heeled, leather sandals. Her lesson? Never wear almost-new shoes when going to the mall.

Hope looked out on the people scurrying to and fro in the large building. Frieda was right. She was trippin'. But who wouldn't? As she thought back to the conference and her weekend with Cy, she felt like Cinderella, who got invited to the ball and whose coach turned into a pumpkin after midnight. Even now, almost a month later, it still seemed like a dream.

Remembering her edict from that afternoon, Hope entered the sanctuary with open eyes and a closed heart. She wouldn't let Cy Taylor's good looks cloud her common sense. She purposely avoided eye contact with him and reminded herself constantly that he was off limits, a reminder that seemed justified as she noticed the tall, attractive woman who was at his side after the conference. Hope tried to remain impassive as Cy took the pulpit and began his lecture on Financing Our Future and strove to keep her attention on the seminar topic. She dismissed the times when she thought she'd caught him looking at her, dropping her eyes down to doodle on the mostly blank notepad. She tried not to notice the piercing eyes, strong, squared shoulders, tapered waist and muscled legs, and tried not to think about the man's tapered fingers or the soft, leather shoes that encased his large feet. *You know what they say about men with big* . . . The words in her mind began forming, causing her to physically shake her head, chasing the thought away before she could hear its conclusion.

Later that day, she learned he was engaged to the woman she'd spotted at the seminar, the one who had followed his every move and seemed to hang onto his every word. *Yeah, she looks more his type.* She was tall and slender with symmetrically perfect features and long, straight hair. It had to be a weave. Surely God couldn't have graced her with a perfect body *and* long hair! Surely in His mercy, He'd leave some imperfection requiring man's feeble if inadequate intervention. It may not be hers, but Hope had to admit, the weave was tight!

As were her clothes, as she remembered the obviously designer suit. Her nails were perfectly shaped and colored in a classic, French-tip design; her shoes looked as if they were brand new and cost not a penny under five hundred dollars. She appeared poised and confident, like a model out of *Vogue* magazine or a music video. They always got the good ones!

Hope fought the feeling of jealousy that rose up unexpectedly at the thought that this woman would be so blessed as to have a man like Cy. It was just as well; he would never go for a woman like her. That was why after the seminar, she'd headed directly to the rehearsal hall, changed clothes and started stretching for dance practice. She focused all her thoughts and energy on the musical and their routine, forcefully blocking out any thought or image of Cy Taylor. She thoroughly enjoyed Pastor Montgomery's message that night and was thankful for the Holy Spirit, because in His presence, Hope's thoughts turned totally away from what's his name.

For once, Hope was thankful for the hectic pace the next day. With so many details still needing attention, she had been unable to attend either the morning or afternoon session. She refused to acknowledge that she secretly wanted the opportunity to see Cy again, if for no more reason than to be able to stare at someone that gorgeous in person. God knew that was probably as close as she'd ever come to someone like him. Hadn't it been rumored that he was a millionaire? It was all the more unlikely that she'd be of any interest to him. As it was, she was praying that Southwestern Bell would let her phone stay on until her next payday. No, it was unlikely that someone who lived from portfolio to portfolio would want someone living from paycheck to paycheck.

Even so, her heart fluttered that evening when she entered the sanctuary and looked up to find his gaze unmistakably fastened on her. She recovered quickly, dropping her eyes and easing up the aisle to take a seat near the back of the church. The man God had for her would be more than another pretty face. Checking her watch, she looked toward the doors. Rashiid had left a message earlier that day saying he might make it to the musical after all.

And in fact, he did. She was glad for the distraction, and after ministering with the Angels of Hope, the last group to come on before Righteous, she was thankful that she had a man to sit by and enjoy the rest of the evening. On top of that, Millicent, who a member had been oh so glad to inform her was the name of Cy's fiancée, had come to the musical looking as though she'd literally just stepped off a haute couture fashion runway. She wore a sleek, black designer dress, with tiny silver threads throughout. The dress was almost ankle length, with a deep, yet modest slit up the back. The bodice also dipped in the back, again stopping before it became ungodly but leaving enough skin to cause a weaker man to lust. Her hair was swept up in an elegant chignon, with tiny tendrils swirling down the sides and in the back. She wore diamond earrings with a matching necklace. Her shoes were silver, with a pointed toe and ankle straps which were, quite frankly, the baddest silver shoes Hope had ever seen. She sat directly behind Queen Bee and Sistah Montgomery, and Hope noticed that Sistah Montgomery spoke to her from time to time. Of course they'd be well acquainted since Cy was one of the associate pastors of the church. As much as she didn't want to admit it, this Millicent woman looked the part of first lady. There was no way around it, and Hope acknowledged these facts reluctantly. The woman was gorgeous.

Hope hadn't seen Millicent or Rashiid before the midnight musical began. Prior to the commencement of services, she had been running around like a chicken with its head cut off, making sure all the various groups were ready to minister. Sistah Stronghart had gotten on her last nerve, issuing orders like an army sergeant, obviously thinking Hope could be in two or three places at the same time. But right before the Angels danced, she had gathered the troupe together for prayer and meditation, and once they'd entered into their own private worship, all the tension and anger and frustration of the day bowed before the presence of God. It was in this spirit she and the young ladies had entered the sanctuary. The first number they ministered to was an upbeat, reggae-tinged, contemporary song entitled "J-E-S-U-S." Over the sounds of a bass-driven hip-hop beat, the 3-4 reggae timing and the rap-infused delivery of the lyrics by the African group Limit X, the Angels whirled and twirled, bringing the young and young at heart to their feet. Standing was the perfect posture for the audience to be in for their next and final selection, a slow, worshipful jazz version of the Baptist Hymn, "Holy, Holy, Holy," performed by the Musical Messengers, gospel's latest number one darlings.

Holy, holy, holy. Lord God Almighty.
Early in the morning, our song shall rise to thee.
Holy, holy, holy. Merciful and mighty.
God in three persons, blessed trinity.

It was as if Jesus Himself entered the room as she danced. Hope could feel His presence envelop her. Indeed, it was as if her feet hardly touched the floor, as if her body became an instrument of the Most High, moving of its own volition while staying in perfect timing and harmony with the other dancers. Tears streamed down her face as the Father seemed to take her in His massive arms, kiss her cheek and whisper words of eternal love and devotion. She knew in those moments that she should never feel lonely and was never alone, that He was always near and would always be with her. She smiled at Him then, and looked into a light so radiant it seemed to fill the entire auditorium. The music seemed to pulsate from within her, and suddenly it was as if she and He were the only ones in the room. No one moved or spoke for several moments after the music ended. For each had entered into their own personal worship with the Savior, their own spiritual serenade led by the Almighty.

Hope's usual excitement in hanging out after service in the

pastors' reception area was dampened by the knowledge that Cy Taylor would probably be there with the lovely Millicent on his arm. Nevertheless, she put on a bright smile, grabbed Rashiid's arm and as always was humbled, giving God all the glory for what they'd witnessed. She'd introduced Pastor King to Rashiid and was shocked when not only did Queen Bee speak to her, but actually complimented her on the AOH ministry. *Wow, wonders never cease,* she remembered thinking before she felt someone's eyes on her.

Cy and Millicent walked over to the Brooks as Hope and Rashiid stood talking to them. Cy was so close Hope could smell his cologne, a subtle, mesmerizing fragrance of sandalwood and spices, musky and poignant even in its toned-down state. She was reserved yet gracious as King introduced them. Cy's large, warm palm engulfed Hope's hand and squeezed it gently. Millicent's handshake was cold, limp. She moved closer to Cy and placed a possessive hand on his arm as she summarily dismissed Hope and engaged in conversation with Sister Vivian, as the Montgomerys had come over to join them.

Soon Millicent, Queen Bee and Sister Vivian were in deep conversation, and Hope turned toward Rashiid, preparing to leave. In that moment, a hand touched her arm, stilling her movements and causing an uncontrolled shiver to shoot up her arm and continue throughout her body. She turned to Cy, who gently and almost imperceptibly stepped away from Millicent and the first ladies, placing his back to them and facing Hope directly. Associate Minister Tyson chose that very same moment to come up to Rashiid, complimenting him on his suit and welcoming him to Mt. Zion. Even though they were in the middle of a crowd, it was as if Hope and Cy had created their own oasis. For a brief moment, the din of noise and mingling masses ceased to exist, and they were alone. It must have been just a few moments, but it felt like forever.

"I enjoyed your dancing. You're incredible." Cy's eyes pulled Hope into their immense depths.

"Praise God," she said softly. Hope's determination to not be moved by Cy was not working.

Cy smiled at her nervousness, knowing that she would be surprised to know that it mirrored his own. "Oh, yes, glory to God for creating someone as lovely as you."

Hope doubted if her wobbly legs could hold her upright, and she squeezed her hands into fists to try and calm her trembling. A thousand words rushed through her mind, but not one of them would come out. Instead, she stood there staring at the man of her dreams like a bump on a stump. *Say something, fool!* "You're too kind," she finally whispered, her eyes lowering as she spoke.

Cy looked around surreptitiously before continuing. Millicent was still engaged in conversation with the first ladies. There must be a God! "I'm staying at the Chateau le Roux," he intoned quietly. "Please call me in the morning. I need to speak with you and, uh, that's not going to be possible tonight."

Hope was flattered for a moment before anger kicked in. The dog! How dare he! His fiancée not five feet from him and here he was trying to hit on her. Well, she was not the one, and she was going to let him know it! She rose up to her full height of five-foot-four and narrowed her eyes for effect as she hissed, "Are you sure your *fiancée* won't mind?" she asked with indignation. Before he could answer, Rashiid rejoined her, and she grabbed his arm and swirled away, leaving Cy standing speechless behind her.

Hope had thought that was the end of it. She was almost glad for the incident because the knowledge that he was a player helped to cool her heated ardor and place more mental distance between them. She'd almost been tempted to go out to breakfast with Rashiid, but her body had other, more pressing ideas. Like sleep. So once again, she'd gone home alone and for once was thankful for the hectic week she'd had. The lack of rest and constant running had allowed her to fall asleep immediately, keeping unwanted thoughts and dreams and unfulfilled promises out of her mind.

No one could have been more shocked when her phone rang the following morning at seven A.M. Hope rolled over to talk to her mama, because only her mama would call her that early on a Saturday morning.

"Hey, Mama," she uttered in a croaked whisper.

There was a moment's pause before a deep voice intoned, "This isn't your mama."

Hope shot straight up in bed, suddenly wide awake. "Who is this?"

"Cy Taylor." Another brief pause. "Good morning."

"Good, uh, good morning." Was she dreaming? She took the phone away from her ear, looked at it and placed it against her ear again. "How did you get my number?"

"I can be fairly resourceful when the circumstances require it. And your statement last night required that I speak with you further, not to mention that I had wanted to speak with you anyway."

"What statement was that?" As if Hope didn't know.

"Why don't you join me for breakfast and we can discuss it?"

Hope's anger began to flair again. That was the problem with handsome men. They thought they could get anybody they wanted. "Look, Mr. Taylor—"

"Please, call me Cy."

"Look, Mr. *Taylor*," Hope repeated emphatically. "You're probably used to getting every skirt that swishes in your direction, but if you think I'm going to rendezvous with a practically married man, you'd better think again!" Hope had thrown back her covers and was now pacing, nude, across her bedroom floor.

Cy wasn't moved. "You're spunky. I like that."

"Look, first of all, I don't appreciate you calling my house like this. Whoever gave you my number was totally out of line and probably had no idea that Millicent was your fiancée. Secondly, I don't know about the women in California, but this woman re-

spects herself and her sisters enough to not hang out with somebody else's man. Now, I don't know your girl personally, but from
what it looks like, she knows you and quite well, I might add. So
do her and me a favor, go back to California and leave me alone!"
Hope was surprising herself with the indignation she felt with this
virtual stranger. Just yesterday she'd almost wet her panties when
the man shook her hand!

Cy remained calm, actually enjoying himself. After so many
women throwing themselves at him, it was refreshing to hear a female try to put him in his place, however misplaced that place she
tried to put him was. "Are you finished?" he asked with a smile in
his voice. "Because if you are, it's my turn."

Hope was silent. She sat back on the bed, grabbing her bed-
spread and covering herself as she did so.

"The person you can get angry at for giving me your phone
number is your pastor, King Brook."

"Pastor?" Hope was incredulous.

"That's right. As far as he knew, you were unattached, and since
he knew I also am single and after I assured him my intentions
were honorable, he had his assistant look your number up so I
could give you a call."

"But I heard . . ."

"Well, you heard wrong. Millicent is not my fiancée. We are
not involved in a relationship of any kind other than that we're
both members of Kingdom Citizens' Christian Center and work
on church-related projects together from time to time."

"But it looked like . . ."

"Looks can be deceiving. Now, are you going to join me for
breakfast or not, because I'm a busy man and if you're not going to
meet me, I can get on a plane and head to . . . a friendlier environment."

Hope smiled for the first time since she picked up the phone.
"Well," she hesitated just to let him know she could. "I *guess* I can
meet you."

"Do you know where this hotel is?"

"I'll find it," she replied.

"Good, is an hour enough time?"

"Yes, I'll see you in an hour."

Hope jumped on the Internet for directions to the hotel. She made it there in just over an hour and, to her surprise and delight, enjoyed a wonderful breakfast with Cy. He was warm and down-to-earth, and though she never would have guessed it, they shared several things in common. For one, his paternal grandparents had lived in Oklahoma, so he and Hope knew many of the same places. They both loved gospel music, especially the more contemporary, nontraditional variety. They both loved to travel, although Hope hadn't traveled nearly as much as Cy. And they both loved God. Cy also seemed impressed with her writing. He was pleasantly surprised to learn she'd written the poetic piece delivered right before their final dance number the night before. He'd actually done a little acting back in his college days, memories of which evoked more than a little laughter as they sat enjoying the morning.

Hope was more than pleased with Cy's company as they sat eating and sharing, a pleasure that continued as he asked her to show him around town. She was a bit worried about how his over six-foot frame would fit into her little MG, but he pressed the seat all the way to the back, tilted the cushion and made himself at home. She took him around the Plaza where his upscale and expensive hotel was located, then down to some of the more touristy sites like the Crown Center Shopping Center and the famed 18th and Vine jazz district. They toured the Negro Baseball League Museum and the Mutual Musicians' Union, the first of its kind for Black jazz musicians. They sat down and listened to an impromptu jazz session in progress before having lunch at Papa's, a neighborhood hole in the wall with the best hamburgers in town. Given his love for jazz music and good food, he was duly impressed with Hope's tour and with her.

They went back to his hotel and spent more time in the lounge area, sipping drinks and getting to know each other. Finally Hope, thinking that surely she was keeping the man from important business, feigned an appointment and said she had to be on her way. Cy looked visibly disappointed. Later, Hope wanted to kick herself because she missed him even before she went through the hotel doors. Before she left, however, Cy had given her his home, office and cell numbers and then stood to walk her to the door. He waited with her as the valet brought her car around, then waited as she stepped inside. He leaned down and looked meaningfully into her eyes. Hope stopped breathing, feeling she would faint if she didn't leave that very moment. Cy sensed her "need to flee" and placed a hand on her arm. The caress, though gentle, sent shards of energy through her. She gripped the steering wheel to keep from throwing her hands around this man and kissing him with the passion of a woman who'd been celibate for far too long.

"Thank you for a wonderful day," he said softly.

"You're welcome," she replied. She started breathing again, inhaling and exhaling in short, jerky beats.

Cy leaned forward slowly and licked his lips. Hope closed her eyes. The kiss was soft and chaste and brief—and on her cheek! Her lips immediately got an attitude. "Until next time?" he whispered, the breath fanning the tendrils of hair around her ears.

Hope swallowed but couldn't speak. Instead she sat mesmerized, staring at his lips. A car pulled in behind them, thankfully jolting her out of immobility. She simply nodded and put her car in gear. She didn't remember the drive home. She entered her apartment as if on a cloud and sank into her couch still dazed. The message light was flashing, and she punched it numbly. She recognized Cy's voice immediately, and once again her breath caught in her throat. At this rate, she'd need CPR every time she was near the man. Then she thought of Cy giving her CPR, and her breathing resumed, quick and erratic. "You are a very special woman, Ms. Hope Jones," he said with certainty. "Thanks again for the day. I look forward to returning the favor soon, by inviting you to Los Angeles."

Hope and Cy had spoken by phone often since the conference at Mount Zion Progressive. It seemed they never ran out of things to talk about, and Cy was knowledgeable about so many topics, Hope could listen to him all day long. He'd wanted her to visit him in Los Angeles right away, but they'd tentatively agreed she'd come two months later, in October, when she could get time off from work. Everything had happened so quickly, so unexpectedly. Maybe this was why Hope was having such a hard time accepting the situation as real. She kept thinking that the clock was going to start chiming twelve and she'd have to run out of the ball, leaving behind a glass slipper.

But it wasn't a glass slipper but a leather sandal that Hope slipped her foot into as she got up from the bench to rejoin Frieda, who judging from the time she'd been inside, had obviously decided to buy the outfit she'd seen in the window along with half of the rest of the store.

God, my Jehovah,
Awesome Wonder

Cy's eye roved impassively over the standing-room-only Sunday morning crowd. Praise and worship was in full swing. If the swelling numbers were any indication, Kingdom Citizens' would definitely need a larger building sooner than anticipated. As it was, the church had gone from one to three morning services per Sunday, and there was talk of adding an extra service to accommodate the thousands of members who attended the midweek prayer hour and Bible study. This thought caused a slight frown to crease Cy's brow. Pastor Montgomery was trying to talk him into taking on a more visible teaching role in the ministry, perhaps even presiding over one of the Sunday services or heading up a midweek service, should one be added. Although Cy would do almost anything to help his friend and spiritual mentor, he knew God was moving him in a different direction, and that in fact, Cy wasn't even sure he would continue in the ministry in his present position. He felt that his would become more of a supportive, behind-the-scenes role, one where his visibility would be limited to the board and business rooms instead of the pulpit.

The fact of the matter was Cy had never been comfortable in his role as a minister, that he'd only agreed to be an associate minister during a time when the church was sorely in need of competent male leadership. The membership had literally exploded in the last three years, and on top of that, Pastor Montgomery's teaching had become more and more in demand both nationally and internationally. Pastor Montgomery was looking for a strong right-hand man, someone he could depend on to continue to lead the congregation during the times when the call of God would lead him around the world. Cy's brow creased again. He was not that man, and the time was swiftly approaching when he would have to let Pastor Montgomery in on this fact.

Cy shifted in his chair and looked at the other ministers sitting in the pulpit. His glance rested on Allen Anderson, a quietly intelligent man in his late fifties, who'd been at the church since its inception. As sincere as Pastor Anderson was, however, and as much as he loved God, Cy knew that he didn't possess the depth Derrick needed to help him lead the masses on a regular basis. He quickly scanned the other three associate ministers sitting around him and just as quickly dismissed them as possibilities. The first, Dave Kroenig, was knowledgeable and charismatic enough. Unfortunately, he was in the middle of a messy divorce, one that would surely overshadow his effectiveness in leading the congregation. Another, Brother Ben Snyder, led such a sin-filled life that Cy was loath to sit next to the man, lest lightning strike him down for being such a hypocrite in the pulpit. Cy knew he wasn't perfect, but Jesus! Was there no end to the testing of God's mercy? Kenneth Brown, a young man in his twenties, showed great promise and, out of all of the other men, was the one whom Cy would embrace most readily. He didn't know whether the man had the maturity necessary to handle a position of such authority, but maybe with mentoring he could in time.

Cy felt an intense stare and turned his attention from the choir to the crowd. Millicent. He'd figured as much, although there were more than a few women during each service who tried to catch his eye. He would never get used to the scrutiny, yet he'd learned to live with it. He managed a slight smile and nodded briefly. Millicent smiled and gestured that she needed to talk to him. What else was new? Maybe meeting her for a quick lunch wouldn't hurt. After all, during the conference in Kansas, it appeared she'd finally gotten over the idea that he was her husband and realized that a friendship was all they'd ever have. She'd spent most of her time there with King's wife and Sister Vivian. Millicent would make someone a good wife, and he sincerely wished her the best. Yes, he'd meet with her and help her out as best he could. She, like all the other women who clamored for his attention, deserved to find happiness in her life, and he would do whatever he could to make that possible.

Cy continued his perusal of the Sunday churchgoers. He checked out the band members, grooving in sync as they led the congregation in glorious praise. He gave a quick nod to Darius Crenshaw, the minister of music who was largely responsible for the success of the Kingdom Citizens' Chorale. Theirs was one of the best and most sought after choirs in the country, and Darius had become a celebrity with the release of his CD, *D&C, Darius and Company*. God had gifted Darius tremendously, and on top of a voice that Gabriel would envy, the man was phenomenal on keyboards, held his own on the saxophone and could pinch hit for the drummer should the need arise. He was self-assured without being cocky. Genuinely kind, with the type of sensitivity women drooled over. Like Cy, Darius had his share of problems with the ladies. He was what women labeled a pretty boy, in addition to being successful and single. They had shared war stories on occasion, and Darius was one of the few Kingdom men able to truly empathize with what Cy went through. Cy thought about Darius for Millicent. Maybe they'd make a love connection. As far as Cy knew, there was no one serious in Darius's life at the moment. He knew that Darius had been married and that his wife, had left him for another man. That undoubtedly had hurt, but that had been a few years ago. Cy knew Darius had dated a couple other women, but it obviously wasn't serious. He also knew that Stacy, who worked in the youth ministry, had aspirations where Darius was concerned, but such feelings had obviously not been mutual between them. Cy remembered hearing a rumor that Darius was gay, but had dismissed it immediately as a vicious lie probably started by a woman scorned. Yeah, Darius would definitely be considered a good catch by any female's standards.

Darius gave the signal, and soon the sanctuary was filled with the illustrious sounds of "God, My Jehovah," one of the original singles from Darius's CD.

God, my Jehovah, Awesome Wonder
Full of power, full of might
God, my Jehovah, Lord, Redeemer
God, my Father, my Delight.

Immediately, worshippers began standing throughout the congregation to become active participants in the praise and worship process. Cy smiled at the looks of reverence and awe on faces lifted toward Christ. His head nodded in time to the beat as his eyes continued to scan the masses. As his eyes took in different women in various stages of worship, another woman's essence filled his mind. Hope. He closed his eyes and smiled as thoughts of their recent conversations bubbled up and into his consciousness. What a delightful surprise she'd proven to be. He'd become more and more enamored each time he talked to her. He couldn't put his finger on what it was that made her different exactly, but somehow she reached places inside him no other woman had been able to touch. She was the only woman in a long time in which he'd thought her name and the word "wife" in the same sentence. That revelation had startled him initially, but he found himself warming to the idea more and more. In fact, he'd decided to share his thoughts with Pastor before long because, even though she didn't know it yet, Hope Jones was going to be his wife.

He opened his eyes, still smiling, and looked directly into the eyes of Millicent Sims. Millicent had thoughts of marriage on her mind as well. Thoughts that included Cy Taylor and did not include Hope Jones.

With or without you,
I'm moving on

Tai poured the glass of wine she'd vowed not to have. She intended to have all her faculties about her when she talked to King, wanted her mind to be clear. But when the clock struck two A.M. and King still wasn't home, she couldn't take it anymore. She reached for calm in the guise of a glass of Merlot.

Tai was too through. King had obviously taken her silence for consent, her kindness for weakness. It was now August, the third month of their impasse, and he hadn't done one thing to let her know he held any desire to see their marriage continue. No, instead the nights away from home became more frequent, he was creeping in later and later in the wee morning hours. After his initial questioning and seeming reluctance to Tai's taking the guest room, he'd actually endorsed it by bringing in some items she had left in the master bedroom closet. Through all of this, Tai remained silent. She said nothing, but she observed everything.

In the past, she'd yell, issue ultimatums and cry. During his blatant affair with Tootie a decade earlier, she and the kids had moved out for a brief period, before she and King reconciled and they bought this place. After the second affair, with Karen, he'd moved out. And now, here she was again. She was estranged and alone, in another room, another bed, apart from her husband. Her quiet demeanor hadn't brought him back to her; instead, it seemed to push him farther away. She'd been fasting and praying and concentrating on God and herself. She'd lost weight, bought a new wardrobe including some fancy negligees that King had yet to see, and further enhanced the updated hairstyle she'd adopted earlier by adding more golden highlights. She'd done so well in her computer class that the instructor had encouraged her to pursue a degree in computers or a related area. She'd continued, and was taking the advanced course.

And she felt good. For the first time in a long time, she felt worthy of respect and adoration. Where before she'd just seen herself as the children's mama, she now felt like a woman, her own woman again, sexy and self-assured. She felt that she had something to offer, not only to her husband, but the body of Christ. Her working with Vivian and the S.O.S. Summit had restored a confidence she hadn't realized was lacking. She was excited about spending the upcoming time in California, excited about God doing a new thing in her life. Because that was how she felt; like God was up to something, something good.

These were wonderful transformations taking place, things a wife wanted to share with her husband. But she and King rarely spent time alone these days. Most of their conversation was limited to the dining room table, and then most talk was directed to Princess and the twins. King had been accepting more and more out-of-town speaking engagements, and more often than not, his secretary knew his schedule better than she did. When King was in town, he spent long hours at the church and on church business. Then, when he was through with God's business, he was spending time with her. His other woman, April.

He'd been the epitome of discretion since the bistro fiasco, but Tai wasn't fooled. Of course, she'd heard about the little witch's visit to the church parking lot and, while not able to prove it, was sure April had King's private number at the church. How could he conduct his adulterous affair from God's house? Just steps away from the pulpit. Was he crazy, or had he just lost his mind? No, Tai knew the affair was still going on and wasn't sure April was the only woman tied to King's affections. Several times in the last month, someone had called the house, only to hang up when Tai answered the phone. Tai had caller ID, but the person blocked their number so she still didn't know who was calling. King assured her it wasn't April, and that he hadn't given anyone else their number. Tai wasn't convinced.

Tai walked from her bedroom down to the kitchen and refilled her glass. She grabbed a bag of popcorn, then, looking at the wall clock in the kitchen, changed her mind. She didn't want to eat this late or this early depending on how one looked at it. Focusing on the time made her angry all over again. What kind of man would be so disrespectful, almost flaunt an affair, coming in at all times of night with no explanation and no remorse? Well, she'd been boo-boo the fool one time too many. It was time to shit or get off the pot.

Working on her outline for the Sanctity of Sisterhood Summit had caused Tai to do some deep thinking regarding her own situation, her own life. What kind of example was she being to the body of Christ, to women in the faith, to be in a situation where adultery was being continually committed and not do anything about it? What kind of example was she setting for her own daughters? That it was all right for their father to sneak around? That turning one's cheek and eyes and ears in another direction and feigning ignorance was the solution? And if it was, for how long? Did love really conquer all, especially when that love was one-sided? In spite of all that had happened, Tai had been willing to fight for the marriage. But she would not, could not do it alone.

She'd simply intended to tell King her upcoming plans regarding her trip to California, but King's late arrival home had allowed her too much time to think, and by the time she heard his footsteps on the stairs, a whole other conversation had formulated in her mind. She'd thought that maybe this time a different tactic would bring different results. And she'd gone back and forth on what she wanted those results to be. Well, now she knew. She was not going to stay where she was not wanted. And she was not going to share her husband.

"We need to talk," Tai stated simply as King passed her in the hall on his way to the master bedroom. He didn't stop or turn around. Tai followed him into the bedroom. "Did you hear me? We need to talk and we need to talk now."

King didn't say a word. He walked over to the sitting area and set down his briefcase. Then he walked over to the dresser and took off his watch, cuff links, tie pin and solid gold bracelet. Still not speaking to or acknowledging Tai, he walked past her to the large, walk-in closet where he started to undress. Tai's patience was wearing thin; in fact, it was gone. She turned and walked from the room. King thought she'd changed her mind about conversing, but she'd only gone to refill her wineglass and to place the bottle in her room for easy access. She walked back into the master bedroom and sat on the edge of their four-poster, brass bed. If looks could kill, King would have been a dead man.

"It's late, Tai, let's talk tomorrow," King stated wearily, walking naked from the closet to the bathroom. After twenty years of marriage he had the audacity to close the door. Without having to think for a second, Tai could picture exactly what he was doing. How he looked when he used the rest room, which hand grabbed the toothbrush and which one the toothpaste, how he held the washcloth to his face after cleansing it with the special soap he used for acne-prone skin, everything about his bathroom ablutions were committed to her memory from years of watching him perform his bedtime ritual. King's closing the door made her feel the slap's sting, a slap that only fueled her unchecked anger. She walked over and pushed open the door. "I'm out of tomorrows, King, we need to talk now."

King finished gargling, spit out the mouthwash, grabbed a washcloth and wiped his mouth and looked at her warily in the mirror before turning around and walking past her toward the bed.

Tai watched his retreat with a clinical albeit not total detachment. Even in her anger, her belly did a mild flip-flop at the sight of his well-toned buttocks gliding above strong, hard thighs and beneath a smooth, muscled back. That feeling lasted for only an nth of a second, followed by a certain nausea at the thought that that ass had probably been hovered over the open thighs of April Summers for most of the night. It certainly hadn't hovered over hers in quite some time, and Tai knew that King's was an ass that had to hover somewhere. Celibacy was not his ministry, not at all. She followed him to the bed and stood over it as he walked around and got under the covers, repositioning his pillows before lying back with the determination of one who wanted nothing more than to sleep at this moment. It was not to be; Tai had some things to say.

"You know, King, I thought it would be different this time. I thought that after I ran into you and your whore at the restaurant that you'd see the error of your ways and change them. I thought you'd come to me seeking forgiveness, apologizing for your transgressions and begging for another chance. I imagined the conversation you'd have with her, letting her know that the affair was over, that it had just been about sex for you, but that your wife and your family meant everything, much too much to throw it all away for some peepee." King looked over questioningly but didn't comment. "Yeah, peepee, pink p-u-s-s-y. That is the color of the one you've been looking at lately, isn't it?" Tai felt her anger mount and tried for a bitter laugh that came out more as a choking, strangling sound. King lay back, closed his eyes and didn't move.

Tai stood for a moment, quietly watching as her husband feigned sleep, or disinterest or both. Similar to when she'd first seen April, Tai's raging anger was replaced by an eerie calm, as if a force outside her was in control. Indeed, only seconds before, she'd empathized with the spouses who murdered their mates in fits of passion, because King's lack of interest in her had caused thoughts of violence to flitter in and out of her mind with increased regularity. But now, suddenly, she was calm. Focused. Determined. But for a split second she had imagined an AK-47 with her finger on the trigger.

Before she could embellish the image in her mind, Tai moved from the bed and crossed over to the sitting area, picking up a picture she and King had taken on their fifteenth anniversary. This had been one of the good years, she thought as memories from that celebration filtered through her mind. The church had given them a trip to Hawaii that year, and this picture had been taken as they were going out to dinner. The woman in the picture seemed like a stranger to Tai, with bright, shining eyes full of love and happiness for the man at her side. King looked especially handsome in his white silk suit with collarless, colorful Versace shirt. One arm was placed protectively on Tai's waist, his other hand resting possessively on her shoulder. Tai remembered how they'd walked on the beach that night, made love under a full moon like two love-starved teenagers. She remembered the joy of their time in paradise, the renewed passion, the renewed commitment, the feeling that their marriage had faced the battles and overcome them; that they had come to the river Jordan and crossed over to the other side. Tai put down the picture and turned back to King, who still lay unmoving. No, they hadn't crossed the river. It was still in front of them. Pharoah's army in the guise of a woman named April was blocking the path behind them, and Moses was nowhere to be found. She walked to the edge of the bed and stood over her husband.

"I'll be in California the entire month of September," she said, having come up with this idea on the spot and voicing it simultaneously. Before, she had planned to fly in every weekend. "While I'm gone, decide whether you want your other women or this family, because you can't have both. I'm through waiting. When I come back, with or without you, I'm moving on." She drained her glass and, like a gauntlet, threw it down on the bed. She then turned and without a backward glance walked out the door.

King waited a moment after the door closed before opening his eyes. He stared at the door and then at the empty wineglass on the bed beside him. Drops of deep red Merlot wine, eerily resembling stains from their marital wounds, dotted the plush comforter. Sleep didn't come immediately for King that night. In fact, as the fingertips of dawn brushed the horizon and slices of sunlight streaked into the room, Tai's calm, quiet words still rang in King's ears while the escape of slumber eluded him.

Girl, you know you need to quit

Vivian and Tai moved slowly through the throng of women still milling around the hotel's lobby. Even though the day's activities had long been over, long enough for Vivian and Tai to retreat to Tai's suite and change into comfortable warm-up outfits, clusters of women still stood in groups talking. They were no doubt adding their thoughts and ideas to the topic that had been discussed in thorough and blatant honesty this day, Sacred Sex. Upon seeing the first ladies pass by, one young lady broke away from her group and walked in their direction. As she neared them, Vivian could see tears in the young lady's eyes. She smiled at Vivian, but her focus was on Tai.

"Sister Tai?" she began tremulously, the intensity of her emotions causing her voice to quiver. "I just wanted to personally thank you for what you said today. You really blessed me. I've always felt so guilty about the affair I had with the head of the deacon board at the last church I attended. I thought . . ." The lady stopped and wiped the tears flowing unabashedly down her face, unable to go on.

"Shhh, it's all right, my sister," Tai intoned gently, taking the young woman by the arm and leading her toward a sitting area in the center of the hotel's lobby. Vivian followed silently. "Admitting

our faults is half the battle, asking forgiveness and moving past our
sins into lives of liberty is the victory we have in Christ."

The woman looked at Tai with admiration and respect. "It's
just that nobody talks about this, not the way you guys did today.
It's like, we know that people cheat and stuff, but we never talk
about the man's role in these relationships, even men in the church
who perpetuate this kind of behavior. I'm not making excuses, but
I was only seventeen when me and this deacon started seeing each
other. He told me if I said anything, I'd be kicked out of the
church. That nobody would believe me. And he was right." The
woman was becoming increasingly emotional, and Tai grabbed her
hand, calming her by steadily patting it while looking straight into
her eyes, into her tormented soul. The woman took a deep breath
and continued. "When I finally got the nerve to go to my pastor
and tell him what was going on, he blamed me. He asked me what
I'd done to encourage the relationship. He said I must have done
something to lead this man on, that I knew he was married, that I
should have said no. He then questioned whether I was even
telling the truth in the first place. I was directing the young adult
choir at the time. They ended up making me give up that position
and all other positions of visibility in the church. Then somebody
leaked that I was trying to ruin this man's marriage by lying. His
wife found out, cornered me and called me everything but a child
of God. I don't blame her—she had every right to be mad. I stayed
away from church for two years."

Tai's heart went out to the young woman before her. How
many other young female lives had been damaged, even ruined, at
the hands of "men of God" who were little more than sexual
predators in God's house? She thought of King and could only
wonder at the women she didn't know who had fallen prey to his
ministrations. She thought of April, and while there was no love
lost between her and King's mistress, she admitted it took two to
tango and reminded herself that April had not spoken vows of

fidelity to her, King had. She could see the faces of women who stared at her husband in awe as he ministered, that looked up in open adoration at the oracles of God coming from the mouth of a Black Adonis. She thought of that handsome face, that sexy smile, those bright, flirtatious eyes. And the thought made her want to puke. Her eyes began to water as the woman continued to weep before her. This was God's precious daughter. Hurt and betrayed in the very place that should have been her refuge. Misused and mistreated by the very ones who should have been leading and guiding her young life into doing great things for God and His Kingdom. Instead, her excitement had been replaced by anger, and her zeal had turned to shame. Tai thought of the woman, this deacon's wife, who'd cursed instead of questioned. Again, she thought of how her behavior toward the young, single women in her church was often cautious at best, her interaction with them often shielded behind a wall of defensiveness and skepticism. She never knew whether theirs was a sincerity to serve God or a desire to sleep with her husband. How many women had she judged unfairly? How many women had she accused in error? The woman now watched quietly as a myriad of emotions played across Tai's face. Tai looked at her and saw all the young, innocent, single women at Mount Zion. She smiled warmly, wiping away the last traces of this dear sister's tears. "I'm glad you came back to God's house," she whispered, pulling the woman into a long hug. "Your sins have been forgiven and God loves you." Tai pulled back to once again look into the woman's eyes. "And so do I."

The woman stood, her eyes now dry and bright with the hope of a new day. Vivian walked over as the woman turned to go. "He whom the Son sets free is free indeed!"

"No doubt," Tai said as she watched the woman walk away with confidence. "No doubt." They continued walking toward the entrance, being stopped every few feet by more thankful summit participants. Finally, they reached the entrance where Vivian's car awaited them. It had been a long, yet fruitful day, and both Vivian and Tai looked forward to an evening of relaxation before the usual strenuous Sunday services the next day.

Traffic was light as Vivian deftly navigated down La Cienega Boulevard, turning right on Slauson Avenue and heading toward the beach community of Playa del Rey via the 90 Freeway. She punched the talk button on her hands-free cell phone to call Derrick, whom she felt she barely saw these days. He'd been incredibly understanding during this busy time, even volunteering to watch the children himself a time or two in lieu of the nanny. Vivian smiled as she thought of the ways she'd pay him back for his consideration.

"Hello?" His voice could still move her.

"Hey, baby."

"Viv, where you at?"

"I'm headed to Penguins in Playa. Tai and I are going to grab a quick bite and then take a walk on the beach to unwind."

"Aw, baby, I was going to take you to dinner tonight. Mother Moseley has taken the kids to a movie, along with a couple of her grandkids."

Vivian could hear the disappointment in his voice. It mirrored her own. Yet, as she stole a quick glance at her friend, she knew this time she was spending with Tai was invaluable. Her friend needed her more than ever, and she knew she could do nothing else but be there. "I tell you what," she continued, lowering her voice and adopting a smoky, sensual tone as she spoke. "You go ahead and grab some dinner, and later, when I get home, I'll make sure you get dessert."

Derrick's low moan was clear evidence that he'd gotten her drift.

"Well, baby, you know nobody serves up dessert like you do. How could I say no to an offer like that?"

"I was hoping you wouldn't be able to."

"You hoped correctly."

"Okay. I'll see you soon. Love you, babe." Vivian clicked off from Derrick and immediately punched in another speed dial number. Her precocious nine-year-old picked up the line.

"Yo, what up?"

"What up?" Vivian asked slowly and pointedly.

"Oh, hi, Mom!" Derrick answered a bit sheepishly, having thought this was his friend Malcolm whom he'd just paged. "I thought you were someone else."

"Not your English teacher, I hope. Derrick, I've told you how I object to you using that ridiculous street language, no matter how cool it is. I want to hear sentences from you—subjects, nouns and verbs. Are you listening?"

"Yes, ma'am."

"Good. How are you doing, baby? Where's your sister?"

"She's over at the video games. Daddy let us go with Miss Moseley to the movies. I'm getting ready to buy some popcorn."

"Well, be a good boy and offer to buy Miss Moseley's snacks, too, okay?"

"Okay."

"And look after your sister. I want you guys to have a good time and not get into any trouble. Do you understand me?"

"I hear you, Mom. I'll be good, promise." Vivian could hear the cashier asking for D-2's order. "I gotta go. Love you."

"Love you, too, baby."

Vivian and Tai entered the quaint, candle-filled restaurant a short time later. It was about an hour before the dinner crowd would start to arrive, so there weren't many others in the establishment. The waiter seated them at a small table by the window and came back a short time later with a glass of Perrier with lime for Vivian and a glass of Merlot for Tai. They decided to split an order of manicotti and ordered individual Caesar salads. A basket of warm Italian bread was placed between them, and small bowls artistically filled with olive oil and balsamic vinegar were deposited in front of them as they spoke.

"Vivian," Tai began, taking a piece of bread and dipping it into the oil and vinegar creation. "Don't ever take for granted how blessed you are to have a good marriage."

Vivian paused, chewing her bread and taking a swallow of water before answering. "I don't. I know Derrick and I are blessed, and I'm grateful. Don't think we don't have our disagreements, because we do. But we're committed to having a successful marriage, and we work very hard to keep it fresh, keep it interesting."

"What do you do? To keep it fresh, I mean."

Vivian hesitated. Tai was her friend and all, but some things just weren't meant to be shared outside the bedroom! "Now, girlfriend, you're asking a lot," she began playfully. "I can't tell you all our secrets, but if I can swear you to secrecy, I will tell you one."

There was a twinkle in Tai's eyes as she leaned forward. "I swear I won't tell a soul."

"Well," Vivian began tentatively, knowing the impact her following statement would make. "I let Derrick sleep with other women."

Tai brought the wine away from her mouth, placing the glass gingerly on the table. She grabbed a napkin to catch the wine she'd been trying to swallow, a drop of which was now running down her cheek. Small splotches of red wine dotted the crisp, white linen tablecloth as well as her baby pink sweats. "Girl, stop! You could have told me anything but this! Derrick and other women?" Tai once again reached for the wineglass and took a long sip, a wide-eyed stare trained on Vivian.

"Sorry, girl! I didn't mean to make you spill your wine," Vivian stated, almost sorry she'd misled Tai. "But it's not what you're thinking."

"Well, what is it then?"

"I'm always the other woman."

"Girl, what *are* you talking about?"

Vivian began again, her voice low, her eyes twinkling. "See, I've got all these outfits representing different women. I've got wigs, glasses, all kinds of costuming to help me transform into whomever Derrick wants to be with that night. If he wants to be with a hootchie, I've got the booty-hugging, jungle-print miniskirt. If he wants a blond beach babe, I've got the waist-length blond wig for him to sink his fingers in and the thong bikini for him to wrap his hands around."

Tai was staring at Vivian as if she were a stranger. Vivian went on.

"If he wants a Las Vegas showgirl, I've got the sequins and the glitter, the feathers and the pumps. If he wants a stripper, well, you get the picture."

Tai, still staring, shook her head slowly from side to side. A slow, earnest smile teetered briefly at the corners of her mouth before widening into a cat-who-ate-the-canary grin. "My, my, my— you *have* been holding out on me, haven't you? Now I find out Mrs. First Lady of the West is wearing Daisy Dukes, thongs and feathers! You go, girl!"

"This actually started several years ago. Derrick was having problems with this woman at church. He was really attracted to her and he told me so. Of course I was upset. No woman likes to know her husband is attracted to somebody else. It made me feel insecure, question my beauty, and his fidelity."

Tai nodded her understanding.

"But in the end, I was glad he told me. Once I was convinced he wasn't sleeping with her, it allowed us to work the problem out together. I asked him what it was about her that attracted him. He told me it was a sexual hunger she radiated, and her legs. I had to admit she was sexy, and always wore these short, tight skirts.

"Well, I decided to fight fire with fire. I went shopping, and when I got finished, I called Derrick. I told him I had thought a lot about his dilemma and had actually found someone with the attributes he lusted after. I convinced him to go to this hotel and talk to the woman, that she was a friend of mine who I felt, after he spent time with her, would free him of his physical obsession with the redhead."

"And he went?"

"Oh, not easily. I had to do a selling job like nobody's business. First I told him she was a therapist and it would only be a mental exercise. He still balked. So I played the money card—said I'd flown her in, paid a large nonrefundable fee, put her up in the Four Seasons and couldn't contact her as she had been instructed not to answer the phone."

Tai leaned back, enjoying Vivian's playful dalliance with deceit. "I bet that got him out of the office."

"Faster than you can say ching-ching."

"And when he knocked on the door, there you were."

"In a fuschia, barely-there halter top and air-constricting miniskirt. I had on four-inch shiny gold pumps. The red wig I wore dusted the top of my behind, and when I kissed him, I left a coat of fire red lipstick on his shocked lips." Vivian laughed at the memory. "We made love all night long. Shortly afterward, Miss Redhead moved her membership, and Derrick never mentioned her again."

The women were silent as the waiter brought out their salads and refilled their glasses. They ate for a while, each deep in thought, before continuing the conversation.

"Maybe that's what I should have done. Been more creative, given him more variety, lost the weight sooner."

Vivian put down her fork and grabbed her friend's hand. "Stop that right now. Don't sit here blaming yourself for King's actions. Remember, you're talking to someone who was with you from the beginning, and no one could have loved King, tried to please King, more than you. His affairs are his fault, his problem, and I don't want you sitting here taking the blame."

"But I am partly to blame." Tai spoke softly but without sadness. Vivian was ready to interrupt, but Tai stopped her. "No, I am.

Believe me, girl, being here has been good for me, away from him, away from the children. It's given me time to think.

"King and I never really had time to ourselves. Michael was already on the way when we got married, and he was barely out of diapers when Princess came along. Almost immediately, my focus became the children and his became the church, and somewhere along the way, we lost focus of each other.

"There were definitely times when I could have been more of a wife to King. But then, after the affairs started, I became so resentful, so full of bitterness, that I stopped really trying. Part of me never really forgave him for the way he hurt me, the way he made me feel inadequate. And at the same time, I now realize that allowing him to make me feel inadequate was too much power to give any man.

"There were times I'd go for weeks without letting him touch me, especially after I found out his ass had been with someone else. Oh, baby, the store would close up quick. And then I started making him wear a condom."

"A condom, Tai?"

"Well, I didn't know where his dick had been. I didn't want to be sleeping with all the people he'd slept with and all the people they'd slept with." Tai's face had taken on a look of defiance.

Vivian hesitated. How could she really blame Tai for that? "I guess I can see where you're coming from," she began hesitantly. "But wow, Tai. I remember Derrick and me trying to use a condom one time, and we were both so frustrated, we quickly gave up that idea. Instead I got on the pill so—"

"It didn't do much for our sex life either," Tai interrupted. "And it would never last long. After a time or two he'd forget to put it on and I'd forget to ask him to. King has always satisfied me in bed, so it didn't take much to make me forget.

"I've had time to really take a keen look back at how, when and why things changed in our marriage. I haven't been a perfect wife, Viv—"

"Nobody is," Vivian interjected.

Tai became quiet, taking in the ocean view. The gentle rhythm of the tide contrasted with the storm in her soul. "I talked to King before I left," she said, still looking out the window. "Told him it was time to decide—her or me."

Vivian studied her friend intently. "What did he say?"

Tai met Vivian's eye. "Nothing."

"Have you talked to him since?"

"Believe it or not, it seems like more now since I've been in L.A. than the last two months I've been home."

"Maybe that's a good sign."

"It could be. We don't discuss anything deep, the kids mostly and the church. The conversations don't last long. No matter what he says, I'm sticking to my decision. It's either April or our marriage. I'm serious. When I go back home, either she goes or I do. And this time, it's going to be for good. I'm going to get a divorce."

Vivian paused as the waiter delivered their mouth-watering manicotti.

"I know that decision didn't come easy," she said as he walked away. "It's a big step."

"Yes, it is, and I'm ready to take it."

"It will be tough on you, and tougher on the children."

"They are what have made this decision so hard. But Michael and Princess know about their father's indiscretions, have for years, and the twins aren't stupid; they know King and I aren't getting along.

"Besides, I like sex. I miss sex. And before I dry up, I'd rather cut my losses, make a clean break and pray that God will send me somebody who will love me faithfully and solely, for the rest of my life."

"You deserve that kind of love, Tai. I want that for you more than anything in the world."

Tai sat back and crossed her arms. "Can I tell you something?"

Vivian didn't miss the gleam that flashed into her friend's eyes. "Sure."

"I've got a secret admirer."

"Unh-unh!"

"Girl, I'm serious."

"Who?"

"I don't know, it's a secret, dummy!"

"Details, girl, give 'em up!"

"Well, I know it's somebody at the college. In the couple weeks before I came here, someone was leaving little niceties on my windshield. A couple cards, a long-stemmed rose, one day a coupon for a smoothie at this trendy juice bar."

"And you have no idea?"

"I have suspicions. There's this professor that always goes out of his way to speak whenever he sees me. And my computer teacher is always flirting with me. He flirts with everybody, though."

"Get outta here! I didn't even know you had Black instructors."

"Did I say they were Black?"

"Oh—my—God."

"That's right, girl, what's good for the goose is good for the gander." Tai started laughing, and Vivian couldn't help but join in.

"Now, look," Vivian began, trying to adopt a seriousness that she didn't feel. "Two wrongs don't make a right."

"Oh, girl. I didn't say I was going to run to the nearest hotel or jump in the first backseat offered. But I do find both men attractive. Come to think of it, I never paid much attention to men of other races before. I never paid attention to anybody, except King."

Vivian shook her head. Tai had thrown a curve.

"The professor's fine—curly, thick brown hair with smoky gray eyes." Tai cocked her head, visually picturing him as she went on. "I'd say he's in his fifties, 'cause he's got touches of gray at the temples and a little streak through his hair. But he must work out because he's in good shape and he works wonders for a pair of jeans."

"Stop!"

"I'm only admiring God's creation!"

"Uh-huh."

"My instructor, Mike, is a little cutie, but I'm really not interested. If he's thirty I'd be surprised. But he's got this crooked, mischievous smile and the blond-haired, blue-eyed hearty looks of a Nordic Viking. He's very affectionate, always grabbing my hand, rubbing my arms. And it's been so long since King's rubbed anything that chile'—"

"Girl, you know you need to quit. You better get to church bright and early tomorrow 'cause you know you need prayer." Tai and Vivian shared a laugh then as they finished their meal and headed for the beach. Vivian found herself hurrying. All that talk of rubbing and grabbing had made her ready for "dessert."

I am the resurrection
and the life

King had just stepped from the shower when he heard the front doors close. *That would be the twins,* he thought as he toweled himself vigorously. He poured a generous dollop of cocoa butter lotion in his hand and rubbed it on his feet and toes before moving up to his calves, knees, thighs, genitals and buttocks. He poured another handful and wiped down his arms, hands and chest. He hated being ashy.

"Daddy! Grandpa's here!" Tabitha bounded up the stairs and yelled through the doorway.

"We already ate, Dad. Gramps took us for tacos." Timothy's shout was heard as he stood next to Tabitha, just outside the door.

Dad's here? What does he want? "It must be something important," King said aloud, and then to the children, "I'm getting dressed. I'll be right out." His brow furrowed as he grabbed his navy blue Calvin Klein jockeys and slid them on, pulling the matching T-shirt over his head. He reached for the freshly starched and pressed jeans, slipping them on and stepping into his Nikes, all in one continuous motion.

King tried to remember the last time his father had come over unexpectedly. He couldn't. He was almost sure the Reverend Doctor Pastor Bishop Overseer Mister Stanley Obadiah Meshach Brook had never dropped off the kids before. Oh, no. His father was definitely from the old school where children, aside from being seen and not heard, were women's work. The fact that he'd taken them out to eat showed that the old man must be softening up with age.

King tucked his white shirt into his jeans and walked over to the dresser. He splashed on some Armani and donned his watch, bracelet and rings. He walked back over to the closet and grabbed a blue sports jacket before heading for the door. His chest seemed to tighten, and an uneasy feeling settled in the pit of his stomach. Why did he get the feeling that his father's visit was not a social call?

"Hey, Dad." King entered the living room to find his father staring at a large family photo of him, Tai and the kids. Uh-oh.

"Son."

King felt oddly uncomfortable. He and his father had never been very close, but they did share an easy-going relationship honed through mutual respect and shared passion in things relating to ministry. The Reverend, as King's mother often called him, was away from home often, either traveling or fulfilling his myriad duties as pastor, district and national leader, advisor, one-time councilman and evangelist. His mother had always been the stabilizing home influence. King and Mama Max were tight. Usually, that was.

"Uh, can I get you something?"

"A glass of water would be fine."

Just then Tabitha bounded down the stairs and into her father's arms. "Hey, Daddy! Ooh, you smell good. Where you going?"

The Reverend turned around as if waiting for an answer to the question himself. "Baby, go get your grandpa a glass of water."

King turned toward his father as Tabitha headed for the kitchen. "So, Dad, what brings you by?"

The Reverend didn't respond. For someone known for his prolific speech, he could sometimes be a man of few words. He turned back toward the family photo while humming "Jesus Keep Me Near the Cross."

"Here you go, Grandpa."

"Thank you, darling. Now, you run along now. Me and your daddy's talking."

King thought that response interesting. Not a word had been spoken.

Tabitha gave her grandfather another hug. "Okay, Grandpa. Thanks again for dinner. It was fun. See ya later." She started up the stairs and then turned back suddenly. "Is Anna watching us again tonight, Daddy?"

Again both she and the Reverend waited for King's response.

"We'll see," King replied noncommittally. He watched his daughter run up the steps. As if for the first time he noticed her rounding bottom, long, slim legs and graceful yet still childlike movements. King blinked. When had his little girl grown up? The twins had just turned twelve. He turned to his father. "They grow up so fast," he started, hoping that the topic of children would keep the conversation safe. "I don't know where the time goes."

The Reverend walked over to the couch and sat down. He took a long drink of water, belched and wiped his mouth with the back of his hand before finishing the glass and setting it on the coffee table. He leaned back against the sofa, put his chin in his hand and stared off into the distance, into a long, long time ago.

"Yeah, time sho' flies," he began slowly, sounding like a preacher even in the confines of his son's living room. His cadence, combined with the honeyed sound of his Southern drawl, drifted like a warm blanket over the room. "Just seems like yesterday y'all were children. One minute your mama was giving you the tittie, the next thing I knew, you was grown."

King smiled warmly and relaxed. He looked at his watch and walked over to the recliner, sitting at the end of it, elbows on knees. Maybe a little chat with his father wouldn't be so bad after all. Maybe now he and his father could establish the closeness he never knew as a child. Besides, April wasn't going anywhere. Of that, he was certain.

"I know what you mean. Looks like I'm going to have to go out and buy a baseball bat to ward off the young men who think they might have a chance with my daughters. They might, but they'll have to come through me."

"Well, they's comin', that's for sho'. That Danny fella must have called the house fifty times today alone."

"Danny Jackson? Deacon Earl Jackson's boy? How old is he, fourteen, fifteen? If he touches Tabitha, Dad, I swear, I'll beat him like he stole something." King's hands flexed at the thought.

"Aw, son, calm down now. He's just a tall thirteen; seems to be a nice enough kid. Know somethin' about the Word, too."

"You met him?"

"His aunt lives a couple doors down from us. He was conveniently visiting her when the kids came over."

King wasn't ready to hear about his baby liking boys. It was too much. It was too soon. "Convenient, indeed. Me and that boy are going to have a talk."

The Reverend looked at King for a long moment and then asked quietly, "And what are you gon' tell him, son?"

King knew it was a loaded question but answered it anyway. "I'm going to tell him to keep his hands off my daughter!"

"Uh-huh." The Reverend rubbed his chin thoughtfully, still looking into the distance. "And who are you gon' keep *your* hands off of?"

Uh-oh. Here we go. So this is the reason for the unexpected visit. King walked over to the large picture window and looked out into the street. Of course, he knew that the Reverend was aware of his indiscretions, that Mama Max and the Reverend shared almost everything. But he and his father had never talked about that or any other personal aspects of his life for that matter. It just wasn't that kind of relationship. No, their conversations had been ones of God and sports, "churchanity" and Mama Max's cooking. They talked about the children, world events, the weather, fishing, but not the personal stuff. This was new territory. King turned around, crossing his arms over his chest and eyeing his father pointedly.

"What's on your mind, Dad?"

The Reverend reached for a peppermint in the crystal dish on the coffee table. He carefully unpeeled the hard candy from the wrapper, eyeing his son as he did so.

"Your mama and I been married a long time," he began. "Going on fifty years. That's a long time to be with one woman." He sat back and perched his elbow on the couch arm, rubbing his chin with his hand, a thoughtful expression on his face. King walked back over to the chair and sat down. Instead of looking at his father, however, he continued to stare out the picture window. He noticed the beautiful colors that danced across the Midwest, Indian summer sky, compliments of a setting sun. A bird flew across the window and perched atop the bushes, neatly manicured to border the house front. The sparrow cocked its head as if looking at King and saying, "Yes, may I help you?" Or was it, "You know you ain't right." Before King could ascertain the correct message, the bird flew away, and his father resumed speaking.

"When your mama and I first married, I had just got my first church. Your mama was a looker back then, boy. We had practically grown up together, you know, our farms being next to each other and all. We were almost what some might call "kissin' cousins" because your mama's great-auntie had married my daddy's brother's cousin's boy."

King looked at his watch. If his dad was going to recount his entire lineage, it could take all night. The Reverend, nonplussed, droned on.

"From our early years, your mama loved God. I can remember many a Sunday at Cherry Hill Baptist Church when your mama would get up there and recite those speeches and thangs, so nice and cute like. Play that piano and sing like an angel. By the time I was twelve years old, I knew I was gonna be a preacher, and not much after that I knew your mama was gon' be my wife."

King tried to hurry the Reverend along without showing his impatience. "Yes, Dad, Mama has told me these stories many times."

"Uh-huh. Well, we worked hard, your mama and me, building the church, building the family. And then when y'all was still wee young'uns, the Reverend Doctor Elijah Smith from Tuscaloosa, Alabama, held a revival meeting in the town's bingo parlor. Changed my life." The Reverend stopped then, his eyes narrowing as he replayed the events of yesterday on his mind's memory video.

Would you get to the point? "Uh, Doctor Smith, huh?" King asked, glancing at his watch, more pointedly this time.

"Yessirree, Doctor Elijah Smith. I was still a young buck, just a snot-nosed preacher, and man, I thought that fella was somethin'. Boy, could he preach! Well, one of the elders told him about me, and he had me bring a prayer that night. When I got finished, wasn't a dry eye in the place.

"Yes, Lawd, after that night, the good Reverend Doctor invited me to join him for the rest of his revivals, and from that day, my ministry took off. Shoot! Just like a rocket. Next thang I knew, I was gone all the time. And next thang I knew, y'all was grown. I can't tell you the respect I have for your mama, boy. She practically raised you by herself."

"As I recall, you were home enough. I think I've still got some marks on my back from your whuppins to prove it." King smiled while making the statement; he'd long ago forgiven his father for what would now be easily termed child abuse.

"Well, you know the Word says spare the rod—"

"Spoil the child," King finished. "I know, I know."

"But in the meantime and in between times, it would get lonely on the road, you know? And I ain't gon' lie to ya,' son, I didn't always do right, wasn't always faithful to your mama. I was young and foolish, full of myself. And these fine, willin' women would throw themselves at my feet as I went from church to church, behinds out to here, tits out to there. Lord a'mercy! Either the temptation was too strong or I was too weak, one or the otha'. I didn't have the good sense to realize them was the devil's morsels I was tastin'. That I should never have sat down at the table, much less took a meal."

King sat in stunned silence at his father's honesty. He'd had his own thoughts about his father's fidelity in the past, but he would have never voiced them. His father was a well-respected pillar of the community, praised as a role model, seen as an icon of leadership in and out of the church. He'd always commanded the utmost respect, in and out of his home. Any thought of impropriety was never so much as whispered. To his knowledge and remembrance, his mother had always treated the Reverend with the utmost respect. His house had not been one of arguments or unkind words. But who knew what went on behind the bedroom doors?

King did remember the women who'd flirt shamelessly with his father when his mother wasn't around. And he particularly remembered this one woman, Miss Callie Something-or-Other, a pretty, dark-skinned woman with long, coal black hair who used to wear frilly dresses with matching hats and sit in the second row of the church, on the far side by the window. King remembered how he'd gone to the church early one Wednesday before Bible study and went looking for his dad in his study. He couldn't have been more than eight or nine. He'd barged in after barely knocking and stood wide-eyed as his father held Miss Something-or-Other in a less-than-Godly embrace. Miss Callie had jumped away from his father, thanking him for his "counsel" and assuring him she felt better. He remembered her wiping away a couple nonexistent tears from her eyes before bolting from the study. He remembered his father whopping him upside the head and threatening him with a "killin'" if he *ever* came into his study without knocking again. King hadn't thought of this incident for decades, and thinking back on it, he remembered that his mother had never liked Miss Callie, and his mama liked almost everybody. King came back to the present to find his father still speaking.

"Then this woman I'd been seeing was staying at the same

hotel with us at the Dallas convention. Somebody told your mama, and she came up to the room, screaming loud enough to wake Abraham from the dead. She threatened the woman, me and everybody else within the sound of her voice. She came home and bought a gun. I thought the woman had lost her mind." The Reverend laughed heartily at the memory. "It was then I thought I'd better straighten up and fly right. The thought of Maxine with a gun was a powerful convincer."

"So you never cheated on Mama again?"

The Reverend took a long time answering. "I wish I could say that was true," he voiced finally. "Just got good at hiding it. No, it took almost losing your mama before I finally realized what my life would be without her, and found out it wouldn't be much."

"You mean the cancer."

His father nodded and rose from the couch. He walked over to the wall and stared up again at the family portrait. "Yeah, when Maxine had that cancer scare, I finally slowed down enough for God to talk to me. And he showed me some thangs. Showed me how I'd gotten my priorities all confused, all twisted in a bunch. How I'd let the church work consume me and hadn't spent enough time with you children, with your mama. It was in trying to take care of you and your brother and sisters while Maxine was in that hospital that helped me appreciate just what she did, how hard she worked. I prayed to God one night in the hospital chapel that if he would give me back Maxine, I'd show Him how much I appreciated her. I been faithful ever since."

The Reverend turned and looked at his son then. "Lookin' back, I realize that all those other women put together couldn't compare with one Maxine Brook. And now I'm so glad that we made it this far and can look back down through the years and see how far God brought us. That we kept our family together, didn't bring in step this and half that. And you know what else, son? Once I made the commitment to really love Maxine and to only be with her, it wasn't as hard as I thought it would be." He walked over to another picture then, a solo picture of Tai taken ten years earlier.

"You got yourself a good woman, boy. Smart, good-lookin', even after all them babies. You know I knowed her daddy for years before she came along. We used to meet at conferences and such. Mama real special, too. It don't take much to find a female, but it ain't every day you find a woman." He continued, as if to himself as he walked toward the kitchen, "I know one thang. If you got a good, Godly woman, one who knows your faults and still loves you, gives ya four fine children and keeps the home fires burnin' while you're out on the battlefield fighting for the Lord, it's only the biggest fool who lets her go. Y'all got any Coca-Cola?" The Reverend headed toward the kitchen humming "Jesus Keep Me Near the Cross" once again.

King didn't go to April's that night. In fact, he didn't go anywhere at all. Hours after his father left he still sat in the oversized armchair, pondering his father's visit. After following his father into the kitchen and grabbing cans of Coke for both of them, he sat at the breakfast nook with the Reverend and talked for over an hour, his father sharing more of himself with King than he had in years—maybe in forever. They talked of safer, less personal topics, too. They talked about his father's church district and the National Baptist Convention, about Mount Zion Progressive and the church's expansion. They talked about the scorching Midwest summer, the lackluster baseball season and who might go to the Superbowl. When his father left, they'd hugged, an act rarely practiced between them. He'd told his father he loved him, and his father had said the same. Their relationship had gone to another, more intimate level. It was a level King aspired to enjoy for some time to come.

Talking about his parents' marriage made King pause to think of his own. For the first time in years, he went back to the begin-

ning. He remembered how in love with him Tai had been, full of
open admiration. The feeling had been mutual; her shy smile and
gentle nature had melted him like butter. He'd been enchanted
with the sprinkle of freckles across her nose and her full, lush
breasts. He remembered how scared she'd been when he talked her
into having sex that night in Boyd Turner's borrowed "deuce and a
quarter" at the Twin Drive-In. How they'd sneak around to be together because Tai's father was not willing to hear of his daughter
marrying King. Even then he had a reputation with the ladies. But
Tai got pregnant and the father relented. King smiled, remembering their simple wedding on her Aunt Beatrice's hundred-acre
farm. Just family and a few friends, but it had been special. He remembered how the sparkle in Tai's eyes had outshone the water reflected in Aunt Bea's catfish pond, how the surrounding rolling,
green hills dotted with lavender and daisies paled in comparison to
Tai's beauty in her empire-styled gown and rounding belly. Tai had
told him how much she loved him and that this was the happiest
day of her life because her dreams were coming true.

He remembered how Tai had been his cheerleader, his cham-
pion in those early years. How she'd go on and on to whomever
would listen about what a great preacher King was, how he was
going to lead millions, be a real preacher's preacher. He remembered how she used to toil with him on his sermons, assisting him
by looking up information and securing reference materials. Then
she'd take the information and type it up in nice, concise outlines.
How she'd draw large, red hearts in the corner to let him know she
was with him in spirit as he preached from the pulpit, and that she
loved him. She'd walk the streets, with little Michael in tow, passing
out flyers inviting people to service. She'd go to the malls and to
restaurants, to movie theaters and grocery stores. She'd hang them
up at beauty parlors and mom-and-pop establishments. She loved
and mothered everyone who came to the church, enveloping the
ministry in a warmth recognized by everyone and for which she

soon became affectionately known as Queen Bee. While barely an adult herself, she still had a mothering influence. Early on, members sought her out for advice because she was a concerned listener, a trusted confidante. It was no wonder, he mused, that she was such an excellent mother to their children. Instinctively she focused on, gave attention to and nurtured them unconditionally. "Then why doesn't she nurture me?" he asked aloud.

Because you're not here.

King knew His voice, but remained silent. He didn't know if he wanted to have this conversation.

You haven't been here for a long time.

"How can you say that, Lord? I *live* here."

No, you exist here. You sleep, eat, shower and change here. You live at the church. You live at April's.

King wasn't trying to hear this. "I *live* here," he repeated emphatically, like a petulant child.

Where your treasure is, there will your heart be also. Is Tai your treasure?

King was silent. Damn, God was playing hardball!

Son?

"You know I love Tai, Lord. She's the mother of my kids. We've been together since we were their age. How can I help but love her?"

I didn't ask you if you loved her. I asked if she was your treasure.

"I love Tai more than I love anyone else. There're just certain things I need that I don't get from her."

And why do you think that is?

"It's not my fault!"

I wasn't going to bring up the f-word, but now that you mention it . . .

King got up, addressed the empty room. "Look, I never said I was perfect."

Well, at least you didn't lie.

King slumped into the chair in a huff. "I've tried my best. I've done my part. There's no use trying to feed a fire that's long gone out."

Many times, son, one looks at a mound that seems but ashes. However, if one stokes the fire, blows wind on it, tiny, glowing embers that are buried beneath the ashes will start to burn, and those embers will become a flame, and that flame can heat a cold room, or a cold heart.

Was it possible? Was there any chance that he could feel for Tai the way he used to? Feel the passion, the tenderness, the romance that was theirs as newlyweds? He could still remember how his heart used to skip a beat when she walked into the room. How her quiet presence had been the calm in the storm of those early church years.

He put his head in his hands, remembering. King had all but given up on his marriage to Tai, and knew she had done the same. Their separate rooms were but an outward manifestation of an inward truth. They shared the same house but lived separate lives. Was there a way that something that seemed so dead could live again?

I am the resurrection and the life. Remember that, son. Remember me.

King went upstairs and undressed. He sat on the edge of the bed, thinking of everything and nothing at all. He looked at the clock on the bedside table. Ten o'clock in Los Angeles. He grabbed the phone and the piece of paper beside it. He tapped the table abstractedly as he waited for Tai to pick up after being connected to her suite. The hotel's voice mail came on. King hung up without leaving a message. But when he went to sleep that night, he dreamt of Tai. It was a good dream; they were talking, laughing. And that, he thought when he awoke the next morning, was a start.

Mums the word

For whatever reason, Millicent had never had many close female friends. From the time she was a young girl growing up in Portland, Oregon, she was often the outsider. Since she was taller than average, awkward and shy, the neighborhood girls would often mistake her introverted nature for arrogance. Because her mother always dressed her like a princess, the other kids thought Millicent's family was rich, but they were solidly middle-class. The fact was her mother, a former model, loved to sew, and though you wouldn't know it, most of Millicent's early wardrobe was home-sewn original designs. Millicent loved how her mom would make sure everything matched, from her undies to her socks to her shoes to the bows in her hair. And speaking of hair, *that* got her in trouble big-time. She couldn't help it that her hair was long and thick, and that her mother kept it immaculate, often giving her Shirley Temple curls with bright, starched bows. More than once she came home crying after her jealous, nappy-headed classmates had knocked her down, pulled her hair and stolen her pretty hair doo-dads. She could remember how the girls would make fun of her, calling her names, picking fights, always instigating. At first she tried to befriend these bullies with offers to play with her dolls or share her cookie and candy treats, but after scores of rejections she

decided that the best offense was a good defense. She started ig-
noring her female classmates and neighbors, choosing to hang out
with the boys instead. They *never* picked on her, and *always* welcomed her to hang out with them. From the time she was twelve
until she was in her late twenties, Millicent always had a boyfriend.
And now, although she admitted a new coworker might be a con-
tender, there was only one man that totally caught her eye and
held her heart. She couldn't wait forever, however, and wanted
something to happen. Right now!

Only, at this moment, Millicent longed for a close female
friend, needed a friend. Who could she turn to? Her friend and
prayer partner, Alison, had recently relocated to the East Coast to
take care of an ailing mother. She was sure no one else she knew
would begin to understand, and she wasn't even sure Alison would
agree with her more recent thoughts which she'd decided not to
share. Who could she trust enough to confide in, with whom could
she share her feelings? Anyone at the church was out of the question.
She had come close to sharing her feelings more fully with Sister
Vivian, but something held her back. *Don't let your right hand know
what your left hand is doing.* That was what the Word said. No, there
was no help there.

Millicent turned from her idle computer screen and looked out
the window of her thirty-story, downtown office building. It was a
clear, beautiful California day, and the view of buildings and streets
and cars and people stretched out endlessly before her. There had
to be somebody, but who?

She thought about her sometime workout partners, Jen and Patricia. Although she wouldn't consider them close friends, they had
developed a warm camaraderie limited primarily to the fitness
center. She felt closer to Jen than to Patricia, but she just couldn't
see making Jen privy to this very personal, very special aspect of
her life. Besides, Jen was always gossiping about somebody, and she
needed someone who could keep a confidence in this situation.
She thought about her coworkers. One by one, the names came

and were checked off in her mind. Again, she liked to keep her private life private, and with the amount of competition already prevalent in the marketing department, she didn't need anyone with any information on her that she didn't necessarily want to get out. In time, the whole world would know, and she herself would shout the announcement from the rooftops. But for now, mum was the word.

Millicent spent the next couple hours talking to potential customers, meeting with clients and putting out fires. After a quick lunch eaten in her office, she pulled out her reports and scanned them again for accuracy. She felt confident that with her plan implemented, the department could hit the numbers she'd forecasted. Yes, she was ready for the meeting, and she was assured the "big boys" would be pleased. She knew already that the vice president, Mr. Burroughs, was impressed with her work and with her. More than once, he'd hinted about her taking a position as director, a position that would place her salary in the six figures but would also involve a good amount of travel as well as outside sales. No, this wasn't the time for Millicent to be under extra pressure and away from home. She needed to be close to the ministry and to Cy.

Cy. Millicent stood up and looked out the window. Cy Taylor, her future husband. A little squiggle of anxiety flashed through her stomach. Could it really be happening? Could she really be right in believing that Cy was the man of her dreams, the man God had chosen to be her husband since eternity?

Millicent walked back over to her desk and sat down. She grabbed the S.O.S. materials she had been working on and placed them in her briefcase. The first three Saturdays of the summer had flown by, and now they were ready for the fourth and final gathering. Millicent would be meeting with Sister Vivian, Sistah Tai and other members of Ladies First later that evening. They would go over details for the final day, including the special luncheon with guest speaker Iyanla Vanzant. Focusing her attention back on the job at hand, she clicked on a computer file and opened it up. She scrolled down the page of information, marketing strategies and suggestions for one of her newest clients, a prestigious investment company whose satisfaction with her work was very important to the firm.

The firm. *Hum.* That was the other question Millicent pondered. Would she continue working after she married Cy? She'd like to continue with some type of financial independence, but, of course, her place would be beside her husband, and since he was very wealthy, money wouldn't be an issue for her. Would he give her an allowance, equal access to a joint bank account? Or would it be a monthly or quarterly sum to deposit in the bank of her choice? There was so much about Cy she didn't know!

One thing she did know through her relationship with Sister Vivian, taking care of a busy husband was a full-time job! Millicent intended to be Cy's right-hand woman. She wanted to help him with everything, especially as he moved farther into the ministry. Millicent smiled as she thought of how well she and Cy worked together. She was certain he would pastor his own church at some point, and then her responsibilities as first lady would be tremendous. Until then, she would ask Sister Vivian to take her under her wing and show her the ropes, and Millicent couldn't think of a better woman to emulate. Vivian had it all, a beautiful home, wonderful husband and fabulous children.

Children! It was something Millicent hadn't considered. Would Cy want children? Would she? At thirty-two, it was something she would have to decide before long. Perhaps it was the fact she was an only child or her limited experience being around children. Or it could be her disdain for the unruly, crying, bratty children she encountered in church and other public places, but the thought of changing a smelly diaper or dabbing an infant's spittle made her stomach churn. She couldn't see herself doing that in a million years. Maybe she and Cy would be content to work for the Kingdom. Maybe their children could be various areas of ministry. She could give back to the human race by being a mentor and role model for teenage girls and young women. Yes, teenagers she could handle, but a toddler? Not as likely. Still, the thought of a child with Cy had its merits. Their baby would be gorgeous. A little boy who looked just like Cy, a son to carry on their legacy and their name. A tangible demonstration of the immense love she and Cy felt for each other. Well, maybe she could handle one child, with an assistant and a nanny, of course.

Goodness, managing the household staff alone would require a great deal of organization. She knew Cy lived in a penthouse, but after their marriage, she was certain he'd think it best for them to buy a home—investing in their future. More appropriate to their status as a married couple, especially with the dinners and holiday parties and other social functions they'd be hosting. They would need a home that adequately displayed their social standing. Millicent thought about the possibilities. Beverly Hills was nice, but overrated. Bel Air was exclusive but overpriced. No, Cy would probably want to have a view of the ocean. Perhaps he'd like a home in the Marina or Playa del Rey or Palos Verdes or lovely Pacific Palisades, with their equally spectacular views of both ocean and mountain. The possibilities were endless, and of course, it also depended on what her husband's desires were. She probably didn't need to put a lot more energy into it until she'd discussed it with him. All these thoughts were making her absolutely giddy. She smiled widely and almost laughed out loud. The new male coworker chose this moment to walk by her doorway.

"I hope that smile is for me." He winked.

Millicent grabbed her reports and headed for the door. *Not!* Passing him, she looked back and returned the wink. "That's for me to know, and you to find out!" She could feel his eyes boring into her backside as she sashayed down the hall and into the conference room.

S.O.S.—The Sanctity of Sisterhood

Strands of Yolanda Adams's singing could be heard coming from the hotel's ample sound system amid the din of voices in the crowded ballroom. All the seats were filled, and many women, some of whom had taken off their shoes or sat on the floor, were lining the walls. Vivian looked out at the expectant audience with a myriad of feelings and emotions. So much had happened in these past four meetings, beyond her wildest expectations. Breakthroughs had been made. Emotionally crippled women were on their way to being whole. The love and compassion and forgiveness of God had replaced shame and depression and guilt. True, the work was only beginning, and not everyone who attended was reached, but many, many lives had been set free by, as the Scriptures declared, "the blood of the lamb and the word of your testimony."

Something else had happened, too. A rapport had developed between the pastors' wives and female congregants that hadn't been there before. Even Vivian had been surprised at the first ladies' honesty in recounting the tests and trials of their personal lives. They had stood naked and not ashamed before these sisters of different cultures and economic backgrounds and bared their souls. Suddenly, the ladies were not these untouchable, seemingly perfect superwomen with perfect families and perfect lives, but they were women just like their members, with the same struggles, the same fears and, as shocking as it was to some, the same failures as everybody else. The pastors' wives had been real with these daughters of God. And in being honest with them, the women were more able to be honest with themselves, to admit their faults and their fears. Vivian understood that the healing hadn't occurred only with the attendees, but that some of the first ladies had experienced healing as well.

That change was no more evident than in her best friend, Tai. Where before, Tai would have played a supporting role, she had emerged as one of the most sought after speakers during the informal times of counseling and group discussions. Her honest portrayal of life as a minister's wife had given the attendees a new understanding of just how complicated and difficult that position was to fill. Vivian still marveled at Tai's speech earlier in the day when she recapped her popular message, "If He Ain't Yo' Husband, It's Defiled," the speech that had replaced Vivian's "Other Women—Ourselves" suggestion and which Tai delivered during the Sacred Sex portion of the conference.

A particularly defining moment came during the question and answer period following each recap. One of the attendees, an attractive, young single woman, had asked why there seemed to be hostility between some pastors' wives and their young, attractive, single church members.

Tai had, from her own experiences, recounted how many times women had befriended her only to find out these women really wanted her husband. Without going into details, she confessed that she had endured infidelity early in her marriage. The audience did a collective gasp when Tai quite boldly stated that it had happened more than once that a female church member had been all too willing to seek copulation instead of counseling behind her husband's office door. She admitted that she didn't know how many of them had succeeded. Without telling them she was even now dealing with an adulterous situation, Tai assured the conference attendees that if they felt a chill in the air surrounding their first ladies, it may be a result of problems with adultery or near adultery in their marriages. While not condoning such behavior by these women, she understood why pastors' wives were often reluctant to let their guard down and befriend the single females in their congregations, especially if they were attractive. She admitted that while single women were most often targeted, there had been affairs between pastors and married parishioners.

She was also careful to stress that not all pastors cheated on their wives and most women in the church were there to seek God and not opportunities to commit adultery. She beseeched the listeners to forgive the pastors' wives who may have shunned their attempts at friendship or halted their advances within the ministry and to understand that pastors' wives were women, too, with the same feelings of intimidation and inadequacy and not-good-enough issues all women faced from time to time. She had turned to the pastors' wives on the roster then and admonished them to not prejudge the women in their congregations and to not put them all in the same category, and to realize that every attractive single woman in the church was not after their husbands. She admitted that sometimes she placed more blame on the woman than she did her husband and that wasn't right. She implored the listeners to understand that women with whom their husbands had affairs looked just like them—sincere, trustworthy, honestly seeking God. They shouted and clapped and prayed and cried and spoke in tongues and then used those same tongues to satisfy men who were not their husbands, men who instead of leading them toward God were leading them to a turned-down bed and a night of illicit ecstasy.

She called on the women within the sound of her voice to take up the spirit of the summit, the sanctity of sisterhood. She asked that a spirit of solidarity be formed in the hearts and lives of women, to denounce the enemy when he came in the form of an

overture from a married man and to "say no to the ho' show." Her
tapes sold out.

Vivian thought of these and other comments she'd heard during the past four weeks as she prepared to make the closing speech.
She had already received more than a dozen requests to host the
S.O.S. Summit in other churches. And she knew she was going to
accept as many invitations as she could. She knew in the very fiber
of her being this had been God's plan all along.

She smiled, thinking of Iyanla Vanzant's luncheon message and
her own personal favorite Iyanla quote, "If you see crazy coming,
cross the street." Iyanla had encouraged the women to respect
themselves and to realize that love of self was essential to loving
God. She encouraged the women attending to get out of crazy relationships, crazy behavior and crazy situations that were disrupt-
ing their happiness. Like a cheerleader for attitude adjustments, she
rallied this family of women to victory in overcoming negative situations in their lives.

First lady Carla Lee approached the podium to introduce Vivian for the final message of the conference. Carla's down-to-earth
personality and straight, honest, often humorous speech made her
another conference favorite. She had single-handedly lifted the
spirits of every overweight woman who'd attended by telling them
that the more there was of them, the more there was to love and
hefty didn't have to mean unhealthy, among other "Carla-dotes."
So many people had requested copies of her lectures that Vivian
had encouraged Carla to write a book containing her zany phrases
and uplifting words. Carla took a moment to scan the audience before speaking, a warm smile on her face reflecting the glow in her
heart. She actually looked like the sun, resplendent in a canary yellow, double-breasted suit.

"Ladies, ladies, ladies!" she began exuberantly. "If this isn't the
most beautiful gathering of women I've seen in my entire life, I'll
pay for lying! Y'all look like you are daughters of the Most High,

His precious brides! My God! I'm seeing a pinnacle of princesses, royal highnesses in the apex of their lives! I see destiny and purpose in your stride and the view of zenith in your eyes! Is this the royal priesthood? My God! I believe I'm in a room filled with women who are more than conquerors, who are above only and not beneath, who are the heads and not the tails and," Carla added slyly, "I mean 'tail' in all ways imaginable."

The crowd, which had gotten to its feet and begun applauding as she spoke, laughed in unison at her last statement. There was whooping and high-fives all over the place. The camaraderie was palpable and exciting—the ladies were on a God-induced high.

"This has been an incredible summit, and well worth it. But like all good things, this has come to an end. I am privileged and delighted to present to you now, for the final remarks, the woman in whom God placed the burden and the vision for what you've just experienced, the woman who has a heart for not only the sisters in her congregation, but for women everywhere. She is a woman who not only talks the talk, but walks the walk. And, baby! Can't nobody walk the walk like Sister Viv!" Carla turned to address her friend. "Girl, you better wear that Donna Karan 'cause you're looking so good, I want to slap you myself!" Vivian shook her head at her boisterous friend, joining with the audience in laughter as Carla turned back to address the crowd. "Women of God, I present my friend and sister in the faith, Sister Vivian Montgomery!"

Most of the crowd was already standing. Those who were not, got to their feet when Vivian approached the podium and showered her with sustained applause. Bouquets of flowers were presented to her amid shouts of "We love you, Sister Vivian" and a few "You go, girl." Vivian's eyes misted as she looked out on the sea of women, a rainbow of beauty and vulnerability, hope and determination. She was embarrassed by the open display of affection and tried several times to quiet the crowd before they took their seats to hear her final comments.

"I feel like the stand-in who accepts the award when the actual winner is not available. Contrary to popular opinion, I'm only partly responsible for putting this conference together. I must tell you, however, that all the honor, all the praise, all the glory, all the kudos and congrats go to my Lord and Savior Jesus Christ. Hallelujah!"

Again, the crowd came to its feet in a cacophony of praise to God. Impromptu praise and worship kicked in, and for a full five minutes, women all over the room sent up their own shout outs and thank yous to The One who had made it all possible. Vivian grabbed a handkerchief and wiped her eyes, waiting for the crowd to calm once more.

"And to my dear Sister Carla Lee, there's no need to slap me, darling, 'cause everybody in this room knows that ain't nobody bad like you!" The crowd cheered again, and many women, especially members of Carla's congregation, stood and hooted their agreement. Carla stood up and did a three-point model turn which got many of the rest of the crowd on their feet again. Carla bowed to the crowd and bowed to Vivian before sitting back down.

Vivian then took the time to personally thank the core members of Ladies First. She presented each one with a bouquet of roses as she called out her name. She thanked Millicent and her assistants and all of the volunteers that had helped the meetings run smoothly.

Lastly, she acknowledged Tai. "And to our first national member, who's been a child of God as long as I've known her, and I've known her since she was fourteen, my friend, my confidante, my covenant sister, Sister Twyla 'Tai' Brook." Vivian gave Tai a big hug as she accepted her roses.

As Tai walked back to her seat, Vivian said, "Ladies, please help me thank these wonderful women of God for their tireless service and sacrifice to the work of the Kingdom. May their labor not be in vain, may their reward come to them one hundredfold. May the desire of their hearts be fulfilled as they delight in Him!" The audience applauded, shouted and whistled their agreement. Again, Vivian waited patiently for the noise to subside.

"When this idea, the Sanctity of Sisterhood, was first put in my heart, I asked God just what He meant by that. What message did He want me to convey? First, He took me to the dictionary and then to His Word and the concordance where He emphasized the meanings 'set apart,' 'inviolable,' 'holy.' One thing that really stuck out in my mind was the opposite of sanctified, which is 'common.' I understood then that God was calling me and the rest of His daughters to a new level of 'uncommonness,' calling us to dare to be different, not go with the flow, to, as one of our segments urged, 'set the standard and dismiss the status quo.' Turn to the sister next to you and tell her, 'I'm uncommon. I'm unusual. I am not the status quo.'" The audience eagerly did so. This had been their mantra throughout the sessions.

"In our research and preparation for the topics, we paid close attention to what the world in general and America in particular saw as 'common.' We saw that sex outside of marriage was common. Unprotected sex was common. Sex with someone other than one's husband or wife was common. We found that common women cared not one iota if a man was involved in a serious relationship, let alone if he was married. Some women even claim to *prefer* married men; pleasure without pain, or so they think. We found that sex without love was common. But what did God teach us, ladies?"

"Sex is sacred" was the shouted response.

"Right!" agreed Vivian. "Turn to another sister and say, 'I'm uncommon. I'm unusual. I am not the status quo.'"

After they did so, Vivian continued with a clear and concise summary of the four-weekend conference and how each Saturday had been designed to bring the attendee to a higher level of sanctity, of relationship and closeness with God. Laughter rang out as she recounted some of the sayings from Carla and Tai's Sacred Sex Saturday. Like one of the favorites, "If he's gonna hit it and quit it, then don't even get wid'it." She reminded the women about the depth of true love: conscious love, sacred love, unconditional love, as taught in Spiritually Speaking. She finished with a national call to sisterhood.

"There is an African proverb which states that the hand that rocks the cradle rules the nation. I believe there is some truth to that. I believe that we as women, respecting each other and our-selves, can go a long way to changing the behavior of our men and society. Yes, it takes two to tango, and no, one of them doesn't have to be you. There are only so many prostitutes, exotic dancers and other forms of professional sex partners. If some of us ladies would start saying no to men who are not our husbands, perhaps we could start saying yes to becoming someone's wife.

"I'm not saying we can make men behave a certain way. I am saying that we can decide today that *we* will act a certain way, and the way we act is sure to influence others. We can decide to be our sister's keeper and to admonish a sister, in love and without judg-ment, when we see her acting common.

"We can, and I hope we do, decide today to love women who are hateful, pray for women who are spiteful, forgive women who are guilty and bless women who are trying. The terms of endear-ment of the day for women are 'b' and 'ho'. We can become that set apart sect within our species that makes a man want to call us 'queen' or more important for a great deal of you, 'wife.'

"We in the church often talk about our relationship with God. We talk about our relationship with family. This conference, this summit, has been specifically designed to talk about and reestablish the relationship between and among women, among sisters.

"Ladies, on behalf of the Ladies First committee and all the other women who worked so diligently to make these meetings happen, I want to thank you for being active participants in chang-ing your lives and the lives around you. Give yourselves a hand. You deserve it." The crowd once again came to its feet in applause.

"Finally, I'd like you all to stand and repeat the Sanctity of Sisterhood pledge with me for the last time in this summit, but certainly not the last time in our lives. Keep this pledge close to your heart and repeat it whenever you feel the need. Call a friend and ask her to say it with you, reach out and let her know, 'I need some help, sistah.' Let's support and encourage and inspire one another. We can do this—we can change the world as we change ourselves! Now, grab the hand of the one next to you, and let's say it together for the world to hear!

> *"I'm uncommon. I'm unusual. I am not the status quo*
> *Set apart, an earthly treasure—'cause my Father deemed it so*
> *Yes I am my sister's keeper and it should be understood*
> *That today we stand united—The Sanctity of Sisterhood!"*

Her divine mate

Vivian moaned contentedly as Derrick massaged the warm, scented oil all over her body. There was a perfect combination of cool breeze from the open bedroom window, mixing with the warmth from the master bedroom fireplace. Derrick's attention was singular, to remove every kink and form of tightness he felt in Vivian's muscles. The Jacuzzi bath had been the first step. This massage was the second. Derrick smiled, his eyes glancing briefly at the bed covered in rose petals, as he thought about the third.

The month of September had flown by in a whirlwind. There was the S.O.S. Summit, the start of a new school year for the children, and a relentlessly hectic travel schedule for Derrick that had included two evangelical trips overseas. Derrick and Vivian rarely saw each other, and when they did, it was hardly possible to spend quality time together. No, their brief interludes of togetherness had been filled with matching schedules, exchanging itineraries and providing brief updates as to each other's progress. The house had been crowded. Aside from the usual in-and-out traffic flow of Kingdom Citizens' members, Vivian's parents had spent the entire month of September with the Montgomerys, and while their help with the children was invaluable, Derrick was looking forward to a slower pace.

He lovingly turned Vivian over on her back as he reached for the oil. "Close your eyes," he spoke gently as Vivian stared at him with such longing and love he could barely finish his present task. He started at her feet, massaging and rubbing each toe, the heels and balls of her feet, rotating the ankles, squeezing and massaging the calves and thighs, all the while planting soft, whispery kisses along the way. He bypassed the place of his personal paradise and stroked her hips and stomach, swirling the oil over and around her navel, up and around her breasts where he dared not linger. He held each arm and as with her legs paid the utmost attention to detail with each finger, wrist, elbow, shoulder. He gently massaged her neck, which was now supple and pliant. Step two was now complete.

Derrick stood and unloosed the belt that held his black, silk robe together, letting it fall in soft, tantalizing swirls of material at his feet. Vivian opened her eyes to see his hand outstretched toward her. She smiled and reached up to grab his hand. Once he'd pulled her to her feet, Derrick swept her off of them once again, picking her up and showering her face with kisses as he stepped up on the master bed platform and laid Vivian gently down in the bed of rose petals. The scent of the petals combined with the scent of the candles Derrick had lit earlier. These combined with the scent of the oils on her body gave Vivian a scented orgasm, with promises of more to follow.

Derrick climbed up on the bed, covering the body he had just massaged. He kissed her fully now, his tongue moving and searching and finding and teasing. Vivian gave back what she had received, her hands tracing every part of her beloved's back and arms and buttocks. She gasped as he bent his head and lovingly worshipped at her breasts. Continuing, he let his tongue follow the trail his hands had forged earlier, slowly, lovingly, completely. As he kissed and caressed her nether lips and suckled her tender nub, Vivian grabbed the sheets and moaned louder, her voice purring like the most satisfied of felines. Derrick took her body to the moon, and the stars surrounded her as she floated back down to earth on a cloud of fulfillment. She had barely caught her breath when he entered her, enticing her to join him in the passion dance created at the beginning of time. He moved slowly, rhythmically, pulling out to the very tip before plunging in fully, deeper and deeper still, again and again and again. Tears formed in Vivian's eyes and ran down the sides of her face; such was the intensity of her love for him. This was her divine mate, her husband. They moved in perfect harmony. It was ecstasy. Derrick cried out in agonized bliss before spilling his seed in the depths of Vivian's soul and collapsing on top of her, the two of them still joined together. And just like that, they fell asleep, resting deeply and dreaming sweetly of more life and love to come.

"Was last night a dream?" Vivian asked as she stepped into the bathroom and kissed Derrick's freshly shaved cheek.

"If it was," he replied, turning to kiss her lightly on the mouth, "I don't ever want to wake up. Baby, I think that was the best love I ever had."

Vivian smiled as she stepped into the shower. She felt like a new woman, revitalized. She made quick work of her shower, knowing the hour was already late and Derrick would want them to leave for the church soon. She grabbed her robe and headed down the hallway to the children's rooms. Once she was sure their getting ready was under way, she went down to the kitchen, put on water for tea and laid out a quickie breakfast spread of bagels, cereal and fruit. Tea in hand, she made her way back to her dressing room where she quickly donned a simple yet stylish ivory-colored suit with matching pumps and jewelry. Her entire ensemble was ivory and gold, right down to her panties.

Once dressed, she again checked in on D-2 and Elisia and found they were also ready. Together they went down to the breakfast nook, each having stopped in the kitchen and grabbed their breakfast of choice. As usual, Derrick did not join them. He rarely ate until after he'd finished the Sunday morning messages. By the time Derrick arrived downstairs, Vivian and the children had eaten, and she had taken care of the breakfast dishes.

"Are you ready, darling?" she asked, even as she reached for her purse and Bible. "D-2, where is your Bible?"

"In the car," he answered simply and patiently, as if he could hardly believe his mother would think he'd leave home without his Word! Vivian watched as father and son headed for the garage, and she smiled at how much D-2 was like his dad. Someday, he was going to make some woman a fine husband, and if the dad's behavior last night was any indication, his wife would indeed be blessed beyond measure!

It was a beautiful morning, and traffic was light as they headed toward Kingdom Citizens' in the heart of the city. They'd been riding only a few minutes when Derrick's cell phone rang. He hit the speaker button, and the sensuously raspy voice of Cy Taylor filled the Jag.

"Minister Montgomery!" he began respectfully.

"Brother Cy, what's up, man?" Derrick responded.

"God is good, man. Is Sister Vivian there with you?"

"Yes, you have the full attention of the entire Montgomery family. Do I need to make this a private conversation?"

"Oh, no, no, that's not necessary. I just needed to speak to both of you today, between services if possible. I was wondering if you could carve out ten minutes for me then."

"It can't wait until this afternoon?"

"It could, but I'd rather not. You'll understand when I talk to you. But don't worry, it's good news."

"Well, that makes me more willing to see you between services!" Derrick joked. "The last thing I need is bad news in the middle of trying to bring the good news!"

"Then you'll give me a couple minutes?"

"Sure man, no problem."

"Hum," Vivian began as Derrick clicked the off button on the cell phone. "Wonder what's on Mr. Taylor's mind."

Derrick looked at his watch as he turned off the highway and began winding through the streets toward the church, representing the last ten minutes of their transport. "I don't know, darling. But we will soon find out."

It is our time

There was a palpable tension emanating from Millicent as Shannon and Maurice stepped back and appraised her. Both stared. Neither spoke.

"Well?" Millicent almost shrieked, except her voice was barely above a whisper.

Shannon found her voice first. "You—look—absolutely—breathtaking."

Maurice, in his flirtatious and feminine fashion, added his opinion. "Honey, I just got three words for you: unh, unh, unh. Girl, if you wasn't marrying somebody else, I'd reverse my faggot ass and marry you myself!" Maurice danced around the room then, punctuating the silence with peals of laughter.

"Maurice! Watch your mouth!" Millicent admonished. But she was smiling.

"Girl, you are looking fierce! That hair and make-up is a wonder to behold, and I am beholding! I don't know who did it, but whoever it is, can't nobody, *nobody*, compete with them."

Shannon cut her eyes at Maurice. "I thought you did her hair and make-up, Maurice?"

Maurice looked like the spider when the moth flew into the web. "Touché," was all he said before walking over to Millicent and patting her head of perfect curls. "Now, once you put the veil on, this flat area will be covered, and you will look like Cinderella herself going to the ball."

Millicent turned and looked in the full-length mirror one last time. She could hardly believe it was her staring back at her. It was as if this was happening to someone else. The day she'd dreamed of her entire life was here. And like any bride, her stomach was a bundle of nerves. She jumped when the phone rang.

"Can you get that, Maurice? I don't want to talk to anyone right now," Millicent said, while reaching for her veil and the ivory silk purse that lay beside it.

"The limo's here," Maurice stated as he hung up the phone. "It's show time, sistah, and you're the star!"

"You're sure you don't want me to go with you?" Shannon asked. "I was planning to go to the beach, but I can go later if you need me."

"No, I'll be fine," Millicent replied, going over to hug her new friend. "I'll have some help once I get there." Ever since Millicent had gone by the bridal shop and asked Shannon's assistance in helping her get ready, they had become fast friends. She'd become a confidante of sorts, and while not sharing everything, Millicent had spoken feelings aloud to Shannon that she'd never shared with anyone else. Not even her intended husband. Shannon had thought some of Millicent's story odd, but she was so taken with this obviously beautiful and successful woman befriending her that she'd just been a quiet, avid listener, keeping her opinions to herself.

Shannon grabbed the bag holding the dress's detached train, and Maurice took Millicent's small suitcase. Millicent looked around the room one more time, took a deep breath and headed toward the front door. A smile spread across her face as she turned to lock the door behind her. *When I step through this door again, I'll be married.*

★   ★   ★

"It's a pleasure to see you again, Hope," Vivian said, smiling warmly. "And I love that suit!"

Hope smiled. "I love yours, too." She'd noticed as soon as she and Cy had entered Minister Montgomery's office that she and Sister Vivian were wearing similar but not identical, ivory-colored suits. Like Vivian, Hope had chosen gold jewelry to accessorize her outfit but had added a splash of color to her ensemble with a gold, slate and salmon-colored scarf. Hope took their being similarly dressed as a good sign. Maybe she and this first lady would get along.

Hope had been hesitant to accept Cy's invitation to visit him in California. Aside from the fact that she didn't have a lot of extra money for travel right now, she didn't think she could control herself if they ever got alone. The man made rational thinking impossible! Eventually, though, Cy's reasoning wore her down, and she decided to accept his most generous offer of an all-expense-paid, extended weekend in Los Angeles.

She'd arrived at LAX on Friday afternoon. The weather was perfect, summer in October. She was whisked by limo to Cy's penthouse where he, having been called to a meeting at the last minute, had informed her to wait. There was a vase of exotic flowers on the table in the entryway, along with a heart-carrying teddy bear and a card welcoming Hope to his not-so-humble abode. That evening they'd gone to a romantic restaurant nestled in the recesses of Topanga Canyon. The food, company and conversation had been delicious. A movie had followed dinner, and they'd enjoyed coffee and dessert in the lobby restaurant of the Ritz Carlton, where Hope was staying.

Saturday had been a visitor's dream and had included an early morning tour of Hollywood, a trip to Disneyland, and an evening of dining and dancing as they sailed on a yacht around the marina.

And now, here she was, in the private domain of one of America's most prolific preachers, calmly chatting with him and the first lady. She wouldn't have been surprised had she looked down and seen glass slippers instead of leather pumps.

Derrick and Cy had been speaking privately and now came over to join the ladies. Cy cleared his throat and placed a possessive hand on Hope's shoulder.

"I know you two are wondering why I asked to meet with you, and I know we don't have a lot of time so I'll get right to the point. Derrick," he began, turning to face his friend fully, "you are more than my pastor. You are my spiritual mentor and friend. Your example in ministry and Christianity is one I work to follow, as you follow Christ.

"I admire the example you set in your personal life with your wife and with your children. I've long said that if I ever got married, I would want a marriage like you and Vivian seem to have— one full of love, ordained by God."

Vivian thought of the love she and Derrick had shared the night before, and if this Black woman could have blushed, she would have been as red as a beet. As it was, the room suddenly felt too warm.

"Well," Cy continued, now turning back to Hope. "I believe I've found that woman." Hope stopped breathing as her head shot up, eyes rounded and filling with tears.

"And as your marriage has been such an inspiration to me and as your friendship has meant so much to me . . ." Cy pulled a box out of his pocket and got on his knee.

"I wanted you and Vivian to witness the moment that will forever change my life, the moment when I ask Hope to be my wife."

As Cy opened the box, streaks of gold and pink and blue danced off of the five-carat diamond nestled in the soft, black velvet. Hope was as still as a statue, her hand over her heart, her mouth a perfect "O," her breath still held. Like Hope, Vivian and Derrick were also shocked into stillness. But they were still breathing.

"Hope," he said simply, "will you marry me?"

Hope exhaled slowly—her answer equally modest, in fact just one word: "Yes."

Like the Red Sea, the Kingdom Citizens' crowd parted as the long, sleek limo glided into the parking lot beside the church. All eyes were on it as the driver stepped out, straightening his jacket and donning his hat before going to the other side to open the passenger door.

Millicent sat frozen in the backseat as the door opened. Suddenly her calm and resolve and confidence left her. *What am I doing? Have I lost my mind?* She glimpsed a crowd of people on the sidewalk, their bodies turned in the direction of the limo. A little girl ran up to the opened limo door and peeked inside.

"Ooh, you're pretty! Are you getting married?" she asked, her eyes and voice full of awe and admiration.

It was enough to jolt Millicent out of immobility. She lifted the hem of her wedding dress and, taking the driver's hand, stepped a satin-covered toe onto the pavement.

You could hear a pin drop as the gawking crowd held its breath awaiting the answer to the question, "Who's that in the limo?" As Millicent stepped out of the limo and stood with back straight and head high, a collective gasp went through the Sunday worshippers, followed by a din of chattering whispers as opinions started flying like pigeons to birdseed.

Millicent dared not look around her. Instead, she walked straight to the side door, the one leading into Kingdom Citizens' suite of offices. The driver followed, loaded down with her suitcase and garment bag carrying the long train. She breathed deeply as she stepped inside the office building. Inside, everyone stared. No one spoke. Millicent continued looking straight ahead as she walked toward the executive offices. She was almost to the door leading to Derrick's office area when his personal assistant, Lionel, stopped her.

"Millicent!" he shouted, quite flustered at what he saw, not to mention that Millicent had come close to interrupting a meeting that Minister Montgomery had insisted not be interrupted. "You look, well, you look, uh, spectacular! I didn't even know you were getting married."

Millicent turned and smiled. "Thank you, Lionel. You look nice today as well." She turned to continue her journey into Derrick's office. "Is Pastor Derrick in his office? I left a message to meet with him between services."

Lionel's smile faded and was replaced with a frown. "Uh, Millicent, Minister Montgomery is, uh, already meeting with someone. He can't be disturbed."

"He didn't get my message?" she asked, as if that could be the only reason she was not being seen at once. She'd never had any problem accessing either her pastor or Sister Vivian, so had not been overly concerned when, during the past week, she'd been unable to reach them. She'd also tried to reach Cy all week, to no avail. But being sure that she'd see them all in church, she'd simply left messages for the Montgomerys and Cy to meet her in the pastor's office between services. Once there, she planned to bare her heart and soul before her husband-to-be and her pastor, assured that once they heard "the Word of the Lord," Cy would quickly agree to be her husband and Derrick would marry them symbolically right then and there. Millicent had taken care of obtaining a marriage license and arranging blood tests so that she and Cy could repeat their vows in a civil ceremony later in the week. This action taken today, with the gown and the limo and the flowers and the veil, was the final feet-to-her-faith act the prophetess had so accurately suggested. After all, she and Cy were already married in spirit; this outward joining was just a technicality.

Lionel was obviously uncomfortable. What was wrong with

him? Once again, Millicent tried to go around him and head for her pastor's private domain.

"Like I said, Millicent. Pastor cannot be disturbed right now." He cleared his throat. "For any reason. He was explicit. Maybe if you wait here, I can have a word with him before he starts the next service. Can you wait?"

Millicent didn't want to, but she nodded her head in the affirmative. She'd waited a lifetime to become someone's wife; a few more minutes wouldn't hurt. She instructed the driver to place her bag near the couch and then told him to wait in the limo for further instructions. She thought that maybe she and Cy would go have a celebratory brunch after their ceremony, then maybe they could take a drive along the ocean-edged Pacific Coast Highway. She knew their honeymoon would have to wait, but tonight. . . . She smiled, and a bit of her nervousness vanished, just thinking about a night with Cy—as his wife.

"No, come this way," Derrick directed as Cy started to lead Hope to the entrance that would take them through the executive offices and toward the front of the church. "We're already late, so you guys might as well come through the pulpit entrance."

Cy grabbed Hope's hand and kissed it as they followed Derrick and Vivian through a second set of doors that led directly into the pulpit of the sanctuary. Rodney, the head usher, was standing just outside the door and led Hope to a seat on the front row. As he walked back toward the pulpit, he was almost run over by a harried-looking Lionel, whose eyes were searching the pulpit anxiously. Seeing Derrick, he made a beeline for his side. Sister Vivian had already taken a seat on the bench she shared with Derrick and their assistants. Derrick was conferring with one of the other ministers as the choir was finishing their offering selection. Lionel waited, shifting his weight from foot to foot, while Derrick concluded his discussion.

"Pastor," he whispered while Derrick was still standing. "I need to talk to you."

Millicent paced impatiently, waiting for Lionel to return. Her nervousness was turning to anger. Where were they? Then she remembered. She'd mentioned only Minister Montgomery to Lionel; she hadn't told him she needed to see Sister Vivian and Cy as well. Darn! What should she do now? She could hear the choir singing and knew the taking up of the offering was almost over. There would be only one more song before Minister Derrick began his sermon. *What do I do?* She continued to pace and ponder her options. She could wait until the service was over and speak to them then. That, however, was a risky proposition since after the last service Minister Derrick and Sister Vivian usually made a beeline for their office before heading home to rest. She also didn't want to risk Cy's leaving without her being able to see him. She thought about leaving and coming back in the evening but quickly nixed that idea. It was now or never. She knew if she left the church grounds, she'd never get up the nerve to do this again. *No*, Millicent thought as she headed for the doors and the front of the church. "This is my wedding day," she vowed. "And I will not be denied."

Vivian rose and walked from the pulpit with as much restraint as she could muster. Inside, her mind was reeling. *What in heaven's name is Millicent doing in the church office in a wedding dress? No, she can't be thinking what I think she's thinking.* "No!" she whispered aloud, and once the door was closed firmly behind her, she sprinted to the lobby of the executive offices where Lionel had left a would-be bride. Before she reached the door that would take her into the lobby, she stopped, took a deep breath and said a quick prayer. She would need some divine help to get through these next

few minutes with Millicent. Lord knew she'd never encountered
this situation before. "Help me, Lord Jesus," she whispered. She
took another breath to steady herself and nodded to Lionel. He
opened the door, and they stepped out into the lobby of the executive offices.

It was empty. Vivian looked around, noticing the garment bag
and suitcase sitting near the couch and a satin purse resting on top
of them. She looked at Lionel, who was also looking around.

"She was right here a minute ago," he said quietly, almost to
himself. "Wait right here, First Lady. Maybe she went to the rest
room or something. I'll check it out."

Vivian was too keyed up to wait. She wasn't getting a good
feeling about this. "Thanks, Lionel, but I think I'd better come
with you."

Hope was quietly taking in the scene around her, still in shock
from what just happened. She was engaged! This was what she'd
wanted her whole life. And Cy was the type of man for whom
she'd prayed. During those first weeks as she'd gotten to know
him, an inner voice had begun to whisper things to her—things
she felt too good to be true. After her mistaken assumption of
Shawn being her future husband, she hadn't dared listen. Now she
knew, without a doubt. It had been God. She stared at the plat-
inum and diamond ring. *I'm getting married!*

Smiling at this thought, she looked up to find Cy's eyes resting
comfortably on her. He smiled and winked. She smiled back. Not
a few women in the audience caught the interaction, and suddenly
Hope was the center of some unwanted and unfriendly attention.
A couple of the women in the choir were looking at her with disdain, and the attractive woman who'd engaged her in such wonderful conversation moments before suddenly leaned in the
opposite direction, placing her large purse between them. *Church
folks are church folks wherever you go,* Hope thought. But they were

just going to have to get over it. Because she was going to become Mrs. Cy Taylor whether anybody liked it or not!

Millicent hesitated for just a moment as she stood at the back of the sanctuary. A small stirring began as the people in the back few rows began to notice her. The choir had just begun to sing another D&C original called "Perfect Love." Millicent felt it was a sign from God. She couldn't have chosen anything more appropriate. The song gave her the push she needed, and she began to glide down the middle aisle. The song's melody was perfect, and she kept her eyes straight ahead, not looking to the left or to the right, as she walked toward her destiny.

"She's not in any of the offices or in any of the classrooms on the other side." Lionel continued to look around as he spoke to Vivian, as if Millicent would reappear out of the air around him. "I looked outside," Lionel continued, "and the limo she came in is still there."

Limo? Vivian shook her head. This was getting more ridiculous by the moment. She stood in contemplation when suddenly it hit her. "Lord, have mercy!" she whispered and headed down the office hallway toward the front of the church. Walking quickly from the side door of the office suites, across the lawn and through the doors to the foyer, she entered when Millicent was already halfway down the aisle. Vivian froze in shock as she watched the unthinkable unfold.

While Vivian stood frozen in the foyer, Derrick maintained a similar position in the pulpit. He'd felt some type of commotion as he sat behind the podium and stood up to see what the fuss was about. By this time, the entire church was talking, and those in the front rows had turned to see what had those in the back rows so excited. Some people had stood to get a better view with many of the members smiling broadly as they watched what they thought was a previously planned affair. "You look beautiful," one whispered as Millicent passed her in the aisle. "I ain't mad atcha!" said another.

Millicent's eyes were still staring straight ahead, although she'd taken note of Cy as soon as she'd entered the sanctuary. *Just let me get down this aisle. Just let me make it to the front.* Millicent's legs were trembling so badly she thought for a moment she wouldn't be able to make it. But when she heard the encouraging comments from the women she passed, it bolstered her confidence. She was only three rows from the front of the church now. She looked into the eyes of her pastor, who had an unreadable expression on his face. Finally, she turned to look at Cy. Had she been buck naked, he couldn't have been looking at her more incredulously. Had Millicent looked down and to her left, she would have seen that Hope's face mirrored Cy's.

Derrick gave an almost imperceptible signal to Darius, and the choir stopped singing even as the music continued to play. Everyone was frozen in suspense now. Derrick, Cy, the ministers in the pulpit, the members out front. Vivian was poised at the door to the sanctuary, her eyes glued to Derrick, waiting for a clue or a cue, whichever came first. Hope was transfixed, along with everyone else who sat in the pews.

"Millicent," Derrick began softly, appropriately discerning that he was dealing with a very delicate situation. He motioned toward the back of the church. "Sister Vivian is waiting for you. She'd like to discuss this with you privately."

Millicent took a few steps toward Cy. She almost felt separated from what was taking place, as if she were watching her own movie, as if this were a dream. Slowly, dramatically, she raised her hand toward him, her once shaking body now remarkably calm. "Husband!" she called out with a loud voice. "It is our time. The time that God ordained for us before the foundation of the world. Come, darling. Come to your bride."

Cy closed his eyes and swallowed hard. *This cannot be happening. If I close my eyes long enough or tight enough, maybe I'll open them to find I'm at home in bed and this was just a bad, bad dream.* Cy opened his eyes and looked into Millicent's face. This was not a dream. He looked down at Hope, who now stared at him wide-eyed. *No, Hope, it isn't what it looks like. There's nothing going on between this woman and me!* He willed Hope to absorb his thoughts. His gaze bore into her eyes, and in that moment, Hope calmed down and sat back quietly in her seat, turning her attention back to Millicent. At this same moment, Millicent looked down and to her left. Hope's face was the last thing Millicent saw before she melted into a heap of silk, satin and tiny seed pearls. Hope didn't move a muscle as mounds of Millicent's wedding dress covered her own ivory and gold shoes.

The ushers rushed forth immediately to take the would-be bride out of the sanctuary and into the privacy of a prayer room, the quickest and most unobtrusive exit, if "unobtrusive" was a word that could be used in this most public of moments. Vivian ducked inside right behind the ushers, and after they'd set Millicent down gingerly on the floor, Vivian instructed them to leave and to please not discuss this with anyone. Even as she said the words, she knew this story would be on the national church wire by day's end. She wouldn't even be surprised if somebody wasn't on their cell phone in the sanctuary, giving a play-by-play as the events unfolded.

Derrick tried with little success to get the service back on track. He instructed Darius and the choir to sing another song. Still sensing distraction, he led the church into a time of prayer and meditation while the sounds of the Kingdom Citizens' band played in the background. The prayer and meditation period centered the crowd a little bit more, but even though he delivered the sermon and got the proper responses of "hallelujah," "amen" and "sho' you right," he doubted whether anyone would remember today's topic. He could barely remember it himself!

Seventy times seven

Tai didn't go back to Kansas immediately. Instead, she took the first week of October to be alone with God at a spiritual retreat and spa nestled in the luxury of Palm Desert, California. There, she spent hours praying and communing with God. When she wasn't with Him, she was being pampered and massaged and wrapped and cleansed. She was manicured and pedicured and exfoliated and exercised. She attended a few classes designed for spiritual healing, and although the instruction was too New Age for her tastes, she still enjoyed the serenity of the surroundings and even heard a word or two that she could embrace. When she left the desert, she'd been cosseted from the rooter to the tooter and felt that no matter what was waiting for her at home, she was ready to face it.

Home. Tai thought about what that word meant as the taxi wound its way through the streets and turned onto her block. She admittedly had no idea what to expect when she walked through the front door, but she was strangely calm regardless. After the encouragingly regular phone calls the first week, she'd rarely heard from King. She knew from daily calls to Mama Max that he'd been out of town several times and that Mama, baby-sitter Anna and Sistah Wanthers had taken care of the children for the most part while she was gone.

The taxi had barely pulled into the driveway when the front door opened and a set of screams burst into the evening air.

"Mama! Mama! You're home!" Timothy and Tabitha surrounded her, filling her arms with hugs and her face with kisses.

Tai dropped to her knees and hugged them fiercely. This was the longest she'd ever been gone from the children, and while she had enjoyed this time to herself—the first time she'd had like this since she was nineteen—she missed her family immensely. Until this very moment she hadn't realized how much.

"We missed you, Mama," Timothy said while grabbing a couple of bags.

"Yeah, Mama, we thought you'd *never* come home." Tabitha was clinging to her mother while pulling her impatiently toward the house.

"I missed you guys, too." Tai turned. "Just a minute, Tabitha!" She laughed, grabbing her purse and turning to pay the cab driver, who'd already taken her larger bags inside. "I'm so happy to be back home." Tai was surprised to realize she meant it. She felt liberated, knowing no matter what, she and the children would be okay. The past month had taught her there was life beyond King Brook, and if necessary, she would jump on that horse called Life and ride it for all it was worth!

And so it was that Tai walked into her home, with Timothy on one side and Tabitha on the other, and got the shock of her life.

The twins' eyes danced as Tai, speechless, looked around the room. The living room had been transformed into a wonderland with silver and gold balloons everywhere. There was a glitter-type substance on the floor, and the white fluorescent bulbs in the lamps had been replaced with colored ones of yellow and blue. The coffee table was laden with gifts, and there was a banner across the back wall with "Welcome home, Mama, Welcome home, Wife" in bold, calligraphy letters. Princess came over and hugged her mom tightly. "Missed you, Mom. Welcome home."

"What's all this?" she squealed, hugging the daughter who was almost as tall as she. She stepped inside the living room and looked around.

"This," King said, coming from the kitchen with an ice pail containing sparkling apple juice, "is a welcome home from the family who missed you very, very much." He set the bucket on a place mat and walked over to his wife, kissing her gently, tentatively, on the lips. "We love you, Tai. Welcome home."

Tai stood dumbfounded. Of all the welcome homes she'd imagined, this had not been one of them. Her insides were a swirl of emotions as she looked at King, looking apprehensive, and then at the children, looking delighted. How could she feel so many things all at once? Love. Confusion. Happiness. Anger. It was a moment before she realized they all stood and stared in silence, waiting for her to speak. She swallowed and found her voice.

"This is, uh, what can I say?" Tai began, squelching the urge to cry even as the tears threatened. "You guys have outdone yourselves." She linked arms with Princess, who was still standing beside her, and winked at the twins. Yes, focusing on the children helped calm her tumultuous emotions. Looking at King did not. So she didn't. Instead, she walked over to the table and picked up a beautifully wrapped gift. "What's all this?"

"It's your welcome home presents," Tabitha patiently explained. "But Daddy let us buy some stuff, too."

"Yes," Princess continued. "Daddy let me get that leather jacket I wanted. And some new jeans."

"Who cares about that?" piped an impatient Timothy. "We all want to see what Mom thinks about her gifts, don't we, everybody?"

"We sure do," agreed King quietly. He hadn't moved until this moment, walking around the present-laden table and taking a seat on the couch. Tai refused to meet the eyes that were searching hers intently.

"Well, in that case," Tai began, grabbing one of the presents and speaking to her eager son, "I guess I better open yours first." She sat down on the opposite end of the couch and opened his gift.

It was lovely. When Tai opened the lid, the classic sounds of "What the World Needs Now Is Love" spilled out of the chrome and glass jewelry box as a shiny red, heart spun round and round. She reached up and hugged her son, losing the battle with the tears that now flowed over her cheeks. "Thank you, darling, it's beautiful," she voiced sincerely. Timothy's face beamed with pride.

A lilac sweater set, pair of gorgeous purple velvet slacks, pair of iridescent crystal earrings with matching necklace, silk-covered blank journal and two spandex workout suits joined Timothy's music box and completed the mound of opened presents covering the coffee table. Except for a Christmas tree, the room looked like Christmas. Tai hesitated as one unopened package remained. A small, square box wrapped in gold-and-white paper and secured with a gold bow. It was from King. Tai further prolonged opening his gift by picking up the music box and placing the crystal earrings inside it. Of course, impatient, observant Timothy would not be deterred.

"Uh, Mom! There's still one present left! C'mon!"

"Can't I take a moment and savor my gifts?" she asked, smiling.

"Mom!" the kids moaned in harmony. Princess continued. "We all want to see what Daddy got you!"

For some reason, Tai wasn't altogether sure she wanted to know what Daddy had bought. Still not looking at King, she reached for the box, slid off the bow and removed the exquisite wrapping paper. A small, black jewelry box beckoned. Tai glanced briefly at King, who was eyeing her intently.

"What is this?" She asked a question that went beyond the contents of the container she held.

"Open it and find out," King whispered.

"Yeah, open it, Mom!" Tabitha squealed.

Tai slowly lifted the lid and gasped. A beautifully designed mother's ring of sapphire, emerald and topaz gems surrounding a radiant-cut two-carat diamond glistened against its ebony back-drop. Tai's emotions swirled. What did this mean? Had some eager children wanting to show their mother love roped King into this gregarious show of affection? Was this an olive branch from a repentant adulterer? Or was this a going away present signaling the end of their marriage? Tai's eyes were veiled as she looked at her husband, but a glimpse of her undeniable love for him seeped through nonetheless.

"It's beautiful, King," she whispered sincerely.

"Just like the woman who will wear it," he smoothly replied.

"Wow, Daddy! Yours is the best gift of all!" Timothy exclaimed.

"Ooh, Mom, can I wear it?" Princess asked, her hands reaching for the box.

"No, you cannot," Tai replied, snatching the box out of Princess's reach.

"It sure is pretty," Tabitha cooed.

"Put it on her, Dad," Timothy suggested, an unwitting mediator in King's attempt at reconciliation.

King hesitated only a moment before complying with his son's request. He stood, reaching for the ring that Tai was removing from its velvet box. As their fingers touched, a shot of electricity went up Tai's arm and her fingers tingled. She closed her eyes against the onslaught of feelings and concentrated on trying to feel nothing at all. King, on the other hand, took full advantage of this opportunity to touch the wife he'd barely acknowledged for the past four months, since Tai had proven King's infidelity. His fingers brushed over hers as he slipped the ring on her right hand. It fit perfectly. In spite of herself, a rush of sexual desire dashed up unbidden and unwanted from her "kundalini," and Tai jumped up from the couch and rushed over to the mirror positioned above the fireplace.

"Ooh, isn't this gorgeous?" she said as she held her ringed finger, a bit breathless as her feelings seesawed between lust and anger, forgiveness and fear. Did King think he could just make it all better with a ring? Did he expect her to forgive, forget and jump back into their marriage as if nothing had happened? And how dare he use the children as a shield. Of course she could be nothing but the thankful recipient with their eager eyes on her. But, baby! It wouldn't be so easy to get back in Tai's good graces. Not so easy at all! She forced a smile to her face as she looked at King in the mirror. "Thank you," she said. It was all she could muster. She needed time to think, to absorb all that was happening.

As if an angel heard her plea, the smell of food wafted from the kitchen at that very moment and caused a necessary diversion. "Is that food I smell?" she asked, turning toward the children and away from King.

"Yes, and we cooked it ourselves!" the twins voiced simultaneously as they came to grab her arms once again. "Hope you're hungry, Mom!" In fact, on the way home, Tai had been starving. But that was before she'd received King's welcome home gift. The ring around her finger felt strangely like a ball and chain. It had taken her breath when she first saw it, and now it took her appetite as well.

Even so, she was able to get enough of the dinner down to show her appreciation. The simple, yet delicious meal of grilled steak, baked potatoes, salad and rolls prepared by King and the kids was obviously a labor of love. Not to be left out completely, Mama Max had contributed her portion by way of a peach cobbler, the kind that made Tai want to slap somebody. Tai's emotions stabilized a bit as the family sat around the table leisurely enjoying the meal. She answered rapid-fire questions from the twins and gave a pared-down description of her five weeks in California. She told them about her and Vivian's star-filled day in Hollywood and how she'd enjoyed a fun afternoon and evening at Universal City Walk and Studios while reminding the children that jealousy would get them nowhere. She reminisced about the regular walks along the beach and made their mouths drool with talk of fresh seafood eaten at seaside restaurants and the California phenomenon called Roscoe's Chicken and Waffles. And all the time she talked, her mind was reeling with the scenario being played out before her. Something she wouldn't have anticipated in a million years. Her emotions were riding a roller coaster. She could barely look at King.

"Your mama has had a wonderful evening and your mama is now exhausted," she said finally, leaving the kitchen only after the children adamantly refused to let her clean up. "Thank you guys for everything," she murmured, hugging the children one by one but only placing a hand briefly on King's shoulder. Focusing her attention on the children she continued. "You'll never know how special this was, how much it meant to me."

King turned then and abruptly left the room. Just when she thought she was getting a grip on her emotions, they twisted again. *What is that about? Is he expecting a hug, too, after all these months?* Tai shrugged, fighting for an armor of indifference to King's unpredictable behavior. It didn't matter, she lied defensively. All was well with her soul. "Good night all!" she sang out with false cheerfulness, kissing Princess, Tabitha and Timothy in turn. "I'm taking a long, hot shower and then I'm off to bed!"

Tai went back through the living room and noticed her luggage had been carried upstairs. She stopped once again and took in the scene around her. She smiled and shook her head, imagining the children fixing up the room. Upon closer examination, she noticed that the banner had loads of hand-drawn hearts and stars and declarations of love from the twins and, she noted with surprise, from King. *King, what are you up to?* Still wondering, Tai turned from the banner and headed upstairs.

Tai opened her guest bedroom door, turned on the light and stopped again. *What is going on?* Tai stepped inside, closed the door and threw her purse on the chair beside the vanity. "Where are my things?" she asked aloud. In an air of confusion, Tai slowly walked around the room, noticing that the books and other knickknacks she'd left on the dresser and bedside table were gone. *Maybe they had a cleaning lady come in.* Tai had noticed the home seemed spotless and thought that Mama Max had probably arranged a cleaning

service to come and do a once-over while she was gone. Tai smiled
to herself. Mama Max was definitely one of a kind. She'd have to
call and thank her later.

With that thought, Tai began undressing and walked over to
the closet to get a robe. Pulling it open, she stopped again. It was
empty. She marched into the bathroom. Her toiletries were
nowhere in sight. As what had obviously occurred began to dawn,
her anger mounted. "Oh, you're pretty sure of yourself, huh, King."
She stood silently for a minute, her hands on her hips. "This
nucka's got a lot of nerve," she spoke while shaking her head to the
empty room. Then she put her blouse back on, zipped up her pants
and headed for the master bedroom.

"King, what's go—" Tai stopped in her tracks. In the master
bedroom, what looked like dozens of white candles in every size,
shape and configuration were lit throughout the room. A new, gold
comforter shimmered seductively in the candlelight. King was sitting at the foot of the bed, wearing an off-white lounging outfit,
his feet bare. Once Tai's senses returned to normal, she could hear
the sounds of The Manhattans in the background, singing the seven-
ties oldie-but-goodie "Maybe We Can Try Again."

King sensed her hesitancy. He understood. He knew he'd been
distant from Tai while she was in California, not to mention the last
few months at home before she'd left. But it wasn't just his busy
schedule, and it wasn't another woman either. While Tai was in a
desert hideaway talking to God, God was in Kansas talking to
King. King had spent countless hours alone, thinking about his life,
the church, his marriage and what was really important to him.
He'd come to the conclusion that in short, he'd been a major ass-
hole and that Tai should be elevated to the level of sainthood for all
the hell he'd put her through. He'd asked God for forgiveness and
promised Him that if Tai would forgive him, too, he'd spend the
rest of his life trying to make up for the hurt he'd caused her. He'd
broken things off with April and removed two women he knew
had ulterior motives from positions close to him in the church. That

included his attractive, personal secretary, Lisa Higgins. Even though Lisa was married, she was flirtatious, and he didn't need the temptation. He'd replaced her with a competent, formerly retired secretary who had worked in the Los Angeles school district for thirty years, gentle-natured, white-haired Sister Pebbley. He'd had more heart-to-hearts with his father in the past five weeks than he'd had his entire life and more than a few long discussions with his mother. He'd even asked the children for forgiveness. And as a keepsake to mark the moment of his marital transformation, he'd bought Tai a perfectly cut emerald and diamond necklace to accompany the mother's ring she'd received. Tai's trip to Los Angeles had given King a taste of how it would be with Tai totally out of his life. "Empty" only began to describe the feeling.

He stood and walked over to Tai, taking her hand and closing the door behind them. "Come here," he said softly. "We need to talk."

Tai snatched her hand out of his grasp. "Why did you move my things?" she asked, skeptical and indignant. "I'm tired, King. I'm ready to take a shower and go to bed. Alone."

King reached for Tai again. She backed away. He dropped his arm and continued. "In a minute, baby. What I have to say can't wait." He walked over to the stereo and turned off the CD. Then he reached once more for Tai, who was still standing by the door. This time she didn't resist him. He walked them over to the bed and sat down. Tai reluctantly complied. King turned to face Tai directly. He looked into her eyes. She stared back, as if seeing his face for the first time. No matter what had happened, no matter what went down, this Negro still had the power to make her wet. She averted her eyes and withdrew her hand from his.

"I'm listening," she said softly.

King nodded and cleared his throat. "I'm sorry," he began, taking a deep breath before continuing. "I'm sorry for everything, Tai, but most of all, I'm sorry for hurting you. I'm sorry for the way I've locked you out of my life emotionally since May. For the way

I've disrespected you and disrespected our family. I'm sorry for all of the time I've spent away from home, and the way you've had to raise the twins almost single-handedly. How I've taken on more and more speaking engagements to escape what I didn't want to face here at home. What I thought was a lost love for you, and for what we had."

Tai turned slowly to face him. "Is that all you're sorry for?" she asked pointedly.

King knew exactly what she meant. "I'm sorry for lying to you."

Tai continued staring at him and said nothing.

"I'm sorry for cheating on you. I'm sorry for the affair, for all the affairs."

Tai turned away from him and remained silent.

"I thought the grass was greener on the other side," he continued.

Tai swung back around angrily. "You've been on the other side before."

King nodded his agreement. "I know, I know. And each time I've sworn to you I'd never do it again."

"And each time you've lied."

How could King deny what Tai said? Truer words had never been spoken. How could he make her see that this time would be different—that this time he could and would change? There was nothing King could say that would make Tai believe him, he deduced. Only time and his changed behavior would recapture Tai's trust. He admitted it would be an uphill journey. A hill he'd created. He sat quietly as the sensation of despair rose up from a place deep inside him. For the first time in their marriage, the thought that Tai may not forgive him crossed his mind. The thought brought with it an irrepressible wave of sadness and fear.

"Three people make a crowded bed, King." Tai got up and walked to the other side of the room to put some space between them. She couldn't think with King so close—feeling his heat, smelling his cologne. But that wasn't the only odor. The scent of true remorse was emanating from King's silence. Tai didn't want to smell remorse. Remorse weakened her defenses, threatened her resolve to not let King back into her heart so easily. No, she didn't want to forgive him. She wanted him to hurt like she'd been hurting. To feel the pain she'd experienced.

What she didn't understand was how much he was already hurting. Giving in to his flesh once again and disappointing God in the process had caused an ache in King's soul that found no comfort. An ache that no one else could ever imagine, would never know. He crossed the room and stood next to Tai. Close to but not invading her personal space.

"From this day forward, you will be the only woman in my bed and in my life, Tai. That is, if there's any way you can find it in your heart to forgive me, to give this marriage one more try."

"From this day forward?" Tai countered incredulously. "Do you really think an apology and a ring are all it takes to mend the rift, no, make that the Grand Canyon that exists between us?"

Ah, yes. Anger. Anger was good. Anger could help calm the warming emotions threatening to outweigh Tai's sense of indignation. She wrapped her thoughts around that anger and, turning on him, burst into dialogue. She swept her hand across the room in exaggerated fashion, indicating the myriad candles lit all around.

"Very romantic atmosphere, King," she spat sarcastically. "How many nights did I try to seduce you, my own husband, only to have you turn your back in rejection? How many times did I try to talk to you, talk about our marriage and your affair? And how many times did you lie about it?

"For months I've done everything humanly possible to make the best of a bad situation, even taking the blame for your sick infidelities. I actually was fool enough to think that somehow your straying ass must have been my fault, something I was doing wrong. I tried to be the woman I thought you wanted, lost weight, changed my hairstyle—not that you noticed."

"I did notice," King interrupted. "It looks, uh, great," he said lamely.

"Ha!" Tai snorted. "A day late and a dollar short with that compliment, you big ape! Well, guess what, King. You can keep your funky compliment. You can keep your apology, and for that matter, you can keep your itty-bitty mistress. Because now that you're so ready to make it work? I'm not so sure this marriage is what *I* want."

Tai was trembling all over as she stomped to the door and snatched it open. She turned and glared at King before continuing in a quiet, deadly tone. "Now, you think on that while you move my stuff back into the guest room!"

King punched the pillow, still tossing and turning hours after Tai's parting words had slashed him like a butcher knife. What had he expected, for Tai to welcome him with open arms? Did he think that like the prodigal son she would throw him a party, give him a robe and a ring? Had he imagined those grilled steaks to be fatted calf? He snorted and, unable to sleep, dragged himself to a sitting position. Turning on the lamp beside the bed, he looked with self-directed disdain at the now extinguished candles taking up every available space in the room. In a fit of anger he jumped from the bed and grabbed a large shopping bag from the closet. He began gathering up the candles and, like missiles to the moon, fired them into the bag one by one. Once that bag filled up he stalked over to the closet and grabbed a plastic bag from the cleaner's. After tying a knot at one end, he walked around the room throwing the remainder of candles inside it. Then he knotted the open end and flung the bag against the closet wall, shattering some of the candles inside. Finally he walked over to the bed and sat down heavily. He put his head in his hands, and before long his tears were escaping, sliding down his arm and across his thigh before landing on the shimmering comforter beneath him. The total helplessness that

King felt was evident in his next thoughts as words he normally would never use came tumbling out of his mouth.

"You have fucked up, man. You have really fucked up this time." He swiped at his eyes angrily, but the tears continued. He crawled back into the bed and lay motionless, staring at the ceiling as the tears slid down his face and stained the bed. *It's gonna take more than dinner and diamonds, my brotha,"* he thought cynically, turning on his side and pounding his pillow forcefully. "A whole lot more," he whispered aloud.

Tai jumped as she heard a loud thump echo from the master bedroom. *What is he doing?* And what had she done? Had she just done something crazy—like thrown her marriage away?

Tai had barely made it to the guest room and turned the shower on full blast before the tears erupted, the water concealing the sobs that exploded from the depths of her being. She had applauded her actions one minute and condemned them the next. In the end, divorcing King was not what she wanted. So why had she gotten so angry when the very thing she'd petitioned God for, King acknowledging he wanted the marriage also, had happened?

Pride, God said.

And He was right. The fact that King thought he could just waltz back into her life, and the fact that he was right, had been a staggering revelation, even knowing how much she loved King. Oh, the anger had felt good at the moment. But the anger Tai felt for King hardly matched the fury she felt with herself. Furious because not ten minutes after her fuming outburst in the bedroom, Tai was ready to forgive King and try again. Outraged because images of how sexy King looked in that lounging outfit came floating into her mind, bringing with them a physical reaction that hardened her nipples. Incredulous that her own emotions and heart would betray her with a need to see King.

Even now, as she listened for more noises to come from the direction of the master bedroom, she wrestled with her emotions. Should she make another go at living with King just when she had reached the point where she could live without him? Did she dare open her heart to him again? I mean, just how many times was she supposed to forgive this man?

Seventy times seven. Just like My Word says.

"Oh, who asked You," Tai whispered angrily, before remembering who she was talking to and adding, "Forgive me, Lord." Tai knew she should forgive King, but knowing what you should do and doing what you should do—as King so aptly demonstrated—were two different things. But Tai had to ask herself. What would she gain by holding out on forgiving King? Would she be any less of a woman if she did it tomorrow instead of two months from now? Did she think that time would remove the essence of April from King's body before she could reclaim it. And what about April? Should she let that bitch waltz into the sunset without a word? Could she trust King to have really ended their liaison? How could she be sure? And then there were her hurt feelings to consider. Yes, she wanted King, but could she love him again? Unconditionally, as she used to, as she was supposed to? She already knew the answer to that question was no, because there was a condition—one with no exceptions. King could never have another affair. As sure as she knew her name, she knew that she could never put up with another act of unfaithfulness. So did that mean she'd put up with this one? Lord, why did life seem more complicated after his apology, instead of less?

The questions continued to bombard Tai's mind relentlessly as she tossed and turned during her sleepless night. When she finally drifted off to sleep, during the early morning hours, her mind was filled with thoughts of a mahogany man with chocolate eyes, a strong body and a nice, thick . . .

Everybody plays the fool

Millicent looked around the childhood room that in years gone by had been her safe haven and where she'd retreated once more after "the incident." Its familiarity had brought immense comfort upon her arrival, even though the canopy bed with frilly white lace of her youth had long been replaced with the more elegant four-poster mahogany design in what was now the guest room. Still, the faux Monet watercolor prints were the same, as was the rocking chair in which she sat. The shelves her father had built a lifetime ago still housed her precious porcelain doll collection, each perfectly etched face giving silent companionship in her abject loneliness. She ran her hand over the brightly colored afghan that warmed her legs against the prewinter chill. She wished there were something that could warm the chill in her heart, something that could fill its emptiness and sooth the dull, continuous ache that beat a melancholy rhythm against her soul.

She placed the unread book of Psalms aside and walked to the window. It was early afternoon, and neighborhood children were walking home from school, some running and playing, others with their heads together in childhood conspiracies of only God knew what. It seemed just yesterday it was her walking home, mostly alone or with one of her boyfriends, or running home after another mean-spirited attack by some of the town's bullies. She re-membered thinking at the time that those were the worst days of her life. If she only knew . . .

I'm the world's biggest fool. Although the thought was constant, it hurt less with each passing day. The pain still felt like a knife wedged deep in her heart, but at least she could breathe again. The tears had dried somewhat, although she wasn't past an outburst now and again. The therapy was helping, as was the antidepressant medication. Still, she had no idea when she'd be able to return to work and, in fact, wasn't sure she could return to Los Angeles at all for fear of running into one of them. A Kingdom Citizens' member who'd witnessed "the incident." *The biggest fool.* Not that they were the only ones privy to what had occurred. No, Millicent wouldn't have been surprised had Oprah called and wanted the 4-1-1 for a show on crazy women stalkers. Or maybe it would be Jan Crouch from Trinity Broadcasting Network wanting to inter-view her for a segment called "Fools Who Miss God." Even her friend Alison, cosseted just outside the small town of Clarkstown, New York, had e-mailed her with a frantic "What's Going On???" message, one she still hadn't answered. She still didn't feel like talk-ing to anybody but her mom and her therapist. She hadn't yet found the words to talk to God. *Fool, fool, fool, fool, fool . . .*

Talking to God was something Millicent wondered if she could ever do again. How could she talk to Him when she obvi-ously had no idea how He sounded? She'd been so convinced it was His voice she'd heard, His words she'd obeyed, and what had it gotten her? A first place spot on the Freak-of-the-Week list at KCCC and a sixty-day leave of absence from her job. Thankfully it was a paid leave, even though she'd had to turn down the promo-tion to director with its six-figure income.

Millicent walked over and sat down heavily on the down-filled mattress. It gave her little comfort. *You're a fool, Millicent, a big, big fool. And everybody knows it.* She lay back, and even though she hated closing her eyes, she did anyway. She hated closing them because she always saw the video. The video called "Millicent Plays the Fool," starring Millicent Sims. She groaned and turned over. She knew it was no use trying to stop it; there were only two buttons on this video machine, "play" and "repeat play."

The video always seemed to start at about the same place, with Millicent in an undignified heap at Hope Jones's feet. Hope's shoes were the first thing she saw as she came to that day, having fainted from the stress of walking down the aisle. *Fool.* Cy's face was etched indelibly in her memory—he looked like he'd seen Satan himself. Pastor Derrick had stood frozen, willing his sanity to transfer to her. It hadn't. She kept walking down the aisle, as in a trance. She remembered hearing the muffled voices, the din of conversations as she walked the road to perdition, the congratulations and compliments on her gown before they realized Insanity, not Beautiful, was walking down the aisle. She'd felt physically ill as she struggled to her feet and away from the woman who represented all she hated, all she'd never have. Yes, those e-mails had reached her, too. The ones announcing the marriage of Hope Jones and Cy Taylor. As if on cue, the tears began as the movie played on. *Everybody plays the fool, but none as bad as you.*

The head usher, two-hundred-and-eighty-five-pound Rodney Lewis, had literally picked Millicent and Vera-the-dress up and whisked them out of the sanctuary as if she were a parasite with leprosy. She'd been deposited into a nearby prayer room with Vivian and the congregation's head nurse, Sistah Flora, who immediately removed her veil and undid the beaded-up bodice of her extravagant gown so she could get some air. They'd placed cloth after cloth of cool water on her forehead; all the while Vivian had prayed in tongues. Millicent was barely aware of her surroundings. It was as if she were being buried alive in a vat of oil. She felt she was sinking farther and farther into an abyss from which she'd never return. She was barely aware of the commotion as she was whisked out one of the church's side doors into the still-waiting limo, with Vivian praying silently by her side. Mother Moseley had accompanied them because as much as she laughed at Millicent's unabashed affections for Cy Taylor, she nevertheless felt an immense compassion for a woman who would go to such lengths for what she believed was God's will. Mother Moseley was convinced that was the only thing that would have led Millicent to do what she'd done because Millicent was many things, but crazy was not one of them. Her purse, suitcase and train-filled garment bag had preceded her and were lying ominously on the limo's smooth black leather seat. The faucet that contained a never-ending supply of tears had been turned on at that moment, and she sobbed quietly against Mother Moseley's bosom as the older woman shushed her and assured her it was gonna be all right. And the tape began, *fool, fool, fool.*

Vivian had found Millicent's keys and let them inside her condo. She took in the wedding day disarray of boxes and bags and toiletries strewn everywhere as she led Millicent into her bedroom, undressed her and tucked her in bed. "You want to talk?" she'd asked Millicent, even as she guessed the negative answer. She left her in a dimly lit room to rest while she and Mother Moseley cleaned up and tried to rid the condo of any evidence of the day's tragic events.

Millicent had remained in bed the rest of the day, not talking to anyone. Vivian had stayed for a while and left, with Vera-the-dress, while Mother Moseley stayed to make sure Millicent didn't do anything foolish. Mother Moseley had rummaged through bare cupboards and a near empty refrigerator and found enough ingredients to put together a tasty vegetable soup—not that anyone tasted it but her. Millicent ate some at Mother Moseley's insistence, but for all her awareness it could have been mud going down her throat. It was several hours after "the incident" and she hadn't stopped crying. In fact, she was getting worse, her sobs turning to moans that turned to groans and then howls. After Mother Moseley prayed and rebuked Satan and prayed some more, with little visible result, she decided to call Sistah Flora and get a little man-made assistance. Having worked in a variety of mental institutions for most of her thirty-five years in nursing, Sistah Flora would know how to handle someone with emotional problems. She came almost immediately, looking like an angel in her white silk suit sans hat and gloves, and administered a mild tranquilizer so that Millicent could sleep. It was also the first peace Mother Moseley had experienced since a dream spelling trouble awakened her earlier that morning. Little did she know that the dream would become a nightmare before the sun set in the evening.

Sistah Flora had suggested Millicent see a specialist immediately to help her deal with the devastation of the weekend's events, and Millicent agreed. She was ushered into a hastily scheduled appointment the next day, and after a two-hour session, the doctor had written a recommendation that Millicent take a two-month leave of absence from her job. Millicent had gone into work late that evening and cleaned out her desk before calling her boss with the news the next day. Shocked didn't begin to describe the reaction her news elicited from her boss and coworkers. Not that Millicent was aware of it—these incidents passed in a haze. All Millicent knew was that she needed to leave the scene of the crime, and all she could think of was her childhood home. She felt that if she could just get back to her Mother, she would live.

The day her flight left for Portland, she'd had a long conversation with Vivian. She'd given her the condensed version of the chain of events that had led her up the aisle in a Vera Wang dress and Manolo Blahnik pumps to the man she thought was destined to be her husband. Vivian had tried to minister to her but realized that only time and God could begin to heal the gaping wound in Millicent's heart. Only then, after the healing began, would Vivian or anyone else be able to reach her effectively. Still, she'd given her several inspirational tapes, including some of her favorites by Joyce Myer, a Midwest minister, and a book of Psalms that included additional daily Bible readings and true life stories of people who'd overcome extreme adversities, up to and including death. She,

Mother Moseley and Sistah Flora had given Millicent a ride to the airport and stayed with her until she passed through security. They'd already spoken with her mother and knew she would be there to greet her daughter as soon as she arrived. And her mother had been there, an oasis in the desert, beckoning Millicent as she walked into the baggage claim area. She'd run and fallen into her mother's arms, and although she didn't know it, the healing began at that moment.

And now, some weeks later, the healing continued. God, the invisible doctor, had never left her side.

Open up, baby

It had been over a month since Tai returned from California to find her world turned upside down by King's amorous behavior. As October gave way to November, King's actions had been exemplary. He'd obviously cancelled some of his out of town speaking engagements because he'd been home every night. At first Tai felt very uncomfortable and was unusually quiet. But old habits die hard, and before long she was joining in on lively evening discussions with King and the children and, although she wasn't ready to admit it, actually enjoying the feeling of family. That feeling had been missing from the Brook household. Just two days ago, Tai had acquiesced and allowed King to move her things from the guest to master bedroom once again. It was there Tai turned to face the man she'd loved before she was even old enough to understand the word. Her mind was filled with jumbled emotions, thoughts and memories fighting for attention. She looked up into eyes the color of chocolate ice cream and scanned the lips that could bring her to ecstasy inside of ten minutes. Although they hadn't been intimate, they'd spent long hours of the night discussing their marriage, their relationship and their lives. King stated over and over again that he'd do whatever it took to save the marriage. She looked at what was being offered to her and wondered if she should walk away from the father of her children, her spiritual covering and former best friend. For the first time, she was strong enough. She knew that she could do it, but not if she *should* do it.

King hadn't pressured her to resume their physical relationship, but he'd let her know in no uncertain terms what he wanted and how he wanted it. And he wanted her. Physically. Mentally. Spiritually. Completely. That was what he said. She thought of how much she'd loved this man, how much she still wanted to love him and how she'd longed to feel those strong, muscular arms around her, holding her, squeezing her, loving her.

And here he was again, reaching out his arms to her, asking for another chance. She didn't step into those arms, however. Instead, she stepped back and away, still holding on to the threads of anger. She knew she was supposed to forgive him. That was what marriage was about. But for a reason she couldn't name, she hesitated. "King, it takes a lot to make up for the hell you've put me through," she said softly. She shook her head slightly before turning around. "I need to take a shower."

Tai sat on the bench in the bathroom, a thick terry towel wrapped around her. She slowly sipped the now warm apple juice, reliving the events of the evening—another evening of King pledging his love. Of all the things she'd imagined as her homecoming a month ago, this had not been one of them. She remembered again, as she had often in the last thirty days, the decorated room, the gifts, the dinner. And this stranger who looked like King but talked like someone she hadn't met before, had stayed past dinner that night and even now was sitting on the king-sized bed just beyond her tile-floored sanctuary. There was sincerity in his eyes, along with a vulnerability that had never been there before. She sensed a spirit of true repentance that hadn't accompanied his other apologies. *What happened while I was away?* Tai pondered the thought. A snapshot of that candle-filled master bedroom scene a month ago flashed into her mind. She imagined King's cocoa-dipped body splashed against that satiny, golden comforter and smiled while the ropes of anger and hurt loosened a little more from around her heart.

So what are you going to do? God asked.

Tai knew what she wanted to do. She wanted to run into that room and jump on that bed and make mad, passionate love to her husband.

So, why don't you?

"I've just gotten myself to the point where I can live without him, and I kind of like it."

Maybe you had to get to the point where you could live without him in order to live with him.

Tai had never looked at it like that. The California trip helped her realize King and the children had been her whole life. She was able to see clearly how she'd put her entire life on hold and turned all of her attention toward them. In the process, she'd lost herself. And once she'd lost herself, she had nothing left to offer King.

Tai stood and dried off while continuing to think. Had King changed, really changed? Tai wanted so much to believe him. She thought how wonderful it would be to have a real family again, a real husband. She thought of April and just as quickly tossed the thought aside. If King could forget her, so could she. Well, maybe not immediately but one day at a time.

Tai thought back to the S.O.S. Summit, when they had explored the meaning of unconditional love in Spiritually Speaking. Tai realized that that was what she had to practice, consciously, and that if she did, their marriage could not only survive, but flourish. With all of his faults, even in his rusted, tarnished armor, King was a good man. He was God's man. He was her man. He was waiting for her on the other side of that door, and she would be a fool not to go and get him. Tai turned, a bottle of lotion in hand, and jumped when she saw King lounging in the doorway. She'd been so deep in thought she hadn't even heard it open. King took in her naked body, the bottle of lotion, the towel at her feet and Tai's surprised expression. He smiled lazily and reached for the bottle. "Can I help you with that?" he asked before grabbing her hand and ushering his wife back into the master bedroom.

"King, really, I can do it myself," Tai said, trying unsuccessfully to grab the lotion from King's upraised hand.

"Come on, baby. I just want to help. I'll rub the lotion on your back. That's all."

"Yeah right," Tai quipped, turning around and resigning herself to melting at King's touch. "Well, I'm waiting. Hurry up, I'm getting cold."

"If you lie down on the bed, you'll be warmer," he suggested. "I promise, Tai. We won't do anything you don't want to do."

"That's what I'm afraid of," Tai whispered before lying facedown on the satiny comforter. She rolled her hands up and down the soft fabric. "This is nice."

"You can thank Mama. She went shopping with me when I told her I wanted to change the feel of the room. Make it special for you."

An involuntary shudder shot through Tai's body as King touched her at the small of her back, the first intimate caress they'd shared in months. He moved his hands in small circles as he worked the lotion into her back, across her arms and down her legs. Tai kept her legs squeezed together so tightly at first that it would take the Jaws of Life to pull them apart. As King prodded gently, Tai failed at all attempts to remain focused. It was hopeless. She was toast.

"Baby, open your legs a little so I can lotion them all over." Tai didn't move. "Tai?" Maybe she was sleeping, King thought. After all, she had mentioned how tired she was earlier in the evening. But if she was asleep, how could she grip her legs so tightly? "Tai, I know you hear me. Open up, baby."

Tai was hoping to hold out, for a little while at least. Yet, here she was, barely fifteen minutes into the seduction, and she was ready to make a vee in the air with her legs and yell out "Welcome home, pardner! Giddy-up!" She eased the muscles in her legs, allowing King to pull them apart. He slowly lotioned one leg first, then the other. He massaged her buttocks and kneaded her shoulders. Suddenly, just as Tai was about to turn over, he got off the bed.

"What are you doing?" Having decided that she would indeed surrender, she was ready to wave the white flag and be taken into captivity.

"Setting the stage," King replied quietly. He reached for the lighter on his dresser and set about lighting the candles he'd purchased to replace the ones he'd thrown away. Tai sat up in bed and watched him move. The candlelight played hopscotch across his naked body, the glow touching parts of his body her hands longed to feel. Their eyes met and held as he walked back to the bed and lay down, facing her. He reached out his hand and outlined her face with his finger. "You are so beautiful," he whispered. "More beautiful now than the day we met." He tentatively touched his lips where his fingers had been. Tai remained motionless, closing her eyes and reveling in King's touch, his feel, his breath, his scent. He kissed her hungrily, as though she were the first meal after a forty-day fast. He grabbed her then and held her close, his throat working up and down as he fought back tears. "Can you ever forgive me, baby? I love you, Tai."

Tai hugged him back, her own eyes shiny. After all they'd been through, she still had some love left for this man. She still wanted him and their marriage. She still wanted to be his first lady and to be Mount Zion's Queen Bee. After taking another hit, the marriage was still standing. She hugged him even tighter. "I forgive you, King Brook." She pulled away from him then to look into his eyes. "I love you, too."

King and Tai embraced, bodies rubbing, hearts touching. They demonstrated how much they loved each other. As it was in the beginning, the two became one—sacred love.

Love was a beautiful thing

Crystal blue water lapped the edges of the white sand beachfront. The lazy ebb and flow of the ocean seemed to rock the Bahamas, and everyone on the island, into a contented lull. Pelicans and seagulls flew overhead, while smaller birds darted in and out of the palm trees and other vibrant, green foliage. Seashells in hues of orange and pink and beige and white dotted the shoreline, interspersed with seaweed and algae. Couples strolled quietly on the beach, and farther down the sandy border, surfers glided in the calm waters, waiting for a windy swell that would allow them to catch the big wave.

Not fifty yards from the ocean front, Derrick, Vivian, Tai and King sat at an upscale, island restaurant enjoying a native dish of peas and rice, fried conch and plantain. They were all sipping non-alcoholic drinks with umbrellas in them, surrounded by cherries and chunks of pineapple.

"I still can't believe she did it," Tai remarked before grabbing another forkful of peas and rice. "Like standing in the middle of the sanctuary was something done every Sunday, like this was normal!"

"Believe it," Vivian replied dryly. Memories of that fateful Sunday could still cause a flip-flop or two in her stomach.

King was sitting back in his chair, a grin on his face. "So, Derrick man, what did you do?"

"Do?" Derrick echoed. "Do? What could I do? I fired up the band and led the church in a round of 'Amazing Grace'!" Everyone laughed as Derrick broke out in an impromptu rendition of the song at the table.

"Man!" King continued. "I bet Cy wanted to go through the floor!"

"Not without his fiancée," Vivian countered. "He was staring at her like he was on *Millionaire* and she was the final lifeline. I really think Hope was his anchor that day. Otherwise the man may have floated outta there on a cloud of disbelief."

"Shoot. Incredibly pissed off would better describe the cloud I saw. If Millicent hadn't fainted, Cy's look would have killed her." Derrick reached over and grabbed a roll. "Can you imagine some woman coming down the aisle talking about 'husband, come to me'? In a room crowded with a thousand people? In a wedding dress?"

"And not just any wedding dress," Vivian continued. "But in a Vera Wang, baby. Sistah went all out."

"Lord, have mercy," Tai said quietly. "I mean, it's so crazy you've got to laugh to keep from crying, but my heart goes out to Millicent. She seemed so together—attractive, intelligent, so on-the-ball. And this came out of nowhere?"

"Not exactly," Vivian admitted. "She'd mentioned something about knowing who her husband was to be, around the time of the summit. We were supposed to discuss it over lunch, but I had to cancel at the last minute, and we never rescheduled.

"We did talk afterward, about how it happened. She became obsessed with Cy and, in her distorted thinking, took all sorts of ordinary events and made them mean something totally different. Her obsession literally drove her crazy. And one day, she just snapped. I wish I could have done something before she did what she did."

Derrick squeezed Vivian's hand. "Baby, she was set on this course. I don't think there's anything anyone could have done."

Vivian went on, trying to find logic where there was none. "I can't imagine the thought process that got Millicent to that point, but she had to have been totally convinced that she was right before taking such drastic action. I mean believing you've heard from God is one thing, but to go out and buy a wedding dress, rent a limo and arrange for a marriage license and blood tests, all without your intended's knowledge, takes the concept of faith to a whole 'nutha level."

"Unh-unh, honey," Derrick interjected. "Like Pastor Price would say, that's not faith, that's foolishness."

"That's sad, is what it is." Tai grew solemn as she imagined Millicent's pain. Tai had felt pain, deep pain. She could relate. She vowed to put the sister on her prayer list.

"You're absolutely right and I miss her terribly. She still isn't returning phone calls, but her mother says she is improving, slowly but surely," Vivian continued. "I send her books and CDs I feel will minister to her. I want her to know that we haven't forgotten her."

King was still more amused than amazed. "So how did you handle the members, Dee? I know you had to talk about it."

"Of course I talked about it. I used it as a catalyst for my evening message that I entitled 'Have You Heard?' "

Tai set down her drink. "No, you didn't!"

"Yes, I did. There was no way I could let something that had gone down in the middle of service in the middle of the church not be handled in the middle of service in the middle of the church. I had to nip that in the bud 'less some lesser soul or mind get on that same train with their bright ideas. There'd been too much plotting and trotting after men by the women in the church anyway—and vice versa. It was a good time for me to address the issue. It was also a good time for me to talk about gossip and judging and unconditional love. On the surface, it blew over rather quickly. Although I'm sure it's still fodder for the gossip mill." His eyes twinkled merrily. "And Cy still breaks out in a sweat when he sees a white dress and it's not first Sunday!"

"You're incorrigible!" Vivian said seriously while her eyes chuckled.

"But Millicent's okay?" Tai queried again, still feeling for her sister.

"I hope so," Vivian responded. "I should try and phone her mother when I get back home."

"It sounds like she needs some professional counseling," King said. "I mean, it's not like I haven't heard of this type of thing before; women coming to the church in wedding gowns and stuff. But to walk down the aisle right before the sermon is set to be preached and demand the hand of somebody who's just proposed to somebody else? Whew! That's too deep for this kid." He looked at Tai. "Good thing we don't have to worry about no crazy mess like that at our church, huh, baby."

Tai rolled her eyes. "In this day and age, nothing would surprise me."

King smiled and kissed her cheek. "So when's the big day. First part of next year, I heard."

"For Cy and Hope's wedding? On Valentine's Day." Vivian, a hopeless romantic, smiled warmly as she thought about the intimate wedding Hope and Cy were planning. They'd decided to get married on a yacht.

"You know they want us both to officiate," Derrick said to King before diving into his dessert. "I told them I couldn't speak for you, but that I'd make sure the fourteenth was open. Who knows? Maybe you and Tai could make a long weekend out of it and have your own lovers' getaway in one of our swanky, five-star hotels."

King reached out and grabbed Tai in a big hug. It seemed he couldn't touch her enough these days. It had barely been two months since their reconciliation, and here, as the new year unfolded, King still felt like a kid with a brand-new toy. "Now, that makes the offer sound infinitely more attractive," King droned while biting Tai's ear. "A getaway with my baby will make the trip worth the money right there."

"Well, Cy Taylor does everything first class," Derrick continued, as if King needed any more encouragement. "I'm sure everything from your flight to your accommodations to the fee for your services will be superb, buddy. Superb!"

Derrick and Vivian and Tai and King walked along the beach as a colorful sunset filled the open sky. There was a comfortable silence—each couple lost in their own world.

Derrick grabbed Vivian and hugged her gently as they walked along the water's edge, their bare feet wading into the sea. It was incredible how much love he had for her after all these years. How her smile could still warm up a room and light up his heart. He patted her booty softly, a booty still firm and shapely thanks to Billy Blanks and his Tae-bo regime. "I love you, woman," he whispered in her ear. Vivian simply looked at him and smiled before turning her gaze once again to the setting sun.

Vivian had been thinking that very thing when Derrick voiced his emotions. It didn't surprise her. After fifteen years, they fit together like hand in glove. They could read each other's thoughts and finish each other's sentences. There was a comfort level with Derrick that Vivian enjoyed with none other, a comfort she looked forward to enjoying for a long, long time. She heard Tai squeal and looked around in time to see King lifting her up and running out into the water, threatening to treat her to an unsolicited swim. "Careful, you two!" Vivian cried happily. "Don't have me performing CPR out here tonight." Like the beauty surrounding them, King and Tai's marriage was proof as to how great, how awesome God really was. With Him, indeed nothing was impossible. If she were a betting woman, she'd have lost her shirt if she'd wagered on her friends' marriage just two months ago. And now to see them frolicking like newlyweds. Well, even with its ups and downs, love was a beautiful thing.

King let his wife down gently, stopping to kiss her as the water flowed around their feet. How he'd ever turned away from this woman he'd never know, but he thanked God every day for the opportunity he'd been given, to try again with Tai and to make it right this time. She looked at him and was reminded of the love of Christ—unconditional. He grabbed Tai's hand as they continued walking down the shoreline. "I thank God for you, baby," he said sincerely. "You're the best gift He could have given me."

Tai smiled and kissed his shoulder, leaning into him as they walked along. Time, she felt, would definitely heal all wounds, and well, that good loving she was getting on the regular wasn't a bad tonic either. So what that a few other women had had him for a night, a week, a month or two? What was that compared to forever? What was that compared to right now? She studied him from the corner of her eye. Damn! He was still fine. Toned and tall, taut and terrific. And when he was thinking with the head above his waist, he was actually the most intelligent man she'd ever met. Not that the other head wasn't good for something. Tai smiled as she thought back to a week ago.

Tai had surprised King, who was working late at the church office, with a picnic dinner. After dinner, one thing had led to another, and after locking the office door, Tai became dessert instead of the oatmeal cookies she'd baked fresh that afternoon.

At first Tai had been hesitant. "Baby, we can't do this! We're in church!" she'd whispered loudly.

"We're in the church *offices*," King replied as he pulled the sweater she was wearing over her head and reached behind her to undo her bra. "Didn't you teach in that conference that sex was sacred?"

"Well," Tai breathed, trying to focus on the question while King did wonderful things with his tongue to her breasts. "Yes, but . . . ooh, baby. I've never done . . . anything . . . like this . . . before."

"Hum," King responded, having relieved Tai of the sexy skirt that matched the sweater and now joined it in a heap on the floor. "Neither have I. Guess there's a first time for everything."

I guess so, she'd thought as King grabbed a couple pillows off the couch and situated her strategically on his large, maple desk. "King! What are you—oh! Ooh, ooh, King . . ." Tai couldn't believe it. She was having sex in the sanctuary, and too busy to see God smile before He left the room and they really got down to business. Even "the God who will never leave" left believing, in His infinite wisdom, that sometimes three really *was* a crowd!

Derrick and Vivian caught up with King and Tai. The sun had gone down, and the air had turned chilly.

"Anybody up for coffee in the lounge?" Vivian asked. "I hear they have an excellent band."

King and Tai glanced at each other. Music sounded like a good idea, but they wanted to make their own. Tai feigned a yawn.

"No, Viv," Tai replied. "I think I'll turn in. It's been a long day."

King mimicked a huge, noisy yawn. "Me, too. Lord knows I'm tired!" He yawned again, even louder this time. Vivian got the message. Little did she know that Derrick's vote was with King and Tai.

"Yeah, I hear you," she said. "Have a good night."

"I'm glad you got their message," Derrick cooed as he and Vivian walked down the hall to their suite, just a few doors down from the Brooks. "Because I've got one of my own."

"Oh, you do, do you?"

Derrick opened the door and waved her inside. "Uh-huh." He stopped just inside the doorway and pulled Vivian into his arms.

Vivian melted into his lean frame. There was no space between them. "And just what is that message, Mr. Derrick Anthony Montgomery?"

"Darling, answering that question," he whispered, pulling Vivian toward the bedroom, "will take all night."

"Umm," Vivian murmured as Derrick placed a trail of kisses from her eyelids to her shoulders and back again. "Well, don't just stand there, baby, get to talking!" And Derrick talked to Vivian, the love of his life, using the unspoken language of lovers throughout time. And Vivian savored every word.

A similar scenario was being played out in the suite just down the hall. King lit the candles he'd requested earlier from the concierge while Tai put on a CD compilation of love songs King had made prior to their trip. The smooth sounds of Al Green's "Let's Stay Together" flowed out of the stereo and mingled with the warm island breeze and the jasmine-scented candles and transported Tai and King to their heaven on earth.

King grabbed Tai and pulled her tightly against him, singing softly in her ear. "I'm so in love with you . . ."

Tai finished the verse as they danced a spry, Kansas City two-step. They were all smiles as they glided to the melody, singing the whole song, word for word.

King was holding her gently now as they rocked to the beat—one two three step, one two three. . . . Tears gathered at the corners of Tai's eyes, a gentle rain storm threatening to shower down on her paradise. King noticed and slowed their movements further. "You're beautiful," he said, kissing the tears that wavered threateningly at each eye's corner. "I love everything about you, what you've done to your hair, this new tight body you brought to the island." He smiled, gently squeezing her buttocks.

"Baby, it's us forever," he continued. They were barely moving now, the only thing flowing faster being Tai's tears. "God has told me what I need to do, and I'm going to show you that this time will be different." The sounds of Champagne echoed his sentiment, saying some people could love each other for life.

"I believe you," Tai said simply. She grabbed King's hand and led him to the sofa. She sat down quietly, and he followed her lead.

They were facing each other, holding hands. "You know I love you, King. And I know it will take time for the wounds to heal. We'll take one day at a time."

King glanced at the bed. "I'm hoping we can start with one night at a time."

Tai smiled. "I hope so, too. I've prayed, and while I know it will not always be easy, I still believe it is possible for us to have a good marriage. We've had one before. I know I'm partly to blame here. It's not all your fault. It's mostly your fault," she added hastily.

"Ah, here we go," King said dramatically, lightening the mood. He wisely changed subjects. "Remember that time when Michael was about three years old. He decided to play soldier with Princess. It had been raining and you went out in the backyard to find her covered with mud and leaves, and he said it was camel-flog?" Both he and Tai laughed softly at the memory.

"Yes, and I wanted to beat his butt because he was as dirty as she was."

"But instead you started rolling on the ground with them, and when I got home, all three of you were looking like little mud children. You were so cute to me that day."

"Yeah, we all jumped in the shower together, singing at the top of our lungs." Tai's face glowed at the memory. "We stayed in there until the water got cold. When we got through that bathroom was a mess!"

"Yeah, but we didn't care. You went in the kitchen and made hot chocolate, and we pulled out potato chips and cookies and Skittles and all kinda junk food and had a picnic on the living room floor. The kids were in heaven!" King pulled Tai up and walked toward the bed. "I want to lie down." He wanted to join Lionel and show Tai she was a lady; once, twice, three times.

Tai followed him quietly, still lost in the memories of happier days. The covers had already been pulled down and Godiva choco-lates placed on their pillows. King got in first and then pulled Tai down and close to him.

Tai laughed softly and continued the story. "We all fell asleep, right on the living room floor. The next morning you were so mad because Princess had somehow lost her diaper during the night and peed on you!" She snuggled closer to King; his scent was intoxicating.

"Humph. I still think you had something to do with that!"

"No, I didn't!" Tai said, laughing freely now.

"Yeah, that's what you said. I still think it was a conspiracy." He pulled her closer, rubbing his lips against hers, gently, lovingly, without demands.

Tai closed her eyes, focusing on the moment. King kissed her eyelids, her nose, her mouth. He hugged her to him and rubbed her back.

"We've had some good times, huh," he whispered against her ear. King began a slow, languorous journey from Tai's ears which he'd traced with his tongue, across her neck, slowly down the valley of her breasts where he rested his head. She hugged him to her, each kiss seeming to relax her a little bit more. He continued, paying homage to first one dark nipple and, after giving it his thorough and undivided attention, moving to the other, pulling, teasing, sucking. He kissed a path to Tai's lips again and kissed her deeply. He worshipped her body with his mouth, adoring her beauty, celebrating her ability to love him still, esteeming her power to forgive. He took his time with her, rubbing and massaging and cuddling and consoling. He kissed her from the freckles on her nose to the soles of her feet. Marvin Gaye had the right idea. It was time for some sexual healing.

Tai moaned in frustration as King rolled over to remove his pants. She shrugged out of the blouse King had unbuttoned on his quest to relive the pleasure of Tai. As he rolled back over, she placed her arms around his neck, looking deeply into the eyes and the soul of the man she'd loved since she was fifteen years old. He rocked her softly, his dick hard between her legs. Thick and throbbing, he lifted himself as Tai opened to receive him. He pleasured the love of his life with deep, steady strokes.

"I love you, King," Tai whispered fervently as King led the way on their dance of love. Slowly, deeply, he possessed her as if he never wanted to let her go.

"I love you, Tai. I love you, baby." King's mind was filled with love for his wife, and there was no one else he'd rather have in his arms.

He smiled as the music lulled them both to sleep. *You're right, Sugarfoot,* he thought. *Heaven must be like this.*

SEX IN THE SANCTUARY

LUTISHIA LOVELY

ABOUT THIS GUIDE

The following questions are intended to
enhance your group's reading of
SEX IN THE SANCTUARY.

DISCUSSION QUESTIONS

1. Does Tai unfairly target and blame the women, as opposed to her husband, for his affairs? Do women in general tend to do this? What has been the experience of your friends, family, coworkers, etc? Your own?

2. Why are some single women willing to sleep with married men? Do single men tend to sleep with married women at the same rate? Why not?

3. Should Tai have left King?

4. Why was Mama Max so upset that King's latest affair was with a White woman?

5. Why did Tai initially feel more devastated that the woman was White?

6. How are Black women affected when Black men date White women? Are Black men affected in the same way, a different way, or not at all when Black women date White men?

7. Do many marriages mirror Derrick and Vivian's? Is it possible to have a successful, monogamous, sexually satisfying, long-term marriage today?

8. How does one know when they've "heard from God?"

9. Are single women in congregations unfairly targeted by other members who think these women are "trying to

get the preacher?" Is it okay for single women to have close, professional, one-on-one interactions with their married pastor?

10. How realistic is it for adult men and women, who've previously been sexually active, to remain celibate until marriage? Do many single women and men in the church make a decision to abstain from sex until married?

11. Was Millicent crazy to think Cy was her future husband? Have you heard preachers talking about "crazy faith"— doing something out of the ordinary to bring about desired results?

12. How should the gift of prophesy be used? Is it okay to look for a prophet, or seer, if seeking an answer to a problem, question or personal situation?

13. What do you think about using such practices or sayings as "name it, claim it," "speaking things into existence," or "faith without works is dead" to justify actions taken towards a desired end?

14. What are your thoughts on the SOS Summit? Are these topics being adequately addressed in church today?

Stay tuned for the next book in this series:
LOVE LIKE HALLELUJAH.
Until then, satisfy your Lutishia Lovely
craving with the following excerpt
from the next installment.

ENJOY!

Remember to forget

Cy moved with calm precision, feeling perfectly at home at Victoria's Secret. He thought it may not be the most traditional gift to give his soon-to-be wife, but he couldn't think of anything he'd rather see her in than a silky negligee, except naked. He knew her body would show off the diamond necklace he'd just purchased at Tiffany's to perfection. He couldn't help but smile as he fingered the wistful fabrics of silk, satin and lace, unmindful of the not-so-covert glances female shoppers slid his way. It hardly mattered. Hope had captured his attention from the moment she'd entered the back of Mount Zion Progressive Baptist Church, a piece of sanctified eye candy wrapped in a shimmering gold designer suit. She was the only woman for him.

The area filled with female admirers as he continued his deliberate perusal. He stopped at a hanging negligee, red and pink flowers against a satiny white background. The top had thin spaghetti straps that held up a transparent gown hitting mid-thigh. The thong had an intricately designed rose vine for the string, a trail he would happily follow once they were on Hope, first with his fingers, then with his tongue . . .

A perky, twenty-something sales rep came over with a knowing smile. "Are roses your favorite flower?" she asked with a grin.

"They could become my favorite," Cy countered easily. "If worn on the right person."

"That's a very popular design, but a woman has to have a really nice figure to pull it off." Instantly aware of how her comment must have sounded, the salesperson hoped she hadn't messed up her chances for a sale.

"Oh, this woman can definitely pull it off, and if she can't . . ." Cy let the unspoken double entendre linger in the air as he casually handed the items to the salesperson.

"Will this be all?" the salesperson asked as she unconsciously moved closer to this live Adonis that had walked into the store and (blessings abound!) into her area.

"No, but I'll keep shopping on my own," Cy murmured as he eyed something else on the other side of the store. The salesperson followed without thought. "I'll let you know if I need any help," he said with meaning.

"No problem, I'm here if you need me." The saleswoman seemed to float away, a look of regret barely concealed behind her cheery smile. Cy was oblivious to the wistful stares his six-foot-two frame elicited from the saleswoman and the other shoppers. His naturally curly jet-black hair may have been hidden under a Lakers cap, but his raw sexuality was in plain sight. He had no idea that his sparkling white smile lit up the room like the noonday sun or that the dimple that flashed to the side of his grin was like a finger beckoning women to come closer.

Cy picked up a bra and panty set that had Hope's name written all over it. It was a soft, lacy pink number. The panty was designed like a pair of shorts, very short shorts, and Cy reacted physically as he thought of Hope's bubble-shaped booty filling them out. He quickly added this set to the black and beige more traditional sets he'd picked up earlier.

While making his way to the perfume counter, another outfit caught his eye. It was a lavender-colored, sheer nightgown with matching floor-length jacket. The beauty was in its simplicity, and he smiled again as he thought of how Hope would look wearing this purple paradise. He held it up and closed his eyes, mentally picturing her ebony splendor wrapped leisurely inside the soft material, rubbing against her soft skin as he kissed her soft lips . . .

Cy felt the presence of someone behind him. Figuring it was the attentive saleswoman, he turned to give his apology at taking so long in making his decisions and for the growing pile of lingerie she'd collected on his behalf. The smile died on his lips, as did the clever banter he'd thought to deliver as he completed the turn and stared into the eyes of the person he'd most like to remember to forget . . . Millicent Sims.